THE OGRE'S LABORATORY

Louis Buss was born in 1963. He studied politics at Durham University and until recently, worked as a teacher. His first novel, *The Luxury of Exile*, won a Betty Trask award in 1996.

by the same author

THE LUXURY OF EXILE

Louis Buss

The Ogre's Laboratory

Jonathan Cape
London

Published by Jonathan Cape 1998

2 4 6 8 10 9 7 5 3 1

First published in Great Britain in 1998 by
Jonathan Cape
Random House, 20 Vauxhall Bridge Road,
London SW1V 2SA

Random House Australia (Pty) Limited
20 Alfred Street, Milsons Point, Sydney,
New South Wales 2061, Australia

Random House New Zealand Limited
18 Poland Road, Glenfield,
Auckland 10, New Zealand

Random House South Africa (Pty) Limited
Endulini, 5A Jubilee Road, Parktown 2193, South Africa

Random House UK Limited Reg. No. 954009

A CIP catalogue record for this book
is available from the British Library

ISBN 0 224 05039 7

Papers used by Random House UK Limited are natural,
recyclable products made from wood grown in sustainable forests.
The manufacturing processes conform to the environmental
regulations of the country of origin.

Typeset by Palimpsest Book Production Limited,
Polmont, Stirlingshire
Printed and bound in Great Britain by
Mackays of Chatham PLC, Chatham, Kent

PART ONE

I

THE CHURCH WAS a leaky old hulk that let in sunshine. It spread in glowing puddles under the doors and soaked through the stained-glass windows. Above the altar, it poured down in one mighty torrent, flooding the place with radiance. As though in awe of it, most of the congregation had knelt and closed their eyes. Some had even leaned forwards to bury their heads in their hands, so that they had all the outward devotion of saints.

As it turned out, there really was a saint in the congregation that day. He was kneeling at the back, unnoticed by anybody, for saints can be rather difficult to spot. This one seemed to be taking particular care not to give himself away. Rather than kneeling with his eyes devoutly closed, he was staring ahead with the blank involvement of a man at the cinema.

The bolt of sunlight which fell onto the altar was so clear and defined against the gloom that it might have come from a projection-room. The priest at its foot was a hologram beamed down from on high. He was a young man who had an uncompromising air more usually associated with middle age. This was partly because his face was thin and hard, yet it also seemed to be something imposed from within. His lips might have been full, almost sensuous, if he'd allowed them to relax. His hair, as black and glossy as the coat of a crow, would have been luxuriantly thick if he'd allowed it to grow. Instead it was severely cropped, parted and combed with fanatical precision. There was a

3

raw, painful-looking rash around his neck, as though he'd deliberately shaved with a blunt razor to punish himself for the sin of being so handsome.

For Father Snow, bowed over the host in his hands, there was no sound. He had reached the centre of his life. The silence commanded him to speak firmly and slowly, giving each word its solemn weight.

'This . . . is . . . my body . . . which will . . . be given up . . . for you.'

He lifted the Host into the bolt of light. It was transfigured. From an enormous distance, he heard one sound: the ringing of the golden bell, symbol of celebration or alarm. The congregation lifted their heads to squint at the white circle. A shoal of dust glittered round it, disappearing at the edges of the beam.

My Lord and my God.

The silence continued while he genuflected and bowed over the altar again to take the cup in his hands. Only when he'd raised that too did the sounds of the last few moments finish their journey into his brain. He realised that a baby had been crying. At some point, there had been a cough, a creak of moving wood. A plane had been flying overhead, cruising to Heathrow through the blue, a tiny boat trailing a long white wake. He could still hear it in the distance, the sound carrying clearly on the crisp autumn air outside.

The solemnity of the consecration stayed with him through the rest of the Mass. He was still absorbed in its mystery when he unlocked the tabernacle and went down to the altar-rail to distribute communion. The congregation formed a queue before him, stepping forwards one by one to hold out their open hands. Father Snow lifted the Host for each of them, staring at it as he did so.

'The body of Christ.'

The recipient would step to one side and another would appear. The process would be repeated, and with each repetition Father Snow would focus his eyes on the Host

4

as though to ignore the unworthiness of those who had come to receive it.

'The body of Christ.'

So they shuffled towards him, the process being repeated again and again without any variation. Nothing strange happened until the very end. From the chalice, Father Snow picked out a Host for the last communicant. His attention was more on the white circle of bread than on the man's face as he said:

'The body of Christ.'

Only when he went to lower the Host into the open hands did he realise that they were not open at all, but joined together just below the communicant's breastbone. Looking at the face, he found eyes closed and lips parted to take communion in the ancient way. The glistening tongue quivered timidly, a little creature afraid to venture from the cave of the old man's mouth.

For old he was, short and rather stooping. He was also, in the manner of saints, overwhelmingly serene. His slight body was clothed in a cheap grey sweater and black trousers. The face was that of a wizened bird which had chosen, for obscure reasons, to starve itself. Despite his age, there was a peculiar softness about his curling white hair, so that it had always looked to Father Snow like the hair of a toddler.

Generally speaking, Father Snow was a dauntingly humourless individual. Now, however, as he placed the Host on the quivering tongue, he all but grinned with pleasure and surprise. For Vincent just to turn up like this was unconventional, unheard of, typical of him. Despite his eccentricity, rather than because of it, he was one of the few people Father Snow genuinely admired.

The old man's mouth closed and his eyes opened as though they were connected to the same inner mechanism. For an instant he looked at Father Snow. There was no flicker of recognition on his face. His expression seemed to warn that this was a solemn moment and that, no matter what they felt, neither of them was allowed to betray it now, even by the slightest sign. The warning was superfluous. Father Snow didn't smile. He had already crushed that particular temptation.

On his way back up to the altar, the priest realised there was a trace of spittle left on his finger, an anointment.

While the final hymn was being sung, Father Snow paced from the altar, as stiff and upright as if he had his neck in a brace. In the sacristy, he quickly changed out of his robes. Then, dressed in his black jacket and dog-collar, he waited in the porch to greet his congregation. This was often a long process, as many of them paused to chat, and one of the obligations imposed by his job was to be friendly. Today he was in a particular hurry to get it over and find out why Vincent was there. Nevertheless, it took a good ten minutes. Standing there at the top of the steps, smiling and shaking hands, he felt like an air-hostess showing her passengers out to the safety of solid ground.

All the while, he kept glancing back into the gloom of the church, where one or two people still knelt at prayer, hunched away from the light. He could see Vincent at the back on the left, bent like a wasted sparrow which had tucked its chin down to keep warm. In the distance, at the far end of the church, the bolt of sunshine still slanted onto the altar, a spotlight on an empty stage.

The last person to leave was old Mrs Murphy, a devout old Catholic. She hobbled slowly into the porch and extended a knobbly hand.

'Morning, Father.'

'Good morning, Mrs Murphy.' At that moment, Father Snow suffered an uncharacteristic loss of restraint. He gestured into the church and lowered his voice conspiratorially. 'Before you go, guess who that is.'

The old woman glanced in at Vincent.

'How should I know?'

'I thought you might have recognised him. It's Vincent Capel.'

Mrs Murphy looked baffled.

'Who's he?'

'The Archbishop of Southwark.'

'No!' Mrs Murphy peered in with more interest. There was nothing to see but a small figure, quite alone and insignificant now in the empty church. He looked more hunched than ever, as though he'd fallen asleep on his knees or was nursing a bullet wound, about to topple forwards. 'That's an archbishop?'

Her tone implied that the holders of that office should be far more imposing personages. Now that he'd done it, Father Snow immediately regretted telling her. It had lowered him to the level of a gossip. Straightening his back still further, he clenched his jaw and froze his lips into a thin line.

'Yes,' he said more quietly. 'That's an archbishop.'

Father Snow said an act of contrition as he walked down the aisle. Vincent remained motionless. With ritual precision, the priest genuflected and knelt beside him, not allowing the pew in front to take any of his weight. He almost spoke, but then thought better of it. The archbishop was deep in prayer, perhaps genuinely unaware that Father Snow had joined him.

For ages they both knelt there, perfectly still. Though he closed his eyes, Father Snow was unable to pray. In the end, he allowed himself to turn and look at Vincent. With a special concentration, he took in the chin, still nestling down into the scrawny neck, the large nose, which would have looked small on anyone else. This was the face which, not long before, had inspired him to become a priest. It had been simply that: the face. No words had passed between them. Father Snow, ordinary Julian Snow in those days, had been sunk in a despair so profound that he'd been on the point of seeking medical help. Vincent, walking down the cathedral aisle in full regalia, had done no more than

7

stare for a moment into the young man's eyes. To Julian, the look had seemed an offer of escape.

Still neither of them moved. Eventually, it occurred to Father Snow that Vincent was completely lost in prayer, to the extent that he'd forgotten where he was. Unable to bear it any longer, he shifted slightly on his knees, causing the wood to creak. Vincent didn't move or open his eyes, but spoke at once:

'Keep still, Julian. You fidget like a child.'

'I'm sorry, your grace.' He hesitated for a moment, blushing. 'Won't you come into the presbytery now?'

Again Vincent remained motionless, his head bowed.

'Can't you kneel and pray with me, just for a few moments?'

It was an echo of Christ's words in the garden of Gethsemane. Vincent would never make such an allusion lightly or by accident. Father Snow wondered again about the reason for this visit. Although he'd always flattered himself that Vincent had a special regard for him, their relationship had never outwardly gone beyond that expected between a bishop and a young priest. When he'd seen Vincent at the altar, Father Snow had dared to hope that the great man had come here simply out of friendship. Now he wasn't so sure.

They knelt there for an hour, although to Father Snow it seemed far longer. He felt fretful and impatient, a child made to wait while the adults finished their business. This was unusual for him, accustomed as he was to imposing silence and solemnity on a restless congregation. Now, though, it was he who was the child, Vincent his superior in every way.

Perhaps because of this, Father Snow still couldn't pray. The small of his back and his knees moved in the usual way through fire into numbness, so that at last he felt he was floating above them, but all he could do was wonder why Vincent had appeared so unexpectedly. Then he went back over the time when he'd found his vocation, remembering

8

the emptiness and desperation of his former life. In the end, all he could manage by way of prayer was to thank God for Vincent.

He opened his eyes and stared at the shaft of sunlight above the altar, watching the shifting glitter of the dust. Like many priests, perhaps because of the demands of sermon-writing, he was constantly searching for symbols. The meaning of the dust was obvious. All human life is ephemeral, futile without God. We move for a short time into the light, glow faintly and, in our millions, disappear.

At last, without speaking, Vincent stirred. Father Snow, having performed a meticulous genuflection, led the way out of the church.

After so long in gloom, the light outside was impossibly bright to Father Snow. Yet there was already a touch of winter coldness in the breeze. Sunday was in the air, a stillness which worked its magic even here in London. Stepping through the doorway with Vincent, Father Snow was reminded of another episcopal visit. It had happened in the 1850s, shortly after the church had been built. That visit had taken place in autumn, too, on Guy Fawkes' night. A crowd of people had been on their way to the Common, where they intended to burn effigies not only of Guy, but also of the Pope and various cardinals. When they heard that a real bishop was dining in the presbytery, they changed their route. Soon the building was besieged by a fancy-dress mob with torches and placards. The bishop had been forced to make an escape through the back garden.

The peace of this present Sunday was almost painful to Father Snow. He found himself wishing, not for the first time, that he'd been called to battle for the Church in more dangerous, more bracing times.

Vincent squinted up for a few moments at the cloudless sky, as though expecting a fly-past of angels. Although the sun was behind him, the thin blue hurt to look at.

'A lovely day,' the archbishop pronounced.

'It is indeed.'

Smiling, Vincent turned towards him. As he had that first time, Father Snow felt himself entirely accepted and understood.

'It's good to see you, Julian. Cheers me up more than I can say.'

'It's not like you to need cheering up, your grace.'

'We'll talk about that later. First, I think we should have lunch.'

The presbytery was a large building. There had at one time been three priests in the parish. Now Father Snow lived there alone. He was addicted to order, to the point where it could almost have been called a vice. The whole place had the severe bleakness of an altar. Like many bachelors, Father Snow wasn't much of a cook. When they arrived, he microwaved two packets of shepherd's pie and took them into the simple dining-room.

'I'm sorry, your grace, but this is all I've got in. If you'd told me you were coming . . .'

Vincent nodded understandingly and began to eat.

'It's delicious.'

That said, he ate only half of it. This, however, was not necessarily a reflection either on the food or on the archbishop's appetite. He excused himself by claiming, most implausibly, to have eaten a gigantic breakfast.

The conversation remained general over lunch. They exchanged a little Church gossip, speculated over the possibility of an early general election. Vincent congratulated Father Snow on a piece he'd written for *Living History*, in which he had examined the influence of the famous medieval monastery at Cluny.

'Any other historical projects lined up?'

'Nothing specific.' Father Snow's voice was as clipped as his movements. 'I'm thinking of doing something more recent, when I get the time. Another piece on local history, perhaps. I never feel I really know a place until I've got inside its past.'

Vincent looked steadily at him.

'And do you ever regret not becoming a professional historian?'

'Not for a moment. I might have made a decent historian, but I hope I make a better priest.'

'Of that I have no doubt.'

Father Snow, who'd been up since six, was starving. He disapproved of himself for being weak enough even to admit his hunger. Leaving a little shepherd's pie on his plate, he went out and made two cups of black coffee without sugar. When he'd sat back down, Vincent leaned forward in his chair and spoke in a different tone.

'You've done great things in this parish, Julian.'

'Do you think so? Sometimes it feels to me as if I've done nothing at all.'

'That's false modesty,' said Vincent gently. 'We both know what you've achieved. The place was as good as dead when you took it over. Now I come to Mass less than a year later and I find the numbers are already up. There's something about you that attracts them.'

All expression drained from Father Snow's face. Compliments, almost as much as criticism, always made him feel uncomfortable. Pausing for a moment, Vincent leaned back in his chair. The light was behind him, slanting at an angle through the window. Beyond, a couple of trees waved their dying leaves despairingly, as though they, like so many others, were trying to appeal to the archbishop for help. Further off some of the tower blocks from which Father Snow was managing now to draw a few more parishioners were visible.

'How would you feel,' said Vincent slowly, 'about continuing your good work in a very different place?'

Father Snow was silent for a while. At last they'd reached the nub.

'I'd be sorry to leave, of course,' he eventually said. 'I've been happy here, your grace . . . or, at least, if I've been unhappy, it's been my own fault, not that of the parish or the people. But, if I'm needed elsewhere . . .'

Vincent nodded.

'I want you to understand that I'm offering you a genuine choice. When I ask you whether you want to go, that's not a veiled order. I don't want to send you against your will.'

This was strange. Such transfers, though often expressed as polite requests, were not usually open to refusal. But then, Vincent's very presence here was strange. Normally, Father Snow would simply have been summoned to see him.

'Where's the parish?'

Vincent shifted in his chair, twisting so that he could stare out of the window. The sun made a white halo of his hair.

'It's a little place called Wodden. I'm not sure whether you'd describe it as a large village or a small town. It's about thirty miles outside London, right in the commuter belt. Quite affluent, peaceful . . . idyllic, as far as one can see. The little Catholic church there serves Wodden itself and several neighbouring villages. Until recently –'

Vincent sighed and turned his face towards the ceiling.

'The parish priest was a man called Charles Conner. I knew him slightly many years ago, when he was in the seminary.'

Father Snow watched intently. Vincent was still staring at the ceiling.

'Last week, Father Conner committed suicide.'

When the archbishop lowered his gaze, there was a look of shock on his face, as though he'd been even more surprised by his words than Father Snow. Then Father Snow realised that the expression wasn't one of shock, after all, but of despair. It only lasted an instant.

They were silent for a while, Vincent staring again out of the window, Father Snow watching him. He had never seemed so bent and old. It was Father Snow who eventually spoke.

'Why?'

Vincent shook his head.

'Nobody knows, and perhaps it's best that nobody ever finds out. All we can do is pray for the poor soul and carry on.'

But Father Snow, for all his self-control, was unable to suppress a ghoulish curiosity. Like a true historian, he wanted to know everything – not just why, but how and where. He was a long way from Vincent's detachment.

'What could make a priest do a thing like that?'

Vincent shook his head.

'It's a mystery. As I say, I knew Charles. He was a good man. All I can hope is that he inexplicably went mad. The alternative is too horrible to contemplate.'

That said, they both fell silent again and contemplated it. This was a fruitless exercise on Father Snow's part. He had no idea what Vincent might have been hinting at.

'We mustn't dwell on this,' said Vincent at last. 'All we can do is pray for him.' He turned from the window, suddenly glowering at Father Snow as though the whole thing had been his fault. 'Besiege heaven with your prayers.'

After that, Father Snow did say a short prayer for the unknown priest. He stared out of the window into the sunshine as he did so, unable at that moment to believe that such things could happen in such a world. Yet the glory of God, however manifest, is not in itself enough to redeem the souls of men, though it lies around them on every side in a laughable abundance. The majority are blind, and even a priest may lose his spiritual sight.

'I've prayed long and hard about this, Julian,' said Vincent, 'wondering what to do.'

'You don't think I'm the right man for the job?'

'Oh, there's no doubt about your being right for the job. What disturbs me is that the job may not be right for

13

you. I constantly worry about the repercussions of such a terrible event . . .'

He paused for a moment, looking at Father Snow as though weighing him up for the first time, wondering whether he was a strong enough tool. Father Snow had a fair idea what Vincent saw. Perhaps the hesitation was understandable.

'In any case,' he said at last, 'the choice is yours. I've already put your name forward, but I can always withdraw it. You can have a week to think about it, if you want.'

'There's no need,' said Father Snow. 'I want to go.'

Vincent laughed.

'Ah, impulsive youth!' He stood up, suddenly old and burdened again. 'Anyway, it's settled. I'll set the wheels in motion.'

'You're not going already?'

'I'm afraid I must. The great irony of this job is that as I get older, ever more calls are made on me.'

Father Snow cast about for a way of making him stay, suddenly foreseeing the loneliness his visit would leave.

'Won't you hear my confession before you go?'

Vincent smiled and wagged a finger.

'You're trying to monopolise me, Julian!'

As he spoke, he sat back down with an air of resignation. Father Snow went and fetched his purple stole. Vincent kissed it and placed it around his neck, incongruous over his cheap sweater. The priest knelt down. As soon as he did so, his knees began to burn, still sore from their ordeal in the church. Removing his mind from them, he spent a few moments preparing himself. Kneeling before Vincent, he felt like a failing battery about to be recharged at the mains.

'Bless me, Father, for I have sinned. It has been five days since my last confession.'

Vincent nodded, staring at the wall so that his ear was facing Father Snow. As he thought of the first sin he had to confess, which was his worst, the one for which he

14

most despised himself, the priest felt almost too ashamed to go on.

'I'm proud.'

Vincent nodded as though this were only to be expected. 'What of?'

'My academic ability, the praise I get for my little historical pieces. And I'm proud of what I've done in this parish. I know that many of them only come now because of me.'

'You have nothing to be proud of. We shine,' Vincent smiled slightly, 'like dust in the sun. A compliment is always paid ultimately to God. It should leave you entirely unaffected, like a comment on the weather. If it makes you uncomfortable, then that, too, is a sign of pride.'

Father Snow lowered his head, blushing again: Vincent must have noticed his own embarrassment earlier.

'What about the more conventional form of vanity?'

When Father Snow lifted his head, he was almost sneering.

'I know that I'm attractive to women,' he said, 'but I never think about it. It means less than nothing.'

'You feel that you've risen above all that?'

'In a way. When I'm hearing confessions, I can't help sometimes feeling a kind of scorn for my parishioners, not because they sin, but just because they lead such futile lives. Everything they experience seems so shallow to me. I don't see why they bother to go on.'

'They go on for ordinary, human reasons, which we should do nothing but admire. For the pleasures of parenthood, work and married love. These things, combined with whatever faith they have been given, are enough for most of them, and that is as it should be.'

Father Snow, whose own limited experience of human love had led him to believe that it was a purely temporary phenomenon, still didn't understand.

'It seems pointless to me, all the same. I don't see how people can live without some greater meaning.'

'That's because God has made you in a certain way and called you to a certain work. The fact that he has made other people different doesn't mean you're superior to them. There's not a human being alive that we have any right to look down on. Christ Himself said He was gentle and humble of heart.'

Father Snow was silent for a moment. For him, this was the central mystery of religion: how the Son of God could have been sincerely humble. Yet Vincent himself was living proof that greatness and humility could not only coexist but actually depend on one another. Now the old man, waiting in front of the sunny window, seemed more serene than ever. Looking at him, Father Snow felt that, if only he could spend enough time with Vincent, humility would come. It would simply rub off on him like an infectious mannerism.

'You have an extreme view of the world, Julian,' said Vincent thoughtfully. 'Perhaps that's no bad thing. But the one sin against which you, more than other people, must be constantly on your guard, is despair. Do you still have bouts of depression?'

Father Snow nodded.

'Occasionally.'

'You must be cheerful at all times. If you can't be cheerful, work. And never let anyone know that you're less than perfectly happy. These are your duties not only as a Catholic and a priest, but simply as a human being.' He shifted slightly. 'What about the sins of the flesh?'

Hardly aware that he was doing it, Father Snow froze his face and straightened his back.

'I'm sometimes tempted,' he said, 'but I never fall.'

Vincent raised an eyebrow.

'What's your secret?'

'Constant mortification and prayer to Our Lady. Then, at night, if temptation does come, I go down into the church and kneel there until it's passed. Sometimes I stay until dawn.'

Vincent sighed.

'It's strange . . . that's exactly the answer I'd hope to hear from any other young priest, yet coming from you it worries me.' He paused and leaned forwards as though trying to tease out the meaning of what he'd just said. 'You're too strong, Julian, that's the trouble, too totally committed and disciplined. I can't help feeling that, if only you had some weakness, some chink in your armour, you'd be a better man . . . not to mention a better priest.'

Father Snow's first impulse on hearing this was to answer back, to object that to be too strong, too good, could hardly be called a fault. Instead, he closed his mouth in a hard line and, with some difficulty, bowed his head.

'You've got a long way to go, Julian, but it can be done. The goal has to be sainthood, nothing less. Always remember that. You'll never get there unless you first plumb the depths of your own weakness.'

Then, for the first time since the confession had started, he turned to face Father Snow.

'Let me be frank. I've got a lot of affection for you. The first time I saw you, before we even met, I had an intuition that you were special. Something in you attracted me, just as it attracts so many others.'

Father Snow, mortified by all Vincent had told him, shook his head.

'I don't believe that.'

'Yes, you do,' said Vincent gently, 'because you know it's true. You've been given great gifts. My initial feeling about you has only been strengthened since we've become friends, and it's as a friend that I'm speaking to you now. I believe that one day you'll achieve great things for the Church, on a national level at least, maybe even worldwide.'

Perhaps it was a measure of Father Snow's immaturity and pride that, although he was surprised to hear this, it didn't seem to him particularly absurd. Then, almost kindly, Vincent crushed him.

'But let me tell you,' he said, 'as a friend . . . if you don't learn humility and genuine admiration of your fellow man, however lowly he may be, then you'd be the last person I'd like to see rise to a position of authority in the Church. If you acquired power as you are now, it would be a disaster for us all.'

This was too much for Father Snow. Staring at the carpet, red in the face, he felt for the first time in his life a real dislike for Vincent, almost hating him. When he tried to speak, he found his voice was choked.

'That's not fair,' he said thickly. 'I know I'm not perfect, but I'm trying to improve. I'm doing my best.'

In contrast to his own, Vincent's voice was quiet and perfectly calm.

'Julian, look at me.' Father Snow didn't move. It was a school-master's ploy, and he felt doubly insulted by it. 'Look at me.'

With a great effort, Father Snow lifted his head. Vincent was leaning forward in his chair, smiling slightly, his soft white curls lit from behind. Father Snow found that it was impossible to look at him and hate him at the same time. He was too fatherly and kind.

'Criticism is hard to take,' said Vincent, 'but it's even harder to give. I hate being hard on you, but somebody has to, and I doubt if anyone else would dare. Take it as a mark of friendship and respect. You've got a long way to go, Julian, that's all. There's no shame in that.'

Staring into his eyes, Father Snow suddenly felt he had a glimpse of Vincent's spiritual simplicity and calm. It made him feel like a stiff, screwed-up man, all cluttered and complicated, a massive lumber-room stuffed with talents, failings and morbid neuroses.

'I wouldn't have come here for anybody else,' said Vincent.

It was the declaration of special regard which Father Snow had always hoped to hear from him. Remembering his recent moment of hatred, he felt a smarting shame. His body seemed to relax and, quite naturally, his head bowed once more towards the floor.

'Thank you, your grace.' He paused for a moment, then added: 'I'm sorry.'

When he'd received absolution, Father Snow escorted the archbishop down to his car. Confession wasn't usually a trauma for him, but today it had been, and he found that it had left him strangely relaxed, at peace. He couldn't help feeling that Vincent, the benign manipulator, had deliberately planned it that way.

The sunlight was softer now outside. Even after such a short meeting, Father Snow was sad to see Vincent go. Loneliness was so familiar to him that he only noticed it after seeing a real friend, and there were few enough of them. The presbytery would be strangely empty when he went back inside.

They stopped and shook hands by the car.

'Good luck down in Wodden.'

'Thanks.'

Vincent smiled.

'You'll certainly find they're a different type of parishioner down there. Far more exalted.'

'In worldly terms.'

'In worldly terms, you could hardly go higher. To start off with, there's the Trevellyan family. Have you heard of them?'

Father Snow inclined his head, unimpressed, yet secretly pleased at the opportunity to call up information from the vast, frozen database of his mind.

'They're old Catholic aristocracy. One of the few families rich enough to remain constant to the faith.'

'For which they deserve our gratitude,' said Vincent, in what Father Snow thought was a rather neutral voice. 'And, as if they weren't enough, there's Gerald Pitman.'

Now Father Snow couldn't hide the fact that he really was impressed.

'Not *the* Gerald Pitman?'

'The very same. So perhaps your eloquence may have more direct effect than you'd imagined. Use it wisely, Julian. Remember that I'm the one who recommended you for the job, in the teeth of much opposition, I may say. There were those who said you were too young for such a sensitive posting. So I'm relying on you to be diplomatic.'

'Are you telling me that Pitman's a Catholic?'

'Yes.'

'You wouldn't have thought it.'

'So much for diplomacy,' said Vincent drily.

When he'd got into the car, he leaned across, opened the window, and extended his hand.

'Pray for me.'

With sudden anguish, Father Snow took the old hand in his own. For the morbid and depressive, in whom the awareness of mortality is itself like a disease, every parting is a bereavement. They are the ones who weep for no reason at bus-stops and front doors, sometimes simply unable to believe that those they have been foolish enough to love will return from the most innocent errand. At the same time, Father Snow had once more the sense that his hero was burdened and alone, going through some private Gethsemane.

'I will.'

'Pray for poor Father Conner, too.' Vincent released his hand. 'Besiege heaven with your prayers.'

That night, at six o'clock, Father Snow said his last Mass of the day. It was still before seven when he elevated the Host, but winter was on the way, and the light was already going. It remained now only in a streak of cloud behind the tower blocks, a streamer of red silk frozen on the wind.

A few minutes later, Father Snow went down to distribute communion. This time, as far as his imperfect vision could perceive, there were no saints waiting in the line.

2

TO THE IRRITATION of certain other road users, Father Snow adhered rigidly to the speed limit. He handled the car like an experienced driver going through the formality of his test. Machines relaxed him. The precision and regularity of their movement was similar to his own. He kept both hands on the wheel, signalled and checked his mirrors assiduously. The drive to Wodden, which most people would have polished off in an hour, took him an hour and a half.

His old 2CV, used to ambling around the side-streets of east London, fared badly on the last leg of the journey. Some of the hills became too steep for third gear, and the priest was forced to crawl up them in second. The road at these points cut deep into the ground, a winding ravine of tarmac with steep banks of sandy earth on either side.

Beyond what Vincent had told him, Father Snow had little idea of what to expect. All he knew was that Father Conner had been looked after by a housekeeper, Flora Dugdale. The idea that a priest should be cared for in this way was, like so many other old traditions, fast deserting the Church. Father Snow himself had never had a housekeeper. Working out what to do about this one would no doubt be the first of many difficult decisions.

For the final mile or so, the road became flatter, only undulating slightly, and the view of the distant hills on the right was obscured by a high and seemingly endless wall. From the directions Flora Dugdale had given him over the phone, Father Snow knew that behind the wall lay the grounds of Flamstead House, ancestral seat of the Trevellyans. He kept glancing across as he drove, hoping for a glimpse inside, and at last he was rewarded. A pair of enormous posts marked what seemed to be the only break in the wall, which rose in two waves of brick to meet them. The wrought-iron gates were open, but no house was visible beyond. All Father Snow could see was a narrow lane which wound between the trees and disappeared over a steep hill. There was a sign giving the prices for the National Trust car-park and admission to the building.

From the top of the gateposts, two stone griffons snarled down at the priest as he drove past, posturing with their stiff legs as though about to climb an invisible ladder. Though corroded and blotched with lichen, they were still impressively threatening, an ancient warning to the common herd. Like a retort, insolent and mocking from a little further down the A25, stood the smiling plastic sign of the Happy Eater.

After a couple of hundred yards, Father Snow turned left onto a smaller road and began to drive downhill. A few minutes later, he entered Wodden. As Vincent had said, it was somewhere between a village and a town, or rather it was a village around which a town had encrusted itself, as though the newer buildings had been irresistibly attracted to the older and more picturesque. There was a high street of shops and banks, their signs incongruously modern against the sagging walls and crooked beams. This led to the green, across which the venerable C of E church and the village pub faced each other as though lazily competing for custom. The road then crossed a very modest river by means of an ancient stone bridge. The river was straddled by a Tudor millhouse, now open for the sale of lunches and cream teas.

Father Snow had to continue away from the green for

a few minutes before he reached the Catholic church of St Mark. By this time, he was driving up a gentle slope and had begun to get his bearings. The village lay in a valley. In the hills behind him were Flamstead House and its huge grounds. Ahead of him, rising above the rooftops, he could see nothing but trees, watching his arrival like a gathering of distant, impassive giants.

St Mark's was a Victorian building. Father Snow, pausing to have a look when he'd got out of the car, dated it almost subconsciously: around 1845, earlier than he would have expected. The presbytery, which had obviously been built at the same time as the church, stood on the left, complete with garage.

The door was opened by a stocky middle-aged woman. The first thing to strike Father Snow about her was her glasses, whose elongated ovals made her look like a bemused duck. Her hair was dyed an unlikely shade of brown and set in severe waves, so that you felt you could have reached out and broken off a curl.

'You must be Father Snow.'

'Yes.'

'I'm Mrs Dugdale.' As they shook hands, Father Snow felt it would be a long time before he was allowed to call her Flora, and part of him was relieved. 'Have you got much to move in?'

'Hardly anything. Just clothes and books, really.'

She nodded, wise in the ways of priests.

'Would you like to get them now, or would you rather come in and sit down for a moment first?'

'I'll come in, if you don't mind, Mrs Dugdale. It's been a long drive.'

'Of course.'

Stepping inside, Father Snow found himself in a fairly spacious hallway. On the left was the staircase. On the right were two doors, one next to him, the other further down. At the end of the passage, a third door opened into what must have been the kitchen: there were brown tiles

23

on the floor and Father Snow could see half of a simple wooden table.

The house had the atmosphere common to all presbyteries: that of the institutional home. There was carpet, but it was of the thin, hard-wearing type used in offices, and it was grey. There were pictures on the walls, but they were all devotional. A small photocopier stood on a table just outside the kitchen door.

Mrs Dugdale opened the door to his right.

'If you'd like to make yourself comfortable in here, Father, I'll go and make some tea.'

It was a living-room painted in pale cream. A sofa and two armchairs, all slightly tatty, stood around a low coffee-table. They were arranged as though in conference with one another. Father Snow had the feeling that his intrusion had produced a sudden silence. Every object in the room seemed to stare in his direction. An escritoire stood in the corner opposite the door. Again, there were the devotional pictures, although one of them had recently been removed from above the fireplace. It must have hung there for a long time, because it had left a rectangular shadow behind.

Father Snow hesitated before he sat down, wondering which had been Father Conner's favourite chair. Having decided that it must have been the armchair nearest the fireplace, he sat himself on the sofa under the window. It was a visitor's place. He sat stiff and upright, as though the sofa might be dirty.

There was a strange smell in the room, though it took him a moment to work out what it was and why it should be so unfamiliar. Then he realised that it was just a hint of wood-smoke, alien to any London house. Automatically, he looked at the fireplace. Two blackened logs lay on a bed of white ash like the remains of a botched cremation. Hanging from a row of hooks were a pair of bellows, a poker, and a toasting fork which might have been put to good use by a very small devil. He wondered whether

Father Conner himself had last hung them there, whether the remains in the grate were those of the last fire he'd made before his death.

When Mrs Dugdale returned, he was praying with a new fervour for Father Conner's soul.

'I hope you like Digestives.' She placed a wooden tray on the low table. 'They're all we've got in, I'm afraid. They were –'

She broke off abruptly, leaving Father Snow to fill in the rest: Father Conner's favourite.

'Digestives will be fine,' he said politely, although personally he hated them. He leaned forward and took one. The habitual formality of his movements made it seem that he was elevating a bloated brown Host. He bit it without much relish, reflecting that it had probably come from a packet the priest himself had started. Indeed, it was slightly stale.

'I'm sorry I haven't cleared the grate,' said Mrs Dugdale, but she was watching him eat as she spoke, giving the impression that it was really the stale biscuit she was apologising for. 'I haven't been back here myself since . . .' She floundered, obviously lost for a word which would nod at Father Conner's suicide without striking up too close a relationship with it. Eventually, the best she could do was: 'the terrible tragedy.'

'That's all right.' Father Snow forced down the last of the biscuit and quickly took a sip of tea. 'I quite understand.'

Mrs Dugdale sat down in the armchair furthest from the fire.

'I've dreaded coming back.'

With that, almost casually, she produced a handkerchief from the pocket of her skirt and began to cry. Father Snow stiffened as though someone had placed a gun against the back of his head. Then, to his own horror, he found himself seized by an almost uncontrollable desire to laugh, like a schoolboy getting the giggles in church. The grimness of the situation was simply too

25

much for him. The china cup and saucer began to rattle in his hand.

'Don't worry, Mrs Dugdale,' he said, barely keeping his voice even. 'God's mercy is infinite.'

At that moment, something unfair happened. Mrs Dugdale, nodding agreement, shifted slightly, causing the old armchair to produce a sound exactly like a fart.

Father Snow gave a snort of laughter, which he quickly tried to disguise as a cough. He leaned forward to put down his cup and saucer, having lost faith in his ability to control them.

Mrs Dugdale apparently noticed none of this. She had raised her strange, oval glasses to wipe her eyes. Her shoulders were shrugging up and down as though in bafflement. With a ruthless effort, Father Snow brought himself under control. He clenched his jaw until it hurt. Then he got up and went to her, moving stiffly and slowly, like a man with a neck injury. He perched himself on the arm of her chair and, unbending slightly, patted her on the back. This he did clumsily and with a little too much force, so that it wasn't clear whether he wanted to lessen her grief or punish her for having displayed it so openly. When he'd patted her three times, he removed his hand.

'All we can do is pray for him,' he said. 'We must trust in God's mercy and the power of prayer. We have a duty, to Father Conner as well as to God, not to fall into despair.'

He paused, having run out of stock phrases. Then he found himself wondering how Vincent would have handled the situation. It would certainly not have been by laughing at the woman's tears. Perhaps he would have so completely conquered the aura of the room that she wouldn't have started crying at all. With him there, it would have been impossible for her to feel such grief, which is only another form of loneliness.

In the end, he repeated Vincent's own words:

'Besiege heaven with your prayers.'

It sounded absurd coming from him, but it seemed

26

to work. Her shoulders became still. Self-hatred gripped Father Snow, but he crushed it, because that too is a sin.

'He was a good man, Father.'

'I have no doubt of that, I promise,' he said, trying to sound kind. 'No doubt at all.'

As though in exhaustion, she laid her head against his side. Once more, he stiffened, horrified.

'Oh, Father, I can't tell you how happy I am to have you here. I'm sure you're going to make everything right again.'

Father Snow silently vowed to say a rosary for her that night, on his knees, in penance.

'I hope so, Mrs Dugdale.'

With a sudden movement, she jerked her head away, as though only now realising where it was. Father Snow shifted slightly, released. The housekeeper sniffed and gave a deep, uneven sigh.

'It's all right, Father,' she mumbled. 'You can call me Flora.'

Father Snow coughed.

'I see,' he said inappropriately. 'All right then. Good.'

When they'd finished their tea, she showed him round the rest of the house. Both of them tried to behave normally, to put the moment of premature intimacy behind them.

Besides the kitchen, there was only one other room to see on the ground floor. It was about the same size as the living-room, but facing in the opposite direction, overlooking the garden through a set of french windows. In front of these was a desk, bare except for a telephone and an old portable typewriter with black and silver keys. There was an intensely mournful silence of the kind one unintentionally leaves by going up to a piano in an empty house and sounding a single note.

'This is the study,' said Flora unnecessarily.

Here there were no pictures, though Father Snow could see white patches where two had been removed.

One wall was entirely taken up by built-in bookshelves, all empty.

'Ah, good,' he said. 'Plenty of room for books.'

'Father Conner's sister had all his things collected . . . afterwards.'

So he'd had one personal picture in the living-room and two in here, along with all his books. Perhaps this was the room where he'd preferred to spend his time. Father Snow wondered whether this was also where the suicide had happened.

'How long was he in the parish?'

'Ten years, almost exactly. He arrived in autumn, too.'

Father Snow went to the window and looked out into the garden. It was small but pretty, secluded by a high, moss-covered wall. At the far end, a willow trailed its branches across the green water of a pond, so that they floated on the surface like hair. The whole place seemed sunk in a dank, vegetable sadness. Far up and away in the distance, from their posts on the encircling hills, the trees waved the last of their leaves down at the home of the dead priest, fluttering untroubled farewells.

'It's a beautiful garden.'

'You should see it in spring, Father. It's a little paradise.'

As she spoke, Father Snow's confidence in his ability to cope with it all was shaken for the first time since he'd left London. He felt unbearably alone, abandoned in an unfamiliar world.

'Shall we go upstairs?' he said.

There Father Snow found the lay-out of the ground floor repeated: a bathroom mirroring the kitchen below, a spare bedroom above the living-room, Father Conner's bedroom above his study. There were no pale rectangles on any of the walls upstairs, not even in Father Conner's bedroom. But above the simple bed was the shape of a crucifix which had been removed. It was a shadow of light, as though it had been burnt into the wall by a burst of radiation.

While they were looking round, Flora told him a little about the village and the routine of St Mark's. Wodden had a small Catholic primary school, but no secondary school at all. The nearest was in Dorking. One of the primary teachers gave extra Sunday school classes in the church. Father Conner had made hospital visits every Tuesday and Thursday, doing a rota with Father Mackenzie over in Dorking. Since before anyone could remember, the Catholic priest from Wodden had gone up to Flamstead House and said Mass in the chapel there at midday each Sunday.

Father Snow found this last duty slightly irritating. Normally such private Masses would be conducted by a priest from one of the religious orders, a man who didn't have a parish of his own to look after. Yet he somehow sensed that there would be no question of a newcomer just down from London breaking with the tradition of centuries. As Vincent had said, he would have to be diplomatic, at least to begin with.

For her own part, Flora did the cleaning and cooked the meals. Lunch was at one, supper at seven.

'Well now, Flora,' said Father Snow hesitantly, afraid of stirring up her emotions again. 'I don't think I'll be needing lunch. Things tend to be so unpredictable during the day that I usually just have a sandwich.'

'Oh, there's nothing unpredictable about Wodden!'

'All the same . . .'

She nodded thoughtfully.

'Things are changing, Father, I know. Women like me don't have much place in the modern Church.' She looked up at him through her peculiar spectacles. 'Do we?'

'Not as you used to have.' He shrugged, trying to think of something kind to say. 'It's just the way the world has gone.'

She sighed.

'Just supper, then. I suppose it's for the best, in a way.

I ought really to spend more time with my husband. He has a heart condition, so he's more or less housebound.'

'You'll be glad of the extra time at home, then.'

Flora winked.

'You wouldn't say that if you'd met my husband!'

Father Snow wanted to be friendly, but didn't want to laugh at a stranger behind his back. He resolved this dilemma by giving a humourless smile which was probably the worst of both worlds.

'No,' Flora continued, 'the truth is, I used to be glad to come here, just to get away. It was always a relief to see poor old Father Conner. Such a gentle man. Quite the opposite of my Jack.'

'Is he a Catholic?'

'Well . . . let's say he was baptised one, but that was a long time ago. You'd have thought a man in his terrible condition would turn his mind to spiritual things, but not him. I can only hope he's leaving it till the last moment.'

Father Snow nodded, trying to give the impression that he was speaking from priestly experience.

'Lots of people do.'

After that, Flora offered to help him move in his things, but he insisted that he could manage on his own. In the end, she gave him the keys and got ready to leave. He saw her to the door. Their roles had been reversed since his arrival. She had welcomed him. Now he was seeing her off. It made him feel strange, escorting someone from a house which was not his home, about to be left alone there.

'Thank you, Father,' she said before she left.

'What for?'

'For coming here. It's upset me more than I can say to think of the place standing empty. Now you're here, I feel we have a future again.' She made a vague gesture towards the sunny lane as though it proved her words: 'Life goes on.'

Then she gazed up at him from the doorstep, again with something childlike and insecure in her middle-aged eyes.

He saw how she was already coming to lean on him, as so many in the parish would. All of them would look to him to reaffirm their faith. Nothing could be more shattering for a group of believers than the suicide of their priest. In him, at least, they'd found the right person. Strengthening faith was one of his specialities.

'Don't worry,' he told her, 'about anything. Everything's going to be all right.'

When he went back into the living-room, every object there seemed once more to fall silent and stare in his direction.

3

FOR SOME TIME after Flora had gone, Father Snow sat on the sofa in the living-room, feeling lost. This first day, hung in the limbo between arriving in the parish and starting his work there, would be a strange one. He was addicted to the discipline of routine, and felt uncomfortable, almost anxious without it.

The silence of the countryside, of the house itself, oppressed him. There was no sound of human life going on outside. The presbytery might have been completely isolated, floating through sunny space. He felt uprooted, though in fact he had no roots. Catholic priests may be moved anywhere at any time. Like the prophets of old, they live in a wilderness.

He stared at the grey ashes in the grate, the brass toasting-fork, the pale rectangle above the mantelpiece. All of these things seemed suddenly filled with Conner's personality, which was now indistinguishable from his last action. They somehow gave a direct knowledge of him which Father Snow couldn't have put into words, but which he felt was more knowledge than he needed or wanted. The curiosity which had until now possessed him vanished. Vincent had been right: it was unwise to try and get to the bottom of such perfect despair.

In the end, the brass tools and the armchair took on a frantic stillness, like children holding their breath. He felt they were trying to communicate with him in the only way they could, dumb witnesses exploding with the burden of what they'd seen. They seemed to fill the room with a tangible atmosphere, as sad as a winter sunset, and as cold.

After a few moments, Father Snow left the house and went into the church, where he spent an hour at prayer. Then, feeling better but still at a loose end, he decided to go and have a look round Flamstead House. Not wanting to be gawped at by the villagers, he changed into ordinary clothes before he left.

He walked down the gentle hill from the presbytery, over the bridge, and up onto the village green. To his surprise, it was from here that he got his first glimpse of the building. Set high above the village, it seemed to have been magically constructed on the trees below it. All that could be made out over that great distance was a long rectangular outline and the glint of windows in the sun. Yet this was enough to excite Father Snow, filling him with a yearning to climb up there and investigate the place.

After that, he walked more quickly. Even so, it took him twenty minutes to make his way along the high street, then up through the newer outskirts and out onto the A25. After he'd passed the posturing griffons on the gateposts, the walk to the house itself took as long again.

The park was enormous and beautifully landscaped. A little mist hung around the trees, as though it were pumped out by some invisible engine to impress the tourists. Herds of deer roamed slowly, adding to the effect. Father Snow had never been so close to deer. There were one or two young stags with furry little antlers, and even he couldn't help thinking that they were like something from a fairy tale.

Once the first undulation of the ground and the first screen of trees were behind him, the house was constantly visible up above, looking down over the gently sloping grass with the dozy indifference of old age. The grandeur of the building came partly from the simplicity of its conception and partly from its sheer size. It was just a

33

long rectangle with three rows of windows. There was a kind of arrogance in realising such a simple idea on such a huge scale, and it worked perfectly. Nobody who saw it could fail to catch their breath.

Having climbed to the level of the house, he stopped and turned around. Below him, he could make out here and there the roofs of the village through the trees. He even thought he could catch a glint of water from the distant stream. Beyond those which surrounded the village, a whole new range of hills had appeared in the distance. They were no more than a pale strip in the sun, slightly blue, as though set back into the sky, but they gave a fantastic sense of freedom and space. The aristocrats who'd chosen to settle here had made wise use of their outrageous power.

The house was entered through a high archway. Inside the archway, on the right, was an ordinary front door. On the left was a little wooden booth, where Father Snow paid his entrance fee and bought a guide. From this he learned that the front part of the building which he'd seen on his way up the hill was not open to the public, still being occupied by the Trevellyans. However, it was not the oldest part of Flamstead, having been added in the late eighteenth century. The original Tudor structure still remained, surrounded on all sides by the newer building, a mansion within a mansion.

Looking up from the booklet, Father Snow stepped into an eighteenth-century courtyard. The Tudor part of the building was entered through another enormous archway on the far side. Its doors were huge and dark, their iron bolts the size of a fist. A normal door had been cut into the wood of the giant ones as though for the use of ordinary human beings.

Beyond lay another courtyard, surrounded by tall red chimneys, typically Tudor. A huge pair of antlers hung from the far wall. They must have been eight or nine feet from tip to tip. He couldn't see how any stag could have carried them on its head. Yet here they were, hanging in the courtyard of an English country house like a trophy from a hunting expedition in the grounds.

The first room he saw inside was the great dining hall with its raised wooden dais. The whole place was panelled in dark oak, ornately carved. From the high musician's gallery, griffons stared down at him. His booklet said, as if anyone would need telling, that the griffon was the symbol of the Trevellyan family. It also told him that Henry VIII was reputed to have dined here during his youth, though the Catholic family had subsequently endured a period of royal disfavour which had lasted on and off until the reign of William and Mary.

After that, Father Snow lost track of time. The other visitors, the signs forbidding photography, the red ropes cordoning off prize exhibits, all seemed to vanish. His normally unemotional face was softened by an expression almost of wonder. Hardly aware that he was doing it, he began running his hand through his hair as he looked around, so that soon even his perfect parting had fallen into disarray.

He saw long dark galleries, stately bedrooms where kings and queens had slept, ancient tapestries ready to crumble at a touch or even a blast of direct sunlight. What really held him, though, were the portraits. They were dotted all over the house, but on the first floor there was one long room which must have contained a hundred of them. Many depicted members of the Trevellyan family, but there were other luminaries as well, from poets to explorers. Father Snow wasn't happy until he'd looked up each name in his booklet. Time and again as he did so he had the sensation of meeting an old friend.

He lingered in that room, staring up at portraits. He felt a nostalgia for their lives which he would never have allowed himself to feel for his own.

In the end, the attendants told him they were closing up. Wintry twilight was already falling by the time he got outside. The distant line of hills had lost all definition. It might have been no more than a band of dim, low-lying cloud, a blue gas above the blackness of the nearer trees.

Before he set off through the park, Father Snow turned for one last look at the house. The next time he came here, it would not be as a tourist, but as a priest. He was going to become part of Flamstead's life, and now that didn't seem to him such a bad thing, after all. Since before the Reformation, an unbroken line of priests had come to say Mass here, and he now saw that to join their number could be regarded as nothing but an honour.

Father Snow hardly noticed the walk back across the park and through the village. His mind was alive with vague ideas for new historical projects which refused to take precise shape. All he knew was that he had to start writing something about Flamstead House as soon as possible. A place like that, where Catholicism had struggled and survived for so many centuries, was the perfect subject for him. It was where history met religion. First, he thought in terms of articles, then in terms of an entire book. All he needed was the focus, the angle from which the thing should be approached.

By the time he got back, it was entirely dark. At first he was surprised to see lights on in the presbytery, but then he realised that, of course, Flora would be inside preparing his supper.

The musty, smoky smell of the house depressed him as soon as he stepped inside. Never having had a housekeeper before, Father Snow found Flora's presence rather awkward. He didn't know whether he was expected to stay in the kitchen and talk to her, or whether he should just wander off into the house and leave her to her work. In the end, since there were things he wanted to know, he decided to go in and chat.

Flora had the business of cooking well under control. While things bubbled away on the cooker behind her, she was sitting at the table, reading a romantic novel. She put it down, perhaps with a little reluctance, as Father Snow entered.

'Hello, Father. I see you haven't moved any of your things in.'

It was true: he'd clean forgotten. Once more, he'd allowed himself to behave like a visitor.

'No. I've been up at Flamstead House most of the afternoon. It's an amazing place.'

'It is that.'

'What are the Trevellyans like?'

'Oh, the children are all grown up and living in London now. We see Lady Trevellyan in the village from time to time, though. She has her shopping to do, just like everybody else.'

'And how about Lord Trevellyan?'

'He keeps himself to himself. Has a reputation for being one of those rich, reclusive types, if you know what I mean. Still, anyone who wants to gawp at him only has to go to Mass up at the house on a Sunday.'

Father Snow was surprised.

'The Masses are public, then?'

'Oh, yes. Lots of people go. It's just like the second Sunday Mass, but held up there instead of here.'

This information further improved Father Snow's opinion of the tradition.

'And what about Gerald Pitman? Do you see much of him?'

'Oh, no. He's away most of the time. They say that he's a friend of Lord Trevellyan's, though. When he is in Wodden on a Sunday, he always goes to Mass up at the house.'

As she spoke, she got up and began to serve Father Snow's dinner. It was steak and kidney pudding, which had no doubt been Father Conner's favourite. While he ate it, Flora began to wash up the pots and pans. He wondered whether this had been her routine with Father Conner. If

37

so, it must have been strange to have a new man there, doing exactly the same things.

When she'd gone, Father Snow decided that it was too late to start moving his things in now. He just drove the 2CV round to the side of the building and parked it in the garage.

Although the garage-door was still open behind him, it was almost completely dark inside when Father Snow turned the headlights off. He got out of the car. Then he just stood there for a moment, his eyes adjusting to the gloom, and looked around him. There was a bare work-bench, but no tools. Under the bench was a can of oil. All he could see on top was what looked like a filthy rag. Then, as they had done in the living-room that afternoon, the objects around him seemed to acquire an intense stillness, dumb things desperate to communicate. Again, there was that air of cold sadness.

Back in the house, Father Snow went into the living-room and started going through the drawers of the escritoire. The silence was profound as he pulled them open, the silence of an abruptly finished conversation. He found bills, newsletters, leaflets and a few letters from parishioners. From all of these he began to get an idea of the parish and the state of its finances, which were far healthier than those of his last parish. Yet there was not a single scrap of paper which would give him any clue about Father Conner. Like the garage and the rest of house, the escritoire had been scrubbed clean, as though deliberately to remove all trace of the man.

It was the same story in the study. Having looked around in vain for a few moments, Father Snow just went and stared through the french windows. The black line of the trees in the distance was receding into the night, a dissolving vapour. The wild was out there, the still countryside whose silence filled the house. Though he was used to loneliness, this intensity of solitude was new to him. He supposed he would get used to it.

Suddenly he was struck by an idea. He went to the old portable typewriter on the desk and stared at its roller, wondering if there might be any trace of Father Conner's last work. Indeed, it was possible to make out the indentations of a few jumbled letters, but he doubted whether sense could be made of them, even in daylight.

One inspiration leading to another, he went back to the living-room and started examining the remains in the grate. But all he found was a few blackened pieces of ash among the white. They cracked under his touch. He had a feeling that they might once have been cardboard or photographic paper, but they were meaningless now.

Going through to the kitchen to make himself a last cup of tea, he saw the guide to Flamstead House where he'd left it on the table. Somehow this one personal possession made the entire room forlorn, as though the little leaflet was a part of himself which couldn't be defended against the sadness of the house. Full of an irrational pity for it, he took it through to the study and put it on one of the shelves, but the effect was even worse in there. Eventually, feeling foolish but somehow unable to bear the thing alone in the emptiness, he went upstairs to hide it away in the bedroom.

The obvious place was the shelf at the top of the wardrobe. As he was pushing the booklet away to the back, well out of sight, Father Snow encountered an obstruction. In a rush of excitement, he grabbed it and pulled it towards him. To his confusion, he found he was holding another guide to Flamstead House.

It was the same as his own, but faded. Father Snow felt a moment of unease at the idea that he'd chosen exactly the same place as his predecessor to hide exactly the same object. He sat down heavily on the bed and stared at the cover of the old booklet. At last he had found something missed by the scrubbing the house had been given after the suicide. In historical terms, he'd uncovered his only primary source.

The pages were blank. He turned them idly, barely bothering to look. Then he got a shock. One page towards the end was covered in doodles. They were made up of the very fine, delicate lines produced by a retractable pencil. At first, Father Snow just stared at them in horror. The shapes were an intense, direct expression of the dead man's personality. His own doodles tended to be hard, angular and structured. These were just a soft confusion, like a collection of strangely shaped clouds.

After he'd got over the initial shock, Father Snow began to wonder why that particular page should have been completely filled while the others were all blank. It was one of the pages which gave details of the portraits in the gallery where he had stood marvelling for so long. Father Snow began reading down the list of names, wondering if one of them might provide a clue. Only by doing this did he find the note which Father Conner had hidden away in his mass of shapes. As soon as he read it, he knew he had the key, the focus for his next piece of writing.

Each portrait on the page was numbered, and the note was written carefully next to number forty-three. The description said:

43. Everard Trevellyan, 3rd Earl of Wodden. 1503–1573.

In other words, this was the Trevellyan who had lived through the Reformation, and, as it appeared, on to a ripe old age. He was the one who would have entertained the young Henry VIII, assuming he'd really visited Flamstead. Beside the brief description of his portrait, the note, written in a neat, faint hand, said:

The English G?

A few hours later, when he had completed his normal observances and said an extra rosary in penance for laughing at Flora, Father Snow climbed into the dead man's bed. The sheets were cold and gave off a musty, unused smell.

Although he was tired by the upheavals of the day, it took him a long time to get to sleep. Even more than the unfamiliar silence of the room, it was the note in the booklet that kept him awake. He wracked his brains to think who or what that 'G' might be, but it was pointless. He couldn't even remember which of the many portraits in the gallery had been of Everard, the third earl.

As his brain grew more tired and less clear, it began to circle like a vulture around the idea of Father Conner. There were now two mysteries surrounding the man. The first was his death. The second was the three faint words in the booklet, apparently the nearest he'd left to a suicide note, although it was hard to see the connection between a Tudor Englishman, a single initial, and the recent suicide of a rural priest.

On the edge of sleep, it seemed obvious to Father Snow that there had to be a connection of some sort. All he had to do was think hard enough and it would suddenly leap out at him. Thinking as hard as he could, he fell asleep and had a nightmare.

He was in the grounds of Flamstead House. A priest in a black cassock was coming towards him, wearing the pair of enormous antlers from the courtyard. Knowing how heavy they must be, Father Snow was intrigued to find out how they were fixed on. The priest stood still, allowing him to go up and have a look. To his horror, he found that they grew right out of the man's head, part of the living bone. Father Snow asked the stranger who he was, suddenly thinking that it must be Father Conner and that he must have committed suicide because of this terrible deformity. Father Snow felt a confused relief at having solved the mystery of his death.

But the priest looked at him seriously.

'No,' he said. 'I am the English G.'

As he spoke, everything went dark. At first, Father Snow thought that night had fallen. Then, lifting his head, he saw that the sky was black with griffons, right down to the hills on the horizon.

4

IT WAS STILL dark when Father Snow got up. Kneeling in Father Conner's bedroom, he said his morning prayers and the first part of his Office. The sadness and solitude of the presbytery were more intense than they had been the day before. A weaker man wouldn't have been able to stand it long.

As it got light, he looked out of the window and found that the hills had vanished. Even the willow at the end of the garden had gone. The house was swaddled in fog, as though it had miraculously ascended into the clouds.

At eight thirty, Father Snow said his first Mass in his new parish. Even for a weekday, the congregation was small. They spoke in quiet voices, as though the fog coiling around the church were some ghostly dragon that they were afraid of awakening. At the end of Mass, he stood in the porch and greeted his new parishioners with as much warmth as he felt was genuine, filing their names carefully away in his mind. They would be impressed next day to find he'd remembered them.

When everyone had left, he walked back to the presbytery, going through the motions of Father Conner's life. There was a strange stillness outside. Fog trickled from the hedges. The quaint cottages had wreathed themselves in it like children pretending to be ghosts.

After breakfast, Father Snow went into the garage to get his address book from the car. Back in the study, he rang the London offices of *Living History*, and asked to be put through to Martin Matthews, the editor.

The line was busy. Father Snow, offered a choice between holding and trying again later, opted to hold, and was rewarded with a rather flat electronic rendering of 'Greensleeves'. Trying not to listen, he sat and stared out into the garden. The willow was just visible now, a fountain of shadow in the fog.

At last Martin's fast, familiar voice came on the line.

'Hello, man of God.'

Father Snow didn't narrow his eyes or clench his jaw. If anything, his expression softened slightly. Martin was an old friend from his pre-ordination days, and one of the few people left courageous enough to adopt a flippant tone with him.

'Hello, Martin.'

'I hope you're not going to try and foist another of your deathly boring articles on me.'

Father Snow's pride would have been hurt if he hadn't been so confident, not so much in Martin's friendship, but in his own abilities.

'You didn't find the Cluny piece interesting?'

'Brilliant, if you happen to be into medieval monasteries. However, just between you and me, Julian, it isn't what the multitudes are clamouring for. Couldn't you do something to boost my circulation? Why don't you work up a new theory about Jack the Ripper?'

'Actually, I wasn't ringing to offer anything at all. I was wondering if you could do me a favour.'

'Say no more, Father. The answer is no.'

'A small one.'

'So, all is not well in the East End, eh? Let me guess. Car nicked? Squatters in church? Am I getting close?'

'I'm not in the East End any more,' said Father Snow, still looking out at the misty shape of the willow. 'I've been moved out to a place called Wodden.'

'What, just like that?'

'Just like that.'

'Wodden . . . Wodden . . .' It was the tone one uses when looking something up in an encyclopaedia, and Father Snow knew that Martin was about to impress him with his compendious knowledge of history. 'Wodden . . . got it! The Trevellyan lot, right?'

'Right.'

'Flamstead House, home of one the great English Catholic families. Fought on the Royalist side in the Civil War. Rumoured to have given shelter to Campion. Erm . . . hang on, there's something else about Wodden. Isn't that where the great Gerald Pitman hangs out?'

'Right again.'

'And he's a Catholic, too.'

'Yes.'

'Met him yet, have you?'

'Not yet.'

'Knee him in the balls for me when you do.' He coughed, perhaps feeling he'd gone too far, and Father Snow was saddened. In the old days, Martin would happily have gone much further. 'Now, why don't you ask me this blasted favour of yours? I can't sit here chewing the fat with you all morning, you know. There are masses to educate.'

'I was wondering if you could tell me anything about Everard Trevellyan. He was the third earl.'

'Sorry, mate, never heard of him. In this case, it's the family that's famous, not the individual members.'

'So if somebody referred to Everard as the English G, that would mean nothing to you?'

'No. Why should anyone want to do that?'

Father Snow briefly explained about the note in the guide, without referring directly to Father Conner's suicide.

'I have to admit I'm intrigued,' said Martin, 'but nothing immediately springs to mind. Can't you tell me anything about this Everard at all?'

'Just his dates: 1503 to 1573.'

'The obvious thing would be to research him a bit and find out who G might be that way. Why don't you just go up to the stately pile and ask the family about it?'

'Yes, I'm going to.'

'Ring me back afterwards and tell me what you've found out. In the meantime, I'll have a bit of a think. If anything springs to mind, I'll get in touch.'

'Thanks a lot, Martin.'

'It's nothing. Just say a prayer for me when you've got a spare moment, eh?'

For the first time since they'd started talking, Father Snow wasn't sure if his friend was joking.

As he put the phone down, Father Snow was assailed by nostalgia. He remembered the old days before his ordination, his old routines, his old acquaintances. Everything had changed beyond recognition when he'd entered the priesthood. Now he was more completely alone. He remembered his mother's horror when he'd told her. The anonymity of the cloth was not what she'd intended for her clever, handsome son.

Then, without any warning, he remembered his father. It had been he, not Julian's mother or grandmother, who'd read the little boy fairy tales as he lay tucked up in bed. Now it sometimes seemed that those moments had formed the closest human contact he'd ever known, moments of complete trust, unappreciated at the time.

After that Father Snow was away for a while in the earliest memories of his childhood. They gave off grief like a gas, and he closed his eyes, allowing it to overcome him. The past is all that matters, in a way. Only memory has any real meaning. Yet Father Snow had always known that nostalgia was no more than self-pity in disguise. As such, it was a vice, and as such, after a few moments of weakness, he crushed it.

Internally offering the work to God, he went to move

his things in from the car. No sooner had he opened the boot than he heard the phone ringing from the house. He hurried back, for a priest never knows what kind of emergency may be waiting on the other end of the line.

'Hello, is that Father Snow?'

'Yes.'

'Good morning, Father. I'm Bill Saunders. I'm the headmaster of St Dominic's primary school.'

The words were spoken in a slow sing-song, the tone so friendly as to be almost patronising. It was as though Father Snow were one of the headmaster's little pupils who'd come to him in tears.

'Ah. Hello.'

'Flora Dugdale told me you'd arrived,' said Saunders kindly, and Father Snow realised the extent to which the village, besides being a community of individuals, was also a single organism, a growth which was already spreading gentle feelers into his life. 'I was wondering if you were free this morning.'

'Yes, so far.'

'How would you like to come and have a nose round the school?'

'I'd love to.'

'Right-ho. Stick tight. I'll potter round and pick you up in about ten minutes.'

So Father Snow had once more to postpone the moving in of his things. Instead, he sat down on the sofa in the living-room and waited. Even at this time in the morning, the silence hissed in his ears. He could hear the occasional drip of water from outside. A lone bird was singing, as though it had got lost in the fog and was putting out a plaintive distress call. After a few moments, it stopped. Father Snow found himself staring at his predecessor's empty armchair, wondering if he too had once waited here for his first meeting with Bill Saunders. The chair stared back, eloquently still.

46

Before the headmaster had arrived, the phone rang again. Father Snow was glad of the distraction.

'Could I speak to Father Snow, please?'

It was a female voice. Though young, it was quiet and respectful, the voice of a dowdy junior librarian.

'Speaking.'

'My name's Susan Fenton, Father. I'm with the *Dorking Advertiser*. I was wondering if I could come round and talk to you some time today.'

'What about?'

'Oh, just things in general.'

The doorbell rang as she spoke.

'All right, if you want. You can come at around one this afternoon.'

'Thank you very much, Father.'

Bill Saunders turned out to be a thin, middle-aged man. He had sparse hair combed over a bald head like pampas grass blown over a stone. In comparison with his gaunt face, his lips were unpleasantly thick, his eyes bogglingly prominent, as though he'd just been punched in the stomach or swallowed something the wrong way. Perhaps to compensate for his appearance, his manner was, as it had been on the phone, superfluously friendly.

'Morning, Father! Great to have you with us!'

They shook hands. As though to make up for being so thin and bony, the hand in Father Snow's gripped hard and pumped enthusiastically.

'Shall we go?'

Father Snow nodded, unable to match the warmth of the other's smile. Saunders led the way to a beige Volvo and opened the door for Father Snow. The inside of the car smelt strongly of dog. On the back seat, he noticed a couple of blankets, and guessed that the smell came from them. Saunders started the engine and drove slowly down the lane towards the centre of the village, peering into the fog, leaning forwards over the wheel like a mantis. After a few moments, he had to put the windscreen-wipers on.

'A typical Wodden morning,' he said cheerfully. 'There's something about this valley that seems to attract mist and fog, particularly at this time of year. It's usually lifted by lunch-time, though.' He glanced across at Father Snow. 'Not quite the sort of thing you're used to, I imagine. They tell me you're a Londoner.'

'Yes.'

'So, what are your first impressions of Wodden?'

'It's a lovely village,' said Father Snow dutifully. 'I didn't think places like this still existed.'

'Oh, they do, they do,' said Saunders, again as if Father Snow were a small child who'd come to him for reassurance. The headmaster licked his thick lips, giving the impression that they'd get gummed together if he didn't keep them moist. 'Old England will always exist, whatever happens. Very little has changed here over the centuries. You'll love it here, believe me. It's a great place! Great people!'

Father Snow wanted to point out that none of it had been great enough to save Father Conner from despair. As though guessing his thoughts, Saunders leaned a little closer to the windscreen, shaking his head.

'It was a terrible thing about Father Conner. The whole village is still in shock.' His head swayed from side to side so that it seemed he was wired up to the wipers. 'Terrible thing, terrible thing.'

'Yes.'

Since Saunders seemed to have said his piece on the subject of the suicide, Father Snow tried to come up with a formula which would tactfully elicit more information. Before he'd had a chance to find one, they had pulled up in front of the school. On the other side of an old stone wall, he saw one long, low, single-storey building, visible only as an outline in the mist. Lights gleamed faintly, unnatural and depressing at that time of day, the lights of a fogbound ship.

'There it is,' said Saunders. 'Nothing grand, as you can

48

see. Of course, we take Catholic children from a number of surrounding villages, as well as Wodden. The routine we got into with Father Conner was Mass for the entire school, over at the church, on the first Friday of every month. I hope that will be all right for you.'

'No problem at all.'

'Good. Just one other thing before we go and have a look around. The little ones all know Father Conner is dead, but they don't know . . . everything.' Father Snow was surprised to hear a headmaster referring to his pupils as 'little ones'. It would have been bad enough coming from a mother. From Saunders it was, like the man's friendliness itself, slightly repellent. 'We thought it was best.'

'I quite understand.'

They stepped into the cold air. Little phantoms of fog streamed from their mouths and drifted away, making it seem that the fog which covered the village was just a single, giant breath. Bushes and trees stood around the playground. The tarmac was pushed up and cracked in places by the roots below. Inside, it was, as far as Father Snow could see, a perfectly unexceptional primary school. There was the usual nasty smell in the corridors. The usual cheerfully clumsy pictures hung on the walls. The children seemed more subdued than those in the East End, or perhaps they were just better behaved. They were certainly disciplined, all standing to attention as soon as Saunders entered the room, obediently chanting good morning to their new parish priest.

'Good *morn*-ing, Father Snow.'

While they were looking round the classes, the bell rang and the whole place emptied into the playground. Father Snow was taken to the staffroom to meet the teachers. One of them, a Miss Histon, attracted his attention because she didn't seem to fit in. She was a young woman in her early twenties with dyed red hair, trendy clothes and large ear-rings. All of this somehow gave her the air of

49

a Londoner, and he couldn't help wondering whether she was a newcomer to Wodden, like himself.

When he'd introduced Father Snow to everyone, Bill Saunders offered him a lift home. The priest refused, saying he preferred to walk. Leaving them to their coffee, he stepped into the busy playground.

The girls were skipping, the boys playing football, lively little ghosts in the mist. Father Snow paused to watch on his way to the gate. At first he was simply stunned by the amount of noise and movement being produced, as any adult would have been. Then his nostalgia returned like a trance. He stood quite still, as though he'd just caught a whiff of a familiar perfume and didn't want to lose it before he'd remembered what it was. His own games at school returned to him. He remembered the huge comfort he had drawn from the idea of his mother waiting for him at home. Then, as though only those few moments out of his entire past life had any real meaning, his mind returned to the memory of his father reading him fairy stories as he lay in bed, to those moments of understanding and trust, unappreciated at the time.

Hardening his face, Father Snow continued towards the gate. Just as he reached it, he heard giggles from behind him, and turned, wondering if he had been the cause.

Screened from the building and the other children by the bushes which surrounded the playground, he saw two girls of about eight. They were waiting there where nobody else could see as though deliberately to ambush him. At first, seeing that they'd got his attention, they glanced at each other. Then the one on the right lifted her skirt. After a moment's pause, more shyly, her partner followed suit.

For a split second, Father Snow was too shocked even to remove his eyes. Then he instinctively flinched, as though from the sight of something painful, turning back towards the gate. Behind him, he heard a renewed burst of giggling, louder now, at once more excited and embarrassed. He realised that he'd handled the situation badly. They'd set out to shock him, and they'd succeeded. For their own sake, he should have just laughed it off, treated it as no more than a bit of naughty, childish fun. But he'd been unable to laugh.

As he walked through the gate, he heard the girls running away behind him, still giggling. Putting a belated smile on his face, he turned to watch them leave, but they had already rejoined the throng of children. Then he found his gaze drawn back to the school building. His eyes scanned the squares of artificial light and suddenly stopped.

Saunders was there, watching him leave. Because of the bushes, he would have been unable to see exactly what the girls had done. But he would have seen Father Snow's reaction, and he would have seen them run giggling away a moment afterwards. Now he was standing perfectly still at the window, and his face, caught without its friendly expression, was as white and hollow as a trick of the mist.

It only lasted a fraction of a second. Then, realising that he'd been seen, Saunders smiled and gave an exaggerated wave, like a mother waving goodbye to a small child. With a nod which would probably have been invisible at that distance, the priest turned and left.

On his way back through the village, Father Snow saw something amazing.

A wind had come up by now and was blowing holes in the mist. There was a hint of watery sunshine breaking through. Crossing the village green, he happened to look up, and when he did so, he saw Flamstead House. It seemed even higher and more distant than before, smaller than a matchbox. The mist had cleared around it, and now the sun was glittering from its windows, flashing down at the common cottages. Yet below the building was a layer of mist which had not yet been blown away, so that it looked as though the great house, with all its gigantic archways and stone griffons, had been constructed on an undulating veil of cloud.

★   ★   ★

51

Back at the presbytery, Father Snow said the second part of his Office and made himself a sandwich. This he ate alone in the kitchen, staring out into the garden and wondering what they would be saying about him now in the school. He knew all too well the kind of first impression he made. They would have thought him a cold fish, distant and severe. Yet they would have been impressed, perhaps even attracted, by his air of certainty.

When he'd finished eating, Father Snow got up from the table, intending to go and move his things in from the car. Instead, acting almost without his own volition, he fell to his knees and bowed his head.

Teach me to love them.

For a long time he brooded on these words, seeing how he still responded to other people too much with the prejudices of an ordinary man, too little with the generosity of a Christian and a priest. Then he prayed to be forgiven for the way he'd looked at the two girls. The sin had caught him by surprise.

A few minutes later, he got up and moved in his things. It didn't take him very long. There were only a few cardboard boxes of books and two suitcases of clothes. At the bottom of one of the boxes, hidden under the books, was a framed photograph. Taking care not to look at it, Father Snow went quickly upstairs, holding the photograph as though it were something insanitary that had to be disposed of. In the bedroom, he opened one of the desk-drawers and put it inside, facing downwards. As he closed the drawer, the doorbell rang.

Downstairs, he found a girl in her early twenties waiting on the doorstep. Father Snow didn't at first realise that she was the journalist who'd rung him that afternoon, because she was somehow not what he'd been expecting. She had straight dark hair, bobbed just above the shoulder. The line of her jaw was so strong and wide as to be almost masculine. As though to compensate, her large mouth and eyes had a pronounced femininity. It was a face too downright odd to have been called beautiful, yet more striking than any mere beauty could have been.

For an instant, they just stood and stared at each other, and Father Snow realised that she, too, had not found exactly what she'd been expecting. Then she extended her hand.

'Father Snow?' Her voice was as serious and respectful as it had been on the phone. 'I'm Susan Fenton.'

Unlike the headmaster's, her handshake was light and brief. There was no make-up on her face. The strong colour of her lips was natural, the touch of red about her cheeks had come purely from the cold air. Her blue, knee-length skirt and matching jacket would have been more suitable for a woman twice her age, as would her eminently sensible shoes.

They went through to the living-room, where she sat on the sofa, holding her handbag on her closed knees. There was something very proper and vaguely anachronistic about the posture. Father Snow took the armchair furthest from the fire. Father Conner's chair remained empty.

'What can I do for you?'

'Well, Father, as I mentioned on the phone, I work for the local paper. One of the jobs we cub reporters get put on is just to go round making routine visits – you know, the hospital, the police and so on, just in case anything interesting has happened.' She gave a cool smile. 'Which, this being Wodden, it never has, of course. Anyway, the Catholic priest is on my list.'

This was strange to Father Snow. There had been no such arrangements with journalists in his old parish. He supposed that in London there had been more than enough knifings and burglaries to fill up the local paper.

'Well,' he said, 'since I only arrived yesterday, I'm afraid I can't tell you much.'

'I understand that. I've only really come round to leave you my card and let you know the way things work.' She shook her head as though astonished at herself. 'I'm sorry, that sounds terribly arrogant, but you know what I mean.'

'Yes.'

'Anything you hear might be of interest to me. You know, right down to the level of cats stuck up trees and all that. I'd be interested in things you arrange, as well. Fêtes, youth-clubs, that kind of thing.'

'All right. If anything comes up, I'll let you know.'

'Thank you, Father.'

They were silent for a moment. Father Snow was surprised to find himself able to sit there quietly, almost relaxed. He'd never felt really at home with young women, particularly since his ordination. The question of sex was always too clumsily prominent. But there was an almost Victorian modesty about Susan which put him at his ease. The handbag on her knees was a defensive wall which, though small, had vast totemic power and could never be breached. It seemed to embody an absolute determination to see him as no more than a priest, and a grim warning that he must behave as one. Perhaps Father Snow was able to relax because he sensed that the merest hint of anything sexual between them would have embarrassed her even more than it would him.

Now, in fact, she seemed to have forgotten him entirely. There was a grave, inward look on her face, as though she had suddenly been overwhelmed by the despair of the building.

'How well did you know Father Conner?' he asked suddenly.

'Not terribly well. I saw him like this for a chat occasionally, but that was all.'

'How would you describe him?'

'Physically? Middle-aged, grey, slightly podgy man. He had a sort of high, wavering voice.'

'And his personality?'

She shifted slightly, as though disturbed by these unexpected questions.

'Oh . . . kind, I would have said . . . hesitant . . . gentle. Probably not particularly brave or strong, although one never can tell, of course. But certainly kind.' For an instant, she looked directly into the priest's eyes. 'You never met him, then?'

'No. The first I heard of him was after his death. I don't even know how it happened.'

This surprised her.

'Nobody's told you?'

'No. There's a certain . . . unwillingness to discuss the details.'

'That's understandable, I suppose. It's only natural that people should want to put such a terrible thing behind them, especially in a place as small as Wodden.' She looked away from him. 'He gassed himself in the garage. He just ran a length of pipe from the exhaust into the car and switched the engine on.' When she turned back, there was an expression of sympathy on her face, as though she hoped to make him feel better about it all. 'It was probably painless. I'm sure he can't have suffered at the end.'

'I hope not.' Father Snow was silent for a moment, remembering the intense sadness he'd felt in the garage the night before. 'Why?'

'I've no idea. They say he'd been depressed, but nobody knows the reason. The inquest was open and shut . . . I did my best to discourage the paper from dwelling on it.'

'Why?' said Father Snow. 'Are you a Catholic?'

'No, I'm not. I just felt –' Her eyes moved around as though the explanation for her feelings was to be found somewhere in the room. She seemed disturbed, in the presence of something she couldn't explain. 'I felt he didn't deserve it, I suppose. It would have been like hounding him after he'd gone. And perhaps I just sympathised with him.' As though coming to a sudden decision, her eyes fixed themselves on her handbag. 'I'd been going through a difficult time myself.'

Father Snow stiffened. The last words had been a

request. She wanted to pour out her problems to him, to open her soul. Even though she was a non-Catholic, he had a duty to listen and give what advice he could. Yet, to his own shame, he backed away.

'I shouldn't ask you this . . .' He paused, wondering whether or not to continue. But Susan seemed at that moment so sincere, so vulnerable, that he felt it couldn't do any harm. 'Was there any hint of scandal surrounding Father Conner?'

Susan shifted and stopped staring at her handbag. She seemed relieved.

'No, and in a way that's the saddest thing of all. As far as anyone can tell, he led an exemplary life.'

As she said that, he seemed to be there with them in the room. In the silence that followed, Father Snow found himself struck again by the unusual width of her face, so close to beauty. He couldn't help admiring her for dressing as she did and wearing no make-up, for trying to play down everything she had rather than make the most of it. It was possible that she genuinely saw herself as unattractive.

'Why had you been through such a difficult time?' he said suddenly.

With a jerk, she lowered her face again. The movement somehow betrayed her immaturity.

'It was nothing.' she said. Still moving quickly, she opened her bag. 'I'll leave you my card.'

Father Snow had missed his chance. There was no telling what good he might have done if he'd taken it earlier. He might even have begun to bring her towards the Church, which is what a priest should try to do for all non-Catholics, even if they are young women.

'Were you brought up here in Wodden?'

She responded to this with an unambiguous, sociable smile, as though warning him off any more personal questions.

'Yes. I've lived here all my life, apart from university.'

'What can you tell me about Everard Trevellyan, the third earl?'

'Nothing at all, I'm afraid. I don't know very much about the Trevellyans. I haven't even been to the house since we went there on a school visit. Why do you ask?'

'It's probably nothing.'

'I see.'

She stood up abruptly, as though hurt by his refusal to tell her, to trust her. This in itself somehow made Father Snow feel that she could indeed be trusted. So he briefly told her about the English G.

'That's strange,' she said when he'd finished. 'I didn't think Father Conner was interested in history.'

'Well, as I said, it's probably nothing.'

'Probably.'

Susan gave him her card and began to walk towards the door. Following, Father Snow couldn't help noticing that her skirt, for all its middle-aged dowdiness, was cut close, revealing the curve of her hips. Perhaps the whole image was subconsciously calculated. She knew that by dressing like a woman who saw herself as ugly she would have men queuing up to tell her that it wasn't true. Yet, even if it were a ploy, it would attract a different kind of man from the ones she'd have got by dressing in a mini-skirt and high heels. Perhaps the whole thing was just a plea to be taken seriously. If it was, then this, too, was something Father Snow admired.

When he opened the front door for her, she paused. They were standing close together in the little porch. Everything outside had come alight. There was still mist, but it was radiant now, as though the sunshine had become solid in the lane. Father Snow noticed that Susan wasn't wearing perfume.

'Are you going to try and find out about this Everard?' she said.

'I don't know.'

She paused, as though wanting to say more. Then she

57

suddenly changed her mind and extended her hand. Her grip was as light and brief as before.

'Goodbye, Father. Thanks for seeing me.'

For the first time since she'd arrived, Father Snow smiled, sensing sorrow in her, and wishing her happiness.

'It was nice to meet you,' he said, and for once he meant it.

For the rest of the day, Father Snow was burdened by what he'd learnt. It was as though, in talking to Susan, he'd had his first meeting with the dead priest. Now he couldn't stop thinking about the poor, grey man with his wavering voice, who had been ineffectual and weak, but kind, kind. The word kept coming back to him: kind. Perhaps Father Conner hadn't been granted the power to do any great good in the world, but he'd done no one any harm. As far as anyone could tell, he'd led an exemplary life.

In other words, the suicide was more disturbing than ever. It was impossible to see what could have driven a man like that to commit the ultimate act of violence against himself. In those last moments, where had his kindness gone?

It was dark by the time Flora came round to make his supper. That night he had steak and chips, eating alone in the kitchen while she did a spot of cleaning. Afterwards, he showed her the faint words pencilled in the booklet and asked if she thought they were in Father Conner's handwriting. She confirmed that they were.

All evening, Father Snow brooded on his predecessor, feeling he was getting to know him at last. When he climbed into bed, the idea of Father Conner kept him awake in the rural silence and darkness. He imagined the poor man kneeling down in this same room each night to pray out of his weakness, going quietly about his business in the presbytery and church, leading his exemplary life.

In the end, Father Snow opened his eyes. His gaze fell on the drawer in the desk, where the photograph lay face down. For the third time that day, he remembered those moments of magical understanding and trust, when his father had sat at his bedside to tell him fairy tales.

With a sudden movement, Father Snow got up and knelt down by his bed, intending to say yet another prayer for poor Father Conner. Instead, he found that all he could do was weep, though perhaps, in the circumstances, that was the only form of prayer available.

5

FATHER SNOW WAS eating supper at the kitchen table when the doorbell rang. Flora, who was just getting ready to go home because her husband had taken a bad turn, bustled out to answer. A few moments later she reappeared, looking solemn.

'Father Snow?'

The priest lowered his fork.

'Lady Trevellyan is waiting in the living-room.'

If she'd told him that a prostitute or a wino was waiting, Father Snow would have left the table without hesitation.

'Right,' he said, returning to his food. 'Tell her I'll be there in a moment.'

'Very good, Father.'

When he'd let her wait for a few minutes, Father Snow went through to the living-room. Lady Trevellyan, in the best tradition of the British upper-class female, was all mud and pearls. The mud was evident on the sides of her sturdy walking shoes and as a faint splash against her quilted green jacket. The pearls encircled the upturned collar of her shirt. No doubt they also adorned her ears, but these were now invisible underneath a patterned silk headscarf. The uniform aside, she was a woman of about Flora Dugdale's age.

When Father Snow came in, she stood up from the sofa by the window and extended her hand.

'Hello, Father. I'm Jane Trevellyan. I do hope I'm not disturbing you.'

'Not at all.' They sat down, Lady Trevellyan back on the sofa, Father Snow in the armchair furthest from the fire. Father Conner's chair remained empty, as usual, as though they were expecting him to join them. 'What can I do for you, Lady Trevellyan?'

She smiled.

'You could start by calling me Jane.'

'I'm sorry. I've never met a proper lady before.'

Taking this as a compliment, she gave a musical little laugh.

'Oh, we're just the same as everyone else, though nobody ever believes it!'

'It sounds almost like being a priest.'

'No,' she said, now with charming solemnity, 'being a priest is serious. We only have to look after buildings and land.'

'Now that the serfs have their liberty.'

'Quite.' She looked at Father Snow as though noticing him for the first time. 'We were all terribly upset about poor Father Conner. Such a dear man.'

Father Snow nodded but said nothing.

'Anyway, Father, I was wondering whether you'd be kind enough to come up and say Mass for us at Flamstead, as Father Conner used to do.'

It wasn't a question. Lady Trevellyan wasn't here to ask, merely to make the arrangements. Father Snow stared past her out of the window as though considering her request.

'Father?' she said hesitantly.

'Private Masses are usually undertaken by a member of one of the religious orders.'

'It's not just for us, of course,' said Lady Trevellyan, with something close to nervousness. 'Lots of people from Wodden and other villages come. Father Conner used to see it just as a second Mass for the parish.'

Father Snow let her wait for a moment more. Then he said:

'All right, then. What time will you expect me?'

Lady Trevellyan slightly changed her position on the sofa.

'Father Conner used to arrive at about quarter to twelve, which gave him time to get ready.' Now that she'd got what she wanted, she seemed to regret her previous manner. She tried to adopt her original, assured tone, but it didn't quite work. 'You'll find everything you need in the sacristy. Just ring the doorbell, and I'll show you where it is.'

'Fine.'

'Oh, there's just one other thing, Father,' she said in an unnaturally casual voice. 'We like to hear Mass sung in Latin. I hope that won't be a problem.'

Perhaps she'd guessed that Father Snow, like most priests of his generation, had never said a Latin Mass in his life. If she'd been hoping to unsettle him, however, she was disappointed.

'Of course not. No problem at all.'

All the same, Father Snow stayed up for hours that night, familiarising himself with the Latin Mass, determined that every syllable he pronounced and every note he sang the following day would be correct. When he was at last satisfied, although it was very late, he went through to the study and had a look in *Who's Who*.

There was almost no information about Lord Trevellyan, beyond that he had gone to Eton and now resided at Flamstead House, Surrey. It appeared that he was only somebody by merit of his birth. Going back a few letters, however, Father Snow found a far more substantial entry.

Gerald Pitman had been born the son of a family doctor in Hove, where he'd attended the local grammar school. From there he'd moved on to Oxford, where he'd been President of the Union and taken a first in PPE. After university, he'd worked for some years in the City. At the tender age of twenty-eight, he'd stood for the Conservatives in an inner-city constituency and lost, but not before he'd got himself on television and impressed plenty of important people in the party. At the next election, he'd stood for Dorking, a safe Conservative seat, and had been its MP ever since.

Once he'd got into Parliament, his rise had been rapid. An extreme right-winger and one of Mrs Thatcher's blue-eyed boys, he'd gone first to the whip's office, then as a junior minister to various departments. At the age of thirty-nine, he'd entered the Cabinet as Minister for National Heritage. Now, two years later, he was Chief Secretary to the Treasury. He lived just outside the village of Wodden in Surrey. He was a practising Catholic, married with three children.

What the book failed to mention was Pitman's charisma. He had a way of standing at the dispatch box which made it seem his own. Few other ministers could match him when it came to sweeping past a throng of reporters and disappearing in a Daimler. Conference, inevitably, loved him. Nobody else could send their Union Jacks into quite the same frenzy. When the leadership fell vacant, he would be among the three front-runners.

Father Snow had difficulty getting to sleep that night. However, this wasn't because he was worrying about Lord Trevellyan, or Gerald Pitman, or the trial of singing the Latin in front of them all. It was history that kept him awake. Tomorrow he might have the chance to find out more about Everard, the English G, and the thought of it, a buried piece of the past, excited him long into the night.

The following morning, having said Mass in the parish church, Father Snow drove up to Flamstead.

There was a strong wind which blasted the air clean. High clouds rode in on it, shining like the souls of the saints. They sailed north and disappeared behind the hills with a strange sense of purpose, as though they were late for some celestial convention just over the horizon.

A few tourists were wandering round the park, having

completed their visit to the house. Father Snow guessed that there were probably far more of them in summer. A young couple, despite the numerous notices forbidding them to do so, were feeding the deer under a tree. Father Snow drove past slowly, enjoying the view, waiting for the moment when the house would appear.

When it did, it was even more beautiful than before. In the weak sunshine, above the grazing deer and ancient trees, the building had taken on a delicate, watery quality. It looked like something set above the ordinary world, enchanted and enchanting. The clouds hurrying above its roof gave the impression that it was moving forwards whilst forever standing still. Autumn leaves, caught by the wind, floated in front of it as if by magic.

Father Snow parked his car with the others dotted around the National Trust car-park and walked into the high archway. There were no visitors queuing for tickets, though he could see an old couple walking across the court-yards towards the enormous antlers, a pair of wondering children.

Set in the wall on his right was the ordinary front door. At its side was a black doorbell with a white button, of the type found in terraced houses all over the country. Like them all, it had a little perspex name-slot underneath. There, hand-written on a strip of paper, just like any other name, was that of the owner: Trevellyan.

When he'd rung, Father Snow looked back across the courtyards. The old couple had disappeared. The huge oak doors which led to the Tudor part of the house were open. As before, he was struck by the size of their enormous iron studs. Across the stones, as in the park outside, fallen leaves were shifting, tumbling, and coming to a halt, the playthings of some unseen wizard. There was no other movement. Only the position of the vast doors themselves suggested that there might be anyone at home. Father Snow felt like a little boy in a fairy tale, tiptoeing into the giant's castle.

The sound of the door opening startled him. Turning, he found Lady Trevellyan waiting. Today she was wearing a thick tweed skirt and a plain sweater, as though in a conscious attempt to appear unglamorous.

'Good morning, Father. Thank you so much for coming.'

He went in and she led him down a long corridor. There were faded friezes set in panels on the walls. These depicted pagan scenes quite out of keeping with the occasion: satyrs tipping back their heads to receive bunches of grapes from scantily-clad nymphs; centaurs playing pan-pipes to lovers half-asleep in shady groves. Between each pair of pictures was a smaller panel showing two griffons facing each other. They passed a gilt table with a phone on it, next to which was an open Yellow Pages, incongruously familiar.

'How many rooms are there?'

'I'm not sure,' said Lady Trevellyan simply. 'Some-where around two hundred, I think, if you count the old house.'

'By which you mean the Tudor building?'

'Yes. We never use that, of course.'

As she spoke, Father Snow heard a distant trundling sound. Looking down the corridor, he saw a small blue pedal-car emerge from one of the rooms and start racing in their direction. The driver was a dark-haired child who somehow looked familiar. He was leaning forwards aggressively, heading straight for them as fast as he could go, pushing a ripple of red carpet before him.

'Gangway!'

Father Snow and Lady Trevellyan stopped walking, but neither of them stepped aside.

'Frightful child,' she said under her breath.

'I'm going to run you over!' he screamed, pedalling more frantically than ever. Lady Trevellyan, losing her nerve, stepped to one side. Father Snow stood his ground. Just before the car reached him, he became vaguely aware of another figure emerging from the same door.

'Jamie! Stop that!'

65

It was too late for Jamie to stop, even if he'd wanted to. He had committed himself now to ramming Father Snow. At the last moment, the priest put out his foot so that the bonnet thudded into his instep and the car came to a satisfyingly abrupt halt. Jamie screamed.

'My foot! You hurt my foot!' Getting out of the car, he began to cry loudly, bending down to rub his injury and hopping about at the same time, so that it looked likely he would have another accident. 'I'm going to tell my father!'

Father Snow immediately regretted what he'd done. It had made him look childish and petty.

'Serves you bloody well right, Jamie. I hope it's broken.'

It was Gerald Pitman. He was dressed in corduroys, brown brogues and a striped shirt open at the neck. He looked older and shorter than Father Snow had imagined, yet he swept down the corridor just as he did on television, brisk and upright, his chin raised, so that one expected to see an entourage appear behind him from the doors on either side. To his own surprise, Father Snow was impressed.

'Father Snow,' said Lady Trevellyan above the sound of Jamie's crying. 'This is Gerald Pitman. Father Snow, our new parish priest.'

'Pleased to meet you, Father.'

'Hello. I do hope I haven't hurt your son.'

Pitman gave a practised smile.

'Don't worry. You did well to stand up to him.'

They looked at each other. Pitman's face seemed to express an exact knowledge of the impression he was making on Father Snow. He knew the priest thought his smile was false, and didn't mind, because everyone thought that, and the smile still went on working. Indeed, he seemed almost proud of his insincerity, as though it were a proof of his power. Pitman knew that whatever he did, however he chose to behave, the priest would never forget this moment. Perhaps it was partly this awareness of the effect he had which made his presence so overwhelming. It seemed to Father Snow that even a foreigner, someone who'd never heard of him, would have instinctively known that Pitman was special.

With a nod that seemed to confirm that he'd hammered himself for ever into Father Snow's mind, Pitman turned away. Holding the child by the hand and the pedal-car by its white steering-wheel, he walked back and disappeared into the doorway from which he'd emerged. Only when the corridor was empty did Father Snow realise that he'd been watching every movement, unable to remove his eyes.

Lady Trevellyan gave a little sniff.

'He's a friend of my husband's.'

At the end of the corridor, they turned left and walked down another. Then at last they entered the chapel, which was built onto the back of the house. The interior was all marble and mosaics, far more splendid than the parish church. Father Snow felt there was an almost Byzantine influence about the decoration. There was also a clandestine air about the place, an indelible residue left by ancient persecution.

Lady Trevellyan showed him into the sacristy and, having checked that there was nothing else he needed to know, left. Father Snow went out to the altar and began getting everything ready. After meeting Gerald Pitman in the flesh, even he was now beginning to feel slightly nervous. He wondered how Father Conner, that shy, wavering man, had coped on his first visit here.

The chapel was full when he stepped out of the sacristy fifteen minutes later. All of them stood up as he appeared. Father Snow walked to the altar and faced them. Then he was silent for a few moments, making it clear that this would be done at his own pace. His mouth was set in its usual hard line, his eyes narrow, his back straight.

Those few seconds gave him a chance to take them in. Most of the faces were new to him, though there were some that seemed vaguely familiar, like the faces of minor actors. The only villager he recognised was Bill Saunders. Lady Trevellyan was standing at the front, Gerald Pitman in the pew behind her with his hands joined and his head bowed. At her side was an enormous man, staring upwards at the windows behind the altar.

When there was complete silence, Father Snow opened his hands and sang:

'*Dominus vobiscum.*'

After that, his nerves vanished. He became entirely a priest. The congregation, no matter how exalted they might be in worldly terms, were only souls. Nobody could say where they all stood in the hierarchy of heaven. For the duration of the Mass, he was the most important of them all. He preached his sermon with as much confidence as ever. As he was speaking, he knew it was going down well. He gripped the congregation as only he at his best could grip. Now it was Pitman who was unable to remove his eyes.

When he emerged from the sacristy afterwards, the chapel was empty. There were two doors, one at the side which led out into the sunshine of the park, and one at the back which led into the house. Not sure which he was supposed to use, he went to the door at the back and looked out into the corridor.

Lady Trevellyan was there, waiting for him. With her was the large man who'd stood at her side during Mass. When Father Snow appeared, he stepped forwards and shook hands.

'Good morning, Father. I'm Nick Trevellyan.'

Close to, he was even more enormous than Father Snow had originally thought. He was a good five inches taller than the priest, who stood at six foot himself. His skin was very pale, almost perfectly white, so that Father Snow remembered being told that his lordship was a recluse, and wondered whether he carried this to the extent of never actually setting foot outside the building. His features, particularly his brow, had the slight heaviness which the features of very large men sometimes have. Yet the most striking thing about him was his hair. He was bald on top and, as though to distract attention from this, had allowed what was left around the sides to grow. Long white ringlets cascaded down over his collar, making him look not only extraordinarily eccentric, but also more patrician and faintly historical. Apart from his hair, he was perfectly, if rather colourfully, turned out. His suit, though in a sober enough blue, was lined with crimson silk. His shirt had a bold orange stripe.

'Thank you very much for coming up this morning, Father.' Reaching inside his jacket, Trevellyan produced a plain white envelope, which he handed to Father Snow. 'Half for you, half for the coffers of the church. Please let us know if it's not enough. We do appreciate all the trouble it is for you to come up here on a Sunday.'

His voice was so quiet as to be strangely at odds with his size. Besides being soft, it was almost painfully mournful, so that you felt it could have reduced you to tears with a casual comment on the weather.

'It can't be too little.' Father Snow put the money into the pocket of his own black jacket. 'But I will let you know if I think it's too much.'

Trevellyan gave an approving nod, as though to indicate that this was just the sort of thing he liked to hear from his priests.

'May I congratulate you on your sermon, Father?' said Lady Trevellyan. 'I'm afraid to say that poor Father Conner wasn't much of a speaker. You, on the other hand, have a real gift.'

Again, Trevellyan gave a single nod, his eyes distant.

'Very moving,' he said, as though remembering some terrible sorrow. 'Very moving.'

'Thank you,' said Father Snow, although he was not particularly flattered by this last comment. He didn't like the idea that his sermons might be considered sentimental.

69

'Won't you have lunch with us, Father?' said Lady Trevellyan. 'Father Conner always did.'

'No, thanks. I'd better be getting back to the presbytery. I might be able to come next week, though, when I've settled in.'

The invitation had been completely unexpected. Father Snow wasn't really sure why he'd refused.

'Next week, then,' said Trevellyan. 'I hope you'll be able to come. It's a sort of family tradition to have the priest to lunch after prayers.'

Father Snow had never actually heard the Mass referred to as prayers before, but he knew that it was a survival from the days of martyrs and priest-holes, when it would have been dangerous to refer to the ceremony by name. Only a family which had remained Catholic from Reformation to Emancipation would have called it prayers today, and only the very highest had been wealthy enough to remain loyal for that long. Through that one word, Father Snow felt he'd been admitted to a charmed circle. At the same time, it produced in him a quickening of historical excitement.

'Well, I'd better be going,' he said. 'I'm dying to have a quick look round the old house before I go back.'

'Really, Father?' said Trevellyan. 'Are you interested in history?'

Father Snow smiled.

'Almost to the point of obsession.'

'Then I must show you round myself.'

This was exactly what Father Snow had wanted.

'Well . . .,' he said uncertainly. 'If you're absolutely sure you can spare the time.'

'Of course, Father. I wouldn't dream of letting you go round on your own.'

'Shall I come with you, Nick?'

Both of them turned to look at Lady Trevellyan. At that moment Father Snow began to notice subtle class divisions of whose existence he'd never been aware. He saw that Lady Trevellyan, despite being so obviously upper-class, was slightly below her husband in the social order. Something told him that she'd been born into wealth but without a title. Seeing her next to her husband, he almost felt ashamed for her.

'No,' said Trevellyan, 'you go and get ready for lunch. I'll see you there later.'

So Father Snow was led back the way he'd come, while Lady Trevellyan said goodbye and disappeared in the opposite direction, going into an unknown part of the house. As they walked down the corridor, Father Snow, for the sake of something to say, told Trevellyan about being charged by Pitman's son in his pedal-car. His lordship gave a gentle laugh.

'Like father, like son!' Then, as though this had suddenly struck him as particularly meaningful, he repeated it. 'Like father, like son.' His voice fell. 'I'll tell you one thing, Father. One of these days, dear Gerald is really going to be in the driving-seat. There'll be plenty of people diving for cover then.'

Trevellyan led him out of the door with its ordinary plastic bell. With a nod to the attendant in the little ticket-booth, he began to lead the way across the first courtyard. There was now a small queue of people waiting to buy tickets, all of whom stared at Trevellyan in open amazement.

Having crossed the first courtyard, they stepped through the enormous doors and entered the smaller courtyard of the Tudor building, the house within a house, hidden away from view behind the elegant seventeenth-century façade which one saw as one approached from the park. The atmosphere was very different here, darker and more claustrophobic. It was Everard's house, and Father Snow found himself absurdly excited at the thought.

Soon they were approaching the gigantic antlers.

'That must have been an enormous stag,' said Father Snow.

'You're right.' The big man stopped and stroked the

bone with a white, long-nailed hand. 'A real monster.'
He looked out across the courtyard. 'I would never have
the heart to hunt in the park, myself, especially these days.
The deer are so trusting, so tame. Sometimes, in the winter
particularly, they come right into these courtyards. It's an
amazing sight.'

Following his gaze, Father Snow saw the scene almost
as a revelation: the deer huddled together in the snowy
courtyard, nostrils steaming, while the pale face of the
recluse watched from an ancient window.

'Who shot this one, then?'

'Nobody knows. There's a sort of family legend that
these particular antlers were a trophy of a man called
Everard Trevellyan, which would make them as old as
the building itself. I personally find that hard to believe.'

'Why?'

'Because there were so many preposterous stories about
that particular earl, both in the family and outside it. He
just seems to have been one of those characters people like
to fantasise about.'

'It's interesting you should say that,' said Father Snow,
'because my predecessor made a reference to him, as well.'

'Really?' said Trevellyan, thoughtfully stroking the antlers. 'Why should poor old Father Conner have mentioned
him?'

'I don't know. It was just a note in a guide to Flamstead,
referring to Everard as the English G.'

'How peculiar. I wonder what he could have meant
by that.' He allowed his hand to drop from the antlers.
'Anyway, let's go inside.'

Father Snow decided to bide his time.

The great hall was empty. Standing with his legs astride
and his hands behind his back, Trevellyan told the story
Father Snow already knew about Henry VIII coming to
dine there. Then, more interestingly, he said that they
had used the room during his own childhood on special
occasions. Since it had been turned over to the National

72

Trust, none of them used it at all. He himself hadn't been in here for months.

'So nobody can remember a time when this was used just as a normal house?'

'No. Of course, when I was a child, we were all free to come in here as much as we liked. We used to play here quite a lot. And, naturally, we all believed the place to be haunted.'

'Why?'

'Just because it was so old, I suppose. And it does have a rather peculiar atmosphere when you come here alone.' Trevellyan was staring up at the ceiling, his voice more mournful than ever. 'We made up so many stories here, played so many fantastic games.'

The group of visitors they'd seen waiting at the ticket booth came in. Trevellyan lowered his head as though embarrassed and led the way towards the stairs.

As they went, Father Snow wondered what it could be like to grow up in such a place. There was a lot to frighten children here, besides the deformed antlers: the monstrous, dark doors, the strange scenes painted on tapestries and walls, the griffons pouncing from every corner. All these things would surely have an effect on the development of a young mind. Perhaps Trevellyan's long hair and loud clothes were just signs of a much deeper, genuine strangeness.

Now he was leading Father Snow into the long gallery where portrait number forty-three was of Everard. Not wanting to show an unnatural interest in his quarry, Father Snow listened politely to what Trevellyan had to say about the other pictures. All of them were people who had at some time or another been friends of the family and visited the house, some more illustrious than others. Eventually, they reached number forty-three, which was almost life-size.

'And there's your . . . what was it that Father Conner called him?'

73

'The English G.'

He was a very young man, his face so perfectly handsome that it seemed the artist must have gone too far in flattering him. A duelling-sword hung loosely from his belt, which was studded with jewels. One hand lay gently on the hilt of the sword. The other was holding out, a little in front of him and just above the jewels of his belt, a golden astrolabe. For all his Tudor dress, his black hair was swept back from his forehead in a style that was peculiarly modern. There was something like derision in the way he stared down at them. Behind him was Flamstead park, complete with a few grazing deer. At his side, contrasting strangely with his elegance, was a savage-looking dog which might have been taken for an overgrown wolf.

'He seems to have been an animal lover,' said Father Snow.

'Who can say? Almost nothing is known about him beyond the way he looked, and we only know that from this and one or two other portraits.'

'Yet you said there are legends about him. Surely they must tell us something?'

Trevellyan sighed.

'Well, the stories, both the family ones and those which, so I've been told, still circulate around the village, hardly paint him in a favourable light. But the most I think we can deduce from them is that he may have had a dissipated youth. That, of course, was no more unusual then than it is now, particularly among the aristocracy, I'm ashamed to say. When a man in his position took things to excess, the villagers obviously delighted in exaggerating his crimes still further.'

There was one part of this which amazed Father Snow, so that he looked back up at the portrait with something close to awe. The astrolabe seemed closer now, as though Everard was holding it out, offering it to them.

'You mean they're still telling stories about him after four hundred years?'

74

'Apparently.'

'And that doesn't intrigue you?'

Trevellyan shrugged.

'As I say, he was just one of those people. He attracted legends, or perhaps he actively encouraged them.'

For a moment more, they stood staring up at the portrait. Everard stared back down at them, as though fully aware that they'd been wondering about him, amused, resolved to keep the truth to himself. Suddenly, although the present earl was far older, it seemed to Father Snow that a family resemblance had survived the centuries. There was the same pallor about the skin, the same slight heaviness of feature. Also, for all his insolence, there was something rather melancholy about the young man's expression. One felt that, if Everard had been able to speak, his voice would have been as soft and lugubrious as his descendant's.

The other striking thing about the present earl, of course, was his height.

'How tall do you think he was?' asked Father Snow, wondering aloud, interested to know how far the resemblances went. 'It's hard to tell from this picture. There's nothing to give you a sense of scale.'

'Which is convenient, as it happens, because it allows the propagation of another of the legends about him.'

Father Snow turned and looked at Trevellyan's heavy white face, while he in turn continued to stare up at his ancestor.

'Go on.'

The earl shrugged, as though embarrassed to associate himself with such nonsense even by repeating it.

'They say he was a giant.'

On the drive back to the presbytery, Father Snow for once broke the speed limit. Never in all his career as a historian had his imagination been so fired, his curiosity so greedily aroused. When he got back, he went straight to the study, found the card Susan had left, and dialled the number.

'Hello. It's Father Snow. I was wondering if I could have a word with you.'

'Of course.'

'You told me that you grew up here in the village, didn't you? Well —'

'Is this about Everard?'

'Yes.'

'I'll come over, then.'

'There's no need for that. I just need to know —'

'It's all right, Father. I only live around the corner. See you in a minute.'

She'd hung up before he had a chance to protest. More slowly, Father Snow put down his own phone, slightly disturbed. Remembering their last conversation, with its hints of traumas in her life, he wondered whether her modest exterior didn't hide something more threatening. He sensed sadness and need behind her prim façade, and knew that he would have to be careful.

Today she was dressed more casually, but her slacks and blouse were still the sort of thing her mother's generation would have worn. Though he was struck again by her dark colouring and the unusual width of her face, she was far less pretty than he remembered. He led the way into the living-room. As before, she sat on the sofa, he in the armchair furthest from the fire. She was smiling, leaning forwards slightly.

'So, what have you discovered?'

'Nothing concrete.' Even as he spoke, though, Father Snow was unable to disguise his own excitement. 'It turns out that, as far as the current earl knows, there is no documentary evidence concerning Everard. However, he did say that there were a number of local legends about him. Some of these he seemed to think might still be circulating in the village.'

Susan frowned and shook her head.

'I've never even heard of Everard. I don't know any stories about any members of the family.'

'You wouldn't necessarily know him by name. Perhaps he had a nickname or something.'

Again, she shook her head.

'No . . . I can't think of anything.'

'He was said to be a giant.'

At this her face cleared, the frown of puzzlement giving way to a look of simple wonder.

'He must have been the Ogre Earl.'

Father Snow waited, feeling a little of her awe communicated to him before he even knew what she was talking about.

'When I was at school, every child in the village had heard of him. I never thought he might actually have been based on a real person. You know, he was the local bogy-man, the one who'd come and get you if you didn't eat up your greens.'

'How was he described to you?'

'As you say, he was a giant, an ogre. When I was a girl, stories about him always got mixed up in my head with Jack and the Beanstalk. I'd imagine Jack ending up in Flamstead and being chased around there by this huge figure with a club who wanted to eat him up. Mind you, there are probably similar stories in almost every English village which has a house like Flamstead nearby.'

'Perhaps . . .' An image of the huge antlers rose into Father Snow's mind. 'How did the stories go?'

'Oh, you know the sort of thing parents use to frighten kids, and kids in turn use to frighten each other. The Ogre Earl lived alone up in the house. In the middle of the night, he'd come down into the village and snatch naughty children, and he was so huge and powerful that nobody would be able to stop him. When he walked through the village the ground would shake and tiles would fall off roofs. All the villagers were terrified of him. He'd take the children up to an enormous hall, full of the bones of his previous victims, and eat them alive. Of course, when my gran told me the story, she'd always have the child saved at the last minute. Still, it was enough to give me the shivers, especially as I could see the house up there from my bedroom window. I was too young then even to know what the words ogre and earl meant. I thought Ogre Earl was all one word.'

Father Snow found his gaze drawn towards the empty armchair, as though he wanted to gauge its reaction to what had been said. With a sudden, unpleasant feeling, he turned away and looked out of the window.

A veil of cloud had been lowered in front of the sun, making it into a pale dissolving disc, a host being lowered by majestic, invisible hands. Even this early in the afternoon, the room was gloomy. Every object, as on the first night, seemed suddenly filled with Father Conner's presence. The brass tools by the fire gleamed dimly in what little light there was. From the corner, the escritoire seemed to stare at Father Snow, a squat shadow waiting to see what he would do.

'So, Father, what's next?'

Her voice was quieter. She was still leaning forwards, her elbows on her knees, her face respectfully intent.

'Next I ring a historian friend of mine and tell him what we've found out.'

'Do you mind if I wait to see what he says?'

'Of course not.'

On his way out, he turned the light on for her. He went through to the study, sat down in front of the ancient typewriter, and rang Martin at home.

'Martin? It's Julian.'

'Well, I knew it had to be divine intervention. I was just about to start changing a nappy.'

'Have you had any more thoughts about Everard Trevellyan?'

'No. What's new at your end?'

'Quite a bit. It turns out that he was the basis for a local legend.'

'What sort of legend?'

78

'That he was a child-eating giant, basically. There's no documentary evidence at all about him, sadly, but –'

'Hang on a minute. This is incredible. You mean to tell me that you've found out that he ate children, and you still can't guess what the English G stands for?'

'No.'

'Come on, Julian, think. Put it all together. We know that this G wasn't English. And I'll give you another clue: he lived a hundred years before Everard.'

For a few moments there was silence while Father Snow stared out into the twilit garden. When he at last got it, he still hesitated, wishing he could somehow undo the knowledge, unwilling to say the filthy name.

'Haven't you got it yet?' said Martin at last.

'Yes, I've got it,' said Father Snow. 'Gilles.'

As he went back into the living-room, Susan looked up with a curiosity her good manners could barely keep in check.

'So, Father,' she said. 'Any luck?'

Father Snow nodded.

'G stands for Gilles.' Her face remained blank. 'Gilles de Rais.'

'I'm none the wiser, I'm afraid.'

'He was one of the most powerful French aristocrats of the early fifteenth century.' Father Snow sat back down in his chair. 'He fought literally side by side with Joan of Arc.'

'And what relevance does that have to Everard?'

'Well, some people believe Gilles was the basis for a fairy tale, as well. Perrault's *Bluebeard*, to be precise.'

'Why do they think that?'

'Because he murdered hundreds of children.'

Susan leaned back in the sofa as though the words had pushed her. She was silent for a while, not looking at him.

'Why?'

79

'He was a paedophile who killed his victims partly to disguise his crimes, partly for pleasure. Also, besides being an unusually devout Catholic, Gilles was a Satanist. The murders were sacrificial. He used parts of the children's bodies in his attempts to summon the Devil.'

Susan was looking at him as though he'd just put forward some particularly quirky religious belief.

'Do you really believe all this?'

'It's historical fact. The Latin transcripts of his trial are still in existence, and they're very detailed.'

'And this monster was a Catholic?'

Father Snow sighed.

'Very much so. He surrounded himself with priests. He loved liturgical ceremonies and music. I seem to remember reading somewhere that he actually travelled around with a kind of portable organ, so that he could have church music whenever he wanted it.'

There was a silence. To Father Snow, the atmosphere of the house was more oppressive than ever. He couldn't help believing that he'd touched the evil which had infected Father Conner, or been touched by it. Somehow, despite all the intervening centuries, there was a direct link.

'Father Conner knew all this,' he said at last. 'What interests me is whether he knew more about your Ogre Earl than we do.'

'You think he might have found out something definite?'

'It seems very likely. When he made that note in the booklet, he put a question mark after it. In other words, he wasn't sure at first whether Everard really was the English Gilles. However, if my instincts are right, he visited the house and bought the booklet shortly after his arrival here. It was one of the first things I did myself after I'd moved in. I can't believe that, having made the initial connection, he didn't try and get at the truth. In all those years, the chances are that he found something.'

'So what are you going to do next?'

'Go and see his sister, I suppose.'

'I never knew he had a sister.'

'Well, he did. She was the one who cleared out all his books and papers after it happened. With any luck, she'll let me have a look through them. I might at least get a few hints as to the way his mind worked.'

'Father . . .' She hesitated, avoiding his eye. 'Would you mind if I came with you?'

She was sitting upright on the sofa with her knees clamped together and her hands clenched in her lap, as though he were the one making improper advances. All Father Snow's defences came up. He straightened and composed his face.

'That might not be a good idea.'

'Don't misunderstand me, Father,' she said quickly. 'I don't mean anything by it, you know. This is an interesting piece of local history and I might be able to write something on it, that's all I meant.'

'I understand,' he said. 'But I see this primarily as a church matter.' He stood up. 'I'm sorry.'

As he rose, Susan seemed to shrink away from him. She remained sitting on the sofa as though his tall, threatening presence had made it impossible for her to stand. She spoke in a small voice.

'You don't need to be afraid of me, you know. Although I'm not a Catholic, I do respect your beliefs, and I admire the way you live. I would never dream of . . .'

She trailed off as though she'd suddenly realised what she was saying. Her embarrassment was infectious. Father Snow felt himself beginning to blush. There was a constriction in his throat which forced him to give a little cough.

'I think you'd better leave,' he said thickly.

'Of course, Father.' She stood up with a jerk. 'It's time I was going.'

They went to the front door, both desperately keeping their distance from each other. Father Snow was outwardly calm, yet his pulse was racing, and he longed for the

moment when she would be gone. Something had been
brought into the open which would have been better left
hidden. Without fumbling, he opened the door for her.

'Goodbye. Thank you for your help.'

Far away above the trees, the veil of cloud had thick-
ened, dissolving the pale disc into a blur. Father Snow
wondered how Vincent would have dealt with Susan.
When he looked back at her, she was staring up at him, soft
and timid. He stared back with something like contempt.

'I'm sorry, Father,' she said. 'Don't think badly of me.'

Father Snow gave a curt nod, but didn't reply. All he
wanted was for her to leave. At last, she walked away, and
he was able, with a deep breath, to close the door.

He couldn't sleep that night. Once more he was burdened
by the awareness that he was in Father Conner's bed.
This time, though, he was also thinking Father Conner's
thoughts. His journey in pursuit of the dead priest had
begun in earnest. He wasn't sure whether the real object
of his interest was Everard or the suicide. Either way, it
was really no proper concern of his as a priest. He'd told
Susan that it was a Church matter, but that wasn't really
true. For whatever reason, the suicide had happened, and
nothing he did could change that fact.

His thoughts turned often to Susan as he lay there,
trying to sleep in the perfect rural darkness and silence,
but then his thoughts turned often to them all. There was
Bill Saunders, wired up to the windscreen-wipers, terrible
thing, terrible thing. The two little girls lifted their skirts.
In the corridor at Flamstead House the satyrs chased the
nymphs in their diaphanous robes. Lord Trevellyan, with
white, long-nailed hands, stroked the enormous antlers,
staring mournfully upwards. Pitman's son pedalled a blue
car down an endless red corridor. Then the great man
himself appeared, striding forwards, chin lifted. Susan sat
upright on the sofa, knees clenched. Standing next to
him, she seemed to cower away: Don't think badly of

me. Father Snow was suddenly drowning, flailing around in dark water at the bottom of which there was a single, motionless image.

In the middle of the night he got up, took the keys, and let himself into the church. The darkness and silence were deeper here, even more enormous and profound than they would have been in the woods outside. Feeling his way into a pew, he knelt down and prayed for peace.

An hour later, the motionless image was still there: a handsome young face, the insolent eyes staring down from under a peculiarly heavy brow, staring down because this was a giant looking at a man of normal height. There was a sleepy confidence about the face, almost an air of amusement. He was daring Father Snow to come after him, to try and discover the truth.

6

WHEN HE'D FINISHED shaving, Father Snow paused to look in the mirror.

The bathroom was at the back of the house, adjacent to his bedroom, its frosted window overlooking the garden. Peering through in daylight, you could make out the fractured shapes of leaves, the pond at the bottom of the lawn, the distant hills. Now there was nothing. Early on an autumn morning, it was still dark outside.

Father Snow's face, with its brown eyes and black hair, was peculiarly at odds with his name. Perhaps he would go grey in middle age; or perhaps the snow was all inside. In his rare moments of vanity, he liked to imagine his appearance as that of a Latin monk, aesthetically thin and intellectual, yet handsome at the same time. He knew his face had a certain magnetism.

Turning from the mirror, he looked down at his naked torso. He'd been something of an athlete at school and university. Like his face, his body was lean, if not perhaps as muscular as it had once been. Looking at it now, he was suddenly filled with a sense of himself as a physical being, the bone and tissue as much a part of him as his invisible, weightless self. He seemed to sink down and inhabit his body.

There he found a recollection of pure well-being. It was so sweet that he stood perfectly still, waiting. He saw a room at night. The streetlamps threw strange shapes of light through the windows, soft and orange, like the pieces of a completed puzzle laid out across the carpet and the bed. It was his old room in a house he'd shared at university. Julian, his former self, was lying in the bed with his hands behind his head, staring out of the window. It was summer. The curtains floated like ghosts trying to enter the room. There was a woman in bed with him. She had laid her head on his chest so that a pool of hair poured over him, cool against his flesh.

Julian was unspeakably happy. He'd adored her for weeks, in awe of her beauty, never thinking he would actually have her. Now they had just made love. This was heaven. Never had the air of a summer's night been so soft and warm. Never had it been so luxurious to lie awake while the rest of the world was asleep. And if this was heaven, Julian was God. The well-being which flooded through him brought an amazing feeling of strength. There was nothing he couldn't do, but there was only one way he wanted to use his power, only one activity that had any meaning in this perfect world.

Father Snow stared at himself in the mirror, stunned by all he had given up. No hands other than his own would ever touch his body again. That joy and warmth was completely lost to him now. If he ever did try to recapture it, it would simply be drowned in guilt. All of that was lost.

The bathroom was cold and all but bare. There were only towels, cheap soap, shampoo and shaving things. Everything spoke of discipline, solitude and cold. He wondered how many times Father Conner had stood here and stared into the mirror at his own face, getting ready to say morning Mass to a small congregation of old women. Perhaps a priest could be driven to suicide just by the loneliness. To keep going through middle age, your faith would have to be monumentally strong. By that time, there would be no turning back. You would live constantly with the knowledge of the life you'd given up. If your faith had been misplaced, none of that sacrifice and suffering would have been worth-while.

The thoughts rushed in on him as though they were someone else's, and he had to struggle to push them away. Of course it was worthwhile. It was the girlfriends at university who had ultimately been a waste of time. After the first few perfect days, those relationships had always started to sour. The fairy tale had repeatedly refused to come true, and Julian had eventually given up on it. He'd been unable to stand any longer the anguish of being abandoned.

It was raining heavily. Torrents of water gushed down the sides of the lane. The rain battered the church as if in a tantrum, wanting to destroy it at once and driven into a frenzy by the idea of how long the process of erosion would take. When Father Snow crossed from the presbytery, running and lowering his head, the air was still grey. A dark, convoluted skyscape was on the move, as though it had all been painted on a single canvas and was being slid behind the hills by unseen stage-hands.

There was an even smaller congregation than usual that morning. The rain must have put some of them off. The scattered responses were barely audible over the sound of it pounding onto the roof and driving against the windows. While they were meandering their way through the Creed, Father Snow saw somebody incongruously young and well-dressed enter the church and, without genuflecting, take a place at one of the back pews.

It was Susan, though he took an instant to realise this, because she looked so different. Under a long, pale raincoat she was wearing a traditional blue skirt and jacket with a white blouse. But her hair had been tied back and, even down the length of the gloomy church, he could see that she was wearing make-up. For the first time since his ordination, there on the altar, Father Snow was consumed with fury. The feeling lasted only an instant. Then, without trying to understand it, he pushed it down. But even at the sublime moment of the consecration, he still hadn't quite managed to forget that she was there, sitting down while everyone else knelt, observing the Mass like an anthropologist at a bizarre tribal ceremony.

When he emerged from the sacristy, she was still sitting in the empty church, waiting for him. Aware of her eyes against his back, he genuflected before the altar, lowered his head and paused for a moment to say a brief prayer of thanks. It was what he always did after Mass. As he stood and turned towards her, the rain gasped against the stained-glass windows.

Susan gave a shy smile as he approached. Father Snow set his face in its habitual hard lines, and walked upright, showing his strength. Her smile withered before him. She averted her eyes as though suddenly ashamed of the obvious transformation in her appearance.

'Good morning,' he said quietly. 'What can I do for you?'

Although Susan didn't move or change her expression, he could almost see her gathering up her courage.

'I was wondering if we could have a quick chat.'

'You'd better come into the presbytery, then.'

He led the way down the aisle. As they left the church, she produced an umbrella and opened it. Then she came close to Father Snow so as to hold it over both their heads. He didn't move away, but automatically glanced up and down the lane to check that nobody was watching. In silence, they walked the few short steps to the presbytery. The rain thumped against the tight skin of the umbrella. The bedraggled cottages seemed to cower under the enormous movement of the sky.

'I'm going to have some tea,' he said when they'd got inside. 'Would you like some?'

'Oh . . . thanks very much,' she said, as though surprised by his hospitality and unreasonably grateful for it.

'Come through to the kitchen, then.'

Leaving her umbrella to drip in the porch, she followed him down the corridor. Father Snow filled the kettle and put it on. When he turned around, he found her sitting at the old wooden table, her raincoat across the back of her chair. Now that he had a proper chance to look at her, he saw how much more mature the make-up made her look. With her hair tied back, there was a nakedness about her face, its lines stronger and more striking than ever. After an instant, he admitted that she was beautiful, and looked away.

'I thought you weren't a Catholic,' he said flatly.

'I'm not.'

'Why did you come to Mass today, then?'

'I wanted to find out if you were going to visit Father Conner's sister.'

'You didn't have to attend Mass to ask me about that.'

She stirred and spoke more quietly.

'I've always been fascinated by Catholicism, even though I don't believe. There's something so powerful behind it all.' She was silent for a moment, and he had once more the sense that she was gathering her courage. 'And perhaps I just wanted to see you in action.'

'You make me sound like a commando.'

He tried to smile, but she went on looking up at him seriously. Father Snow didn't like the way things were going at all. This was already the third visit she'd made to the presbytery. In a place like Wodden, it would be all too easy for unpleasant rumours to spread before people had understood the kind of priest he was. It would be the worst possible start to life in his new parish.

'You really do believe it all, don't you?'

'Of course I do. I wouldn't be a priest otherwise.'

'No, but I mean you really believe it. Anyone could see that, just from watching you. You really believe that when you hold that bread up it becomes the body of Jesus.'

'Yes,' he said simply. 'I believe that to be true.'

'I admire you for that.'

Susan went on staring up at him for a moment, then spoke in a different tone.

'Anyway, are you visiting Father Conner's sister?'

The kettle boiled and Father Snow made the tea in silence, letting her wait. When it was ready, he put the two mugs on the table and sat down opposite her.

'Why are you so interested in Father Conner?'

'I'm not. As I told you before, I think he should be left in peace. But I am interested in Everard, the Trevellyans and Gerald Pitman. If I could dig something up on him, it might get me off the *Dorking Advertiser* and into Fleet Street.'

Father Snow smiled. From what he'd seen of Susan, he found it hard to imagine her in Fleet Street. This deferential, almost prudish girl would never survive in such a world. Yet he was starting to see that there was a certain quiet pushiness behind her deference. Remembering their awkward, blushing conversation of the previous night, he wondered whether there wasn't also, behind her apparent prudishness, that ability to be suddenly quite shameless which is often found in the very shy. All in all, with her striking face, clenched knees and dowdy clothes, she was something of an enigma. He wondered what had happened to her.

'You're getting carried away,' he said. 'This is history, not current affairs. If there's any scandal to be uncovered here, it involves a man who died in the sixteenth century.'

'All the same, I'd like to come . . . if that's all right with you, Father.'

She leaned forwards to take a sip of her tea, holding the mug in both hands, changing in an instant from a sophisticated young woman to a little girl taking shelter from the rain. Father Snow felt she was like a novice fencer trying to confuse the enemy with a clumsy feint. It was as if, after a lifetime of being dull and prim, she'd suddenly decided to employ the untested weapon of her sexuality. Disturbed, he stood up and went to the window.

Though the air was lighter now, it was still raining heavily outside. The endless dark skyscape was still being drawn swiftly away over the hills.

'Well?'

When he turned back, he found her looking up at him over the rim of her mug, her eyes wide and solemn. If his instincts were right, and she was really developing some kind of crush on him, it would have to be ruthlessly stamped on before it became an embarrassment. Yet this could only be done if she overcame her shyness and told him what she felt. She had to be smoked out. At least by taking her with him he would have a chance to get it all over and done with away from the prying eyes of the village.

'I'll ring Flora and see if she's got the address.'

It turned out that Eileen Dodson, née Conner, lived in the southern suburbs of London. Even in Father Snow's 2CV, it would only take them an hour or so to drive there. He wanted to phone before going, but Susan talked him out of it. If they phoned, Eileen might try and put them off. However, as soon as she actually saw Father Snow on her doorstep, she would be only too happy to let him in. Father Snow had to admit that she was probably right.

He told Susan to wait in the presbytery porch while he ran through the rain to get the car out. As usual, some superstitious part of him seemed to feel Father Conner's presence in the garage – a grey aura. It seemed stronger than ever today, trapped in the little space like a genie in a jar.

The 2CV had a sunroof, which leaked on the passenger's side. All the way up to London, Susan was forced to sit at a strange angle to avoid the water dripping onto her smart blue jacket. She read the map while Father Snow concentrated on his driving, leaning forwards to peer through the little upright windscreen. Neither of them spoke very much. Perhaps, like him, Susan was subdued by the weather and the idea that they were going to rummage through the effects of a suicide.

The place, when they finally arrived, did nothing to lighten their mood. Eileen lived on one of the main roads which ran into London from the south. It was a busy dual carriageway in both directions. In the middle was a peeling iron fence. The only way to cross on foot was over a concrete bridge. The road was entirely straight and flat, giving the place the emptiness of a surrealist painting. On either side was a row of identical semi-detached houses, which seemed to be repeated to the horizon. The cars sped up and down as though desperate to reach somewhere more interesting. Spray rose all around so that it seemed the road was steaming.

They pulled off the dual carriageway into the little slip-road where Eileen lived. When Father Snow had parked, Susan closed the map and looked glumly around her. The rain drummed on the sunroof as though to remind them of its presence, proud that it had pursued them all the way from Wodden.

'What an awful place.'

'You stay here,' said Father Snow. 'I'll go and talk to her.'

'Can't I come in with you?'

'Absolutely not. This woman has suffered a bereavement. She might welcome a visit from a priest, but the last thing she needs is a party of tourists. You'll have to stay here.'

'I'd really rather come, if you don't mind, Father,' she said gently. 'I think the presence of another woman might actually reassure her. You can trust me to handle the situation sensitively.'

'All right, then.' Father Snow was vaguely aware of irritation, and wondered whether she'd deliberately set out to produce it in him. 'In that case, you go alone and I'll wait here. All I can tell you is this: there's no way we're both going together.'

'What was the point of my coming, then?'

'Good question.'

Father Snow turned to look at her. She was staring straight ahead through the windscreen, which streamed as though they were in a car-wash. The rise and fall of her chest was plainly visible under her neatly tailored jacket. As he noticed this, he was suddenly seized by a violent but vague impulse towards her. He didn't know whether he wanted to hit her or hold her so hard that the breath was squeezed from her lungs.

'Go on, then,' she said tightly. 'Go alone.'

When he got out of the car, Father Snow shocked himself by slamming the door. After that, he just stood there taking deep breaths, his head lifted as though he'd come to study the dark movement of the clouds. He didn't understand his own fury, because the nature of fury was to bring confusion with it. All he knew was the rain streaming down his cheeks.

A moment later, he opened the door again and leaned down to look into the car. Susan was still sitting exactly as he'd left her, staring forwards. She didn't turn when he opened the door.

'I'm sorry,' he said.

'No. I'm the one who should be sorry.'

'Why?'

'Because I shouldn't have come.'

'Perhaps not, but I'm the one who should have stopped you.' He paused and then, out of his confusion, said something foolhardy: 'Priests should always be careful of spending time with young women.'

Now she turned towards him, as though to let him see how beautiful she was.

'I should have stayed away.'

'It doesn't matter. No harm's been done.'

But she gave him a look full of sadness, almost of

yearning, the look he'd been dreading since they first met.

'Don't you understand? I'm not really interested in Father Conner's papers. I came because I wanted to spend the day with you. I didn't sleep a wink last night, thinking about it.'

Father Snow just stood there, leaning down towards the car. The rain was beginning to soak through his black jacket. Behind him, he could hear the roar of the dual-carriageway. Susan was still staring up at him. He knew that he should say or do something, but found himself unable to act, frozen as if under an unexpected enchantment. When she spoke, her words seemed to travel straight into his mind, in a way which made them more immediate than ordinary words, as though they'd had no more external existence than the sound of his own thoughts.

'I think I'm falling in love with you.'

Father Snow returned to his senses with a jolt.

'Don't be ridiculous.'

Even he was surprised by the degree of savagery in his voice. Susan flinched away, leaning her head against the back of the seat and screwing up her face. All Father Snow's contempt for her returned.

'I'm going now. I'll be back in under half an hour. By that time I expect you to have got a grip on yourself.'

When Father Snow had gently closed the car door, he drew himself up, straightened his back and composed his face into its usual uncompromising expression. Yet in spite of these measures, he found himself blinded by a number of contradictory emotions as he began to walk away through the rain. For Susan he still felt contempt and a little irritation. There was sympathy as well, though, and the desire to help her. Her desperate declaration only confirmed what her clothes and manner had already suggested. Her dowdiness was somehow a plea, her tight reserve the result of some unbearable need. No normal, well-adjusted girl would have said it.

Alongside these feelings, and more dangerous than them all, was a happiness that Father Snow was unable immediately to suppress. Perhaps it was a primal, chemical thing, a legacy left by millennia of urgent biological necessity. Perhaps no young man could see that look in the eyes of an attractive young woman and hear her say those words without feeling happy. Father Snow saw then how easy it is for those who live in the ordinary world to think themselves in love. On the basis of one moment like this, they rearrange their lives and set off in pursuit of the fairy tale. When they feel this floating happiness, which is just what any young man would feel, they think the magic has begun. Yet a priest is at once less than a normal man, and more. Father Snow knew that all emotions, even happiness, can be redirected or denied.

All this occupied him so much that for a few moments he entirely forgot where he was. When he came to himself, he found that he was walking in the old way, perfectly upright, with slow precision. Yet it was pouring with rain. Any normal person would have been bolting for cover. He was aware that Susan would be watching him from the car. Now that he'd started walking like that, it would be doubly absurd to break suddenly into a run. So he paced on through the rain as though he were part of a procession down a cathedral aisle.

He'd gone on for some time before it occurred to him to wonder exactly where he was going. Taking the address from his pocket, he found that Eileen lived at number three hundred and forty-three. Checking the nearest house on his right, he saw to his annoyance that he'd already gone much too far. So he was forced to retrace his steps, pacing through the rain. Once, he glanced at Susan. She was staring at him through the streaming windscreen. When he saw her, Father Snow felt that the sudden turmoil she'd produced in him was itself part of his journey in pursuit of Father Conner.

To begin with, it seemed that there was nobody at home. After the first ring, he waited for a full minute, staring blankly at the traffic smouldering up and down the dual-carriageway. Then he rang again, making a deliberate effort not to look in Susan's direction. He was about to give up and go back to the car when he thought he heard, over the roar of the traffic, a faint voice.

'Coming!'

Not sure whether it had been his imagination, Father Snow bent down, looked through the letter-box, and saw Eileen. With the aid of two walking-sticks, she was making her way towards the door over an unpleasantly patterned carpet. Her movements were unbelievably slow. Although he only looked for a moment, feeling it was rude to stare at her through the letter-box, that impression of slowness stayed with Father Snow as he stood upright. It reminded him of those children's bicycle races in which the idea is to keep moving whilst being the last to reach the end.

Eventually she opened the door, without removing the chain, and spoke through the six-inch gap.

'Who is it?'

Even this close to, her voice was barely audible over the sound of traffic and rain.

'Mrs Dodson?'

'Yes?'

'I'm Father Snow, the new parish priest down at Wodden. Flora Dugdale gave me your address.'

'Who?'

'Flora Dugdale. She used to be your brother's house-keeper.'

'Ah, yes.'

'I was wondering whether I could have a quick word with you.'

'What about?'

'Your brother.'

There was a pause. All Father Snow could see of Eileen Dodson through the gap in the door was the bottom of one of her walking-sticks, a piece of varnished wood ending in a thick rubber stopper. As he looked at it, the stick was withdrawn from view.

'You'd best come in.'

The rattle of the chain went on for a long time, as though she were unable to get it off. Then, at last, very slowly, the door opened. Eileen Dodson was a short, slight woman, stooping forwards onto her sticks. Her shoulders were rounded almost to the point of deformity. Her permed red hair was going thin, so that the shape of her skull was clearly visible in the hard grey light from the door. As soon as he saw her, Father Snow realised why she moved so slowly and spoke so quietly: she could hardly breathe.

'Come in, Father.'

'Thank you.'

He stepped into the hall and closed the door behind him. Only when it receded did he realise what a strain the sound of traffic had become.

'This way.'

They began the long journey through the hall. Compared to the rest of her movements, the jerks of Eileen's sticks were almost comically fast. They moved about a foot at a time, stabbing down into the carpet as though she'd spotted a particularly nasty insect there. The carpet itself was every bit as hideous as it had seemed through the letter-box, and was perfectly complemented by the rest of the furnishings. All of it was old, but none of it antique. Everything was done in that ghastly bad taste which the elderly in particular seem to consider homely. There was an invalid lift on the stairs.

Father Snow had plenty of time to look about him. They walked in silence, Eileen battling on with her two sticks like a parody of a cross-country skier. It was hard not to look down on the house and its owner. Besides the difference in age, there was an obvious gulf of education

96

and class. Father Snow said a prayer for humility. He was going on to say one for the sick woman when he was interrupted by the memory of Susan, young, beautiful and healthy, waiting for him outside in the rain.

At last they reached the sitting-room. Here there was an enormous three-piece suite done in grey crushed velvet. The gas fire had a hood of imitation beaten gold. There were two pictures, one of a stormy sea, one of a cat with unfeasibly large eyes. A real cat lay curled on the sofa, fast asleep, perhaps because the room was very warm. There were horse-brasses and china everywhere. The overall effect was such as to make even the simple crucifix above the mantelpiece look tasteless.

'Have a seat, Father.'

Father Snow lowered himself into one of the armchairs, Eileen into another, which he could see was where she spent most of her time. At its foot, the TV remote control lay on top of a pile of papers and puzzle-magazines. On one side, near the wall, was a kettle and a tray with things for making tea. On the other stood an enormous iron cylinder almost as tall as Father Snow himself. Among all the homely fluffiness, it looked horribly industrial, part of some nightmare which had remained on waking and couldn't be made to go away. It was scuffed and chipped around the bottom. Father Snow wondered how many deathbeds it had stood beside, a grim witness to the passing of things less durable and cold.

As soon as she'd sat down, making a movement of her hand to show that Father Snow should wait, she turned to the cylinder. A moment later, Father Snow heard the hiss of gas. The sound, associated with explosions and poison, made him feel uneasy. His instinct was to get up and turn it off at once. Eileen reached down the side of her chair without looking and produced a transparent plastic oxygen mask. Closing her eyes, she clamped it to her face and began to take deep, intent breaths. This went on for a couple of minutes. Father Snow watched, feeling the weight of her claustrophobia settle on him, the sensation of being trapped and unable to breathe.

When she removed the mask and turned the gas off, Eileen's voice was a little stronger, so that Father Snow was able to hear the vague trace of an Irish accent.

'Emphysema,' she explained. 'Smoked all me life . . . thirty a day . . . paying for it now.'

Her tone was matter of fact, but he sensed bitterness behind it. There was a pause, for even those few short words seemed to have robbed Eileen Dodson of breath. From outside, through the double-glazing, came the relentless thunder of traffic on the wet road.

'So, Father. You want to know about Charles.'

'Yes. I –'

'He didn't commit . . . suicide . . . no way.'

Father Snow nodded.

'What kind of man was he?'

Eileen paused, looking up at the ceiling, perhaps wanting to choose exactly the right words on which to expend her limited supplies of breath.

'Soft,' she eventually said. Then, realising that this might be taken as a negative, she was forced to add an uneconomical proviso. 'But in the best way you could want . . . We always knew he . . . wasn't going to go far in life. He wasn't that type . . . no ambition. But I'll tell you one thing, Father . . . He loved God . . . loved the Church. You couldn't . . . have wished . . . for a better . . . parish priest.'

With that, she retreated behind her mask for a few moments, closing her eyes. While he was waiting for her to finish, Father Snow noticed a black-and-white photograph on the mantelpiece. It showed a middle-aged man with grey hair, wearing a pullover and holding a pipe which had gone out. When Eileen lowered her mask, Father Snow pointed to the picture.

'Is that him?'

'Yes. That's Charles . . . Go on . . . have a look. You'll see what . . . sort of man he was.'

Father Snow got up and went to have a closer look at the picture. She'd been right: a personality did seem to be written there. It was the first photo Father Snow had seen of him, and he looked at it with a mixture of horror and awe. The priest was smiling broadly, but almost shyly. He seemed to have a sort of endearing uncertainty about himself. Yet, in spite of what Eileen had said about his not having committed suicide, Father Snow felt he read a little sadness there. Perhaps there were darker signs, too, which he was unable to decipher.

He turned back.

'You can see that he's a good man.'

'That you can.'

'Was he happy in Wodden?'

Eileen shrugged.

'As far as I know . . . Are you?'

'Well, I've only been there a few days.'

'Why are you here, then, Father?'

'Flora Dugdale told me that you'd cleared out Father Conner's things . . .'

Father Snow hesitated, only now realising that this was impossible. Eileen was in no condition to walk down the corridor, let along undertake house clearances.

'Yes,' she said. 'Went down with my son after . . . the funeral.' Then, with a kind of pride, she added: 'Haven't left the house since.'

'I see. Well, the thing is, I believe Father Conner was working on something I might be interested in. I'm a historian, you see. Was he interested in history at all?'

Eileen made to laugh, then suddenly stopped, as though realising what a reckless waste of breath it would be.

'History? Charles? Last week's football results . . . more like. No. He wasn't one of your . . . intellectuals.'

There was a hint of disapproval about this last remark. Eileen had obviously decided that Father Snow was one of your intellectuals. Once more, despite all her sufferings, he felt a rush of scorn for her. This time, it spread to

99

her brother. Perhaps he, like her, had seen his own lack of education as a source of perverse pride. As much as from her words and the photograph, he had learned a lot about Father Conner from the house, its location and its furnishings. Casting a quick glance around, he saw that there was not a single book in the room.

'Anyway,' he went on, 'although he might not usually have been interested in history, I think your brother got involved in some sort of historical investigation. So I was wondering if I might have a quick look through his books. Obviously, I don't want to see any personal papers. It would just help to know what he was reading.'

'You think this is connected with his death?'

'No,' said Father Snow. 'This is purely historical.'

'It's all out in . . . the shed. Help yourself.'

'Thank you very much.'

'You can get out through the kitchen. Wipe your feet, mind . . . on the way back.'

There was a strange smell in the kitchen, although it was perfectly clean and tidy. The cabinets and cooker seemed to date from the 1930s, when the house itself had been built. The plastic handles and knobs were yellowed. Father Snow let himself out into the small garden. It was still raining. The grass was slippery; he nearly fell as he hurried towards the shed at the far end of the lawn.

The shed smelt of creosote. A few gardening tools hung along the walls. The rain drummed loudly on the wooden roof. Priests don't accumulate many belongings. They go lightly through the world. What Father Conner had left fitted into six cardboard boxes and a suitcase. Assuming that the case contained clothes, Father Snow ignored it and started going through the boxes.

The first two contained books, all of which emphasised the fact that Father Conner hadn't been one of your intellectuals. Most of them were thrillers with lurid covers. There were one or two theological works, but they were hardly heavyweight. There was a battered black bible, which Father Snow put gently to one side. The next box contained papers, mainly letters from parishioners, bills and the like. There was a box of personal belongings, shaving tackle, pens, pipes and other oddments. Then came another box of books. At the bottom of this was a green box-file.

When Father Snow opened the file, he found inside, held in place by the sprung metal clip, another book. It was as though this one had been hived off from the rest so that it wouldn't contaminate them. The title made his heart jump.

WITCHES, GIANTS AND OGRES
The Origins and Meaning of Fairy Tales

The cover showed a witch on her broomstick flying across a full moon. Opening the book, he scanned down the list of chapter headings. Sure enough, Gilles had a section all to himself:

Gilles de Rais: The Original Bluebeard?

It was the first certain evidence he'd found that Father Conner really had known about Gilles and been interested in him. Father Snow turned to the chapter. There wasn't time to read it through now, but he wanted to know if Father Conner had left any revealing notes. However, flicking through the pages, he found nothing, nothing to point him towards Everard or the next step he should take. As far as he could see, it was a standard account of Gilles' life. Going to the back of the book, he checked the index for any reference to Everard Trevellyan or Wodden. There was nothing.

Putting the book down, he glanced at the box-file once more. When he'd opened it, he'd thought the book alone in there, but now he saw something else, something so familiar that it was almost like a part of himself. It was a small, laminated card with a colour photograph underneath the plastic. The photograph showed a smiling, almost boyishly excited Father Conner. The card was for the British Library.

There was no reason why a man whose reading hardly seemed to go beyond thrillers should need to use the largest library in the country. The only conclusion was that his visit had had something to do with Gilles and Everard. The card had been issued a year previously, and it was the sort which was only valid for one day. In other words, Father Conner had gone once, found what he'd been looking for, and not visited again. Then he'd put the card away in a special place, with the book about witches and ogres from which he'd probably learned about Gilles.

Father Snow stared at the card for a long time, slowly piecing together what his predecessor at Wodden had done. Some time after his arrival in the parish, he'd heard the story of the Ogre Earl from one of the villagers who'd been frightened by it as a child. Intrigued by the idea of a child-eating giant, he'd bought his book about the origin of fairy tales, no doubt hoping for some reference to Flamstead. Instead of that, he'd learnt the story of Gilles de Rais, the French ogre. At that point he probably still wouldn't have known which earl the stories had been based on, or even if they'd had any historical basis at all. He'd gone to visit the house, seen the portrait of Everard with his enormous dog, and written the question Father Snow had found in the margin of the guide.

Then he had made some jump which Father Snow had so far been unable to make. It had taken him to the British Library with a goal specific enough to be achieved in one day. On the basis of what Father Snow had found in the shed, it had to be some clue hidden away in the book. After all, that one volume had been separated from the rest and put in a box with the British Library card. To a non-academic, the card would be a kind of trophy. Father Conner had been a historian for a day, had conducted an investigation into Everard which perhaps nobody else had ever thought of conducting. He'd bluffed his way into the British Library and satisfied his curiosity. Then, back at the presbytery in Wodden, he'd put the book and the card aside as relics of a special occasion. A year after making that intellectual leap which had connected Gilles, Everard and the British Library, he'd committed suicide.

The idea had never been more disturbing to Father Snow than it was now, standing in the shed among the dead man's belongings. Remembering his last conversation with Susan, he felt insecure, almost afraid. Without thinking, he reached out for the battered black bible which he'd left on top of the other books. Opening it near the back, wanting to read something from the New Testament, he got a shock. Since his arrival in Wodden, he'd searched for the truth about Father Conner and found only silence. Now, suddenly, the priest spoke to him directly, with an outpouring of words.

The first page he looked at was crammed with notes, all written in that fine, retractable pencil Father Conner had used to write the note in the guide to Flamstead. He might not have been one of your intellectuals, but Charles Conner had certainly spent a lot of time with his bible. Shame filled Father Snow for the way he'd looked down on the dead priest and his sister. He had no right to judge a woman by the carpet she chose, or a priest by the kind of novels he read.

There wasn't much light in the shed, and Father Snow had to hold the bible close to his face to read the first note. It was next to the story where Peter tries to walk to Jesus across the water. In the margin, Father Conner had written: *Beautiful!*

An image of the priest's face, smiling shyly as it was in the photograph, filled Father Snow's mind like an admonishment. Now he felt that Father Conner's cheap novels, his pipe, his sister's awful house, were things not to be looked down on, but admired. They spoke of a simplicity which Father Snow himself would never attain, because he was one of your intellectuals, and there is always a kind of corruption in that.

The other notes all had the same unashamed directness, which struck at the young priest's heart. *Help me always to do this*, Father Conner had written by the phrase 'suffer little children'. By the Sermon on the Mount he had written: *All the wisdom we need in life*. And then, in the margin next to the crucifixion, he had said simply: *My Lord and my God*.

When he read that, Father Snow fell to his knees in the shed and prayed for his dead colleague as he had never prayed before, offering his own soul if Father Conner's could be saved. He prayed for himself, too, and then for the whole of mankind, seeing how much help they needed in a world where even a man of Father Conner's obvious simplicity and goodness could be driven to the ultimate despair.

7

PHYSICAL DISCOMFORT STOPPED Father Snow from praying too long. It was cold in the shed and the floor was hard and splintery, so that sharp points of wood stuck through his trousers. These, like his jacket, were still wet. As he stood upright, he heard once more the sound of the rain on the wooden roof, and shivered.

Putting everything back as he had left it, he hurried across the garden, taking with him only the book about fairy tales. At the door to the kitchen, he spent a long time wiping his feet. When he finally crossed the room, he glanced back over his shoulder to check he'd left no mark on the floor.

Eileen was still in her armchair. She had her mask on again and was breathing deeply. Her head was lolling to one side and she was staring through the window at the rainy road, drowsy as a baby with its bottle. She didn't notice Father Snow arrive.

'I've finished now, Mrs Dodson,' he said. Removing her mask, she looked up at him. Again, the hiss of gas made him uncomfortable. 'Thank you very much.'

'Did you find what . . . you were looking for?'

'Well, I was wondering if I might borrow this.'

Father Snow showed her the book, but she just made a vague gesture of dismissal, without bothering to read the title.

'Help yourself. I'm sure Charles . . . wouldn't have

minded. Never denied anything to anyone . . . poor old Charles.'

Remembering the notes in the margin of the bible, Father Snow nodded.

'I have no doubt of that. I only wish I'd met him.'

For the first time since he'd arrived, Eileen Dodson showed some signs of agitation. She shifted slightly in her chair, her eyes lifting with a kind of appeal to Father Snow, who was still standing by the sitting-room door.

'Father . . .' She paused, but he didn't know whether she was embarrassed, afraid, or simply overcome by her emotions. 'Is my brother . . . saved?'

'Yes.' For the first time since Vincent had told him about the suicide, Father Snow had no doubt about this himself. No God would damn the man who smiled shyly down from the mantelpiece, let alone the man who had made those private notes in his bible. 'You need have no doubt about that. None of us can know what terrible tragedy happened in his last moments, what it was that unbalanced his mind, yet I'm sure that's what happened.'

'I hope God . . . understands it, Father, because . . . I can't.' She was still staring up at him, her voice thinner and weaker than ever, but again there was that note of bitterness. 'How could he leave me . . . alone like this?'

'He didn't know what he was doing, Eileen. Don't judge him. Just try and find it in you to forgive him.'

'I'll try, Father.' For a moment, her chin trembled, but then her face became suddenly impassive. She turned away from him to look out of the grey window again. 'I'm not well enough . . . to be upset about him. Can you see yourself out?'

'Mrs Dodson . . .' Reaching down for her mask, she waved him away. Father Snow hesitated, wondering what he could do to help her. 'If there's ever anything you need . . .'

Putting the mask in place, she gave a dismissive nod, as though she had no time for such pleasantries. Then she began to breathe deeply, staring out of the window through drowsy eyes. As Father Snow left, her head was beginning to loll.

If anything, the rain outside was harder than before. The wind was sweeping it in giant grey ghosts above the roofs. As he closed the front door, Father Snow could see Susan waiting for him in the car a little further down the road. She was staring straight ahead, her face blank, as though it had been washed clean by the rain. Further off, the spray hung over the dual-carriageway like fog. It occurred to Father Snow that this was the strangest day of his life.

Holding the book about fairy tales under his black jacket, he ran back towards the car. Then, with his usual calm expression, he climbed carefully down into the driving seat. Susan was looking across at him. He had forgotten that she was wearing make-up, that her dark hair was tied back. The sight of her produced an unexpected surge of emotion, a turbulence in which he floundered for a moment before regaining his self-control.

'Father —' As she said it he gave her that look of his which few people dared to go against. It seemed to shrivel her. She returned her gaze to the windscreen. 'You've been ages.'

'Mrs Dodson's very ill. There was quite a lot to look through.'

'Did you find anything?'

'Just this,' he said, handing her the book, 'and a British Library reading card. The book has a chapter on Gilles.'

Susan began flicking through the pages. Father Snow looked at her in silence, wondering what was to be done. He was struck by how entirely alone they were. Their isolation filled the car like air pressure in a tunnel. The desire to hold her came across him, a dizziness which passed when he looked away.

'What are the Thomason tracts?' she said.

'Eh?'

'The Thomason tracts. It's underlined in the notes at the back of the book.'

'Give it here!' He snatched the book from her. 'Where?'

Leaning across so that he could smell her skin, Susan pointed out the note. The words had been underlined in Father Conner's faint retractable pencil.

'That must be it,' said Father Snow. 'It would be a secondary source, of course, and about the most unreliable you could imagine, but that must be what he used. That's why he went to the British Library. He'd found something in the Thomason tracts.'

'What are you waiting for? Let's go.' Father Snow turned towards her, and she looked away, embarrassed. 'I mean, if you still don't mind my coming with you, that is.'

Reassured by her shame, he gave a curt nod and started the car. Neither of them spoke until they were on the dual-carriageway, picking up speed.

'What are these Thomason tracts, in any case?'

'How much do you know about the interregnum?'

'As much as your average schoolgirl, I suppose.'

'Well, the main thing here is that censorship was lifted for the first time since the invention of the printing press. Generally, historians look on it as a time of intellectual flourishing. Unheard-of democratic ideas began to be thrown around. But there was a darker side, as well, which is often overlooked.'

'Great. So who was Thomason?'

'I suppose you could call him the curator of the darker side.'

Driving as slowly and carefully as ever, Father Snow explained. One of the most dramatic effects of the lifting of censorship was the emergence of the pulp pamphlet or newsbook as a form of mass expression. These ancestors of the modern tabloid had contained stories of the most lurid type imaginable. They were usually printed in London then hawked around the provinces by travelling salesmen. This was in an age at once uneducated and turbulent, when simple minds were casting round to explain the apparent collapse of their world. The newsbooks provided such explanation, though it was of the most primitive, superstitious and sensational kind.

Many of them, for example, told stories of hideous prodigies: men born with their heads in their chests or hands growing out of their knees, cats with human faces. Village ponds filled mysteriously with blood and huge ghostly armies were seen to fight in the sky. All of these stories were related as true, with exact times and places provided. The moral to be learnt depended on the writer of the pamphlet. A royalist, for example, would try to show that by killing Charles, men had toppled God's order on earth and that now God was paying men back by toppling the natural order. There were writers with a religious agenda, too, hurling allegations of child murder and satanic possession at rival sects. Nothing was considered too gross. Witches, of course, were a common theme, and it was during this period that the witch-hunts were at their peak. Anything written in these pamphlets, no matter how hideous or preposterous, was probably believed. These were people, after all, who still thought that trees were responsible for wind, roaring and waving their arms to produce it.

'Fascinating,' said Susan when he'd told her all this. 'But you still haven't explained about Thomason.'

'Thomason was a bookseller during the interregnum. He collected literally thousands of pamphlets, which are currently in the British Library. So you can see why it's probably a secondary source. The whole thing happened about a century after Everard. And you can see, as well, that it's probably unreliable. Nobody would want to put too much faith into anything written in one of Thomason's newsbooks.'

'Father Conner thought there was something in it, though.'

Father Snow frowned. Every time Susan mentioned the

dead priest, he felt she was interfering, poking her nose into a tragedy which was purely a matter for the Church.

'Why does that book quote from the Thomason tracts, in any case?'

'I'll have a look.' There was a pause while she found the right place. 'It's the chapter on witches. A quote from one of the pamphlets . . .'

She trailed off.

'Go on.'

'It's about how witch-hunters used to examine the private parts of their suspects.' There was an excruciating pause. 'For suck marks.'

Father Snow leaned a little closer to the windscreen. He was blushing. The idea that Susan was looking at him and had noticed this only made him blush the more.

'Father, about what I said earlier —'

'I don't want to talk about it.' Father Snow made an effort to keep his voice calm, to show no weakness. 'I don't know what your problem is, but I want to make it quite clear that I am not the solution.'

'I know that,' she said quietly. 'I know it's hopeless, but I can't help what I feel.'

'Yes, you can. All of us can. You just have to make an effort.'

He glanced towards her as he spoke. She'd been staring at him, but immediately turned away when she saw the expression on his face.

'You hate me, don't you?'

'Of course not.' Irritation made him clench the wheel as though trying to throttle it. 'What a stupid thing to say.'

'I'm so sorry.'

The embarrassment and contrition slightly softened Father Snow, so that a little of his irritation turned to pity. This was dangerous, because it made him want to tell her that he really didn't hate her at all, that, on the contrary, he found her attractive, which was why he had to be so hard with her. Then he somehow began telling her in his mind all the things he found attractive in her: her quiet voice, her serious, respectful manner, the way she dressed and moved, her obvious lack of vanity, not to mention her unusual yet almost beautiful face, the curve of her hips, her breasts. As his mind ran over all this, it began to seem to him that, if he hadn't been a priest, she would have been the girl he'd always dreamed of meeting.

When things got to this point, Father Snow brought himself back under control. With a conscious effort, he relaxed his grip on the steering-wheel.

'You're not to try and see me again after today. Is that understood?'

'Yes, Father,' she said obediently. 'Thanks for letting me come with you, all the same.'

Father Snow gave a firm little nod, but he was thinking of the moment when he'd leant down towards the car in the rain, the magic moment when an ordinary man would have believed himself in love.

After that, neither of them spoke until they reached the museum. Father Snow pulled up in front of the gates and took out his wallet.

'Are you allowed just to drive straight in?'

He was relieved to hear that the emotion was gone from her voice, that she was making an effort to behave normally.

'Not really.' Father Snow was looking through his wallet. 'A friend of mine lets me use his pass.'

He found the pass and raised it to the windscreen. Without really bothering to examine it, the uniformed attendant nodded through the rain. A moment later Father Snow had parked right in front of the famous building. By now he was beginning to regret that he hadn't just gone and found a meter. Susan might think that he was trying to impress her, and he wasn't entirely sure that she'd be wrong.

The force of the rain only came home to them once they

were out of the car. Susan opened her umbrella. Before she could offer to hold it over his head, Father Snow was gone, moving so quickly that she had to half run to keep up. He led her up the steps, among the crowds of tourists in their garish anoraks. No matter what he did, he was bound to make an impression on her today. Until now she'd only known him as an outsider, somebody finding his feet in a new environment. This was the first time she'd seen him on his home ground.

Once he'd reached the shelter of the echoing entrance hall, Father Snow slowed his pace a little. He led her through the door where the tourists weren't allowed to go and into the little office on the left. Here there was a delay, because Susan needed two passport photographs. So Father Snow had to wait while she hurried back out into the downpour to find a machine. By this time he was becoming agitated. The atmosphere of the place, the silent proximity of that vast body of knowledge, had quickened his historian's instinct. He wanted to get in at once and begin the search.

Eventually, she came back, breathless, and was issued with her pass. As they left the office, she was staring down at her laminated photograph.

'I can see why Father Conner kept his safe. Coming in here must really have felt like a special occasion.'

A moment later they entered the enormous circular room and Father Snow forgot everything in the simple pleasure of being back. Almost as much as on entering a church, he had the sense of complete familiarity and belonging. Since it was impossible to take books out of the library, all his research had actually been done on the spot. Like Karl Marx, he had his own preferred desk. The furniture and the smells were as familiar as those of home. Indeed, there was something of the cathedral about that enormous blue dome. It was like entering a giant Roman basilica, which seemed to dwarf the murmuring human voices beneath its roof whilst abruptly amplifying any louder sound. If you dropped a book on your desk, the ceiling would throw back an unexpectedly loud echo, as though protesting at the noise.

Father Snow led Susan straight across the room and through the door on its far side. She followed in silence, accepting that he knew where to go. They went down a corridor and up an iron spiral staircase, emerging into the gallery of the North Library. This was smaller than the Reading Room itself, but impressive nonetheless. Here the ceiling was supported by pillars. Tall standing lights grew from the floor like giant flowers which reached right to the level of the gallery. At the top of each stalk was a bowl brimming with light.

On the last shelf at the far end of the gallery, they finally reached their quarry: the index of early English books. First they looked under 'Wodden' in the title index, but there was nothing at all that referred to the village. Then they tried under 'Trevellyan', but again drew a blank. It was the same story with 'Everard', so Father Snow switched to the subject index and looked under 'giant'. Here he found only one entry, which referred to the wrong part of the country. After that, beginning to feel stupid, he looked under 'ogre' and 'child murder', again without success. Then Susan had the idea of looking under 'Flamstead', but there was nothing.

Father Snow sat there for a moment with the books open before him, beginning to feel the depression of a frustrated search, which was always to him a kind of humiliation. Somewhere along the line, he'd made a mistake and allowed himself to set off in pursuit of something that didn't exist.

'Can't you think of anything else?' whispered Susan.

'No. I can't see where else it would be.'

Unwilling to give up, they sat there for a few minutes staring at the open books and thinking. The books seemed to stare back out of an intense silence and stillness, as though they were willing Father Snow to use them correctly, to look in the right place. As he stared at them, he became certain that they contained the answer. Somewhere among all those hundreds of thousands of entries there was one which would explain everything, not only about Everard, but also about Father Conner. All he had to do was look in the right place.

'It's no good,' said Susan eventually. 'My mind's a blank.'

'Mine too,' said Father Snow, but it wasn't really true. He now felt something stirring just beneath the surface, something he'd already seen as they were scanning down the list of entries, something which had come up from the vast index and was floating round in his head, trying to find the right memory to connect with.

'We might as well head back, then,' said Susan despondently.

They replaced the books on their shelf and began to walk slowly back along the gallery towards the spiral staircase. Father Snow was thinking about the dead priest, trying to see how his mind had worked. He'd been no historian, yet he'd just read a book which might have given him a scrap of specialist knowledge. Now Father Snow felt that, while they'd been looking through the catalogue, just such a specialist word had passed his eyes without being consciously read by his brain.

When they'd got about halfway to the stairs, he suddenly stopped and stared out across the bowls of brimming light. On the other side of the gallery a young man was sitting in front of one of the huge microfiche screens, winding the spool on by hand, so that it looked as if he was operating a miniature butter-churn.

'Got it!'

A number of scholars looked up from their work like cows disturbed at grass. Father Snow went quickly back, got down the title index, opened it, and began rapidly turning the pages. His heart was racing. For him, this was a moment of high drama.

Completely still, he bent down silently over the book. Then, elated, he stood upright and pointed at what he'd found in the list of titles:

The Ettin of Wodden.

'What's an ettin?' whispered Susan.

'Wait.'

Father Snow hurried back down the gallery to the main desk. Once there, he began scribbling out a request form, filling in the shelf mark for the microfiche of pamphlets which contained his find. When he'd handed it in, he led her back towards the spiral staircase.

'Where are we going now?'

'To have lunch in the canteen. It'll take them a while to get the microfilm, and I'm hungry.'

They went back the way they had come, down the corridor and across the Reading Room beneath the echoing dome. In the canteen, they ordered sandwiches, tea and buns, and sat down facing each other across the cheap wooden trays.

'So, what's an ettin?'

Father Snow finished his first mouthful of sandwich before answering.

'It's a word Father Conner would probably only have known by reading that book of his.'

'But what does it mean?'

'A giant, of course. I didn't originally think of looking under it because I just assumed it would have passed out of use by the interregnum. Ettin's an Anglo-Saxon word.'

'Ah. I see.'

As soon as there was silence between them, Father Snow began to feel awkward. Seeing that he had to keep up a normal conversation at all costs, he looked around the canteen, trying to think of something to say.

'So, are you excited about our discovery?'

'Yes, very. It's almost scary.'

'Why?'

'I suppose it's hard for you to imagine just what the

Ogre Earl means to a child growing up in Wodden. You know, when I was very young, I really believed in him, although my parents told me not to. I just knew he was up there in that huge old house. All my friends felt the same way, too. I remember we once went on a school trip to Flamstead. We must have been about seven by that time, so we were old enough to laugh at the stories, but we were still young enough to be afraid, especially when we were actually inside the place.'

Father Snow remembered his own feelings on visiting the house that Sunday. If a grown man could be impressed by the enormous doors opening on the courtyard and the gigantic set of antlers, the effect on a child would surely be devastating.

'And to think,' Susan went on, 'that the Ogre Earl was a real person who we're going to read about in a few minutes . . .' She laughed. 'It gives me the shivers!'

Father Snow, too, felt a little irrational apprehension mixed in with his excitement, though it had nothing to do with childhood fears. He was thinking of Father Conner, wondering if he too had come down here for tea while he was waiting to read the pamphlet about Everard. Whether he had or not didn't really matter, of course. On an intellectual level, Father Snow was following him exactly. Standing on the edge of the same discoveries, he felt like a detective re-enacting the movements of a victim, afraid that the killer might strike again.

'I don't know your name,' said Susan suddenly.

'It's Julian.'

'Julian. And am I allowed to call you that?'

'No.' He stood up. 'Look, I'm going back. The microfilm will probably have arrived by now.'

'Can't we even sit and have a cup of coffee together?'

'No.'

Leaving his food unfinished, Father Snow left the canteen. He went without looking around, as though to prove that he didn't care whether Susan came with him or not.

Yet all the way he wondered whether she had immediately got up to follow him, leaving her lunch unfinished. Only when he stopped at the desk in the distant gallery of the North Library did he find that she had.

A small cardboard box was waiting for them on the desk. Father Snow took it to one of the microfiche units and sat down on a tall swivelling chair. The spool of film inside the box was protected by a strip of cardboard tied with a small string. As he undid it, Father Snow felt certain that he was the first person to use this particular reel since Father Conner. The last fingers to tie this string had been those of his predecessor.

Father Snow fed the film into the machine. When he switched it on, white light filled the enormous screen. Tiny imperfections appeared, made luminous and magnified to many times their normal size. At that moment, the priest had an irrational sense of having been lured here. It was Everard who had summoned him and who in a moment would begin to broadcast his story across the centuries. Everard, not Father Snow, was using the technology. In a moment it would receive a transmission from the past, from a time of superstition and horror, a fairy-tale age. As soon as the screen was alight, the ogre had them in his grip.

8

IT WAS STRANGE to sit in front of that screen, winding the first part of the film slowly onto its receiving spool. He'd done it often enough after ordering a microfiche, but the circumstances were very different now. To begin with, there was Susan, sitting down next to him, close enough to look over his shoulder as he operated the controls. Then there was the nature of the microfiche itself. After years of sober, meticulous historical research, he suddenly found himself careering off in pursuit of a fairy tale. Yet at the back of his mind was the hope that he really would discover historical truths, that in Everard he'd found the point where fairy tale and history merged.

When film was feeding through properly, Father Snow pressed the switch and wound it on at full speed. The machine made a small screaming noise. Ancient pamphlets began to flood across the screen, blurring before his eyes. The movement made him feel a little sick. It was like looking through the window of a speeding train without being able to fix your gaze on any of the objects hurtling past outside. At the same time, because the pages streamed from left to right, he had the unsettling sensation that the train was moving backwards, carrying him at breakneck speed into the distant past.

It went on for ages, since Everard's pamphlet was buried right at the end of the spool. Eventually Father Snow stopped so that he could read one of the reference numbers and find out how far they had to go. The movement slowed to a crawl. Then the frantic rush began again. This happened a number of times until they eventually came near to their destination. Then Father Snow started turning the spool by hand, so that the train chugged slowly along, allowing them to have a look at the scenery of the strange world into which it had carried them.

The first pamphlet Father Snow noticed was about an anabaptist who had decapitated her seven-week-old child then asked her Presbyterian husband to baptise its head. A few more slid past, all in a very similar vein, peddling absurd stories of prodigies, apparitions and witches, with a generous helping of sex and murder for good measure. Their only historical value was to reveal the mass mentality of the age. Father Snow would never normally have dreamed of going to them in search of information.

At last, everything came to a halt. The magnified cover of Everard's pamphlet filled the screen, glowing with a soft light which somehow retained the yellowish colour of parchment. It was mainly taken up by a crude black-and-white woodcut. This showed the giant himself. He bore no resemblance to the portrait of Everard in Flamstead House. This character might have stepped straight out of a fairy tale. He had high boots, long hair and a shaggy beard. Another figure had been drawn next to him, presumably to give an idea of scale. He barely reached above the giant's waist. In one hand the monster held a club the size of a man's leg. In the other, raised like a trophy, he held by the hair a severed human head, still dripping with blood, which might have been the head of a child.

The title of the pamphlet was written above the wood-cut:

The Ettin of Wodden:

Being the most Strange, True, and certain History of a mighty Ettin or Giant; together with his Life, Death and recent Return to make mischieve amoung the good people of the Parish, perticularly amoung the CHILDREN.

Then, beneath the gory illustration, was a further note:

119

Certified in a Letter from a Gentleman of that Country, to his Brother (a merchant) in London.

London: *Printed by* R. Austin, *for* W. Ley, *at* PAUL's *Chain, 1651.*

When he'd taken in the cover, Father Snow turned and gave Susan a look, raising his eyebrows to show how ridiculous he thought the whole thing was. In fact, now that he actually saw the pamphlet, he felt slightly absurd for having gone to so much trouble to find it, as though tracking the thing down was tantamount to giving it some kind of credence.

'Do you really want to read this?'

'Of course I do!' she hissed. 'Go on!'

'Prepare,' said Father Snow as he turned the spool, 'to be amazed.'

My Dear Brother, all our children here bee tooke with an Illnesse of great violence and malignancy, I mean the children of the village and mine own too. Some bee attackt by dreadfull feavors, some go with growthes of great bignesse on their faces and necks, some cannot arise but lye moaning all daye, five are Dead this past weeke. All are afraide and full of wonder. This distemper or as it may be curse striketh onely at the children.

Now wee have neere here a very fine and noble POPEISH family, which is calld Trevellyan and which lives in a house fitt for Giants. Two weekes past, mine own dear daughter, being sick with the feavor whence I have wrott, did awake us all by a frightfull Scream. Upon going unto her, we found her garments all soaked, but the girl her selfe quite cold, from which you can plainly see that it was a sweate of feare. Then shee spake, saying shee had dreamd of that same POPEISH house, which is calld FLAMSTEAD. There shee had seen a man like a tree in bignesse; with long hair like the hair of a Lion; wielding an huge Clubbe; the manner of his dresse most perticular. This Giant had come after her so that shee feard for her life.

This were not strange, but that ALL *my children dreamd the same, and* ALL *the children in our village here taken by the Illnesse, wherefore none can account.*

Last weeke I mett a stranger upon the road. This gentleman was a Doctor of Physick calld hither from London to attend a great and weathy Nobleman. When I told him of the strange affliction of our children, his countenance became grave, for the house hee attended was that same FLAMSTEAD, *whose Master, my Lord Walter Trevellyan, had layde neere Death. From that great man the doctor heard Wonders the relation of which alone were enough to affright him. Of these Wonders, brother, I now give thee a full relation, that thou may better understand the evil times wherein wee live.*

The true and certified grandsire of my Lord Walter Trevellyan was one Everard Trevellyan. This Nobleman was an Ettin or Giant, his hight being fully 10 foot, and his head as big as half a bushell. Hee built FLAMSTEAD *house to his own proportion, and all things there are huge, as the doctor willingly attested. The Ettin was bredd-up before the last King Henry and livd to a great age, dyeing in the dayes of Elizabeth. Hee had much learning, being the possesser of neere an hundred books, and knowing Black Artes wherewith he could controll Nature and produce therein prodigys like unto him selfe. Indeede, hee was one of the most evil men of all times, a very Hogre, for he consummed the Flesh of children. These he stole at night from our own village, descendeing like a wolfe on sleeping lambes, and so mighty was hee that none could stopp him, for all were afraide. Never was there a truer sign of the evils of the* CATHOLICK *religion.*

After a long life of great wickednesse, the Monster at last mett his end at the hande of a childe. Though his Ettinish appetites were undiminishd, his bodie was weakend with age and lustfullnesse. One night he took a childe, one James Jackson, indendeing to doe murder on him at FLAMSTEAD *house. Guessing his fate, James stoutly*

*tooke up a sword and ran the old Ettin through. The
Giant, ancient and full of weaknesse as hee was, fell dead
on the spott.*

*All this was certified as true unto my selfe by the doctor,
Timothy Darting, of London. Mr Darting further saw the
Ettin's secrett and private chambers at FLAMSTEAD,
where hee practist his Magyck, and attests that therein bee
wonders whereof he is afraide to tell.*

Just as Father Snow read this part, Susan jumped up at
his side and, without saying anything, hurried away down
the gallery. Uncertain of whether he should follow or not,
he watched as she sat down in front of a computer terminal
and began to type. He went back to the leaflet, which he'd
nearly finished.

*The strangest newes of all, brother, is that the Ettin, dead
these sixty yeares, is now returnd. The doctor him selfe was
of the opinion that our daughter's illnesse was not to be cured
by any earthly means, but was the work of an evil Spirit.
Hee informd me that in dark times the Ettin would return
on the same nights he did murder while alive. These are
evil times indeed, brother, for last night I saw the prodigy
my selfe, strideing down the road through the village. In
one hand hee had an enormous Clubbe, in the other hee
carryd the head of a babe. Though hee was a spirit, formd
as t'were of mist or white smoake, there was a sound like
that of thunder at his stepp. Nor was this a phansy of mine
own, for sundrie others in our village saw the same figure,
amoung them Charles Clark, Minister of this Parish, who
beheld him fording the stream by the Old Mill.*

*Thou knowest, brother, that I speak Truth. I woud never
bee false or lye unto mine own brother. These things are
true, strange and wonderfull events, not dreams putt about
to afright the fulish.*

*I begg thee pray for me and pray for our children, that
they may not be punishd for the caos of the age.*

Looking up, Father Snow found that Susan had disappeared. He rewound the spool, watching the pages fly past as though this would enable the journey to be completed in reverse and return him to the rational world. Yet as he put the little roll of film back in its cardboard box, his mind was still full of strange, unsettling images.

When he'd returned the microfiche, there was still no sign of Susan. After looking around for a moment, he went down the spiral stairs and back towards the Reading Room. Before he'd reached the end of the corridor, she appeared ahead of him, almost running, triumphantly waving a request-form in one hand, a look of elation and excitement on her face.

'Where have you been?'

'They've got a book by the doctor!' she said, barely able to keep her voice down.

'What doctor?'

'Timothy Darting, the doctor who treated Walter Trevellyan. He wrote a book of memoirs and medical observations. It's here in the main collection. They told me it would take them about an hour to get it.' She could barely stand still. 'How are we going to wait a whole hour? It's unbearable.'

'What are you so excited about?' said Father Snow, speaking quietly to make it clear that he was not excited himself.

'That pamphlet, of course! It was amazing! And you wait, this next book will be more amazing still.'

Father Snow sighed.

'Let's talk about it down in the canteen.'

So they went back downstairs and ordered fresh supplies of tea and sandwiches. The noise of the place was almost painful after the silence of the library.

'You didn't believe any of that rubbish, did you?' said Father Snow when they'd sat down.

123

'Not literally, no, of course not. But I can imagine that it was based on truth. It has that ring about it.'

'A ten-foot, child-eating ogre coming back fifty years after his death and making all the children in a village sick? That's your idea of the ring of truth, is it?'

'Not the part about him coming back, of course. But the rest could be an exaggeration of a true story. Gilles de Rais was real, after all, wasn't he? Surely Father Conner was quite right to wonder whether we mightn't have had an English version.'

'It may be a distant possibility, but you can't rely on that pamphlet for evidence. Just look at the other ones from the same stable. They were written to make a profit by frightening the gullible, and also to put across a point of view. This particular one is blatantly an anti-Catholic tract. That's why the writer wrote it, which leads me to think that he probably made the whole thing up.'

'But Flamstead is a real house, and Everard was a real person. If you were going to make something up, why not go the whole hog and produce a complete fabrication? And why set it in the past, when it would be so much more frightening to say that the giant was still alive?'

Father Snow thought for a moment. The truth was that most of the newsbooks had set their horrific stories in the present, intending to show the disorder of the times. The writer of *The Ettin of Wodden* had tried to draw a similar conclusion, but it had lost its force somewhat. This monster, after all, had committed his murders in the golden age of the Tudors.

'Perhaps he thought a ghost would be more frightening than a living person.'

'Hardly. I think he realised that was the weakest part of his story. It looks to me as though he tagged the ghost idea onto an account he really heard from Darting, which might well have been true.'

Father Snow shrugged.

'I still think it's all extremely implausible.'

124

'Another thing,' Susan went on, her excitement undiminished, 'did you notice the name of the child who was supposed to have killed the ettin?'

'No, I can't remember it.'

'James Jackson.'

She gave him a look full of triumphant meaning.

'So what?'

'Don't you see? He was Jack, of course. Jack the giant killer.' Father Snow gave a tight smile.

'Don't be ridiculous.'

Susan looked at him strangely when he said that, and he realised that they were the words he'd used by the dual carriageway that morning, when she'd told him that she loved him.

'It's not ridiculous,' she said softly, so that he had the uncomfortable feeling she was no longer speaking about Everard. 'Why shouldn't a fairy tale contain a kernel of truth?'

'Because those stories are as old as the hills. Jack and the Beanstalk, in particular, is obviously connected to the most ancient of myths. Cultures all over the world have legends about a tree linking heaven and earth, which was cut down so that nobody could climb it any more. Here in England there was certainly a similar belief in pagan times, which is still celebrated in the symbol of the maypole. It all goes back a long, long way before Everard Trevellyan.'

'So you think that the name James Jackson was just a coincidence?'

'Of course it was. Countless folk-stories use the name Jack, in any case. It wasn't really a name at all, just a kind of shorthand by which to refer to the hero.'

Realising that Susan was staring at him, Father Snow looked away.

'Can I borrow your car-keys?' she said.

'What for?'

'I want to have another look at Father Conner's book

and see what it says about the origin of Jack and the Beanstalk.'

With a shrug, Father Snow got out the keys and handed them to her.

'All right, but I promise you you're wasting your time. There's no possible connection with Everard.'

When she was gone, he sat and thought about her for a long time. Her reaction to the pamphlet was a further clue as to what lay behind her plain clothes and clenched knees. She longed to believe the fantastic and improbable. Perhaps that was why she was willing to believe in love at first sight, not only with a priest, but with a priest like Father Snow, who was so obviously beyond her reach. The more desperate and hopeless the fairy tale was, the more magical it would seem when it finally came true. Although he still felt scorn for the whole thing, he couldn't help also feeling touched. No other woman since his ordination had dared try this sort of thing with him so openly.

In the end, he thought about what would happen that evening. It would be dark by the time they got back. When the 2CV pulled up outside the presbytery, Susan would try and invite herself inside. She would do it respectfully and hesitantly, shy and furiously ashamed, yet unable to help herself. Father Snow would refuse, and then the whole thing would be over. In a few days, his life would have returned to normal.

When he went back up, he found her in the Reading Room, bent over Father Conner's book about fairy tales. Timothy Darting's book had not yet arrived.

As soon as he sat down next to her, she looked up and started talking, her excitement undiminished.

'Jack and the Beanstalk originated in England,' she whispered, 'from where it spread around the world. They're a bit vague about how old it is, although even the oldest written versions which survive are relatively recent. There's nothing to prove it's any older than Everard.'

'Except common sense.'

'I don't see why. His legend could easily have got tagged onto your Tree of Life story.'

Father Snow didn't argue any more. He sat there in silence while Susan went back to the pamphlet, which she must by now have read a number of times. Father Snow wondered if he didn't play the sceptic precisely because, like her, he wanted to believe the fairy tale. Perhaps in him the need to believe was even greater, dangerously strong, so that it had to be suppressed at all costs. Nothing could be more magically alluring than the idea that those stories his father had told him had, in some absolute sense, been true.

Timothy Darting's book, when it finally arrived, was bound in unexciting, grazed brown leather. The speckled frontispiece declared that it contained the memoirs of a medical life, both for the illumination of those young men considering taking up the profession, and for the edification of the general public.

They began searching for references to Flamstead and the Trevellyans, Susan turning the pages and Father Snow looking over her shoulder. As promised, the book contained Darting's experience of various cases, along with his medical opinions and recommendations, which – as one would have expected from a seventeenth-century doctor – were at once comical and terrifying. At the same time, Father Snow couldn't deny that, by the standards of his day, Timothy Darting had been both educated and sceptical, pouring scorn on many of the more absurd beliefs of his contemporaries. Compared to the writer of the pamphlet, one would have called him a beacon of reason.

The book had been written in the doctor's later years and followed his life chronologically. They skimmed through the early part, and reached the story of how he had been called in to attend a wealthy London merchant. All the established doctors had despaired of the case, but the young Darting had effected a miracle cure.

127

This successe was the begining of my fame. Soon I was calld upon to attend the great and rich, not onely in London, but in the Provinces beside. Here it was that I encounterd the strangest and most wonderfull experience of my early career, nay, of my entire life.

'Got it,' said Susan.

Father Snow nodded but said nothing. He was already reading.

Were I to relate these things from memory, my readers might consider them the prodigys of an old man's dotage. Therefore, I shall here offer the reader the accompt I wrott at the time, wherein hee shall find the words of a man young and sound in bodie and minde, for the yeare was 1651, and I had but four and twenty. In the long gap of time, I have oft considerd what I learned and heard. In spight of my age, and though I bee a doctor and a man of education, I can still offer no relation of these things which is conformable to Reason.

January 5th, 1651

To Flamstead, a great house neere Wodden, in the county of Surrey. Here am I to attend my Lord Walter Trevellyan, who is tooke with a most violent feavor. The house is extreamly strange. All things here are built large – dores, windows, court yards – as t'were for an other race of men. In the court hang the horns of a mighty Stagg, huger than any I did ever see, so that the minde faintes picturing the monster whereof they came. The beaste stood a full eighteen handes by my reckoning. Snowe lyes deep on the house and all around, and falls still from the skye, as t'will never cease. His lordship is exceeding sick. Hee raveth and seeth not the world around him, neither can he hear. This night I bled him copiously. I feare that he will die.

At this point, Father Snow stopped reading for a moment to arm himself with scepticism. He already sensed that Darting might make a convincing witness. More than that, he was struck almost to the point of amazement by his account of Flamstead. The place had made exactly the same impression on Darting, writing more than three hundred years before, as it had made on Father Snow himself. In those days, of course, when large buildings were rare, the house must have had even more impact. As he'd been reading, Father Snow had found himself picturing the young man's arrival with a strange clarity. He saw the snow lying thick on the Tudor roofs, highlighting the lines of the bare trees and the enormous antlers in the courtyard, which were still there and still astounding after all those years. He saw, as though he'd been there himself, the exact tone of the grey sky from which the flakes still teemed. In the largest bedroom of the house there would have been an enormous log fire. There, his huge bed covered in furs, the great lord lay raving.

January 6th, 1651

The feavor cometh and goeth as it will. For houres together, his lordshipp perceiveth nothing. In this sad state, hee speaketh much. Some names and words there bee so oft repeated that they may perchance have some meaning or connexion with his illnesse. They are like writing in a foreign language whereof I can understand nothing.

Then the feavor goeth, and my lord's braine seemeth clear. Hee perceiveth me, knoweth my name and my professioun and can make some little talk. Today he asked me if I beeleive on Ghosts and Phantomes. 'Nay, my lord, I'me not one of the common, credulousse men to bee so easily deluded.' 'Thou shouldst beeleive,' replyed hee, 'for t'was a Ghost put me in this state,' and fell again to raving and became apopletick.

The snowe cometh on, ever deeper. I have ordered his lordshipp's bed bee piled high with furs.

January 7th, 1651

Today my charge is much recovered. He sitteth in bed, taketh a little gruel, and talketh most strangely, though the raving fit bee gone. Hee askd mee the reason of his illnesse. I told him it was the mischieve of an evil humour borne on the frozen air of winter, whereon he laughed most merrily. 'T' was none of your humours!'

'Why, then, my lord, why hast thou layde in this feavor these two fulle weekes?'

Wherewith he grew pale and sayd that, two weekes past, he had seen his grandsire, the sight of whome layde him down sicke. It were not strange, said I, that a man shoud see his grandsire. Nay, replyed my Lord, but that same has bin deade these fifty yeares. And anon he gave me the following accompt:

'My grandsire, Everard Trevellyan, was born ere King Henry came to the throne. In childhood I use to see him oft enough. Hee was a Giant, standyng fully seven foote tall, with long hair like that of a lion, but all white, and the clawes of a lion on his handes. I was sore afraide whene'er hee came neere, and this pleasd him mightily, for he revelld in the feare of children. He use to say: "Henry Tudor was afraide of me, boye, and so shouldst thou bee." For Henry came here in his youth to enjoy my grandsire's hospitality. They went a-hunting side by side, and returnd all bloudy, my grandsire likeing to hunt not with the bow nor yet with the knife, but with a mighty Clubbe or his own two handes, and this arte he shewd unto Henry, who liked it greatly. And my grandsire told me how he was wont to open the belly of a stagg with his two handes and eat its liveing entrails, and Henry did doe likewise, and they returnd to the house all red with bloud. And anon my grandsire shewd the King how to kill a stricken deer as the wolfe does, which is with the teeth of the mouth, and they returnd with bloud on their faces and their beards stiffe with bloud. But then my grandsire shewd Henry that which hee liked not, in such wise that he fledd in feare and never returnd to this house, nor woud he dare raise armes against my grandsire. All this my grandsire told unto mee him selfe, the which I beeleived, being but a childe.'

'And beeleive you so now, my lord?'

'Have I not seen him these two weekes past, in the great hall where he use to feast, with bloud on his handes and armes, and the bloud pouring as a very fountayne from his beard?'

Wherefrom I coud conclude none other than that his lordshipp is melancholy mad. When I asked how t'was that Everard Trevellyan had filld so stout a heart as Henry Tudor's with feare, my lord fell silent.

January 8th, 1651

My Lord Trevellyan is fulle recoverd, for which hee gave mee a great abondance of thanks, saying, 'Thou hast saved my life, boy, and shalt bee richlie paid for't.' This night I did dinne in the great hall, my lord attended by her ladyshipp, theyr children and theyr many servants. To honour me, he sate me at his side. Anon I asked him again how his grandsire had affrighted the heart of Henry Tudor. 'Nay, boy,' quoth he, 'tis best thou knowest not.' Yet later, when my lord was in his cups, he sent away both familie and attendaunts, and spake to me alone.

'This is the very hall where my grandsire suppd with King Henry, and they revelld much, in drunkenesse and lust, and the Ettin, my grandsire, spake unto Henry of the dark artes whereof he knewe and his own evilnesse. All this, as Henry thought, was but in jest. My grandsire owned he was wont to slake his disire on young children, whereafter hee ate theyr flesh, dranke theyr blood, and ground up theyr bones, the which had Magyckal propertys. Whereon Henry laughed in his drunkenesse, which sore angerd my grandsire. And my grandsire in rage and pride shewd him that which made him beeleive and filld his hearte with feare.'

My Lord spake much more on his grandsire, saying that his mighty and evil spirit still livd in this house. In life hee had always sworne that death woud never overcom him. By the exercise of perticular Black Artes, he vowd to enchant a certain part of his own house in such wise that death coud not come thither, wherein hee woud remaine for ever, and so it is, says my lord Trevellyan. As the times grow more or lesse evil, so the spirit of the Ettin waxes and wanes. In these days of war and civile turbulence, hee has grown mighty powerfull and spread sicknesse amoung all the liveing children of the town, some of whome have died. Many are the Priests and Ministers who have come to Flamstead to drive out the evil Spirit from his enchanted chamber. All have faild. One was struck blind. One fell to pukeing and vomiting when hee enterd the great hall. Others lost theyr mindes.

Much else I heard — that the Giant used his Artes to create prodigys in Nature, such as the monstrous Stagg the antlers whereof I have already seen, enormous dogs, and other, stranger things — but none of it did I beeleive, the reason being that my lord was in his cups and all he said was the childe of drunkenesse. When I said that I beeleived him not, my Lord bid me hold my cluck. He snatchd up a torch and vowed to shew me that night that which Henry saw, so that I might beeleive and my heart too be filld with feare.

Whereon he ledd me unto a chamber cunningly conceald high in the house, so that none coud find it but that they know it bee there. This hall was fulle of wonders such as I never saw nor hope to see again. First my lord shewd mee certain strange Devices and Machines, which hee owned hee did not understand. Then I beheld a cat with the head and winges of a hawke. This magyck creature is calld the Gryphon, which is the signe of the Trevellyans. The monster was like in size to a dog. Though the torch was bright enough, I coud detect no artiface by which the Prodigy had ben made, the diverse parts all seeming those of one animal entire. The Ettin bredd these horrors, my lord informed me, as an other man might brede cattle, letting them to roam freely about the park in great flocks. Yet nor was this the most awfull thing in that strange room.

For anon my lord ledd mee to a large cauldron of metal and bade mee look inside, wherein I beheld the severd head of a young girl. I guessd her to have been no more than eight years on this earth before her death. The head was immerst in yellow water, like piss, the eyes open and most horrible. My lord informd me shee had layde so for neere on an hundred years, and the flesh quite uncorrupted, by the Artes of his grandsire, her murderer, the Ettin, Everard Trevellyan.

At the next wonder, I cryed aloude and thought I must fainte away. The torch danced so, that at the first I coud not comprehend what horror t'was I saw. Then I perceivd the bodys of two children standing straight. Yet theyr bodys had nor bones nor flesh, being composed onely of the little rivers and streams which carry the bloud. It were as the living bloud had frozen like rock, whereafter the rest of the body had bin melted away. By what Arte this had bin accomplisht, I cannot say. Afraide as I was, I stood astounded for some minutes, examineing this hidden and secrett structure of the bloud, wherefrom I now know that, even unto our fingers, *there are tiny channels of red and blue, no bigger than threads, which carry the bloud to every part. In the neck and neere the heart, these channels are thick and massd, tangld together like the roots of a mighty tree. All this I saw standing alone in front of me as though supported by thinne aire, all in the forme of a childe.*

Anon I was shewd a likenesse of Everard Trevellyan, paintd by him selfe in his old age, yet done with great mastry and skille. Hee was extreamly large, with grey hair to his shoulders, and black eyes. His fingers had clawes like those of an Eagle. Beneath the picture, Lord Trevellyan shewd me an enormous peice of wood. This was his grandsire's Clubbe, and many had died under it, both animals and children, and the very wood was black and heavy with theyr bloud.

I'me not drunke, nor yet am I mad, though I feel I may shortly bee so. All these things I saw this very night. Now I cannot slepe, but only write to still my minde, but there is no comfort in the writing of these horrors. Tomorrow I'll leave this place, for I feare the Hogre still dwells here in his secrett chamber, not to be seen, but onely felt as an intollerable feare.

January 9th, 1651

On the road I mett a fellow from the village of Wodden. All the children there are sicke. His own daughter dreamd last night of Flamstead House, where she beeleived her selfe pursued by an Ettin. I left the village and returnd to London, hapy to scape with my wits.

The rain had started again when Father Snow and Susan left the British Museum, but it was lighter than before. Darkness had by that time fallen over London. The rain floated down into the aura of the lights, seeming to melt into a fog around them. The tarmac shone like black rubber. Wet metal gleamed everywhere. The streets were full of people hurrying home from work, stooping forwards slightly under their umbrellas.

It was the modern world, as mundane as ever, and it seemed at first completely unreal to Father Snow. He'd only recently been immersed in the age of enchantment, when even a scientist like Darting had been ready to believe in ghosts, giants and griffons. Perhaps Susan, too, felt a little of the same disorientation, for she remained silent as they walked slowly to the car.

'So what do you think?' she said, when they'd got inside out of the rain. It was the first time either of them had spoken since handing back the book and leaving the Reading Room.

'I don't know.' Father Snow sat in silence for a while, collecting his thoughts. 'It certainly was an extraordinary piece of writing. It's also fair to say that this Darting seems like a reasonably reliable witness. However, that doesn't mean a word of what he said is true.'

'Why not?'

Father Snow started the car and began to drive off down Museum Street, beginning the long haul to Wodden. The idea of going back depressed him.

'Well, let's take an example, shall we? Take the claim that Everard went on these barbaric hunting trips with Henry VIII. This tale comes to us from Darting, who heard it from Walter Trevellyan, who in turn heard it from the Ogre Earl himself. Now, if you start with the premise that people love to frighten one another, you see our problem. Everard probably embellished his story to frighten his grandson, who in turn embellished it for Darting, who in turn embellished it for us. The most I'd be willing to conclude from all that is that Henry might once have visited Flamstead and gone on a hunting trip with Everard. The same is true of the entire story.'

'What about the strange stuff Darting saw in the secret room?'

'There could be explanations for all that, as well. For example, he saw something that looked like a child's head, but he saw it in torch-light, under coloured liquid. If we accept that Everard and his grandson loved frightening people, then it's quite easy to imagine how one of them could have set up a convincing enough illusion. The

134

bodies made of veins could have been models constructed by someone interested in anatomy. It would have been difficult, of course, but it's not impossible. We know that Everard had great learning. What else did Darting see? A portrait of an old man with long hair and nails, and a large piece of wood.'

'And a stuffed griffon.'

'Which is precisely the weakest part of the whole story, because that particular wonder was definitely a fake. People in those days would have fallen for it readily enough, but we know it can't have been real. And if one of the ogre's artifacts was a fake, that surely casts doubt on all the rest.'

'I suppose you're right.'

After that, they were silent for the entire journey. Father Snow's memory moved between what they'd just read and the hopeless declaration of love Susan had made that morning. No doubt her own thoughts were moving along similar lines. He kept seeing himself leaning down towards the car, the rain soaking through his jacket. All in all, it had been a strange day.

Indeed, there was still a peculiar atmosphere in the car. The rain poured endlessly against the windscreen and trickled down through the leaking roof. There was a lot of traffic going out of London, a long line of red lights ahead of them, glowing as they slowed down. As they got closer to the village, the question of how he was going to stop her coming into the presbytery when they arrived became uppermost in Father Snow's mind. He was ready to be as ruthless as necessary to keep her away.

All this occupied him so much that he all but forgot where he was, automatically following the road. Then, suddenly looming above him in the glow of the headlights, he saw the two stone griffons on the gateposts of Flamstead House. Whatever myths might obscure him, one thing about Everard was certain: he had built Flamstead and set the mythical creatures here to guard the gateway. Father Snow only glimpsed them for a moment as he drove past, but it seemed to him that they said more about Everard's character than all he'd read that day. They were prancing on their hind legs, their wings spread and their beaks open, symbols of aristocracy, power, and overweening pride, enduring this rainy night as they had endured thousands of others since the time of their maker.

Father Snow turned left down the lane. The last trial of the day was approaching. All he had to do was get her safely out of the car and it would be over. He drove down the High Street and past the gloomy village green. Soon they were passing the Old Mill, driving across the bridge. He remembered how the pamphlet had reported the ghost of the giant fording the stream.

Then, unexpectedly, Susan broke the silence which had lasted since London.

'Could you drop me off here? I only live around the corner.'

'Of course.'

Father Snow stopped the car. Susan took off her seatbelt and turned towards him. The light from the street caught her jaw, making a pale crescent of it in the shadows. Its width made the point of her chin more feminine and pretty.

'Thanks for taking me with you.'

Her voice, raised above the sound of the engine, was strangely loud and hard in the dark.

'Not at all.'

As he had that morning, Father Snow felt the desire to hold her. It was only what any man would have felt, though perhaps the darkness made it worse. All he had to do for it to end was to lean across and kiss her, to take her in his arms. He would turn the engine off first. Then the car would fill with the sound of their clothes rubbing against each other.

When Susan next spoke, it was in the same hard voice.

'I didn't really mean what I said this morning, you know.'

Father Snow took a deep, quiet breath, relieved. She'd finally got the message.

'I'm glad to hear it,' he said.

'You must think I'm so silly.'

He turned towards her, feeling at last that it was safe to smile.

'Not at all. It's only natural. Everyone has these feelings.'

'Except you, apparently.'

Father Snow wasn't going to allow himself to be trapped so easily. He turned away from her and shrugged.

'I've chosen a different way. Whether they like it or not, the people around me have an obligation to respect that choice.'

'Yes, I understand that, Father. And from now on, I will respect it, I promise.'

This sudden determination in her was what Father Snow had been trying to achieve all day. Now that he'd got what he wanted, a part of him was saddened, though perhaps that was only natural, as well.

Cold, moist air flowed into the car as Susan got out of the car. Father Snow drove back to the empty presbytery.

In the garage, he paused for a moment to think about Father Conner. From that point of view, the day had been a failure. If anything, the suicide was more mysterious than ever.

A few minutes later, he went into the dark presbytery and through to the kitchen, turning on lights as he went. Flora had left him some supper, but he only ate a couple of mouthfuls. For some reason, he had no appetite.

Leaving the kitchen, Father Snow went into the living-room and sat down on the sofa under the window. Everything was as he'd left it that morning: the brass tools in the fireplace, the pale square where Father Conner's picture had hung, the escritoire in the corner. The very silence was the same. Loneliness filled him. The intensity of it was such that he began to wish Susan had come back with him, after all, just for a few minutes. At least she would have driven away the atmosphere of the place.

After a few moments, he found himself wondering what she was doing, what sort of life she had gone back to. No doubt she was thinking about him, too. Perhaps she was trying to resist the temptation of ringing him up or coming round. Then Father Snow began listening for the sound of the phone or the doorbell. He was disgusted at his own weakness, yet unable at that moment to resist. The day had somehow exhausted him. The house made things more difficult, as well. Perhaps he only listened in the hope that something would break its crushing silence. Things would be better once he'd settled down there, got into the routine of life in his new parish. This temporary weakness would pass.

Susan didn't ring. Father Snow, to his shame, felt more disappointment than relief. The rural silence deepened by the second. Eventually, the solitude, to which he was generally accustomed, became a torment. He went up to the bathroom and cleaned his teeth. There, in the cold, bachelor emptiness, he looked at himself for a few moments in the mirror.

In the bedroom, Father Snow fell to his knees, but said none of his usual prayers. He was too exhausted somehow. All he could do was fire one bolt of love and faith into the silence, one desperate plea.

As soon as he climbed into bed, he remembered once more how he had leaned down towards the car in the rain. Slowly, as though he were walking step by step down a staircase into deepening darkness, he felt himself falling asleep.

Towards the end, somewhere between sleep and waking, between the sea and the shore, where the waves pulled at his ankles, Everard Trevellyan came to him. He saw the enormous old man with his long white hair, his club heavy with blood. Then he was in the room of wonders, where the bodies of two children were preserved only as networks of veins. These things, for all their horror, somehow delighted him. Susan's face appeared and spoke: He was Jack, of course. Jack the giant killer, of course. Father Snow's rational mind struggled against this nonsense, but it was clumsy with exhaustion, so that thinking logically had become like trying to type in boxing-gloves.

Then the first wave of the sea rolled in, rising cold and dark up to his chest, carrying a memory. It was from the foggy day when he'd visited the primary school. On his way back to the presbytery, the wind had come up. From down on the village green he had seen Flamstead House high above him, floating on the layers of mist, a castle in the clouds.

9

FATHER SNOW WOKE up early, got straight out of bed and went about his work.

It was dark outside when he left the presbytery. Up and down the narrow lane, Wodden's answer to a main road, the streetlights spread their haloes on the damp air. Their illumination served only to emphasise the absolute emptiness of the lane. It was sad to think of them shining like that all night, throwing their helpful light down on a road which nobody would use. The low buildings were all dark. Few people would be out of bed for some time yet.

Father Snow went into the church and turned on the lights. It was cold in there, barely warmer than outside. Bowing his head, he spent a long time at prayer.

He was still kneeling there when he heard a noise behind him. Instinctively turning, he saw a young woman entering the chapel. It wasn't Susan. Only after he'd turned did he realise that he'd been worried it was her.

After that, Father Snow couldn't concentrate. He had recognised the young woman, but was unable to place her. There had been so many new faces over the past few days. She had short dyed hair and a thin, intelligent face. He groped for her name. At last he realised that it was Melanie Histon, the trendy teacher he'd met when he'd visited the primary school.

By that time his concentration had been broken entirely. In any case, it would soon be time to start preparing for morning Mass. Getting stiffly up, he genuflected, then walked down the aisle towards her. She wasn't kneeling, but sitting in a pew with her head bowed, staring at her knees. She was wearing large ear-rings and a loose, fluffy sweater.

'Good morning, Melanie.'

She replied without lifting her head.

'Morning, Father.'

'You're up very early.'

'Yes.' She was still staring downwards. 'I couldn't sleep.'

'Oh dear. What's the matter?'

In answer, she shook her head hard at her knees, as though resolutely denying them something, and Father Snow realised that she was crying. He stiffened, wanting to escape. 'Is there anything I can do?'

Again she shook her head. Father Snow sat cautiously down at her side.

'Problems at home?'

'Work,' she said tearfully. 'Problems at work.'

'What kind of problems?'

Now at last she turned towards him. He noticed that she had freckles.

'I shouldn't really tell you . . .'

'No reason why not. That's what I'm here for, after all, and I promise you it won't go any further.'

'Well, it's my boss.'

'Bill Saunders?'

She nodded.

'He's making my life a misery.'

'In what way?'

'He's just got it in for me,' she said, suddenly speaking more quickly. 'He criticises everything I do, he tries to turn everyone against me. His outlook's very different from mine, you see. Perhaps it's because I'm not from around here.'

'Really? Where are you from?'

'London. Anyway, Bill and I hold different views on

everything. Teaching, politics, religion, you name it. I know he's going to sack me as soon as he gets a chance.'

'Have you spoken to him about it?'

'No, I can't. It's nothing you can put your finger on, you see. That's the awful thing.'

Father Snow was silent for a moment. Even in his old parish, there had been the constant danger of getting sucked into such disputes, of taking sides and losing friends. In a small town like Wodden, the risks would be even greater. Whatever his own feelings about the headmaster, the most important thing in these early days was to be diplomatic.

'I hardly know Bill Saunders,' he said. 'I've only met him once. But if he is treating you as you say, then I'm sure the fault is entirely on his side. It simply means he hasn't really understood you yet, that's all. You just have to give him time.'

Father Snow hesitated, taking a moment to try and gauge her spiritual state before he started turning the situation to good use. The vital thing was always not to go too far.

'Pray for him, Melanie. Difficulties like these are sent by God for our own good. If you overcome this one, both of you will become better people.'

She turned towards him, as though this was really the sort of thing she'd come to hear.

'Yes, Father.'

Encouraged, Father Snow spoke without really thinking, perhaps moved by God.

'Would you like confession now that you're here? You'd be surprised how much good it can do when things are getting you down.'

She shrank like an abused dog from a friendly movement.

'No, thank you, Father. Not today.'

He smiled, standing up to leave.

'Perhaps on Saturday, then.' For a moment he paused, looking down at her, letting her feel his strength. 'I'll pray for you.'

Father Snow turned and walked to the sacristy with all his old stiffness and assurance. He knew that he'd done God's work, sowing a seed in the girl's mind. It might take years to bear fruit, but he felt sure that one day she would go to confession. It was possible that, with one short conversation, he'd saved a soul for eternity.

Melanie stayed for Mass, but didn't approach the altar to receive communion, leading him to think again that perhaps confession was what she really needed. Although the congregation was small, as always on a weekday, it was a good, uplifting Mass for Father Snow.

When he got back to the presbytery, he stood for a few moments staring out into the garden. Grey light was coming up behind the hills, a pallor in the clouds. Everything outside was still wet and dark from the rain of the day before, the rain that had fallen on the dual carriageway. Sadness seemed to coat the dank garden like an invisible moss. He wondered what the weather had been like when Father Conner committed suicide. Perhaps the slightest difference in the quality of the light or the moisture in the atmosphere could mean the difference between life and death, damnation and salvation.

Father Snow stood and waited for his own melancholy to pass as though it were a moment of giddiness or nausea. When it had gone, he left the room and got on with his work.

During the next week, he began to get a feeling for Wodden and to understand what his life would be like there. In many ways, he was able to recreate the routine of his old parish. Immediately after morning Mass, he had breakfast, then spent a couple of quiet hours doing paperwork, answering the correspondence which had built up after Father Conner's death, preparing his sermon. If he had any time left in the two hours after breakfast, it was given over to spiritual reading. History, being his personal indulgence, had to be left till the evening.

Mondays were to be his day off. On Tuesday and Thursday he visited the local hospital. In London he had sometimes come up against hostility from matrons and administrators on such visits, but here everyone seemed co-operative enough. They obligingly gave him a list of all their Catholic patients. There were no obstacles set in his way; he was free to visit them all. Father Snow made sure that with each patient, no matter how minor their ailment, he turned the conversation to spiritual matters. At each bedside he knelt and said a short prayer before leaving.

There were various other threads of Father Conner's work to pick up. Two baptisms had been postponed; Father Snow had to re-schedule them. A couple who were to be married the following year had had their course of instruction interrupted; he agreed to see them on Wednesday evenings. A pre-Christmas jumble sale was being organised for the benefit of the church; he was asked to fix dates, approve leaflets, and exhort his parishioners the following Sunday. Melanie Histon's class at the primary school were being prepared to receive their First Communion, so he would be required to go round on Friday mornings and help in their instruction.

Although it was a busy week, it seemed to him by the end of it that there was something missing in Wodden. At first he couldn't work out what it was, but then he realised that it was the strange quietness of the presbytery. The phone and the doorbell hardly ever rang. In his old parish there had never been a moment's peace. People had bothered him constantly with their problems. Here, though, there was silence. The whole parish seemed to be quite contented and calm. Perhaps it was simply because they were unwilling to open up their personal lives to a complete stranger, especially one who seemed so uncompromising and cold. Father Snow knew, however, that those very qualities which at the moment put them off him would eventually attract them. They would seek him out precisely because he was so removed.

For the moment, though, everyone left him in peace. In the silent evenings, he was free to think. For all his ruthless efforts to distract himself with meditation, reading and prayer, his mind often turned back to Susan. This was understandable. Moving to his new parish had been particularly unsettling. Besieged as he was by loneliness, he was unable to crush his inevitable human desires with quite his usual efficiency. It would be better once he'd found his feet in Wodden. All he had to do was wait for the unpleasant sensation to pass.

Outwardly, his life was as ordered and calm as ever. The presbytery had the severe tidiness of any house inhabited by Father Snow. He seemed entirely controlled and self-contained. Yet he would often find himself just sitting down in the midst of all that order and picturing her face. He remembered how different she had looked with her make-up on and her hair up. Though he knew now that she'd been trying to attract him, it was impossible to feel anger. A mere seductress or a flirt would have been easy to deal with. But Susan was respectful and sincere, drawn to him in spite of herself. She probably wanted the attraction as little as he did. Like him, she knew that it was wrong, but she lacked his experience and self-control, and instead of anger he could feel nothing but a perilous sympathy.

Behind it all, somewhere far away at the back of his mind, was the memory of what they'd discovered about Everard. Although his rational brain had dismissed all that, the fantastic story had lodged firmly in his subconscious, as fairy tales are wont to do. Often he would dream about the gigantic ogre, back from a hunting trip in the snow, blood caked in his beard. Or he would find himself in the room of wonders, where the giant's club leaned against a wall and the tangled veins of two Tudor children stood independent of their bodies.

In the morning, waking from such dreams and still half

believing them, Father Snow found it almost incredible that on Sunday he would say Mass in Everard's house and have lunch with his direct descendant.

Before that happened, on the Thursday of his first full week in Wodden, Father Snow went to visit Jack Dugdale.

There was still a painful awkwardness in his relations with Flora. Unless they were talking specifically about the church or spiritual matters, he had little to say to her. He could deal with her as a soul, but not as a person. Of course, it was pleasant to have his meals cooked for him, but he would by far have preferred his solitude.

The rain started up again on Thursday, this time with all the stage effects of thunder and lightning. The garden was waterlogged, the blades of grass hammered under spreading pools, pale in the darkness. The trees leapt from the hills as tormented silhouettes, wringing their hands at the sky. Then the thunder rolled low and fast over Wodden, an enormous plane whose pilot wanted to terrify the inhabitants, a bellowing demon.

After supper, Father Snow stood at the french windows in the study and watched the bubbles drift on the pools of water outside. When he'd been there a few minutes, the door opened behind him.

'Father?'

He turned around to see Flora standing there. It was the first time she'd ever disturbed him in his study. For all her middle age and her motherly stoutness, she looked at that moment like a frightened child, unable to sleep in the storm, come down to seek comfort from her parents.

'Yes, Flora?'

'I'm all finished now.' She paused for a moment, again like a child, afraid to admit her fear. 'I was wondering if you could give me a lift home.'

'I'm so sorry, Flora. I had no idea you'd walked here. Of course I wouldn't let you walk back on a night like this.'

'It's not so much the weather, Father . . . I've got an umbrella.'

'What is it, then?'

'I was wondering if you could have a word with my husband. He's very ill, Father. The doctors haven't got much hope for him. He's on the list for a transplant, but it doesn't seem likely he'll get one. They give preference to younger applicants, you see. He was brought up a Catholic, but he hasn't set foot in church since the day we were married. Father Conner could never get through to him, but I think you might.'

She poured it all out like a prepared speech. Father Snow gave a businesslike nod.

'I'll go and get the car out.'

The drive took only five minutes. The rain pouring down the windscreen reminded him of going up to the British Library with Susan. It had only been three days ago. On the way, he checked with Flora that Jack himself understood the full gravity of his condition. Father Snow had heard of priests making disastrous blunders in these situations.

'I haven't hidden anything from him, Father,' she said. 'If you knew Jack, you'd know it would be pointless to try.'

After that they drove in silence. Once or twice, Father Snow glanced across to look at Flora, taking in her stiff perm and her peculiar oval glasses, touched by the simplicity and frankness of her faith. At these times more than any other, he felt like the representative of Christ, who had often been called to the houses of the faithful on such missions. He prayed he would be able to do a little good.

The Dugdales lived in a typical little Wodden cottage. It was small and cosy. There was a front garden with a low hedge and a wooden gate. The light through the ancient leaded windows looked warm and inviting. The effect was only ruined by a satellite dish, angled upwards from the wall as though it were some instrument designed to measure the intensity of the storm.

147

Father Snow parked the car and they both hurried up the garden path. Even those few seconds were enough to dampen his jacket and leave his black hair plastered across his brow.

'Jack?' called Flora as she opened the door. She sounded nervous. 'We've got a visitor!'

There was no answer. She showed him into the front-room. It was as small and homely as one would have expected from outside. The old walls, too lumpy and uneven for wallpaper, were painted white. The place was stiflingly warm. Besides the log fire which blazed in the grate, Father Snow noticed a long radiator under the window, and guessed that it was on.

Jack Dugdale was sitting on the sofa watching a game of football on TV. He was wearing a dressing-gown and tartan slippers. Something told Father Snow that the man sat like that all day, without bothering to dress. He looked far older than his wife, bald and liver-spotted, with a scrawny neck and glittering, chicken's eyes.

'This is Father Snow, Jack. He's the new parish priest.'

Father Snow walked towards the sofa, extending his hand.

'Hello, Mr Dugdale.'

Dugdale didn't take his eyes from the screen. Nor did he extend his hand, so that Father Snow was left standing awkwardly for a moment before removing his own. Rain beat against the window. The football crowd cheered.

'I'll make some tea, shall I?' said Flora.

Father Snow gave a little nod, and made a small sign which meant that she should give them some time alone. Flora left the room.

'Do you mind if I sit down?'

The dark eyes flickered from the game, as though to check there were chairs in the room.

'Suit yourself.'

Father Snow sat quietly down and looked at the screen

for a few moments. Arsenal were playing Manchester United.

'Are you an Arsenal fan, Mr Dugdale?'

For the first time, the old man turned towards his visitor, staring directly at him, as though to prove a point. The eyes, besides being now deliberately direct, were venomous. Father Snow forced himself to meet them as gently as he could.

'I hate football,' said Dugdale. 'Can't bloody stand it.'

He turned back to the screen.

'Just watching for something to do, are you?'

'What do you think? I'm stuck in here all day. I can hardly manage to get up the stairs. I can only leave the house in a wheelchair, and I'm buggered if I'm going to do that.' His eyes flicked back to Father Snow, perhaps to see if he'd been offended by the bad language. 'So of course I watch TV.' He gave a brief, unpleasant smile. 'In any case, it's nice to have something to hate.'

It was obvious that he wasn't about to be won over by polite conversation, so Father Snow tried a different tack.

'And you hate priests, do you?'

'Whatever gives you that idea?'

'Your lack of basic civility,' said Father Snow evenly. 'Or do you treat all your visitors like that?'

'You're no visitor of mine. I know why my wife has dragged you over here. She wants me to go back to church, see the error of my ways, confess, and all that crap. Well, she's wasting her time. And so are you.'

For all that he knew Dugdale's rudeness to be the result of fear, Father Snow could put up with it no longer. He got up, crossed the room, and turned off the television.

'Hey! Who the bloody hell do you think you are?'

'I'm somebody who's come out on a filthy night to help you, Mr Dugdale. Now you're going to shut up and give me five minutes of your time.'

This was obviously not what the old man had been expecting; it was certainly not what Father Snow's kindly

149

predecessor would have done. Dugdale leaned back on his sofa, staring up at the priest with an intensity of hatred which was almost frightening. In the silence where the TV had been, they could hear the rain lashing the cottage.

'Right. You've got five minutes. Save my soul, then turn the TV back on.'

Father Snow remained standing in front of the screen, aware of the impact his tall black figure would have in the little room.

'You're dying, Mr Dugdale. You've got to face facts. You probably won't be alive this time next year. Do you understand what that means?'

'I know as much about it as you or anybody else. In any case, I don't believe everything these doctors say.'

'Don't delude yourself with that false hope. I've dealt with a number of cases like this, and in almost all of them the patient died when the doctor predicted. Sometimes to the very day.'

'So what do you suggest?'

'Confess and receive communion. None of us like to face this, but the fact is that if you die in a state of mortal sin, you may go to hell. If you make a good confession, you'll be saved. It's a small price to pay for eternity.'

'You really believe that?'

'Oh, yes. I believe it absolutely, and so do you. You're just too terrified to face your belief. I'm not here for my own satisfaction, Mr Dugdale. I'm here to offer you the greatest gift anyone could give. I can hear your confession now and leave you a happy man. I promise you, nothing you have to say will shock me.'

Jack Dugdale went on staring up out of steady black eyes. All the priest's instincts told him that the man was in a state of very grievous sin, though he was unable to guess at its exact nature. He was dealing with a soul in the jaws of hell. A wrong word from him, and all would be lost.

In silence, they faced each other. The rain poured down outside. Then there was a flash of lightning and a roll of thunder roared over the roof. As though this had been a signal, Dugdale spoke.

'How old are you, sonny?'

Father Snow became suddenly aware again of the uncomfortable heat in the room.

'Twenty-eight.'

Jack Dugdale shook his head as though amazed.

'Twenty-eight! And I'm expected to call you father, at my age, to listen to your advice. Don't come in here and tell me you wouldn't be shocked by anything I've got to say.' He leaned forwards, smiling. 'If I told you the half of it, you'd probably lose your mind.'

At that moment, it was as though he'd changed into a different being, as though the eel in him had poked its head between the rocks. Father Snow had never felt himself in the presence of such malevolence. It made the room feel suddenly colder.

'Whether I'm shocked or not, let me hear your confession.'

Dugdale sagged back, looking away; the thing hid itself again. He was just a pathetic old invalid, ungracious and grumpy.

'No. I'm keeping my so-called sins to myself. I'm sick of this silly little game now, so you might as well leave. Don't bother coming back.'

'Very well. If you change your mind, let me know. You can call me twenty-four hours a day.'

Father Snow bent down and turned the TV back on. The miniaturised roar of the crowd returned to the room. When he got to the door, he paused and looked back at the dying man on the sofa.

'I'll pray for you.'

Dugdale's eyes, already immersed in the screen, flickered momentarily, and the word must have escaped without his volition, for there was no irony in it:

'Thanks.'

Father Snow walked down the corridor and found Flora

in the kitchen, staring out at the rain. He felt a terrible pity for her, a good, ordinary woman doomed to live with such a man. Yet even she probably didn't realise the true darkness of her husband's nature. There are some things which only reveal themselves to priests and which only priests have eyes to see.

'We've made a bit of progress, Flora,' he said kindly, 'but not much. I think he'll come round in the end, though. He's basically a good man.'

Her smile of gratitude was the only real reward Father Snow got from the whole exercise. He stood there stiffly for a moment, suddenly wishing he could squeeze her shoulder or hold her hand. In the end, he gave her a little nod, and left.

Outside, the wind had started to tear the remaining leaves off the trees and hurl them across the sky, millions of shadows swirling and floating like banknotes from a runaway train. Father Snow drove slowly. When he arrived at the presbytery, he saw a figure waiting for him in the lighted porch.

He forced himself to stay calm as he got out of the car, though he still couldn't be sure. But as he approached, he saw that it was really her. It was Susan. She'd come this time without her umbrella. There was no make-up on her face. Her hair hung in rat's tails.

Stepping into the porch was like stepping into a cave behind a waterfall. She moved towards him with a kind of involuntary jerk.

'I had to come,' she said in a low voice. 'I had to see you.'

Father Snow became more upright and distant than ever.

'What can I do for you?'

She drew back from him as though suddenly realising that her behaviour had been improper.

'I'm sorry, Father . . . Do you think I could come in for a minute? I'd like to talk to you.'

'Talk to me here.'

Susan became agitated. She took a deep breath before she spoke, her eyes wandering as though she were addressing an invisible audience.

'I don't know what's wrong with me,' she said. 'I don't usually behave like this. But I can't eat or sleep. All I can do is think about you.' Her eyes stopped moving and fixed themselves on his face. 'I just can't stop thinking about you.'

Father Snow allowed himself the small sin of looking into her eyes. They seemed almost desperate. It was incredible that he should have been the cause of such feeling in such an attractive girl. Part of him longed to take her inside and find out what was the matter with her, to give her what help he could. He became aware of the water splattering as it cascaded over the side of the porch.

'I think you'd better go.'

'Won't you let me in, just for a minute?'

'I can't do that, I'm afraid. I'm terribly busy tonight.' Taking out his keys, he stepped past her and opened the door. 'You'll have to go home.'

Susan just stood there, obviously ashamed, yet unable to leave.

'I only want to talk to you.'

Turning on the doorstep, Father Snow shouted in a voice which carried above the sound of the storm:

'Leave me alone!'

There was a glimpse of her face, astonished and hurt, before he slammed the door on it.

It took Father Snow only an instant to compose himself again. Then he went calmly upstairs to say the rest of that day's Office. He knelt upright in his usual way, with the usual impassive expression on his face. Nobody who saw him would have guessed, and he barely admitted even to himself, that he was reeling from the shock of happiness.

★   ★   ★

153

The encounter with Susan did have one good effect. The following day, having put it off all week, Father Snow went and introduced himself to the priest in the neighbouring parish. More than at any time since his ordination, he felt himself in need of spiritual guidance.

The church in Dorking was far larger than that in Wodden, a looming Edwardian building with a spacious car-park. The presbytery was built on similar lines. No doubt it had once housed three or four priests looked after by a full-time housekeeper and a cleaner, a little religious community in itself. Now there was only one priest left.

In some ways, Father Snow's life in his new parish would hinge on this man. A priest can only really have an equal relationship, a real friendship, with a fellow-priest. With his parishioners there is always one last, insurmountable barrier.

The door was opened by a stocky, scowling man in his forties. He had brisk movements and a gruff, aggressive voice. His black hair formed a pronounced widow's peak, like that of a vampire in a fifties horror film. His bulbous nose was red and pock-marked. Father Snow's heart sank.

'Hello, Father. I'm Julian Snow. I'm the new parish priest over at Wodden.'

'I was wondering when you'd turn up.' His tone made Father Snow wonder whether it had been rude not to get in contact sooner. 'Ralph Mackenzie.' The name was barked like an insult. 'You might as well call me Ralph from the start. I'll call you by your first name, too, provided I don't forget it. Which I already have, come to think of it.'

'It's Julian.'

'Course it is.'

They shook hands. Ralph's grip was brief and energetic, but damp.

'Come in, then.' Father Snow followed him down the hallway. 'Will you be wanting confession?'

Father Snow coughed.

154

'Yes.'

'Right. Let's get that out of the way straight off, then we can relax.'

The enormous front room managed to look empty without looking particularly tidy or clean. The walls were bare apart from one large crucifix with a painted wooden figure. Blood trickled like sweat down the sides of his face. Father Snow had rarely felt so unwilling to confess. He always liked to feel that his confessor was also his superior, not in terms of rank or age, but in terms of spiritual development.

The big, ruddy face remained impassive as Father Snow tried to explain his confused feelings for Susan, neither condemning nor understanding, apparently not even listening at all. When the story was finished, he didn't comment or offer advice, but merely asked whether Father Snow had any other sins to confess. So Father Snow went through the litany of his other faults. They were less dramatic, but more depressing. At each confession, they were almost unchanged.

Only when he'd finished did Ralph speak.

'Is this woman a Catholic?'

'No.'

'Then you have absolutely no excuse for seeing her. Bar your door to her entirely. If she says she wants to convert, which is a trick they often try, send her over here to me. I'll sort her out.'

Father Snow felt slightly insulted by this. Ralph seemed to be saying he was more than capable of dealing with the situation which had unsettled the younger priest. Irritated, he bowed his head. Ralph, meanwhile, carried on telling him what to do.

'You may feel that you're madly in love with her, and that this proves you never had a vocation. That's nonsense. You'd fall out of love quickly enough once you'd broken your vows and moved in with her. Believe me, she'd just become a very ordinary, humdrum girl. You'd be bored with her inside a month. Don't throw your life away for that.'

This uninspired advice was delivered with the same gruffness as before. Ralph was obviously trying to play the part of the older priest who'd seen it all, but he couldn't quite pull it off. When he'd given Father Snow absolution, he stood immediately up.

'Right, Julian, or whatever your bloody name is, wait there while I go and get the drinks in.'

A moment later he returned holding two tumblers and two bottles, one of whisky and one of vodka.

'Have to keep the holy elixir hidden away from the parishioners,' he explained confidentially. 'Wouldn't want them thinking we're human beings or anything, would we? Right.' He slammed a glass down in front of Father Snow. 'What's your poison?'

'Tea,' said Father Snow flatly.

Ralph scowled.

'I'll pretend I didn't hear that. You can join me in a drop of vodka, and you're to drink it all up like a good boy.'

He began to pour.

'I never drink alcohol,' said Father Snow. 'I really would prefer tea, if you don't mind.'

Ralph straightened the bottle and stared at him out of small, glassy eyes. The rough bonhomie was gone from his voice.

'A young priest should never refuse a drink, especially if it's offered by an older priest. Otherwise the older priest may feel he's being criticised in some way, and the younger one may end up looking like a sanctimonious little git.'

'No criticism is intended,' said Father Snow, although he could countenance priests drinking only the smallest quantities. 'But I'm not used to it, and I've got to drive home in a minute.'

'Listen, my lad, one of the great advantages of the cloth is that the police don't usually bother you. I make it a rule always to get fully tanked up before I drive anywhere. Say a quick prayer to St Christopher, then go like the clappers, that's my policy.'

Father Snow found that it required courage to answer back.

'I prefer to stick to the speed-limit.'

Ralph stared down at him for a moment. Sitting stiffly at the table with the glass of vodka in front of him, Father Snow began to feel awkward.

'God, you must get up a lot of people's noses.'

Father Snow shrugged, but said nothing. He was starting to blush.

'Well, I'll leave the glass there, in case you change your mind.' Ralph threw himself back into an armchair, took his own tumbler in his large hand, and knocked half of it back in one. 'Ah! Your good health!'

Father Snow stared with deliberate distaste at the vodka on the table in front of him.

'Cheers,' he said.

'So, you're the poor bugger who's been sent in to pick up the pieces after Charles, are you?' He grinned broadly, enjoying himself. Now he was trying to shock with coarseness. Father Snow gave no sign of having noticed. 'How are you finding it over in Wodden?'

'Well, it's very different from my last parish, I must say.'

'And where was that?'

'In the East End.'

Ralph laughed.

'Very different!'

They were silent for a moment, Ralph swilling his drink around and staring down at it as he did so, as though savouring his sheer possession of it. Father Snow watched, feeling like a puritanical killjoy, pompous and immature.

'I was speaking to an archbishop about you the other day,' said Ralph at last.

'What! Which archbishop?'

'Vincent Capel.'

Father Snow was astonished.

'You know Vincent?'

Ralph smiled at the reaction, as though it was exactly what he'd expected.

'Yes, poor sinner that I am, I know the holy Vincent. We go back a long way.' He was still staring down at his glass. 'Unfortunately, I haven't yet been able to follow him into sainthood, as you've obviously noticed.'

There was a silence. Father Snow was too embarrassed to move. Eventually, Ralph looked up.

'He asked me to keep an eye on you, see how you were settling in.' It seemed to Father Snow that there was bitterness in his voice. 'Speaks very highly of you, he does.'

'I don't know why.'

'Even Vincent can make mistakes,' said Ralph drily. He took another swig of vodka then stared thoughtfully at the carpet for a moment. 'Sorry. I didn't mean that.' He looked up and gave Father Snow a big smile. 'Look, let's not fall out over a silly little drink on our first night, eh?'

'No, let's not.'

'So, tell me how you're settling in over there.'

'Not too badly.' Father Snow wanted to stop there, but forced himself to make an effort. 'I must say, it's a bit depressing being in a place where something so terrible has happened.'

'Yes . . . poor Charles,' said Ralph, then, as though suddenly realising that he might be in danger of appearing sentimental, added: 'Silly bugger. I suppose, as a new boy, you're trying to do everything much as he did?'

'More or less.'

'So you're saying Mass up at that accursed house?'

'Flamstead, you mean?'

'That's the one.'

'Yes, I am.'

'There's no reason why you should, you know. It's no responsibility of yours.'

'Why do you think Father Conner did it, then?'

Ralph leaned forwards to fill his glass. Then he swilled the drink and stared down at it again, considering. Finally, seeming to come to a decision, he looked up.

'I'll tell you about Charles. He was a good bloke, you couldn't hope to meet a better. And I'm not saying that just because he's dead, either, because that isn't my way. Yet for all his goodness, or perhaps because of it, he was soft. Like many of these innocent types, he was easily impressed, and he was completely bowled over by those Trevellyans. Had lunch with them almost every Sunday. I hope you won't be doing the same.'

Father Snow looked at him steadily, prepared to accept more criticism.

'Well, I did agree to go the day after tomorrow, actually.'

'Don't make a habit of it. When you've got a house like that in your parish, full of high-ups, it's all too easy to lose touch with reality. Poor old Charles was always coming over here full of the latest political gossip, you know, what Gerald Pitman had said in Cabinet the week before, and all that. I have no doubt that it was mainly rubbish, but Charles, being Charles, was dazzled by it all.'

'Was he interested in the history of the family?'

'Unhealthily so. In one of them particularly, whose name I can't remember. Charles said he'd been an ogre. That was shortly before he went mad.'

There was silence. A car passed in the road outside. The young priest found himself staring up at the huge crucifix on the bare wall. Christ's painted head was bent as though to catch their conversation.

'I didn't realise that's what happened.'

Ralph sighed.

'It started a couple of weeks before his death. He came in here raving about some secret room which he believed existed in Flamstead House. The ogre's laboratory, he called it. He said he'd known of its existence for some time, but now he had to find it, because the ogre was still there. Well, I might have believed that in itself. I've been called to enough houses which obviously had evil spirits in them, and I've seen again and again the good that exorcism can do . . . You look sceptical, Julian.'

Father Snow shrugged. He felt they were approaching the uncomfortable territory where religion met superstition.

'I wouldn't know. I've never attended an exorcism.'

Ralph was staring at him out of bleary little eyes.

'Think yourself lucky.' He took another swig. 'In any case, I don't believe there was any evil spirit involved here. Poor old Charles was obviously losing his mind. I can see that clearly now. Perhaps I should have paid more attention to it then.'

For the first time Father Snow felt the beginnings of sympathy for him.

'It's hard to see what you could have done.'

'Had him transferred out of Wodden. That's what I should have done. As I've said, there was great weakness in him, and rubbing shoulders with the likes of Pitman and Trevellyan is a heady drug. It had obviously all got too much. Of course, I had no idea it would have such terrible consequences.'

Ralph paused. It occurred to Father Snow that perhaps the vodka was the reason he was talking so freely and that it was leading him to embellish his story.

'The following week he came round in a terrible state. He said he'd been to the house, taken measurements, and found the exact location of the room. There was a lot of other stuff as well, typical paranoid delusions. He said that he had information which could bring down the government, that he was being watched by MI5. They were emptying his rubbish, they'd broken into his house and been through his things, all that stuff. It was awful. I did my best to calm him down, but it didn't seem to do much good. I decided that, if he was in the same

160

state the following week, I'd get him professional help. The following week, as it turned out, was too late.'

The big priest drained his glass. Father Snow cast around for words of comfort, and found nothing but curiosity.

'What was the information which would bring down the government?'

'He wouldn't say, of course. Far too dangerous.' Ralph shook his head. 'I couldn't sleep for ages after he died, and not just because of my own guilt. The idea of it happening to Charles, of all people, was the most horrible thing. It was as though it had happened to a child.'

They were silent for a long time after that. Ralph finished his drink and poured himself another. The glass in front of Father Snow remained untouched. The painted figure listened to the silence, its attitude encouraging them to continue with their conversation, to become friends. Unfortunately, Father Snow couldn't think of anything further to say. The longer the silence continued, the more uncomfortable he felt. Eventually he started making movements to leave.

'Won't you have just one sip of that before you go?' said Ralph. It was almost as though he were pleading now. 'Just to keep me company?'

Only now did Father Snow realise that, for Ralph, the offer of the drink had also been a way of offering his friendship. It had been wrong to refuse point-blank. So, as he stood, he lifted the glass and took a small sip. The vodka burned his throat like a recrimination. Ralph, watching his face, was delighted.

'That's the boy!' He laughed heartily. 'Now you're more prepared for the drive back!'

They went to the door. As Father Snow walked to his car, Ralph watched from the doorstep. While the younger priest was still in earshot, he called:

'Julian!' Father Snow turned around. 'Remember what I said! Just one quick prayer, then drive like the clappers!'

As he spoke, he raised his heavy arm above his head,

fist clenched, as though in a gesture of victory or defiance.

The image stayed with Father Snow all the way back to Wodden. He drove slowly. His depression was deeper than it had been at any point since his transfer. There were no friends for him here. He thought of the broken priest turning around after he'd gone, lowering his arm, and returning to the huge, empty presbytery, originally designed to accommodate many priests together. Then he found himself thinking of all the presbyteries around the country. He pictured them as a string of forts manned by a withered army, a skeleton force waiting for the enemy to launch its last offensive.

When he got back to his own presbytery, where one of the troops had so recently gone mad and lost all hope, his spirits fell still lower. Again he pictured that network of all but deserted buildings, sinking into dereliction. They reminded him of the villas abandoned all over England in the decline of the Roman Empire, when the great civilisation had retreated back over the sea, taking all organisation and learning with it, leaving the country to centuries of savagery.

10

ON HIS WAY back to the presbytery after morning Mass, Father Snow found himself peering down the lane as though the place itself might explain Father Conner's madness. The picturesque cottages and the ancient stone bridge beamed innocently in the sunshine, smiling at the absurdity of his suspicions.

Since it was Saturday, he had to return to the church after breakfast to hear confessions. It was one of his least favourite tasks. For long periods, nobody would come to him. When they did, he had to listen to the same repetitive lists of sins. Besides tedium, there was the added strain of responsibility, the need to find the right words and tone. If he failed to do that, he might drive them away from the Church forever, and it would have been better if they'd never come. He always left the confessional feeling drained.

Today, after an initial rush, there was a lull. Father Snow opened the little doors in front of him and looked out into the church. It was empty. Across the aisle, he could see candles flickering, droplets of light in a sea of sunshine. Trying to use these quiet moments for prayer, he found himself instead thinking of how Susan had waited at his doorway, bedraggled in the rain. If anyone else had come to him in that state, he would never have turned them away. Slamming the door on her had demonstrated nothing but insecurity. It was almost as if her infatuation had been an infectious disease against which, even after his years of celibacy and discipline, he did not feel entirely immune.

Someone knelt down at his side. Father Snow's first reaction was irritation at having his reverie interrupted. Then he realised how much he'd been enjoying his thoughts of Susan, luxuriating in them. Here in the confessional, he'd fallen into temptation.

'Bless me Father, for I have sinned.'

When he heard the voice, Father Snow allowed himself a moment of professional pride. It was Melanie Histon. The few words he'd said to her on Tuesday had produced results.

'It's been . . . about twelve years since my last confession.'

Father Snow gave a nod. Then he waited silently, staring in front of him and asking God to give her courage.

'Father, I'm —' There was a creak of wood, a rustle of material. 'This is very difficult for me. I'm not usually so embarrassed about it.'

'It's alright. Take your time.'

When she next spoke, her whisper was almost inaudible.

'The reason I haven't been to confession for so long is . . .' There was another creak of wood and her voice fell still lower. 'I'm attracted to other women.'

Father Snow nodded. Perhaps thinking that he hadn't heard, Melanie said:

'I'm a lesbian.'

'I understand,' said Father Snow. 'Go on.'

'I haven't got a girlfriend at the moment. I had two in London, before I came down here.'

'When was that?'

'About six months ago.'

'And did you sleep with them?'

'Yes, Father.'

He nodded, but said nothing.

'It led me to drift away from the Church. I was very religious when I was a girl. Then, in my teens, I felt that the two things couldn't go together. One of the reasons I left London was to try and work out what to do about it all.'

Father Snow was silent, trying to find some gentle way of saying what had to be said. After a few moments he decided that there was no gentle way.

'Homosexuality is wrong,' he said. 'Never believe the blandishments of people who say otherwise yet call themselves Christians. They will lead you into grievous sin and imperil the salvation of your soul. Yet God, while deeming homosexuality a sin, has created you a homosexual, and this must seem very unfair to you at times. All I would say is this: God never asks the impossible. Those he asks to struggle are those he loves the most. He loves you more than other people because of what you are, not less. If you really have sexual feelings only for women, then perhaps he's asking you to sacrifice that form of love.' He paused, groping for the right words, but nothing came to him. 'You're a good person, and I know you'll win through in the end. I promise you, you'll be always in my prayers.'

'Thank you, Father.'

She was crying. Father Snow decided not to ask her if she had any other sins to confess. She'd done enough for the moment.

'You've made a good confession. Bow your head now while I give you absolution.'

He was depressed for the rest of the day. This wasn't because he felt he'd been too hard on Melanie. Father Snow knew that people turned to the Church in search of absolute moral guidance, and he never had any hesitation in giving it to them. Yet her confession had left him with the feeling that only the broken and confused are driven to seek refuge in God, only those who can't find comfort in the ordinary world. He thought of Ralph, drinking himself to sleep each night in his huge presbytery, and of Father Conner slipping into madness. He thought, too, of himself, slamming the door in Susan's face.

★   ★   ★

165

The park had never looked more lovely than when he drove slowly through it the next morning. The huge trees were all but bare, each twig picked out by a cold, meticulous sun. It was really beginning to feel like winter now. Herds of deer roamed slowly in the distance, giving the whole place an air of lazy peace, making the legends easier to believe. Henry VIII had come hunting here with Everard. The giant had introduced the king to a purer kind of savagery. Father Snow almost saw them, roaring aloud as their horses thundered beneath the trees.

The building itself was like a dream. If he'd been told about such a place without actually seeing one, he would have found its existence difficult to believe. Yet there it was, with its hundreds of windows and its fabulous stone carvings, far larger and more beautiful than life. Of course, as he drove up the hill Father Snow could only see the later building, behind which Everard's house was hidden. Darting, peering through the snow, would have seen something very different: a mighty Tudor mansion, a more naked statement of feudal power, the perfect home for an ogre.

This time Father Snow didn't have to ring for Lady Trevellyan to show him the way. He walked around the house and entered the chapel through the door which opened onto the park. Alone, he knelt for a few moments before the altar, preparing himself spiritually. Then he started getting everything ready. His concentration on the Mass he was about to celebrate was slightly disturbed by thoughts of the lunch which would follow it.

When he stepped out onto the altar fifteen minutes later, Father Snow couldn't help looking quickly around the congregation. Pitman wasn't there this week. However, the presence of Lord Trevellyan was more than distraction enough. He was standing right at the front with his wife by his side. At first, Father Snow thought he'd had a haircut. The long white curls which had hung from the sides of his bald head were gone. But then the Earl slightly turned and he saw that they'd been tied back in a pony-tail.

After Mass, Lord and Lady Trevellyan waited for him outside. They shook hands and Trevellyan handed him an envelope.

'Let's go and have lunch,' he said, and the three of them set off down the corridor. 'So, Father, how are you settling down in Wodden?'

Father Snow repeated the answer which was by now becoming routine.

'Well, it's very different after my last parish, I must say.'

'And where was that?'

'In London. The East End.'

'Ah. I don't care much for London, myself. Can't stand all those crowds of people.'

'My husband likes to keep himself to himself,' said Lady Trevellyan. 'I think that if he had his way he'd lock himself up here entirely and live as a recluse. As it is, he hardly ever sets foot outside the house. Do you dear?'

Trevellyan gave her an almost pitying look, but said nothing. He showed them into a panelled room which was small by the standards of Flamstead, but would have been palatial anywhere else.

'Here's what my wife loves,' he said to the priest in a low voice. 'Company!'

There were about ten people sitting around the table, all of whom stood up as they entered. The only one Father Snow recognised was Bill Saunders. Near the head of the table was a huge log-fire. On the walls hung portraits, presumably of his lordship's ancestors.

The chairs were all of ornately carved wood. Three of them were empty. Lady Trevellyan went and stood behind the one at the foot of the table, while her husband stood at its head. The third empty chair was on his right, opposite Bill Saunders, whose thick lips were smiling in reassuring welcome.

'You sit here, Father,' said Trevellyan. 'This is the priest's place.'

Not sure of what to do next, Father Snow just copied his hosts and stood still behind his chair. Now everyone was standing, silent, apparently waiting for something. After a moment, he realised that they were all looking at him.

Trevellyan only allowed the embarrassment to continue for a split second before he spoke.

'If you'd like to say grace, Father, then we can begin.'

Father Snow blushed. He'd been so worried about committing some lapse of etiquette that he'd forgotten he was among Catholics.

'Of course.'

Fortunately, he remembered that they would expect it in Latin, and managed to produce the words. Still nobody moved. They all stood looking at him as before. He wondered desperately what else could possibly be required of him.

'Please sit down, Father,' said Trevellyan in a low voice.

It was one of those rare moments when Father Snow lost his composure. He fumbled with his chair, pulling it clumsily away from the table. The terrible silence and stillness continued. Only when he was quite definitely seated did the room come back to life. Everybody else sat down and Father Snow was introduced to them all, though his discomfort was such that he remembered none of their names. There were four men and their wives. Apart from him, only Bill Saunders seemed to have come alone.

'Great to see you again, Father,' said Saunders when the introductions were over.

Composing himself, Father Snow gave a nod.

'Hello, Bill.'

Conversations started up around the table. A pretty girl of about twenty appeared and began serving soup.

'She's just an au-pair,' said Trevellyan, as though apologising. 'We haven't had any staff here since I was a child.'

Father Snow nodded, unsure of how he should respond.

'A building of this size is terribly expensive to maintain, you see,' Trevellyan went on. 'That's why we've had to turn the old house over to the National Trust. Sooner or later we're going to have to start selling things off, or rent out one of the wings. The whole place is riddled with rot, of course. There are rooms here which stand empty for months on end. I understand there's a whole colony of bats living in the south roof. People have even reported seeing foxes running down some of the more remote corridors, though I personally find that hard to believe.'

He'd spoken more sadly than ever, leaning back in his chair, managing to endow himself and his home with a sort of mournful magic. Then he ruined it all by repeating something he'd said on the priest's last visit.

'The deer are quite happy to come in and roam around the courtyards, especially in winter. Perhaps they think the house is uninhabited.'

'Perhaps,' said Father Snow.

As they spoke, he was beginning to understand why his predecessor had been drawn to have lunch here every Sunday. After a week spent down in the empty presbytery, it must have been tempting to enter this fantastic world whose important inhabitants treated their priest with such respect.

Father Snow took a sip of his soup. It was delicious. Trevellyan leaned towards him and spoke more quietly, so that only he and Bill Saunders could hear.

'So, Father, are you still interested in my ancestors?'

'Yes. As I told you before, I'm a bit of an amateur historian. I always look into the local history when I move to a new place.'

'I see. And in Wodden it's Everard Trevellyan who's become the centre of your interest. Am I right?'

'I must admit, he's an intriguing character.'

Trevellyan smiled.

'So everyone says. Well, have you got any great revelations for us?'

Father Snow hesitated. Apart from Trevellyan, only Bill Saunders was listening. The headmaster managed to continue smiling even as he was sucking soup through his glistening lips.

'I've found out a few things. Do you know about seventeenth-century newsbooks?'

Trevellyan nodded, looking down as he took soup from his bowl.

'Of course. I think we may have a small collection of them upstairs in the library, actually.'

'Really? I'd love to have a look at them one day.'

Trevellyan smiled.

'I'm sure that could be arranged. In any case, tell us what you've found out.'

So Father Snow explained what they'd discovered at the British Library. He did it briefly, leaving out the more gory and sensational details, which he would have been embarrassed to repeat.

'That's fascinating, Father,' said Saunders when he'd finished. 'I knew the legends of an Ogre Earl, of course, but I'd no idea they might have been based on a real person.'

'The story is still popular in the village, then?'

Saunders laughed.

'You'd better believe it! Half the poor little things down at the school are terrified of Flamstead to this day!'

Trevellyan was silent, staring down at his empty soup bowl.

'Of course,' said Father Snow, 'neither of the sources I found was really reliable. The pamphlet was obviously sheer sensationalism. Darting's account was third-hand, and no doubt much embellished in the telling.'

'So you think there's nothing in it?' said Trevellyan, looking up.

'Of course not. As you told me before, he was just

an aristocrat who had a dissipated youth. The rest is all exaggeration, tales to frighten children.'

'And Protestant propaganda,' said Trevellyan. 'Our family was one of the few in this country which had the wealth and faith to remain true to the Church. That's what my ancestors should be remembered for. Instead, centuries later, they're rewarded with the continuation of this evil gossip.'

'But these days it's all just a bit of harmless fun,' said Father Snow reasonably. 'Even if people did believe the legend, what difference would it make? Everard's been dead for four hundred years.'

'But the family is still alive, Father, and it's by its ancestors that a family like mine is judged. Can you honestly say that, after all you've discovered about the third earl, you still see the present one in exactly the same way?'

Resting his chin on one long-nailed hand, he leant back in his chair as though allowing Father Snow to examine him.

'No, I don't. But then I can't help feeling that you deliberately invite a comparison.'

'I assure you, Father, nothing could be more odious to me than a comparison with that monster.'

'I'm sorry,' said Father Snow, noting the unintentional admission that Everard had been a monster, and feeling strangely thrilled by it. 'No offence intended.'

'None taken, Father.'

After that, all three of them were silent until the second course arrived, when Trevellyan turned towards Saunders.

'So, Bill, how are things going down in the school?'

'Still having a few problems with the staff, I'm afraid. Well, one member of staff in particular.'

Father Snow went on eating as though he wasn't interested.

'This new girl?' said Trevellyan. It seemed that, for

a recluse, he was surprisingly well up on village gossip.

'Melanie Histon, yes. She's a lovely lass, but she's going to have to go sooner or later, I'm afraid.'

'Why?' said Father Snow. Saunders gave him an even larger smile than usual.

'Nothing for you to worry yourself about, Father. I can deal with it.'

'All the same, I'd like to know, if you don't mind. It is a Catholic school, after all, and I am the Catholic priest.'

Saunders stopped smiling.

'Her ideas about teaching don't really fit, Father, that's all. Besides which, she's what you might call a radical feminist, obsessed with gender roles, stereotyping and so on. Now, I don't deny that these things may have their place, but that place is not in a primary school. The last thing very young children need is somebody like that trying to mould them according to her ideology. I like her, as I say, couldn't like her more, but I can't help thinking we made a dreadful mistake in ever taking her on.'

'You've met her, have you, Father?' said Trevellyan.

'Yes, I have.'

'And what do you think of her?'

'She's a good woman. She may be a radical feminist, I don't know, but I do know that she's serious about her religion.' He paused, reminding himself how unwise it was to take sides. At the same time, he felt it was his duty to defend Melanie. 'Perhaps she just needs a little time to find her feet in Wodden. She probably needs to unbend a little. But it may be that the village should unbend a bit in her direction, too. I think it would be a great pity if we lost her.'

'There's something else,' said Saunders, then stopped.

'Go on,' said Father Snow.

'There are rumours about her . . . well, her sexuality, to put it bluntly.'

'What sort of rumours?'

172

'They say that she's a lesbian.'

Father Snow gave Saunders his hardest look.

'So what if she is?'

The headmaster stared back.

'Well, call me old-fashioned, Father, but I don't like the idea of a person like that being responsible for young children. It's all very well for you, as a historian, to look into medieval monsters. As a headmaster, my concerns have to be rather closer to home. I have to think of the little ones in my care.'

Father Snow put down his knife and fork.

'That's a disgraceful slur, and I'd like you to retract it at once.'

His tone silenced the other conversations at the table. Uncertainly, Bill Saunders looked towards Trevellyan. The big man was sitting with his chin on his fist, looking bored.

'He's right, Bill. You can't go round saying things like that without evidence.'

'All right,' said Saunders. 'I'm sorry.'

'Good,' said Father Snow. 'And, believe me, if Melanie Histon loses her job, I for one shall want to know the reason.'

Trevellyan sighed.

'I hope you two aren't going to fall out over this. One of the reasons I invited you both was so that you could get to know each other.'

After a moment's hesitation, Saunders managed to produce his smile, although it was now more obviously false than ever.

'Of course we're not going to fall out. It's all forgotten already, isn't it, Father?'

As his anger receded, Father Snow realised what sort of impression he must have made. None of them would have expected such a young newcomer to start making scenes, least of all in Flamstead House. He decided, rather belatedly, to be diplomatic.

'Of course, Bill. It's forgotten. All I'm asking is that you should give her a little time.'

Nothing seemed real to Father Snow when he got back to the presbytery that afternoon. For a couple of hours he'd been magically whisked up into a world more glamorous and exciting than his own. Now, just as magically, he'd been transported back down to his lonely little house. The place seemed more bleak and depressing than ever.

In the living-room he sat and looked at Father Conner's empty chair. His predecessor must often have sat there with this same feeling of anticlimax and depression, Cinderella back from the ball. He'd been fêted by the great house, but now he was back, just an ordinary rural priest after all. Somewhere that magical world was still going on without him. It was only natural that he should have wanted to make the fantastic journey to Flamstead again the following week. Yet it was still difficult to see how such small doses of unreality could have unbalanced a man's mind.

After evening Mass, Flora Dugdale came and cooked him supper. They had a brief chat about her husband. Physically, Jack was deteriorating. Spiritually, he was making no progress. Father Snow told her never to give up hope, although in this case he had little hope himself.

When Flora had gone, he opened the french windows and let himself out into the dark garden. The silence astonished him. Far away, from the hills which surrounded the village, he heard the calling of an owl. The sound carried as though it were indoors. He saw how the village lay enclosed in a vast bowl of hills and trees. Perhaps it was partly this geological isolation which had enabled Everard to keep the place under his spell for so long.

When he looked up, it seemed that another bowl of identical size had been laid like a protective cover over the one which held Wodden. The blue was graded so that on one side it was almost black, on the other almost white. The stars coming out up there seemed to be arranged in occult symbols. There was a group of gently twinkling lights lower down and to his left, as though a cluster of stars had fallen and got lodged high in the hills. It took him a moment to realise that they were the lights of Flamstead.

After that, he stared up at them for a long time. He was remembering the fairy stories his father had told him. In particular, he remembered Jack and the Beanstalk. For some reason, that had been the one he'd wanted to hear again and again. Of course he would have liked to believe that in some way it had all been real, that it had happened here. He would have liked that more than anything. Perhaps the very reason for his standing here in a presbytery garden wearing a dog-collar was that he still needed a fairy tale, and there was only one left which he now felt able to believe.

Lowering his head and straightening his back, Father Snow went indoors to say the last of his day's Office. But the emptiness of the house, the lack of wife or children, made him think again about the strangeness of his life. Only the misfits are called by God, those who can't find any comfort in the ordinary world.

It took a massive effort of will to make himself settle down to prayer. After a few moments, he was disturbed by another image. It was his mother on the day when he'd told her of his intention to become a priest. His memory exaggerated her horror. The scene had some strange resonance with what he'd felt in the garden, with the cluster of lights shining down from the hills, but he couldn't work out what it was. Then his mother's place was somehow taken by Susan. He realised that the struggle was beginning again, and suddenly doubted his ability to see it through.

Forgetting his Office for a moment, Father Snow immersed himself in a prayer for peace which was almost desperate in its intensity. It worked like magic, and he was allowed to complete his observances in the normal way. Shortly after he'd finished, the doorbell rang.

As he went to answer, Father Snow already knew that it could only be her. Nobody else in Wodden would think to bother him at this time of night.

He was right. When he opened the door, he found her standing there in her dull clothes and sensible shoes. Her eyes were lifted towards him from her lowered face, so that they seemed at once more vulnerable and more provocative. The priest assumed his hard expression.

'Please don't send me away again.' Her voice was unsteady, full of weakness. 'I only want to see you for a moment.'

'What about?' he said flatly.

'I've got some things to tell you about Everard.'

Father Snow's heart pounded as though trying to wake him up.

'All right. Come in.'

As he stood aside to let her pass, he saw the stars again, looking down into the closed sphere of hills and sky. He remembered himself standing in the garden, staring up at them. Then he found himself missing the life he'd had an hour before, looking back at it with the kind of acute nostalgia he usually only felt when he thought about his father.

II

FLORA HAD LIT a fire in the front room. The flames were low now, but the undersides of the logs were all brittle embers, glassy and shimmering. Their glow could be felt from the doorway.

Susan put down her bag and sat herself neatly on the sofa, knees together, hands on lap. Her hair was as it had been on their first meeting, a long, straight bob which hung to her shoulders. He felt that it was the sort of style an ugly girl would have chosen to try and hide as much as possible of her face.

'What do you want to tell me?'

She smiled at him with a kind of shy excitement.

'Wait a minute.' She leaned down to look for something in her bag. When she sat upright, she was holding a large glossy book, and still smiling. 'I think I've found Everard's secret room.'

'Really?'

'You don't sound very impressed.'

'Well, I assume you haven't actually seen it.'

Susan placed the book on her lap like a prim primary-schoolmistress preparing to read a story.

'No, but I think I've worked out where it must be. Come here and I'll show you.'

With a movement of her head, she indicated the empty place next to her on the sofa, then quickly avoided his eye. Mainly to spare her further embarrassment, Father Snow stood up, determined to pretend that everything was normal and innocent? Yet when he began to walk towards her, his movements came in a series of disconnected jerks, so that he wondered whether he wasn't in fact embarrassed himself. Then he was sitting next to her, close enough to take her in his arms, and his nostrils were taunted by an infuriatingly delicate scent.

The book on Susan's lap was called *Stately Homes of Britain*. Opening it, she produced a sheet of paper.

'I went up to Flamstead yesterday and paced out the distances of the rooms. It took me a long time to put all the measurements together, but this is what I eventually worked out.'

She handed him the paper, which showed an assortment of rectangles arranged around a central square.

'Do you recognise it?'

'No.'

'It's the first floor of Everard's house. This is the long gallery, the one with all the portraits in. When you go upstairs, you walk along here first. Then you turn left at the end and go through the series of bedrooms. The last one is the big one where Henry VIII is supposed to have slept. Left again here, and through another gallery, where they've got all those mouldering tapestries. Then left again, and through this enormous room, the one with the old billiard-table in it, and you're back where you started. You've gone round in a square.'

Father Snow was hardly listening. He felt a strange giddiness.

'I see.'

'It's a sort of optical illusion. When you're walking round, you think that the bedrooms back onto the billiard-room. But when you take the measurements, you realise that they can't. Everything's too narrow. There's a void in the middle of it all, which seems to be a perfect square with each side about twelve foot. I looked carefully, but I couldn't see any door leading in that direction. It could be that there's one hidden behind a tapestry, but I doubt it. Darting's account suggested something more cunning than that.'

Father Snow shook his head and smiled down at the piece of paper on his lap.

'The ogre's laboratory!'

'You could call it that, I suppose.'

Susan opened her book and started turning the pages, so that he could feel the light movements of her elbow. He hadn't realised quite how close they were sitting. Feeling that to move away would say too much, he stayed where he was. Then he was suddenly frozen, unable to breathe normally. In the silence it seemed to him that he was panting, a dog which had settled too close to the fire.

When she'd found the page she was looking for, Susan removed the piece of paper from his lap. Whether by accident or design, the backs of her fingers brushed against his thigh. He felt the touch with a strange intensity, as though that part of his body was suddenly more alive than the rest. Then, where the paper had been, she placed the open book.

'This is an aerial picture of Flamstead.'

As he looked down, Father Snow for a moment had the strange feeling that he really was floating high above the house. He could see, in the long line of windows at the front of the building, those of the room where he'd had lunch that afternoon. Behind were the two courtyards he knew, the Tudor one with its huge antlers, and the more recent addition. Yet now he realised that these were only a fraction of a network of courtyards, the rest of which were closed to the public. The size of the place was staggering. From the air, the architectural trickery was obvious. The Tudor structure had been buried right in the heart of it all, something darker and more solid that seemed to have thrown out the rest of the structure like a vast, elaborate fantasy.

Then Susan's hand appeared somehow without destroying the illusion of flight, so that it was like the hand of a giant hovering over the building. Her finger descended right to the centre of it all and pressed. A strange sensation crawled up Father Snow's leg.

'The void I found is here,' she said. 'What can you see?'

She removed her hand, allowing him to look. There was a tiny, faint square right at the centre of the building. When he saw it, even Father Snow couldn't help thinking for a moment that perhaps this was a fairy castle, after all.

'It looks like a trap-door.'

'Exactly. And it's right above the empty space I showed you on my plan. So Darting wasn't exaggerating or lying. There really is a hidden room.'

For a moment, Father Snow could do no more than look. It was as though he'd been turned to stone. At last he closed the book and handed it back.

'Very interesting.'

'Aren't you excited? Don't you want to try and get in there?'

'No, I'm not excited, because I still think the whole story is nonsense. As for getting in there, I can hardly ask Lord Trevellyan to let me go clambering around on his roofs, can I?'

'No, you're probably right.' Leaning forwards, she replaced the book and the plan in her bag. 'I just thought you'd be interested, Father.'

Father Snow didn't answer. He was staring into the shimmering fire so as not to look at her, wondering how he could now get her to leave. The first vital step would be to return to his place in the armchair, yet somehow he hesitated. For a long moment, he just sat and did nothing. Then he realised that he'd missed his opportunity to move. After such a long pause, it would be too awkward and absurd suddenly to get up. Once more he felt himself frozen and crushed, labouring for breath. They just sat there side by side, not looking at each other. He knew that the silence had to be broken, but each passing second made it more impossible to speak. Eventually, as a preliminary, he shifted slightly so that the sofa creaked. Then, as though that small sound had been enough to break the spell, Susan herself spoke.

'Father, I've been thinking . . .' There was another silence, during which Father Snow didn't look at her, for fear of embarrassing them both. 'I've decided not to try and see you again.'

Father Snow coughed.

'I think that's for the best.'

When she next spoke, Susan sounded on the edge of tears.

'There's so much I'd like to say before I go.' Father Snow closed his eyes, not out of embarrassment, but out of some other feeling aroused by the sincerity of her voice. 'I'd like to explain everything to you, but it's so difficult.'

'Why me?' said Father Snow. 'Why should you want to explain these things to me?'

'I don't know. I don't really understand it myself. Perhaps it's just because I can see that you're a good man, a gentleman. I think there's something a bit old-fashioned about us both. I just know that, if we could ever be together, you'd never let me down.'

'And you've been let down, have you?'

'Yes. About as badly as anyone could be, I suppose.'

Now at last Father Snow turned towards her. There was something different about her face, something at once more open and more sad. At this, their final meeting, Susan had finally lost her reserve.

'And because you'd been let down,' he said, 'you decided to latch onto me, a sort of fantasy figure to take the place of a real man.'

But Susan was shaking her head.

'It was nothing so simple as that. If it was, I'd have been able to deal with it.'

'What was it then?'

'I just fell in love with you. That first time you opened the door for me and I saw you standing there, all stiff and formal, giving me that look of yours . . . It was like being struck by lightning.'

Father Snow would have liked to sneer, to tell her how ridiculous he thought this was. Yet somehow, seeing her there in front of him and hearing the emotion in her voice, it didn't seem quite so ridiculous, after all. She was staring straight at him, and he didn't look away, so that he wondered whether he, too, hadn't lost a little of his reserve.

'Of course, I told myself that it was silly and wrong, that I should leave you alone. I've always rather looked down on those silly girls who get crushes on people they can't have. But I couldn't resist coming to hear you say Mass, just once. And seeing you up there on the altar, which should have made me realise how hopeless the whole thing was, only made me love you more. I admired you so much for the life you live, you see. And now that I've seen how absolutely you live it, I admire you even more.'

'So it was really the priesthood that attracted you?'

'No. I fell for you in spite of that, not because of it. If you'd been a train-driver or a street-cleaner, I think it would still have happened. If you'd opened the door for me in a set of grubby overalls, the lightning would still have struck.'

'But I was wearing a dog-collar. And, as I hope you've now understood, my devotion to the cloth is absolute.'

'I know. I sensed that even then. But I just couldn't believe that you didn't share my feelings. I always thought that love at first sight had to work both ways.'

Father Snow was silent, thinking about the moment when he'd leaned down towards the car in the rain, wondering. He thought also about how the image of her face had kept interfering with his prayers and disturbing his sleep. Yet it had all been the result of his loneliness in a new place, nothing more.

'I was serious, Father. I'm not going to try and see you again. But before I go, I just need to know . . .' She stopped and looked away from him as though now, after all she'd said, she had at last been overcome by shame. 'Do you really feel nothing for me?'

'No,' said Father Snow. 'I have no . . . special feelings for you.'

Susan closed her eyes and leaned her head against the back of the sofa. In spite of his denial, or perhaps because of it, Father Snow felt himself flooded with affection for her. He'd been right: her infatuation was an infectious disease against which he was not entirely immune. Her description of her feelings had somehow carried him away until he felt himself sharing in them. Now he would have given anything to make her happy. Perhaps, in another life, he might have done so.

'There's no reason why you should find me attractive,' said Susan, without opening her eyes. 'Nobody else does.'

Hearing her say that, seeing her there in her plain clothes with her unbecoming haircut, was too much for Father Snow. His heart went out to her, and she had never seemed to him more beautiful. Then he found himself reaching out and giving her hand a sympathetic squeeze.

Susan opened her eyes and smiled at him sadly.

'It's all right,' she said. 'You don't need to feel sorry for me.'

Father Snow said nothing, yet he didn't immediately remove his hand. As when she'd brushed her fingers against his thigh, the part of his body she was touching seemed suddenly more alive than the rest. It was like a dash of colour appearing in a black-and-white picture, a patch of spring in the snow. He vaguely realised that he was holding hands with her and staring into her eyes, and wondered how things had come to this. All he wanted was to tell her that she was the most beautiful woman he'd ever met.

'I don't feel sorry for you.'

Perhaps he would have said more, but at that moment the telephone rang, and his hand jerked away from hers.

As he reached for the receiver he found that he was shaking.

'Hello?'

'Julian? Ralph Mackenzie.'

Father Snow's heart sank.

'Oh, hello, Ralph. What can I do for you?'

'Not much. I was just sitting here, looking at an empty bottle and wondering how you are.'

'I'm fine, thanks.'

'Fancy coming over here to open a new one?'

It was a renewed offer of friendship. Given how badly their first meeting had gone, Father Snow was in no position to refuse.

'I'd love to, Ralph. Thanks.'

Outside the living-room door, he composed himself like an actor getting into character. When he opened the door, he looked as straight and uncompromising as ever.

'I've got to go out.'

Without saying anything Susan got up, put on her coat and picked up her bag. Then she came to join him in the hall. As Father Snow stood aside to let her through the door, their bodies came within inches of each other. There she stopped and looked up at him in such a way that he thought she might start crying.

'I'm sorry about all this, Father. I won't bother you again.'

Father Snow realised that this really was a final parting. To his own surprise, he found he couldn't bear to see her go. He gave a little nod.

'Goodbye, then,' she said.

He stepped round her, keeping his back straight so that no part of his body should touch hers, and opened the front door.

'Goodbye.'

It ended suddenly. Father Snow closed the door and was alone. He went back to his armchair. The loneliness of the whole building seemed to concentrate itself on the spot where she'd been sitting. Father Snow screwed up his eyes. In another life, he might have made her happy.

After a few moments, he got a grip on himself. His feelings were irrelevant. The battle had been won, that was the important thing. He went and got the 2CV from the garage. But as he turned onto the lane, she materialised in the swing of the headlights. She was just standing there waiting in the cold, her bag held in both hands like a bridesmaid's posy. As he drove past she simply watched.

The roads were almost empty. There were no lights on the lane which led up to the A25. Father Snow's headlamps were magic lanterns projecting shadowy images of cottages and trees. A few minutes later he began driving slowly along the main road towards Dorking.

Ralph was already drunk when he arrived. They sat in the same large, bare room as before. He allowed Ralph to pour him a small whisky, which he then managed to make last for the rest of the evening. Father Snow felt as little liking for Ralph as before. The older priest did the talking, not seeming to care, or perhaps simply not noticing, that his guest just sat there stiffly most of the time, staring down at his drink.

Ralph talked shop, complaining about the less agreeable aspects of their work: arguments with hospital staff and social workers, parishioners who tried to borrow money, old women who rang at supper time then kept you on the phone for hours, lapsed Catholics who only turned up at the church for christenings or funerals and then treated the place like a hotel lobby.

'I've almost come to blows with some of the buggers before now.'

'Really?' said Father Snow.

'I mean, if you're going to call yourself a Catholic, at least make a bit of an effort. Eh?'

'Yes.'

'Anyway, how are things over in Wodden?'

'Not too bad.'

There was a silence, during which Ralph stared at Father Snow and Father Snow stared at his drink.

'You're not much of a talker, are you, Julian?' said Ralph at last.

'Sorry. I'm just a bit preoccupied this evening.'

'What about?'

'Nothing. Nothing important.'

'Are you all right? You seem a bit depressed.' Ralph leaned closer, examining him. 'You seem to have had all the stuffing knocked out of you.'

'Look, I'm fine. Just leave me alone.'

Ralph stood up and went to look out of the window, although there was nothing to see except a pale reflection of the room hanging in darkness. He spoke without turning.

'You might as well leave. I'm sorry to have dragged you out like this.'

Father Snow felt himself falling into despair. He stared at Ralph's broad back.

'Ralph –'

'It's all right, just go. You should be tucked up in bed with your saintly cup of cocoa by now, in any case.'

Father Snow sat still. A moment later, Ralph turned back towards him, smiling.

'I've got a few things to be getting on with myself. Come on, I'll show you out.'

So the young priest stood up, leaving his unfinished drink on the table like a last insult for Ralph to deal with when he'd gone. As they left the room, Ralph slapped him on the back, and said without irony:

'It was good to see you, Julian. Come again when you're in a more chatty mood.'

Father Snow felt his life had been used up.

Back at the presbytery, he spent a long time praying for strength. Then he went to bed and lay awake for hours, unable to stop thinking. In the end, he went downstairs and stared at the place where she had sat. Finally, remembering the plan and the photograph she'd shown him, he went out into the garden and gazed up at the cluster of lights in the hills until he was exhausted enough to sleep.

It was unfortunate that the following day was Monday, the day in Father Snow's week set aside for rest. He got up at his usual time, performed his usual observances, then went to the church for morning Mass. There was a spiteful frost outside. The winter had really begun. There was a hollow quality about the cold, something perfectly empty and still, which suggested that there might even be an early fall of snow.

Back at the presbytery after Mass, he found himself unable to settle to anything. The emptiness of the building was too intense. He realised how until now he'd used his thoughts of Susan as a kind of company. Now all he could do was sit there and remember the night before. For all his efforts, he couldn't feel ashamed or disgusted by what he'd said and done. Instead, he felt lightheaded and ill; lonelier than before. Perhaps this was love, which is supposed to change our lives.

He remembered, too, how Ralph had slapped him on the back and thanked him for coming. There had been a kind of generosity in that. Yet now Susan was gone, the idea of friendship with Ralph was somehow more repugnant than ever.

At some point in the afternoon, Father Snow found that he could stand the silence of the presbytery no longer. There was nowhere for him to go today, but he had to go somewhere. So he put on some casual clothes and left.

The cold hit him as soon as he got outside. The sky was grey. Although it was pointless, he was unable to stop himself looking for Susan as he walked through the village. There was no sign of her. Indeed, there were very few people around. The sudden frost seemed to have sent the place into hibernation.

Before long, Father Snow had reached the A25, from

where there was only one place to go. As he walked past the griffons, he wondered how often Father Conner had been driven up here by the boredom and sadness of the presbytery. Perhaps it had been a regular thing with him to walk this way, hatching increasingly elaborate fantasies and plots, slowly losing his grip.

The park was empty. There weren't even any deer to be seen. The rising ground was sprinkled with frost. The house itself looked entirely deserted. It might really have been no more than an enormous ruin given over to foxes and bats.

Father Snow paid his fee at the little booth. There were hardly any visitors. He walked through the great dining-room. Despite all the legends, it seemed to him like no more than a large room.

After looking round for a few moments, he went upstairs, past the carved griffons at the bottom of the bannisters, and paced down the long gallery. If Susan was right, the secret room was behind the portraits and panels on his left. He paused for a moment to look at the picture of Everard. There was no doubt that he'd been a very tall man. The fact that he'd chosen to be painted with such an enormous, savage dog proved perhaps that he'd enjoyed frightening people, nothing more. The golden astrolabe might have indicated an interest in science. His face seemed sadder today.

Turning from the portrait, he continued on his way, walking through the rooms which formed the square Susan had shown him, always aware of what might lie on his left, wondering. He recalled Darting's list of the marvels he'd been shown in the laboratory: the strange machines, the head in the barrel, the bodies made of veins, the giant's club. Perhaps they were all still there, mouldering away.

When he'd walked round three sides of the square, he entered the last room and started to head back past the antique billiard-table. There was nothing more to be seen.

The room was empty, apart from an old attendant sitting in one corner, apparently asleep with his eyes open. As he walked away, Father Snow heard a short laugh. He turned around, but the attendant was sitting exactly as before, his expression and posture unaltered, staring into nothing. Father Snow walked on, back towards the long gallery, then stopped in his tracks.

Standing in front of the portrait of Everard, staring upwards into the wistful face, was the massive figure of his descendant. Father Snow stood perfectly still, instinctively wanting to keep his presence here a secret. There was no logical reason for this, except perhaps that he'd unintentionally crept up on Trevellyan at a private moment. From where the priest stood, the big man's face was entirely hidden by his fall of white hair.

Neither of them moved, and Father Snow, watching unobserved, felt an irrational thrill. He was the child who'd crept into the castle and now stood in the very presence of the giant. They were alone, except that, behind the boy, one of the creatures of the place lay under a spell. If the ogre happened to turn around now, the pursuit would begin.

It only lasted an instant. Then Trevellyan, apparently coming to a sudden decision, began to walk down the long gallery away from Father Snow, heading in the direction of the historic bedrooms. His steps were large and purposeful, making a slow, heavy sound against the wood. There was an aura of power and ownership about him which Father Snow had never noticed before.

On his way back home through the park, Father Snow met Melanie Histon. She was going in the opposite direction, walking up towards the house. They had a short chat. She said that things were going a little better at the school. When he asked her why she was visiting Flamstead, she told him that the children had been having nightmares about it.

12

THE COLD DEEPENED. Wodden lay in the grip of a frozen spell. In the mornings, the frost on the grass made it look as if there had been snow, though there had as yet been none. There was ice everywhere. It hung from the eaves of the cottages and tinkled in the trees. Father Snow's black figure made a striking contrast as it paced across the white of the village green. He seemed, if anything, more controlled and self-contained than ever. Nobody who saw him would have guessed that his life was in turmoil.

After a few minutes, he had reached the school. He was there to speak to Melanie Histon's class, who were preparing for their first communion. The grim, awkward man was surprisingly good with children. He spoke to them calmly and seriously, telling them about the importance of the sacraments they were soon to receive and explaining the biblical origins of each. His presence could hold a class as firmly as it could a congregation. Bill Saunders' little ones hardly moved as they listened to him. They'd just come in from the playground and their faces were still red from the cold outside.

When he'd said all he had to say, Father Snow looked down at them for a moment, wondering. Then, to show that now they were going to have an informal chat, he moved forwards and perched himself on the edge of the teacher's desk.

'As some of you may know, I'm a newcomer to Wodden. I've only been living here a few weeks, and

I was wondering if anyone could tell me a bit about the village.'

Then he let a number of them tell him about the place in their own way, describing the shops, the village green and pub, their own houses. Father Snow pretended that all this was new and useful information, and they were soon vying with each other to produce a new fact. He got them to make guesses at how many people lived in the village and how old some of the buildings were.

'And can anyone tell me which is the largest house in Wodden?'

Most of them raised their hands. He chose one of the girls to answer.

'Flamstead House, Father. It's enormous.'

A few of the others gave knowing nods.

'What's it like, then?'

'It's got a really big door all made of iron and wood, about as big as our whole house. And there's about a thousand windows and a garden full of deer.'

Many of the others still had their hands up. Father Snow chose one of the boys.

'There's a huge pair of horns, Father, off a stag, hanging up on one of the walls.'

'And what's it like inside?'

'All old and wooden, with lots of old pictures.'

'Has everybody visited the house, then?'

In a clamour, they told him that they'd been together on a school trip the previous term. Some added that they'd already been with their parents, in any case.

'So who lives there?'

The room sprouted arms. Father Snow let one of the boys answer.

'A giant, Father.'

There was laughter.

'That's just a fairy tale, like Sleeping Beauty,' said a girl from the other side of the class.

'Who really lives there, then?' asked Father Snow.

'A lord, which is a very rich man,' she said, as though quoting a lesson learnt by heart, 'from a very old family.'

'There is a giant,' said the boy unhappily. 'I saw him when I went there with my mum and dad.'

'Really?' said Father Snow. 'What did he look like?'

'He was very tall and white with long hair, like Father Christmas, except he was bald on top. My dad told me he was the giant of Flamstead.'

'That wasn't a giant,' said the girl. 'It was just a big man.'

'That's what a giant is!' he cried triumphantly.

'How many other people here believe in the giant?'

No hands were raised. The one believer was alone.

'But you've all heard of him?' There were nods around the class. 'How many of you have ever dreamt about Flamstead House or the giant?'

About half of them put their hands up. Father Snow just stood and stared. The children of Wodden were still dreaming about Everard, just as the newsbook had said. It was as if he really had stepped back into the seventeenth century, into a world of superstition and magic.

'All right. You can put your hands down now.'

He would have liked to question them further, but he'd already taken up too much of the time they should have been devoting to proper schoolwork.

'I've got to go now,' he said. 'Thank you very much for telling me about the village. Perhaps we'll continue our conversation next time.'

As he was getting ready to leave, a boy who had not yet said anything spoke up from the back of the class.

'My dad says that there isn't any giant.' All the others turned round to look at him, as though he were some oracle who would settle the matter once and for all. He had dark curly hair and a quiet, grown-up voice. 'There used to be, though. He lived hundreds of years ago and his ghost is still up there in the house.'

There was silence. This was obviously one theory that

192

they felt unable to laugh off, no matter how much they would have liked to. The tone of voice, the speaker's grown-up gravity, had frightened them. It was obvious as they turned back towards the priest. One of the girls spoke up:

'Do you believe in ghosts, Father?'

Very slowly, Father Snow went back to his place behind the desk. They watched in complete silence.

'Now,' he said, 'I want you all to listen to me very carefully, because this is important. There are no such things as ghosts. What does the Church say happens to a person when they die?'

The same girl answered:

'They go to heaven, Father.'

'That's right. There are no exceptions to that rule. Not one dead person is allowed to stay here. There's only one person in the world that we can't see. Can anybody tell me who that is?'

The boy who answered was the one who, alone of them all, had confessed to believing in the giant.

'Jesus,' he said.

Father Snow turned towards the child and smiled.

'What's your name?'

The boy looked surprised.

'David, Father.'

'You're a good boy, David, and because of your answer, I promise you, you have nothing to be afraid of in this world. Nobody who gives the same answer ever needs to be afraid, because Jesus will always look after them. There's not a ghost or giant that can hurt them.'

At that moment, he wondered how he must appear to them: an adult in a black uniform, somewhere between a teacher, a parent and a policeman, yet carrying with him an air of mystery which none of those others possessed. Nobody else could tell them about ghosts with such authority. They watched in silence as he left the room.

He walked quickly on his way back to the presbytery, for

193

it was freezing cold outside, that morning's ice unmelted on the pavements. The low sky made it like walking through a cave. Huge, misshapen icicles hung from the eaves of the cottages. Only the catatonia of snow was needed to complete the effect. Then one would be able to believe anything of the place. It would become once more the enchanted village the newsbook had described, where all the children slept fitfully under the ogre's spell, disturbed by a communal dream.

For the rest of that day, he couldn't settle to anything. He'd been unable to pray or work seriously since his final parting from Susan. All he could do was force himself to go through the motions. His thoughts, and perhaps his heart, were elsewhere. Part of him was astonished that this had happened, almost outraged. Yet when he thought of the kind of person she was, it all seemed dangerously natural, almost inevitable. More than anything, he was burdened by the knowledge that he'd left her more unhappy than before. If she'd been more balanced and secure, he'd never have fallen under this spell.

In the end, he began to see a way out, though it perhaps entailed a kind of sin. All afternoon, he thought about it, wondering if it would work. By the evening, his thoughts had hardened, almost without his realising, into an intention.

After supper, when Flora had left the presbytery, Father Snow went into the study and phoned Susan. Her disembodied voice in the earpiece seemed a distillation of her femininity. It shook him almost as much as her presence on the sofa had done.

'It's Father Snow,' he said. 'I'd like to see you, if you've got a moment.'

'I don't believe it.' She sounded weak, as though she'd just heard some piece of terrible news. 'Yes, I've got a moment. Of course I have. I'll be straight over.'

'No. Not here.'

'Where then?'

'Do you know the Happy Eater up on the A25?'

'You're joking, aren't you?'

'No.'

'But, I mean, couldn't we go somewhere a little more . . . ?'

'No. I'll see you there in half an hour.'

She sighed.

'All right, then.'

Father Snow went upstairs and changed. It would be the first time she'd seen him in ordinary clothes, stripped of the impersonal black which perhaps for her held some sort of glamour. He chose a brown sports-jacket and a pair of beige slacks. Both were unfashionably cut, the trousers having a hint of width about the ankle. After a moment's thought, he added a polyester tie, doing it up so tightly that it looked like an act of aggression. Since it was so cold outside, he put on a quilted anorak over the jacket.

Susan was already there waiting for him when he arrived. She had chosen a table facing the window and was watching the traffic on the A25. The first thing to strike him about her was that, as on the day when they'd visited the British Museum, she'd tied her hair back. There was a kind of naivety about this that Father Snow found touching. At the same time, he couldn't deny that it made her more attractive. He felt sick with nerves and guilt.

As he walked between the tables towards her, he glanced furtively at the other customers. There was nobody he recognised. One of the reasons he'd chosen this place was that it was outside the village and used mainly by people driving to or from London. The waitresses, too, all seemed to be strangers. For all that, Father Snow felt painfully conspicuous. The clothes he was wearing seemed an inadequate disguise. Everybody would be able to see, just from the way he moved, from the expression in his eyes, that he was a priest.

When he sat down in front of her, he did so with his usual ceremonial care.

'Thank you for coming.'

She said nothing, but just stared at him. It reminded him of how she had stood in the headlights, having waited in the cold just to watch him drive away from the presbytery.

A waitress appeared. Father Snow ordered coffee and a cake. Susan, without seeming to give the matter any thought, did the same. Neither of them spoke while they were waiting, not wanting to start a conversation which they would have to suspend when the waitress returned. Father Snow looked around him, taking in the cheap ashtrays, the laminated menus. Even the wood of the tables somehow looked like plastic. There was a faint sound of muzak, bland and soporific. A little condensation had formed on the windows. The occasional swish of a car passing was like the snore of a comatose giant stretched in the cold outside.

When the coffee and cakes had arrived and the waitress had left them alone, Father Snow saw that there could be no putting it off any longer. As always when forced to deal with emotions, he straightened himself and retreated into formality.

'I've asked you to come here because I wasn't completely honest with you when we last met.'

He stopped, dismayed to find his pulse up, his breath short, his face hot.

'How do you mean?'

The only way to do it was to look away and pretend she wasn't there.

'I mean that my feelings are in fact much the same as yours. At least, the symptoms, if I may call them that, are almost identical.'

When he looked back, he found that she had leaned forwards. Her lips were parted. There was an intense look on her face, a mixture of yearning and surprise.

'I think about you all the time,' he found himself

196

saying, though this was not part of the conversation he'd planned. 'I can't eat or sleep properly. I can't get on with anything.'

'I don't believe it,' she said.

Father Snow went back to his prepared speech.

'However, I want one thing to be clear from the outset. I'm not going to have an affair with you. From that point of view, you're simply wasting your time with me.'

Susan didn't seem to have heard. She was still gazing at him with exactly the same expression on her face.

'Tell me that you love me.'

Father Snow looked away from her with an expression of distaste.

'I can't do that.'

'Why not?'

'I just can't. In any case, I don't think it's true.'

'Have you had lots of girlfriends?'

'Of course not.'

'Before you became a priest, I mean.'

Father Snow's eyes wandered around the café as though looking for an escape route. This wasn't going at all as he'd intended.

'About as many as you've had boys, I imagine.'

'Only one, then.'

Father Snow couldn't hide his surprise. Susan stared down at her plate, apparently ashamed at her lack of promiscuity.

'I met him while I was at school and went out with him all through university. We only split up a few months ago.'

'Why?' said Father Snow, glad to remove the focus of the conversation from himself.

'He just walked out on me.' Her voice was strangely unemotional. 'We were engaged by that time. We were going to get married next summer. Everyone knew about it: our families, our friends, everyone. They were all expecting it. They all said what a lovely couple we made.

197

Then he just called it all off. It turned out that he'd been seeing someone else.'

Avoiding his eye, she put sugar in her coffee, screwing up the little paper bag with sudden aggression and grinding it into the ashtray. Father Snow watched in silence.

'I try not to think badly of him,' said Susan. 'But I just haven't been able to put myself back together. It was worse than if he'd died. It made me feel so ugly and worthless. I thought nobody would ever be interested in me again.'

Then she looked up as though suddenly remembering the silent presence of Father Snow. When their eyes met, the magic words almost escaped him. With a desperate effort, he began to rationalise. Everything now was easy to explain. He understood the modesty of her dress and her shuttered, defensive air. She was a child who had almost no experience of the game. Having been once badly hurt, she was afraid to try again with a real man, so she had fixed everything on Father Snow, neutered by the priesthood. He was a kind of halfway house between being alone and having a real relationship, a place for her to rest and restore her confidence. For his own part, he'd simply been won over by her need.

Yet for all that they were still looking into each other's eyes, and Father Snow could almost have believed himself in the presence of something that no analysis could explain. He could almost have believed this romantic child had been right, that it was like being struck by lightning, an inexplicable thing.

'I wanted it to be perfect,' she said, 'and for a while it was. But then he let me down.' Still looking at Father Snow, she shook her head. 'I wanted it to be like the fairy tales.'

'That's what everybody wants,' said Father Snow. 'It's a disappointment we all have to go through.'

'Have you been through it?'

'Oh, yes,' said Father Snow. He looked away from her. 'I understand how you feel. I know about being abandoned.'

The word had been too strong. It left a long silence behind it. A car passed on the road outside. Father Snow felt obscurely ashamed of himself. He thought that when they next spoke it would be more conversational, at a lower level of intensity. But he had underestimated Susan's romantic endurance.

'I'm glad he left me, now,' she said. 'He never made me feel like this, and I can see now that this is what I should have felt all along. Did your girlfriends make you feel like this?'

Father Snow took a sip of coffee, spilling a little as he replaced the cup.

'This is a very different situation.'

When he said that, she seemed to become desperate.

'What are we going to do?'

'Wait for it to pass,' said Father Snow. 'Until it does, I'm prepared to meet you once a week, like this.'

'Really? You mean I can really see you every week?'

'Until things go back to normal, yes.'

She was beaming at him, apparently overjoyed.

'And if things don't go back to normal?'

'They will. In a few months' time, we'll both be embarrassed about it all.'

'But what if we aren't? What if we still feel the same way in a year?'

Father Snow straightened.

'Then I will be prepared to reconsider the situation. However, the only possibility for any closer relationship between us would be if I left the priesthood and we got married. Even after a year, I wouldn't consider having an affair with you while continuing as a priest.'

Susan was staring at him with open affection, perhaps even with admiration. It made him more uncomfortable than ever. At the same time, her expression was slightly surprised, as though she couldn't believe the strength of her own feelings.

'I love you so much,' she said.

With a little cough, Father Snow looked away.

'We'll see about that.'

When they left the Happy Eater and stepped out into the car-park they found that it was snowing. The sight of it brought both of them to a halt. It was the most perfect kind of snow, large flakes falling through still air. It reminded Father Snow of the handful of other such moments he'd experienced in various places. Above all, it reminded him of his childhood. All such repetitions point back to that. There's always a little of the same wonder, though it naturally dwindles as the years go by.

After watching the flakes for a few moments, Father Snow had the strange feeling that they in fact stood motionless while he himself floated upwards through them. To bring himself back to earth, he looked away, down the A25. He could see the gateposts of Flamstead, their griffons suffering the snow with snarling immobility, just as they had suffered thousands of storms and sunny days. Through the trees, the lights of the house itself were just visible, like the lights of a jet coming in low over the hills.

Susan walked forwards, lifting her face towards the snow as though to receive a blessing from on high.

'You see? This is a fairy tale, after all.'

'I'll be here at the same time next week,' said Father Snow. 'Obviously, you're under no obligation to come.'

She turned towards him with a sudden, impulsive movement, so that he feared she was going to take his hands or throw her arms around him.

'Tell me that you love me.'

Father Snow felt that, if he could just say it, all the happiness in life would be his. For a moment he allowed himself to look down into her face. Her expression might have been one of intense sadness or joy. Then, suddenly realising that his own face was assuming an identical expression, he shook his head and turned away. As he walked towards the car, he heard her voice from behind him:

200

'This has been the happiest night of my life.'

All the same, she sounded sad. He drove slowly back to the presbytery, wondering if he'd done the right thing. She was even more innocent and romantic than he'd imagined, more desperate to realise her girlhood dreams. The priesthood was somehow at the heart of it all. Besides making him unobtainable and unthreatening, it gave him the allure of a fairy-tale figure, a man frozen or turned to stone, waiting to be brought back to life by the love of the right woman.

She was wrong. Father Snow knew that his feelings for her would quickly disappear. All the way home, he was dogged by pity and guilt. He could only hope that, by the time it was all over, her confidence would have been restored. He would be her springboard back into the ordinary world, into the rough and tumble of normal human relationships.

Almost as soon as he got back to the presbytery, the phone rang.

'Julian! Where on earth have you been? I've been trying to ring for ages.'

It was Ralph. For the first time since they'd met, Father Snow was almost pleased to hear his voice.

'I was out visiting.'

'Well, you're back now, and not a moment too soon. Go straight out, get in that clapped-out old heap of yours, and get round here pronto. I've got a surprise for you.'

'What kind of surprise?'

'A bloody surprising one, but not surprising enough to survive my telling you what it is. So you'd better just get round here and find out, hadn't you?'

It was a drive Father Snow would never forget. He had to go slowly, because the snow was already starting to settle. Its silence was all around him. To him that night it seemed like a glimpse of the spiritual world, a hint of God's great serenity. Even the old engine seemed respectfully to muffle its noise. The windscreen wipers swished with methodical aggression, and the flakes simply disappeared before them, so that it seemed they hadn't been physical at all. Ahead, they appeared out of nowhere and hung motionless in the headlights for an instant before the car smashed through them.

Ralph answered the door almost as soon as Father Snow rang the bell, an urgent finger held to his lips, as though to chide him for the noise.

'What's the matter?'

'Be quiet!' hissed Ralph. His face was red, perhaps from the exertion of keeping his voice to a whisper. His sharp widow's peak seemed to lower at Father Snow, a warning frown. 'Don't make a sound!'

'Why?'

'You'll see! Come inside!'

They crept in as though they were carrying the silence of the snow inside with them. In a mime of triumph, Ralph opened the door to his sitting room.

'There!' he hissed. 'How's that for a surprise?'

At first, Father Snow couldn't see what he was talking about. Then, going into the room, he found that Vincent Capel was sitting in the armchair by the fire, asleep.

He was even older and smaller than Father Snow remembered. His body was so thin that it looked as if a shabby old pair of trousers and a sweater had been thrown down into the armchair and, by a freak chance, landed in the shape of a man. His face, the face of some wasted bird, was even more frail than his body. The vulnerability of sleep made him look like a baby, completely trusting and relaxed, so that Father Snow felt strangely protective towards him.

Ralph came and stood by his side.

'He's here!' he whispered, and to Father Snow he was suddenly like a clumsy great dog, full of excitement and innocent pride. He could barely keep his voice down; it seemed his big shining face would burst open. 'He's come to visit us!'

Father Snow just nodded, unable to speak. Overcome by drunken emotion, Ralph came forwards and gave him a bear-hug in his huge arms. At first, Father Snow just stood and endured it, too horrified to move. Then he found it in him to give Ralph's shoulder a gentle, condescending pat.

After that, while Vincent snoozed, they sat at the table and went through the usual routine of Ralph drinking and Father Snow pretending to do so. They talked in whispers. Outside, the snow still fell, filling everything with silence. Looking at the old man by the fire, it was impossible not to imagine that the millions of flakes, slow and unreal, were no more than an involuntary projection of his sleeping mind and would vanish as soon as he woke up.

13

THE TWO PRIESTS spoke in quiet voices about Vincent while they were waiting for him to wake up. At last they had found something in common. Ralph explained that Vincent had come down on the train that afternoon. The primary purpose of his visit was to find out how Father Snow was getting on in his new parish, but he'd broken his journey to see Ralph. They were old friends; Vincent had once been Ralph's bishop.

Then Ralph started reminiscing about Vincent. Twenty years before, when he'd gone to his first parish in Vincent's diocese, the bishop had already become a legend among his priests. There were so many stories about him that it was impossible to distinguish myth from reality. For example, they said that, during the Depression, the young Vincent set up a shelter in London for the poor. One of the men, arriving back drunk one night, started a fire in his room which quickly spread through the building. As if by magic, Vincent arrived on the scene long before the fire brigade and set about rescuing people, getting himself seriously burned in the process. Some of them claimed to have seen the scars. Ralph had never seen them himself.

There were other, more fantastic stories, too. The briefest of conversations with Vincent was said to have converted any number of hardened atheists. Some people even claimed full-scale miracles for him, saying that he'd cured those for whom the doctors had long since given up hope, simply by kneeling and praying at their bedsides.

None of this had ever been put to the test. They were stories which circulated mainly inside the priesthood, and in that enclosed circle they obviously grew with the telling. For his own part, Ralph had only had one direct experience of any such power in Vincent.

It happened when Vincent, in typical Vincent fashion, made an unexpected visit to Ralph's parish. He said he was sick of being a bishop, that he wanted to do some 'good priestly work', so Ralph took him on a hospital visit. The first person they saw was a very old man, left paralysed by a major stroke. He'd contracted a chest infection and there was little doubt that he would shortly die. Although Ralph had been the man's parish priest for some years, it was on Vincent that his eyes fixed themselves as soon as the pair appeared on the ward. As they approached, the man lifted his arm. Taking his hand, Vincent knelt down by the bed.

'It's you,' the man said. After that, he just stared at Vincent for a long time, his head lolling on the pillow.

'Then what happened?'

'I did the Last Rites,' said Ralph. 'The poor bastard died about ten minutes afterwards, still holding Vincent's hand and staring at him.'

Father Snow found Ralph's stories depressing. He felt he'd had another insight into the weakness of his fellow priests. The miracles of the Gospels weren't enough for them. They needed something now, something fantastic to bolster up their faith. It was precisely this tendency towards superstition which enabled the rationalists to scoff.

'Do you believe he cured people?'

Ralph turned and looked at the old man by the fire as though studying him would produce the answer. He was still asleep, head slumped forward, lips parted.

'I don't know.' He turned back. 'All I do know is that he has a unique quality about him, an ability to inspire faith. Perhaps that's the important thing, in the end. Perhaps it's not the actual performance of a miracle that matters, but the ability to make people believe one could be performed.'

By Ralph's standards, especially after a few drinks, this seemed to Father Snow a rather impressive piece of reasoning.

'Perhaps.'

They fell silent after that. Father Snow was remembering the moment when Vincent's eyes had found his across the cathedral, the moment which had changed his life. Until now, he'd always explained it in terms of his own psychological condition. He'd felt particularly depressed and lost that day, groping for direction and meaning. Now none of that seemed to lessen the strangeness of the event.

When he looked back at Vincent, Father Snow had an unfamiliar feeling of unease, almost of fear. He remembered how his transfer to Wodden had been signalled not by a summons to the bishop's residence but by the appearance of Vincent, dressed in an old sweater, at the back of the queue for communion one Sunday morning. This led him back to their last conversation, after lunch in his old presbytery, when Vincent had said that one day Father Snow might revitalise the English Church.

Then he remembered what else Vincent had said that day: unless he learnt humility, genuine love of his fellow man, Father Snow would be the last person he'd like to see rise to a position of authority. Looking back over his time in Wodden, particularly his relationship with Ralph, Father Snow felt he'd made little progress in that direction. The realisation brought an unexpected pang of sorrow and guilt, and at that moment, as though he'd felt some echo of it, Vincent awoke.

'I must have nodded off.'

He looked around him for a moment, obviously unable to understand where he was, not at first even noticing the two figures sitting at the table. He had that expression of gentle confusion which makes the old seem so vulnerable when they awake. His face cleared when he noticed Father Snow.

'Julian! There you are!'

Father Snow got up and walked towards the armchair by the fire. It was strange to see the inconsequential little figure there after all he'd heard from Ralph. His new knowledge about Vincent brought other feelings, too. Now he knew that he was not the only one to admire the old man, that their relationship was not unique. Ralph and many like him had looked up to Vincent before Father Snow had even been born. He was just another face in the crowd.

Without getting up, the bishop raised his hand. His eyes were still a little inward and distant, but he was smiling. Father Snow had forgotten the magic of his smile.

'It's really nice to see you, Julian.'

'Thank you, your grace.'

Vincent shook his head chidingly.

'Now, now, this isn't an episcopal visit, you know. I'm here as a friend, not a figurehead. It's Vincent this weekend.' He turned and spoke to Ralph: 'The problem with young people today is that they have too much respect for authority, don't you think?'

Ralph raised his glass.

'Far too much.'

Father Snow just stood there, looking down and wondering.

'What have you been telling him about me, Ralph?'

'Just a bit of ancient history. That's what Julian loves, you know.'

Vincent laughed, then turned back to Father Snow. Suddenly the young priest felt that they were entirely alone together. It seemed that the only thing which interested Vincent at that moment was him. In a worldly man, the effect this had on Father Snow would have been called charm.

'Don't have too much respect for authority, Julian. It's good that you should respect me as a bishop and an older

207

man, but friendship is always the most important thing. Never let anything come in the way of that.'

Father Snow nodded, unable to speak. It had just struck him that this visit was the first concrete sign of friendship he'd ever had from Vincent.

Leaning forwards slightly in his chair, the old man lowered his voice so that only Father Snow should hear.

'All men deserve our Christian love, but only one man deserves our adoration. Even the very best of us bear only a vague resemblance to Him.'

They stayed at Ralph's for another half hour after that, all of them gathered round the fire. Ralph and Vincent made most of the conversation, talking about old times, bringing up the names of people and places which meant nothing to Father Snow. He sat there quietly, trying to accept the situation with humility, without feeling bitter and excluded. From the way Vincent behaved, you would have thought that Ralph was the most important person in the room. He listened intently while Ralph was telling some amusing story, laughed delightedly when it was over and then, rather than talking himself, encouraged him to go on.

The result was that Ralph showed himself to Father Snow in a completely new light. He was no longer just a drunken, middle-aged priest living alone in a large presbytery. Now he was a man of experience and wit, the sort of man who held the floor at dinner-parties. Father Snow realised that his own awkward formality, his refusal to relax and have a drink, had until now prevented Ralph from being himself. In the end, Ralph's jokes and exuberance became like a deliberate accusation.

At last Vincent decided it was time to go, and all three of them stood up. As they headed for the door, Ralph infuriated Father Snow by slapping him on the back.

'Thanks for listening to the reminiscences of an old fart.'

Vincent spluttered, covering his mouth as though he knew he ought not really to encourage such naughtiness.

'Ralph, you really are incorrigible!'

'No,' said Ralph wistfully, 'I was corriged long ago.'

'Well, you have mellowed slightly, I'll give you that. As long as you don't get yourself too drunk to drive, I'm satisfied.'

'I'll see what I can do.'

'I'm serious, Ralph. A priest should be ready to jump in his car twenty-four hours a day. Are you listening to me, now?'

'Yes, your grace.'

They'd reached the front door. When Ralph had opened it, Vincent stood and stared outside.

'It's snowed!'

'While you were asleep.'

'Why didn't you tell me, you rotten lot? I would have gone out for a walk.' Standing at the top of the steps, the old man spread his arms as though in benediction. 'Isn't it lovely?'

Without speaking, Father Snow walked down the steps and left the two old friends to their farewells. When he reached the car, he turned around to see Vincent shaking Ralph by the hand and saying something to him. Ralph, suddenly serious, was looking down into the old face and nodding. Then he started speaking himself, apparently angry. At one point, he glanced towards Father Snow.

At last Vincent came down the steps, frail and careful in the snow. Ralph stayed in the doorway to wave goodbye as they drove away.

'Isn't he marvellous?' said Vincent, waving through the window. 'It always cheers me up to see him.' He twisted round in his seat to keep on waving until the presbytery was out of sight, although Ralph probably wouldn't be able to see. 'He's so full of life.'

'And drink.'

With a sigh, Vincent turned back in his seat.

'I understand that you two haven't been getting on very well together. And I'm afraid, Julian, that most of the fault has been on your side. You've offended dear old Ralph in just about every possible way.'

Father Snow stared at the white road, blushing.

'I don't drink,' he muttered. 'Ralph seems to have taken that as some kind of comment on himself.'

'Ralph's hardly the touchy type, Julian. I don't think he'd have taken it the wrong way unless, perhaps without realising, you wanted him to.'

For a few moments after that they drove on in silence. Father Snow stared ahead of him, hating Ralph as though the whole thing had been his fault, almost hating Vincent for taking Ralph's side.

'As a priest, you can't choose your colleagues,' said Vincent, 'but they should be the greatest friends you have. Try and see things from Ralph's point of view. He's much older and more experienced than you. He feels you owe him your respect, yet he's not really sure if he deserves it. Always remember the effect your strength could have on a man like that. Unless you treat him gently, you'll only make him feel inferior and insecure.'

Father Snow succumbed to self-hatred.

'I don't see why anyone should feel inferior to me.'

'Because in you great failings are outweighed by even greater strengths. And the failings can be overcome, Julian, believe me. You'll eventually see Ralph as one of your closest friends.' Father Snow saw a small movement in the corner of his eye, and knew that Vincent had turned to look at him. 'All failings can be overcome.'

After that, Vincent began to talk about his past. It was the snow that set him off, telling Father Snow about how he'd used to go tobogganing with his brothers and sisters as a child. That got him on to his parents, who'd raised a large family on almost no money at all. For some time he sang their praises, and became just a little old man, reminiscing as all of them do. All the while, Father Snow was driving carefully, staring at the road ahead and keeping his wheels in the two black paths of slush left by earlier cars. The snow had stopped now. Only the occasional tiny white speck drifted into the windscreen.

'We should always respect parents,' Vincent was saying. 'Nobody does more good in a parish, or in the world, than a good Catholic parent. Although our calling may be higher in some ways, we should always look up to them for what they do.'

As he was speaking, they passed the gates of Flamstead House. The old man peered round to look at the tall posts with their rampant griffons, now capped with a few inches of snow. It was how Timothy Darting must have seen them centuries before.

'Is that the home of the famous Trevellyans, then?'

'Yes. We're nearly in Wodden now.'

After that, Vincent fell silent, and Father Snow knew he was thinking of Father Conner. As they entered the village, he found himself seeing it all through Vincent's eyes, the eyes of a stranger. It reminded him of his own arrival in the parish, though it was even more picturesque in the snow. Once they were off the main road, there were no more tracks of slush to follow. The snow was almost virgin. They went along the narrow high street at a crawl. Lights were still on in the ancient houses. One or two people were trudging back from the pub, their shoulders hunched.

The village green was just a featureless white square. Only memory told Father Snow where the road ended and the grass began. The war memorial had lost its meaning, a monolith left by some vanished civilisation. Very slowly, they crossed the stone bridge and began to climb the hill towards the presbytery. Just before they arrived, Vincent spoke.

'Where did it happen?'

His voice was quite different from what it had been till now, weak and strained. Father Snow wondered what it had cost him to come here, what grief such a man might be capable of feeling.

'In the garage.'

'How?'

'He ran a pipe round from the exhaust into the car.'

Vincent said nothing, but just sat quietly, staring through the windscreen. Father Snow stopped the car, opened the garage door, and drove in. When he'd switched off the engine, he turned and saw that Vincent's chin had dropped down to his chest. His eyes were closed, and he spoke without opening them.

'Would you go and wait outside for a minute, Julian?'

Father Snow got out of the car and went into the stillness of the snow. For his own part, he was unable to think of Father Conner. Being with Vincent had made him realise how far he had to travel spiritually. He resolved to treat Ralph better in the future, to try to unbend towards him. Vincent's presence, as always, was both a blessing and a trial. It seemed incredible that he should be here at all, let alone for a whole weekend. He wondered about Vincent's reasons for arranging the visit, and about God's reasons, too, assuming there was any difference. Then it seemed to him that the snow had been laid out as a ceremonial welcome. Even the great trees on the horizon were done out in white, beaming respectful silence across the village.

When he at last emerged from the garage, Vincent looked tired. Without thinking, Father Snow began to lead the way to the presbytery.

'Julian!'

Turning round, he saw Vincent still standing by the garage door, smiling sadly.

'Yes?'

'I must make a visit to the Blessed Sacrament before I can go inside.'

'Of course.'

Ashamed of his mistake, he crunched back through the snow and led the way into the church. Inside, Vincent

212

knelt and prayed for a long time, chin fallen, eyes closed, a roosting bird. Father Snow began to feel restless. This time, however, he didn't make the mistake of suggesting they should leave. Kneeling quietly, he did his best to pray. As before, he found himself remembering the garden of Gethsemane, where the disciples had fallen asleep.

At last they got Vincent's bag from the car and entered the presbytery. Vincent went all round the house, blessing each room in turn. Then they returned to the sitting-room, where he sat heavily down on the sofa and sighed, as though the whole thing had exhausted him.

'Poor Charles.'

Father Snow sat down in the armchair opposite and they were silent for a few moments. As it had on his first few nights, the presbytery seemed suddenly once more full of Father Conner's presence. He was watching from the brass tools hung up by the fire, the white rectangle above the mantelpiece, the empty armchair.

'So, Julian, how have you been getting on here?'

Father Snow was silent for a moment, wondering where to start. In the end, he decided to get the most embarrassing part out of the way first. He stared at his feet.

'There's a girl who's been causing me a few problems.'

'Ah! Isn't there always?'

This answer surprised Father Snow. He couldn't imagine that Vincent had ever had to cope with such entanglements. When he looked up, the old man was smiling.

'How are you supposed to deal with it?' said Father Snow. 'I mean, when somebody really latches onto you?'

Vincent shrugged.

'There's no set way, of course. It depends on the people and the situation. What do you feel for her, on your part?'

Once more, Father Snow looked away, but he was unable to stop himself blushing like a thirteen-year-old.

'I don't know.'

'Put it this way: if you weren't a priest, would you consider yourself in love with her?'

213

The question was far too direct for Father Snow. He coughed. There was a lump of embarrassment in his throat which made it difficult to speak.

'Perhaps.'

'And how are you dealing with it?'

'I've told her she can see me once a week for a cup of coffee, no more.'

'And where will you be having these cups of coffee?'

'At the Happy Eater.'

Vincent laughed, but Father Snow was past seeing anything funny in the situation.

'Do you think I've done the wrong thing?'

Vincent stopped laughing but went on smiling.

'You're obviously mad about this girl, no matter what you say. That means your vocation is in peril. A weaker priest might even have fallen already. But you're dealing with the problem just as I would have expected, trying to bulldoze it into a corner.'

'And how do you think I should deal with it?'

'You need to learn to relax with your emotions, Julian. That's the lesson to be learnt from your problems with Ralph, as well.'

'How can I achieve that?'

'By not being afraid of what you feel. That's difficult for a young priest, because it only comes with an absolute certainty in your vocation. Ralph, no matter what little weaknesses he may have, has reached that state. Only when you've reached it, too, will you be free of problems like this. Your girl is only attracted to you because she senses that there may be a weakness behind all your apparent strength. If you were really certain of your vocation, she'd realise it was pointless and leave you alone.'

Father Snow saw the truth of this, and it brought him close to despair.

'Perhaps I never really had a vocation, after all, then.'

'I didn't say that. Lots of priests have to go through this kind of test. Some of them endure it many times, but the first is always the hardest. If you can come through this, Julian, I think you'll be a priest for life.'

After that, Father Snow told Vincent everything else that had happened since his arrival in Wooden. It was the first time he'd told the story to an outsider. He started at the beginning, with the discovery of Father Conner's note about the English Gilles and how it had led him to follow the dead priest in pursuit of Everard. Vincent listened in absolute stillness as he explained Father Conner's obsession with the ogre's laboratory and his slide into madness.

'It's interesting,' said Vincent, 'that Charles seems to have found a political dimension to the whole thing . . . Do you see much of Gerald Pitman?'

'Hardly anything. I bumped into him once in a corridor, and he's been to Mass a couple of times, but he rarely seems to be in the village. I've never actually had a conversation with him.'

'So, as far as you can tell, this is just a normal village with a rather colourful past.'

'Well, there is one other thing . . .'

Father Snow paused, embarrassed to mention it.

'What?'

'I visited the school this afternoon. It turns out that lots of the children there have nightmares about Flamstead House. They seem afraid that Everard is still up there.'

Vincent smiled.

'Children have an almost infinite capacity for belief. If most of them didn't lose it, we'd be living in a very different world.'

Looking towards the window, Father Snow saw shadows teeming quietly through the light which poured from the room.

'I'd like to visit this house of yours and meet the present owners, if possible. Do you think you could arrange that?'

'Yes. We could probably have lunch with them on Sunday, if you like. They're always inviting me.'

'Perfect.' The old man stretched and suppressed a yawn. 'This is all very strange.'

But Father Snow was still looking out of the window. 'It's snowing again.'

'Good! Then this time we must certainly go for a walk . . . unless you feel too tired?'

'No, I'm fine.'

It was true. Thanks to Susan, Father Snow had had a troubled week and slept badly, yet he felt invigorated by Vincent's company. It was incredible to him that such a small old man could radiate such energy.

They walked together in silence through the snow, up the lane towards the village green. The place was entirely deserted now. The pub had long since closed. Lying against the hedge at the side of the lane, as though it had been left there for him, Vincent found a long stick about a foot taller than he was himself. This he took for support. Father Snow wasn't sure whether it made him look like a bishop walking with his crozier or a wizard on his way to shatter an enchantment.

They went on through the floating snow. If anything, it was thicker than before, the flakes heavier. They dropped through the still air like pebbles through water. On the wide space of the village green, Father Snow stopped and pointed up at the distant lights behind the trees.

'That's Flamstead.'

Vincent stared upwards, leaning on his stick.

'The ogre's laboratory, eh?'

Then they just stood there for a while, silent, the snow luminous around them. It was coming down so thickly that the hills which surrounded the village were invisible now. The lights of Flamstead, gleaming through the crowded air, seemed to be floating on nothing.

'This is a strange place,' said Vincent. He closed his eyes and lifted his face. When he spoke again, he did so without opening his eyes, so that it seemed he was rambling, talking in his sleep. 'There's a sadness about it, I think. But then I suppose that must always be true. Paradise itself wouldn't be complete without grief, as far as I can see. After all, even Jesus wept.' Leaning on his stick, he opened his eyes and turned towards Father Snow. 'There must be terrible sadness in heaven, you know.'

A few moments later, they turned and walked back to the presbytery along the white lane.

14

VINCENT'S PRESENCE MADE that weekend feel to Father Snow like something between a holiday and a retreat. Although they hadn't gone to bed until the early hours, Vincent got up to attend morning Mass. Then, when Father Snow had finished hearing confessions, they said the Office and the rosary together. Today there was something more solemn and momentous about the familiar prayers. Father Snow felt he was being charged with grace.

In the afternoon, they went for a walk through the village and had tea at the old mill. Most of the time, Vincent was lively and talkative, as he had been at Ralph's the night before, but there were moments when he fell silent and seemed to forget where he was.

Back at the presbytery, Father Snow rang Flamstead and spoke to Lady Trevellyan. When he told her that he had a friend staying and asked if they could both come to lunch after Mass the following day, she agreed with perfect patrician courtesy.

'It's all fixed,' he said as he put down the phone. 'You're coming to lunch at Flamstead tomorrow.'

Vincent fell into one of his silences.

That evening, Flora came round to cook supper. When she shook hands with Vincent, although Father Snow only introduced him by his first name, she gave a little bow.

'Are you a priest as well, sir?'

'Yes, Flora, I am.'

She looked questioningly at Father Snow, obviously sensing that this was not the whole story.

'Vincent's an archbishop. He performed my ordination.'

Flora came over all flustered.

'Oh, dear. What am I supposed to call you? Is it your excellency or your grace?'

'Your Vincent will be fine,' said Vincent.

'Very good, your Vincent,' said Flora, and it wasn't clear whether she was joking.

The first part of the evening was an ordeal for her. Fortunately, she didn't burn anything, and Vincent's praise of the supper she served him was obviously sincere. While she was washing up, he went out to talk to her. Father Snow, who'd never been quite sure what to do with himself at these times, followed to see how Vincent behaved. It was quite simple. The old man just picked up a dishcloth and did the drying. Soon Flora was chatting to him as she never had to Father Snow, telling him about life in Wodden, Jack's illness, her childhood, the death of her parents.

Ignored by them both, Father Snow sat stiffly at the table and listened. He realised that it was fear of this human outpouring which had kept him away from Flora after supper each night. The only way he felt comfortable about looking into a human heart was through the protective grille of the confessional. Vincent made it all seem so easy and natural. This night would be special for Flora now, a story to be constantly retold: the time an archbishop did my drying-up. She would explain what a lovely man he'd been, so humble and friendly, not at all the type to stand on ceremony. Vincent had probably done more for her faith in that half hour than Father Snow had since his arrival in the parish.

When she'd gone, they lit a fire and sat side by side on the sofa staring into its flames, drinking endless cups of tea. There was something almost fatherly about Vincent that night. Now he was interested no longer in Wodden and the Trevellyans, but in Father Snow himself, asking about his childhood, his parents, his time at university.

As soon as Vincent stopped questioning him, Father Snow found himself thinking about Susan. He remembered how he had seen her sitting in the Happy Eater with her hair up, waiting for him. Her face appeared to him, wearing the same look of surprised yearning it had worn that evening. Then he saw himself, as he so often had before, leaning down towards the car in the rain.

'What's she like, then?'

Father Snow turned from the fire.

'Who?'

'This girl of yours, of course.'

'Nothing special.'

Vincent laughed.

When he went downstairs the following morning, long before dawn, Father Snow was surprised to find the old man up and dressed. He was sitting at the desk in the study, staring out through the french windows into the dark. When Father Snow entered the room, he remained motionless in the chair.

'You're up early.'

'I couldn't sleep,' said Vincent. 'I've been awake all night.'

'Why?'

Vincent went on staring outside.

'I'm nervous about today.'

Since Vincent insisted that they should walk rather than drive, the pair of them set off for Flamstead as soon as Father Snow had said his morning Mass. There had been a fresh fall of snow during the night. Vincent took with him the stick he'd found on their previous walk, swinging it energetically as they made their way through the village.

Only when they'd walked through the tall gateposts and into the park did the sheer volume of the snow become obvious. It lay all around them as far as the eye could see. In the village it had been pretty, but here it was imposing, its silence dramatic.

Flamstead itself had never looked more suited to the role of fairy mansion. When it came into view, Vincent stopped, leaned on his stick, and stared at it across the white expanse.

'What a beautiful house.'

Standing at the top of its snow-covered hill, the building had taken on the stillness of a painting. The drive which led to it had disappeared. There was no sign left of the modern world. They might have stepped back into the days of Timothy Darting, when Walter Trevellyan had lain inside, his bed piled with furs. Yet, for all that it was especially impressive today, the house seemed more desolate than ever. Father Snow wondered whether, even in its prime all those hundreds of years ago, it had somehow managed to seem like a ruin.

They went round the side of the house to the chapel. Before going in, Vincent left his stick propped against the wall. Inside, he knelt at prayer while Father Snow got everything ready. Waiting in the little sacristy, listening to the small sounds of the congregation arriving, Father Snow himself began to feel nervous. The first person he saw when he at last stepped up to the altar was Gerald Pitman. He was standing just behind Trevellyan with his hands devoutly joined. Father Snow ignored him and immersed himself in the Mass.

When the congregation came forward to take communion, however, he did notice one thing. Vincent was one of the last to reach the altar. Pitman, who had already received, was kneeling with his head bowed only a few feet from Father Snow. When Vincent walked past, Pitman looked up and stared at him.

After Mass, Father Snow emerged from the sacristy to find Vincent alone in the chapel. As he approached, the old man got up and genuflected. Then they walked together towards the doors which led into the house, and Vincent said:

'Let's get it over with.'

Trevellyan was waiting for them in the corridor. He was leaning against a window-sill and staring into the snowy courtyard beyond. His wife was waiting just behind him, looking away from him so that it seemed they'd just had an argument. Hearing them arrive, Trevellyan turned heavily, as though moving under an invisible weight. He was wearing a beautiful navy-blue jacket and a sky-blue cravat fixed with a golden pin. His hair was undone.

As Father Snow did the introductions, Trevellyan and his wife looked at Vincent with understandable curiosity. Although his black coat and grey sweater were perfectly clean, Vincent had a schoolboy's knack of making them look scruffy. He might have been anything from an absent-minded Oxford don to a well-off tramp. When he shook hands with Trevellyan, the difference in size was comical. Vincent barely reached Trevellyan's shoulder.

'It's very kind of you to have me to lunch today, Nick.' Trevellyan seemed slightly taken aback by this. 'You don't mind if I call you Nick, do you? I find titles such a bore.'

Lady Trevellyan gave Father Snow a look, as though to ask where he had dug up this peculiar little man. Her husband seemed entirely fascinated by Vincent.

'You're quite right,' he said. 'Titles are a bore. But may we know if you have one yourself?'

'Yes, I do. Archbishop of Southwark.'

Trevellyan seemed to relax a little now that the riddle was solved. He gave a small smile.

'Then we're the ones who should thank you for coming to lunch. Shall we go?'

He started to lead the way down the corridor, side by side with Vincent while Father Snow and Lady Trevellyan followed. From behind, the difference in size between the two men was even more marked. Trevellyan had joined his hands behind his back as though to emphasise the width of his shoulders and was bending his head courteously towards his guest.

'Do you have any particular reason for visiting Wodden, Vincent?'

'Not really. I just wanted to see Julian and have a little break. Perhaps it's also a way of paying my last respects to Charles Conner.'

'Poor Father Conner,' said Trevellyan, his voice more mournful than ever. 'Such a tragedy. Such a mystery, too.'

'Indeed. Now that I've seen the place for myself, I can hardly believe such a thing could happen here.'

Outside the dining-room they stopped while Lady Trevellyan took their coats. Then they went inside. Eight guests were waiting around the table. Most of them Father Snow recognised from his previous visit: a merchant banker, a barrister, a property developer and their respective wives, all local luminaries. Apart from them, sitting in the chair to the left of Trevellyan's, where Bill Saunders had sat before, was Gerald Pitman.

It was a jolt for Father Snow. He'd never thought that Pitman would have the time or inclination to attend one of these lunches, but now he saw that this was what he'd been hoping for, or dreading, since his arrival in the village. At last he was going to meet the great man properly. His presence seemed to have brought a certain expectant tension to the room, as though everyone sensed that this would be a memorable occasion. As before, Father Snow had the impression that Pitman knew exactly the effect he was having, and that this knowledge in itself was part of his power.

Sitting on Pitman's left, like an accessory, was a young man in a striped suit, a red silk handkerchief flowering shyly from his breast-pocket. Pitman himself was dressed in a loose tweed jacket, his shirt open at the neck. It took a moment for Father Snow to accept that this perfectly ordinary human being was really Pitman. He seemed

223

almost ridiculously small, as though Father Snow had subconsciously expected his physical presence, in keeping with his fame and power, to be that of a giant.

Everyone stood up as they entered. Today there were four empty places at the table. There was silence as they approached. Father Snow watched Vincent uneasily, remembering the embarrassment of his own first lunch here and wondering if he would need telling what to do. The old man needed no such help. Without hesitation, he went and stood behind the place of honour on Trevellyan's right, then waited quietly, facing Pitman across the table. Father Snow stood next to him, so that he and the smart young man were facing each other like a pair of seconds.

The appearance of this peculiar little figure caused a few surprised looks to be cast around the table. Only Pitman seemed to take it in his stride. He stood looking quietly at Vincent, and Father Snow wondered whether they'd already met. For his own part, Vincent just stood there. Again it occurred to Father Snow that he might not know what was expected of him. Turning towards him, however, he found that Vincent had his eyes closed. He was just waiting for everyone to be completely still. When they were, he said grace in Latin. Father Snow had by that time closed his own eyes, so he didn't see how much astonishment this caused.

At the end of grace, Vincent didn't sit down. Father Snow opened his eyes. People were looking towards Trevellyan, wondering if he would say anything, wanting to get on with their lunch. Vincent's eyes were still closed. He was standing with his head bowed and his hands folded, oblivious of them all. He knew well enough that he had to sit down first, but he hadn't finished grace yet. One by one, the others around the table realised what was happening and adopted once more the attitudes appropriate to prayer. When they were all still, Vincent spoke.

'There are many wealthy and powerful people gathered around this table. Let us therefore pray that we may never lose sight of Christ's humility. Let us also remember the poor, so that we may eat the food that God has provided with due gratitude.'

After that, he kept them on their feet for what seemed an eternity. For all that he knew Vincent well enough by now, Father Snow was impressed. To most of the important people there, he was no more than a shabby little stranger. Yet when Father Snow sneaked a glimpse through his lashes, he found that even Pitman was dutifully standing with his head bowed, just as though he really was praying for the humility of Christ.

Even when Vincent eventually sat down, the other guests didn't immediately follow. Perhaps they'd passed through resentment into complete resignation, or perhaps they had simply drifted off into their own thoughts, gone into a trance like children in a boring lesson. It took them a moment to realise that he'd released them. Then there was general noise and movement as they took their seats. Vincent leaned over and, in a low voice, said something about prayer to Trevellyan which Father Snow couldn't completely catch. Though he slouched back in his chair as usual, Trevellyan looked solemn for a while after that, his chin resting on his fist.

When they'd all sat down, instead of the usual hubbub breaking out, there was silence. One or two of them looked towards Trevellyan, but he just sat staring into nothing. In the end, it was left to Lady Trevellyan to introduce Vincent to them all and explain who he was.

If anything, the silence which followed this revelation was more profound than before. Everyone looked towards the head of the table. It was obvious that they expected one of the three men there to start the conversation. It was Pitman who eventually did so. Before speaking, he arranged himself in his chair as though preparing for a television interview, making a couple of small adjustments to his clothing and adopting a posture which managed to be relaxed without being insolent.

Father Snow almost expected him to feel his lapel for a microphone.

'I hope you don't mind my asking, your grace,' he said, with all evidence of humility and respect, 'but was your prayer after grace intended as some kind of political exhortation?'

Everyone looked at Vincent, except Trevellyan, who was staring into space as though he'd lost his hearing.

'Not at all,' said Vincent mildly. 'I would never demean prayer by using it to make a political point. My exhortation was on a purely personal level.'

This seemed to wake Trevellyan up. He gave an amused smile.

'You find politics demeaning, then?'

'Far from it. Politicians do essential work and many of them achieve great good in the world. All I meant was that one shouldn't trivialise prayer by using it to take political sides.'

'And which political side do you take, your grace?' said Pitman. 'Are you a supporter of the government?'

Vincent smiled and was silent for a moment or two. Everyone was waiting to hear what he would say, though two or three separate conversations would usually have started up by now.

'I never discuss politics,' said Vincent. 'Only religion. My job is to amend lives and save souls. The worldly conditions in which those souls exist are irrelevant to me, except in so far as I have a duty to relieve their suffering. If one political party causes more inequality and poverty than another, who am I to complain? These are often the best conditions for encouraging faith. Look at the strength of the Church in eastern Europe.'

'Surely, though,' said Pitman, 'you must have some political opinions of your own?'

'Of course.'

'But you never discuss them?'

'Only with people at my own level in the Church. To

air my opinions outside might be taken in the wrong way. The politician's weapon is argument. Ours is prayer, and nothing but prayer.'

'So,' said Trevellyan, and Father Snow had never seen him take so much interest in a conversation, 'you absolutely refuse to tell us what you think?'

'All right,' said Vincent with a smile, 'I'll give you a political opinion. All politicians should kneel down each night and pray for humility. In other words, they should do what all of us must do for the salvation of our souls. If they took care of that, the political problems would be solved soon enough. It might even be rather interesting.'

Now it was Pitman's turn to try and catch him out.

'So you think that, at the moment, politics is unholy?'

'Of course,' said Vincent, spreading his hands regretfully. 'This is an unholy world. And it's the rich, not the poor, who get the worst of it.' There seemed to be a sudden, absolute silence as he looked around the table. 'In spiritual terms, the rich labour under an intolerable burden. They're hamstrung from the beginning of the race.' The silence continued. 'They're like passengers preparing for a shipwreck by locking themselves into suits of armour.'

For some time after that the only sound was a muted percussion of knives and forks. Most of them avoided Vincent's eye, concentrating on their food. Pitman was looking at him and smiling, as though he found the situation hugely entertaining, but Trevellyan had stopped eating and was staring at the old man with a kind of awe.

'You're brave enough to speak your mind,' he said at last, speaking slowly, as though he'd never before encountered this quality.

'I'm only doing what has to be done. God will hold me to account for every soul at this table. There are times when silence is the easiest and gravest of sins.'

There was another pause before Pitman asked his next question, which concerned the West's moral culpability for the problems of the Third World. And so it went on for the

227

rest of lunch. No other conversations started around the table. Everyone there seemed solely interested in Vincent. Only Pitman and Trevellyan spoke to him directly, and their cross-examination seemed to Father Snow full of biblical resonance.

At no time did Vincent try to do the polite thing, to ask them questions about themselves. He seemed quite content to go on being the centre of attention, apparently relaxed. In another man, such an attitude might have been offensive. In Vincent, so obviously concerned with God and the Church above himself, it was simply an added charm. Even Pitman seemed to accept that he'd been overshadowed.

Father Snow himself was totally eclipsed. He didn't say a word the whole time, nor did he want to. The only disappointment from his point of view was that he didn't feel he was really meeting Gerald Pitman. All he saw was the public persona he already knew so well. As much as Vincent, Pitman was cunning, careful not to let anything slip. Father Snow wondered if he always behaved like this in the presence of strangers, and guessed that he probably did. Unless you were a close friend, meeting the minister was the same as watching him on TV. All you got was the smooth image and the evasive word. The only difference was his presence itself, which continued to produce an excited tension.

Over coffee, they were still talking to Vincent, asking him about the Church of England, women priests and celibacy. At one point, a phone rang in the smart young man's inside pocket. He excused himself politely, then almost ran from the room, pulling the phone out as he went. A few minutes later, he returned and murmured something to Pitman, who nodded without taking his eyes off Vincent.

When he'd finished what he was saying, Vincent looked at his watch.

'How time flies! I hope you will all excuse me, but I

have some private business to discuss with my host and hostess.'

This surprised Father Snow as much as anybody else. Vincent stood up, leaving Trevellyan and his wife with little alternative but to follow suit.

Before he left, Vincent didn't thank them for a lovely lunch or say how much he'd enjoyed talking to them. Instead, addressing his remarks to the whole table, he said:

'I'm sure you all realise that this hasn't been an idle conversation. All the questions asked here have had their purpose just as much as my replies. Every question about religion is prompted by God. He expects us to give due consideration to the answers, and amend our lives accordingly.'

They all looked at him in astonishment, as though suddenly struck again by the fact that a little old man had appeared out of nowhere and started lecturing them.

Perhaps appreciating the impression he was making, Vincent smiled.

'Here endeth the lesson!' he said. 'And I shall pray for you all.'

The four of them left the room as they had entered it: Trevellyan and Vincent in front, Lady Trevellyan and Father Snow behind. In the corridor, Trevellyan stopped and turned to Vincent.

'So, Vincent, what is it you want to talk to us about?'

'Could we go somewhere a little more private? I assure you, it will only take a few minutes.'

Trevellyan looked down at him for a moment, obviously reluctant.

'All right, then.'

He led them a little way down the corridor and then into a room on the right, overlooking the park. It was like a grossly exaggerated version of a normal sitting-room, with two sofas and some armchairs arranged around a coffee-table, a TV and video in one corner. Vincent paid no attention to the antiques, the pictures, the enormous gilt mirror on one wall, the splendid view of the snowy grounds outside. Without seeming to notice where he was, he sat down in the seat he was offered. All his attention was focused on Trevellyan and his wife.

'That was a very impressive performance you gave over lunch,' said Trevellyan.

'So it was meant to be. People can't be too impressed by religion.'

'I think, more than anything, they were impressed by you.'

Vincent smiled.

'Ah! What am I?'

'Exactly,' said Trevellyan, looking at him thoughtfully. 'What are you?'

After that, Father Snow had the feeling that he and Lady Trevellyan were entirely excluded from what was happening. The two older men seemed interested only in each other, like a couple who'd suddenly and unexpectedly fallen in love.

'I want to talk to you,' said Vincent, 'about a matter which I realise you may regard as a rather delicate one. Before we begin, let me assure you that anything you tell me will be in the strictest confidence. If there's one thing we priests can do, it's keep a secret.'

Trevellyan glanced at Father Snow.

'All right, though I don't see what could be so delicate.'

'It's very simple,' said Vincent. 'A priest and an old friend of mine has recently committed suicide in this parish. Father Snow tells me he had developed an obsessive interest in one of your ancestors. I'd just like to hear the story of that particular man, as it were, from the horse's mouth.'

Trevellyan leaned back in his chair, frowning.

'What relevance could that have to Father Conner's death?'

'In all probability, it has none. However, as I say, Charles was an old friend, and it might give me an insight into his state of mind.'

After that, Trevellyan fell silent, apparently unaware of the other three, who sat and watched him. At last Vincent spoke again.

'It's all ancient history, Nick,' he said. 'I quite understand how a man in your position might worry that people will judge him in the light of his ancestors, but I assure you that none of us will. And, in any case, as I've said, nothing you tell us will go any further.'

There was another silence. Father Snow found himself looking out of the window. Sunlight glared back at him from the snow.

'What I'm going to tell you,' said Trevellyan, 'is known to nobody outside my family, though many have suspected, including Father Conner, it would seem. Everard Trevellyan was indeed an evil man. We have the documentary evidence to prove it, for one of his many perversions was to write detailed accounts of all he did.'

'You never told me about this, Nick,' said Lady Trevellyan.

'I've never told anybody. My own father never told anyone but me. In recent years, my family has done everything it could to repress that particular piece of its past.'

Father Snow wasn't looking out of the window now. At the mention of ancient documents, his historian's instinct had quickened.

'He was a child-molester and murderer,' said Trevellyan. 'Of that there is little doubt. How many he killed it's impossible to say, but probably a great many. Even their deaths weren't the end, though, for he would go on to use their bodies in various ways. Parts of them he would eat. Parts he would use in his experiments. He was deeply involved both with ordinary science and the occult, though in those days the distinction between the two was not as clear as it is today.'

231

'But he was a Catholic,' said Lady Trevellyan. 'Wasn't he the one who kept the family Catholic through the Reformation?'

The other three turned towards her as though they'd been interrupted by a child. With a pitying look, Trevellyan spread his hands.

'Only a Catholic, a true believer, could ever be really tempted by pure evil. One can't be attracted to darkness without also seeing the attraction of light.' He sighed. 'Who knows? Perhaps, even in the depths of his evil, he still hoped for some deathbed salvation. All of us are sinners, after all. What did he do but sin with more conviction than most?'

Vincent stirred, no doubt wanting to make some theological interjection, but he remained silent.

'In any case, he was one of the original ogres. In this country, and particularly round here, he lives on in fairy tales. That's part of the fascination he exerts on those who discover his history. Some of them even maintain that this is the house on which Jack and the Beanstalk was based. The Victorians, I believe, were particularly keen on the idea.'

Now it was Father Snow who interrupted.

'And you don't believe it?'

'I'm no folklorist.' Trevellyan shrugged. 'There do seem to be some strange coincidences. By all accounts, he was a very large man. Perhaps the position of the house is significant, too. On foggy days it does sometimes appear to be floating. But all such speculation is pointless. It's one of those things which will never be proved. My own personal view is that they are coincidences, no more.'

'And this hidden room,' said Vincent, 'this ogre's laboratory. Does that exist?'

Trevellyan seemed to hesitate, frowning at the carpet. Then he nodded.

'It's opposite the portrait of Everard in the old house. It's little more than a glorified cupboard, though, and it certainly doesn't contain the marvels some people have claimed for it.'

'You've been there, then?'

Trevellyan lifted his gaze towards Vincent.

'Only once.'

There was silence. All of them stared at the huge man in his armchair, not slouching back now, but bent down towards them and speaking sadly and quietly, as though afraid of what too loud a voice might do.

'The tragedy is that, in many ways, Everard was a great man. There's no telling what he might have achieved if he'd been free from vice. What exactly he did achieve is impossible to tell, since he loved to impress as much as to terrify, and his writings are obviously full of exaggeration. Yet I'm convinced that some of his discoveries and experiments were far ahead of their time.'

'Very interesting,' said Vincent. 'It's all very interesting.' He paused, apparently trying to come to a decision, like a doctor mulling over a list of symptoms. 'I'd like to visit his room,' he eventually said. 'If you've no objection, that is.'

'It's not so easy, I'm afraid. The only access is through a trapdoor in the roof.'

'I don't actually want to go inside. I want to go no further than Father Conner did.'

'That's simple. The old part of the house is open to the public. Thousands of people walk round the walls of Everard's room each year without even knowing that it's there.'

'Fine, then that's what I'd like to do. However, I'd rather go alone. I don't want crowds of people around.'

Trevellyan gave him a strange look.

'You'll have to come back in the evening then. We've got a spare pair of keys which my wife can give to Father Snow.' He looked towards her. 'Do you think you could do that for me?'

'Of course.'

Father Snow and Lady Trevellyan stood up and quietly left the room.

'This is all rather creepy,' she said as they walked down the corridor. 'I knew there were some funny stories about this house, but I had no idea such horrible things had happened here.'

They stepped out through the front door with its ordinary little bell. It was the way Father Snow had come on his first visit. Lady Trevellyan crossed to the National Trust booth and bent down to speak to the attendant. Looking to his right, Father Snow saw that a straight black path had been dug through the snow which covered the courtyard. A small group of visitors stood wondering at the antlers on the far wall.

A moment later, Lady Trevellyan handed him a set of keys and a number scrawled on a scrap of paper. As they went back down the corridor, she explained that the number was the code for the alarm system. Then she told him which key was which and how to turn the alarm back on when they left.

At the door to the room where they had left Vincent with Trevellyan, she stopped.

'Why do you think Vincent is so keen to visit the house alone?'

'I don't know,' said Father Snow. 'He didn't mention it to me before we came.'

'Very strange. Anyway, I'd better be getting back to my guests.'

'Of course.'

'Tell Vincent how lovely it was to meet him. Tell him we'd love him to come back, as soon as he possibly can. Perhaps he could even say Mass for us one day.'

'Yes. That would be nice.'

'You will remember to tell him, won't you?'

'Of course.'

When he opened the door, Father Snow found that Trevellyan had got up from his place and was standing at the window with his hands behind his back. The room was full of light thrown inside by the snow. Vincent was still sitting as before. He was speaking, but fell silent when Father Snow entered. Trevellyan turned from the window at the sound of the door. His face was strangely twisted, as though he'd been shot.

Without needing to be told, Father Snow retreated into the corridor, quietly closing the door again behind him.

When Vincent eventually opened the door, Father Snow caught a glimpse of Trevellyan inside. He was still standing with his back to them, motionless, staring out of the window at his enormous park. Vincent looked old and drawn.

'Come on,' he said. 'Let's go.'

As they were walking through the park, Father Snow said:

'Why do you want to visit the laboratory?'

Vincent glanced at him, then walked on a little more quickly, thrusting his stick into the snow.

'It's something I have to do for Charles.'

His tone warned Father Snow not to ask any further questions. They walked through the village and back to the presbytery in silence. All the way, Father Snow thought about Jack and the Beanstalk. He kept remembering the hands going up in Melanie's classroom. There was something else, though, some deeper, more personal meaning to the fairy tale which he couldn't tease out, something from his adult life.

In the end, it came to him. It was the memory of his mother's horrified face when he'd told her of his intention to become a priest. At that moment he'd been Jack, returning home in disgrace, having bartered everything of value for a magic seed which would enable him to climb into the clouds.

15

VINCENT'S DECISION TO visit Flamstead that night meant that he wouldn't be able to leave Wodden until the following morning. Back at the presbytery, he spent a long time on the phone in the study, changing his plans. After that, he went outside and paced around the snowy garden with the thoughtful agitation of a chess-player between moves. Every now and again he would stop and stare up at the house in the hills, praying aloud, or perhaps just muttering to himself. Father Snow, watching him from the study, began to feel uneasy.

At last Vincent marched in from the garden, his little face red from the cold. Like a general rapping out commands, he gave a list of things he wanted packed in a bag. All Father Snow's worst suspicions were confirmed as he listened. Without seeming to notice his reaction, Vincent disappeared upstairs, saying he didn't want to be disturbed. Father Snow spent the rest of the afternoon alone.

Vincent didn't come back downstairs until Flora arrived that evening. She was surprised and pleased to find that he was still there. Vincent himself was strange, more lively and talkative than Father Snow had ever seen him. It was as though he was over-compensating, desperately trying to hide the agitation which had been so obvious earlier. Father Snow remained his usual calm self.

As soon as Flora had left, Vincent fell silent again. For twenty minutes, he just sat at the kitchen table with his eyes closed, Father Snow waiting quietly at his side. In the end, just before nine, he asked if he could borrow some clerical clothes. Father Snow took him upstairs, gave him the clothes and left him to get changed.

When he came down, the old man looked really comical. The clothes were far too big for him. The shoulders of the black jacket fell halfway to his elbows. Though he'd rolled the sleeves a number of times, they still flopped over his wrists. The trousers were as baggy as a clown's. The dog collar hung loose around his scrawny, bird's neck. In the hall, he bent down to check that everything he'd asked for was in the bag. Looking at his soft white curls, Father Snow felt a surge of affection for him, about which there was a trace of pity.

Having gone carefully though everything in the bag, Vincent snapped it shut and straightened. Now the most comical thing about him was the fixed, grim expression on his face.

'Right,' he said. 'I'm off.'

'Don't you want me to come with you?'

'No. You'd better stay here.'

'Why?'

'Because you're not ready for this.'

The solemnity of his voice was too much. Father Snow spluttered.

'What's so funny?'

'I'm sorry, Vincent. It's just that those clothes are rather big for you.'

For once, Vincent didn't appreciate the joke.

'You think I'm slightly absurd, don't you, Julian?'

'Not at all. It's just the clothes.'

'Yes, you do,' said Vincent, beginning to lose his temper. 'You think I'm just an old fool off on an old fool's errand. Well, maybe you're right, but you could at least have the decency to hide it.'

Father Snow was taken aback by the tone. He'd never heard anger in Vincent's voice before, or dreamed such a thing might be possible.

'I don't think that,' he said, not smiling now.

'It's pointless for you to deny it. The unfortunate thing about you, Julian, is that everything about you proclaims your scorn for the rest of the human race. Just look at the way you're standing. Look at the expression on your face. I can see why you drive poor old Ralph round the bend. You're so insufferably smug.' He clenched his fists and shook his head with frustration. 'You'd try the patience of a saint!'

As he spoke, Father Snow became uncomfortably aware of himself, standing stiff and upright in the hallway. He lowered his chin a little, but was so shocked and stung by Vincent's attack that he couldn't find it in him to speak.

'You want to come, do you?' Vincent was almost shouting now. 'You want to come with me? Come, then. You call yourself a priest. Come and show us what you're made of. Come and watch the old fool at work. It'll give you a laugh, if nothing else.'

With that, he picked up his bag and marched out of the presbytery, leaving the door open behind him. Father Snow watched him leave, unable to speak or move. He was blushing so much that his head felt swollen up like a balloon. There was a lump in his throat.

Outside in the snow, Vincent turned around and bellowed:

'Come on!'

Father Snow walked stiffly outside, feeling that every careful movement he made was a betrayal of pride and awkwardness and the inability to get on with people. He went into the garage, moved the car in front of the presbytery, then got out to close the garage door. When he came back, Vincent was already sitting in the passenger seat. Only when he'd taken his own place in the car did Father Snow realise that the old man had switched the engine off. When he spoke, it was once more in his usual, gentle voice.

'I'm sorry for losing my temper, Julian. I don't know what came over me.'

'It's all right,' said Father Snow. 'I deserved it.'

'No, you didn't. Nobody deserves to be talked to like that, least of all you. You know I didn't mean it, don't you?'

Father Snow shrugged.

'In all my years as a bishop,' said Vincent, turning towards him, 'I've never felt such admiration and liking for a young priest. It's quite understandable that you find me ridiculous. Perhaps your curse is to be surrounded by people less capable than yourself.'

'Don't say that, Vincent. You know it isn't true. I just have . . . an awkward manner about me.'

'I know, I know,' said Vincent, smiling now. 'In a funny way, that's part of your charm. That's why I'd rather see you stop being a priest than stop being my friend. Tell me you forgive me.'

Father Snow's face suddenly screwed up. He turned his head away.

'Of course I do.'

'It's just that I'm rather tense this evening.' Vincent was silent for a moment. 'Actually, I'm scared stiff, if you want to know the truth.'

As he said that, Father Snow remembered what Walter Trevellyan had told Timothy Darting three hundred years before: a succession of priests had made visits like this to Flamstead. Some had lost their minds, while others, like Father Conner, had taken their own lives.

'Are you sure you want to come?'

Even now, Father Snow couldn't help smiling.

'Of course.'

He started the engine and they began to crawl away through the snow.

This was the first time he'd visited Flamstead at night, and it was a very different experience. As they turned off the A25, headlights swinging, the two stone griffons suddenly seemed to loom above them out of the darkness. Their heads and wings were touched with white, as though they'd just landed after a long flight high in the frozen air. The gateposts on which they'd settled looked taller than during the day. Then the 2CV clattered over the cattle-grid, and the threshold was crossed.

The drive to the house through the park seemed longer, too. Father Snow had to stare ahead, concentrating on the twists and turns in the lane, which existed now as no more than two tracks of churned slush. Low white banks lay on either side, so that he felt like a pilot about to nose above the clouds. It was a relief when he at last saw lights up ahead and knew they were approaching the house.

In the sudden silence after he cut the engine, they both sat still for a moment. To the right of the car the building filled their entire field of vision. Only one or two of the windows were lit, their curtains drawn, and this paucity of illumination seemed to highlight how preposterously large the place was.

Without saying anything, Vincent got out of the car. Father Snow followed. Only when he was outside did the brightness of the moon come home to him. Reflected from the snow, it would almost have been enough to read by. The park was visible as far as the horizon in that unreal light. From here, the vast area of snow looked more than ever like an undulating mass of cloud, so that he imagined the trunks of the trees plummeting for thousands of feet beneath it. All he could see was their giant heads thrust up through the surface, intricate black ideograms. Behind him, he could feel the presence of the house, the dark acres of corridors and empty rooms.

'Come here, Father Snow,' said Vincent, lapsing for some reason into the formal form of address.

Father Snow went and stood by the archbishop, who had moved a little way from the car and was standing with his back to the house, staring out across the luminous expanse of snow.

'We'll say a short prayer before we go in.'

As Father Snow composed himself, he was struck by the fact that a casual observer, seeing the two men standing side by side, might have thought they were preparing to pray to the moon. Yet when Vincent started to speak, his voice was very low, more as though he were murmuring into someone's ear than calling on a distant planet.

'Lord, you know that we are here to do your work. Fill us with your gentleness and strength in the struggle which lies ahead. Help us to remember that you are at our side, whatever happens.' After a moment's pause, he echoed the words from the Office: 'Protect us from the demons which roam the earth in search of men's souls.'

After that, they both stood there in silence. Father Snow, for all that the whole enterprise was still ridiculous to him, felt strangely close to God as he stared out across the moonlit park.

Eventually Vincent spoke.

'Father Snow?'

Turning, he saw the little old man in his oversized clothes and found them slightly less silly than before.

'Yes?'

'This is your last chance to turn back. There's no shame in deciding to wait here.'

Again, Father Snow couldn't stop himself smiling.

'I don't mind coming.'

With a shrug, Vincent picked up his bag and, in silence, led the way towards the house. As they walked through the first of the two courtyards, Father Snow wondered whether Trevellyan was up there, watching them go in, as his ancestors, if the legends were to be believed, had watched other priests go the same way. Yet he didn't feel he was being watched. There was just a sense of complete emptiness, which seemed to deepen as they progressed.

The huge doors to Everard's part of the house were open as if in welcome, and this somehow made the place seem even more deserted. When they entered the Tudor courtyard, there were no more lights. Only the moon showed them the way, but that was more than enough. The snow crunched loudly under their feet, as though it had been laid there to warn of intruders. The tall chimneys ignored the noise, standing so perfectly still that it seemed they were doing it deliberately. Ahead, the antlers were visible, casting deformed shadows across the wall.

Father Snow found himself averting his eyes as he walked past them. He had to make an effort not to quicken his pace. Taking the bunch of keys from his pocket and choosing the one Lady Trevellyan had shown him, he opened the heavy oak door. The alarm began to beep. It was on his left, a white box with flashing lights. Switching on the main lights, he keyed in the magic code from the scrap of paper. The beeping stopped. Vincent came and joined him in the hallway.

'Where's this awful laboratory place supposed to be?'

'Upstairs,' said Father Snow.

He led the way through the doorway on the right, which gave onto the huge dining hall. Long rectangles of moonlight lay across the floor. The raised dais where Everard had caroused with Henry VIII was just visible.

Turning on lights as they went, they climbed the stairs, past the two carved griffons at the bottom of the bannisters, frozen as they clawed the air. The ancient floorboards creaked beneath their feet, and Father Snow smiled. At the top of the stairs, they entered the long gallery of pictures. When they turned on the lights, they could see, at the far end, a pile of white leaflets left on one of the attendant's chairs.

'As far as I understand it,' said Father Snow in a normal voice, 'the laboratory is behind the wall on the left.'

'Good. The first thing I want to do is walk right around it and turn on all the lights.'

Vincent's own voice had been far from normal, quavering, barely above a whisper. Father Snow began to lead him round. Before they reached the end of the first gallery, he stopped in front of Everard's portrait.

'The ogre himself.'

They both paused to stare up at the picture. Although Everard was standing exactly as he had for centuries, one hand on the hilt of his sword and the other holding the astrolabe, the silence of the house and the darkness surrounding it seemed to have wrought a subtle change in him. Now that there was nothing to distract from the image, it was more immediate and motionless. Each second that Father Snow spent staring upwards seemed to heighten the contradiction between the portrait's lifelike presence and its stillness, until it seemed incredible that Everard could just go on standing there without moving. The expression on his face intensified, as though gathering itself for movement, but still nothing happened. Then the moment passed and it was suddenly just a picture again, flat and lifeless.

Vincent was still looking up into the handsome, sneering face. He spoke with something like awe.

'Even in an ancient picture like this, the monster can't quite hide himself.'

They began walking from room to room, turning on lights as they went. There was an intensity to the silence which emphasised every noise. Father Snow could hear not only their feet on the wooden boards, but also the rustle of their clothing, even the sound of his own breath. It gave him a small thrill of fear which was made pleasurable by the knowledge that nothing frightening could happen here. He was almost beginning to enjoy himself.

Soon they'd come full circle, surrounding the hidden square of the laboratory with a larger square of illumination. Standing in the last room they'd lit up, Vincent took his stole from his pocket and draped it around his neck, so that the fancy-dress and its absurdity were complete. Then he just stood facing the laboratory with his chin dropped down towards his chest. It was the roosting position in which Father Snow had so often seen him pray. This seemed to go on forever, but Father

Snow, standing a few paces off, waited without making a sound.

Eventually Vincent crouched down and snapped the catches on his case. A moment later he stood and, with a precise flick of his wrist and forearm, sprayed holy water like buckshot against the wall of the laboratory.

Father Snow saw all this with a strange, slow clarity. He saw Vincent's white curls, the folded sleeve of the black jacket performing an arc in the air, the water glittering for an instant as it flew, and his pleasurable little fear exploded into panic.

The sudden force of it was like a blow. It gripped him in the stomach so that he felt a desperate need to urinate. He heard the blood rushing through his ears as an impossibly deep bass note. The desire to flee coursed through him, but he stood perfectly still, as though turned to stone. Then it seemed to him that the panic and the deep sound which accompanied it were not only inside him, but outside as well, behind the wall. It was as though his terror had been externalised, projected out into the real world.

There it took on the shape of a personality which sent his own fear back at him in waves. The image of something intricate and perfectly black leapt into his mind and was immediately thrown outwards. It had utter hatred for them, yet a strange kind of affection, too, the affection of a bully for his victims. Above all, it was sardonic.

Father Snow knew that he was imagining all this, yet it was so clear to him that he wasn't sure whether his eyes were open or closed. With an effort he convinced himself that they were open. He was standing in front of a panelled wall. Vincent was bending back down to his case, moving very slowly. As he stood straight, he turned back towards Father Snow, floating round. There was a book in his hand. In the same way of seeing which had shown him the personality behind the wall, Father Snow perceived Vincent as a pure light balanced against it, tiny but intense, one star in the void. His voice was almost drowned by the bass note in Father Snow's ears, which now boomed and resonated fit to shake the windows from their panes.

'Leave, Father Snow!'

As though in a dream, Father Snow heard the words and understood them without understanding. He just stood rooted to the spot, his mind filled by its imagining of the thing behind the wall. For all its sardonic hatred of him and for all the terror it inspired, there was something overwhelmingly attractive about it, so that a part of him wanted to move closer just while the rest of him wanted to run away. He stood in frantic equilibrium.

'I'm all right,' he said, raising his voice above the noise in his ears. 'I'm not afraid.'

Then it was Vincent's face which filled his mind.

'Just go! Run!'

Father Snow turned, but didn't run. He began to walk stiffly away. His progress was very slow, because he was somehow finding it difficult to lift his feet from the floor. In fact, he wondered whether he wasn't just walking on the spot. Then a sledgehammer of white light hit him square in the back, so that he was forced to run in order to keep his balance, and once he'd started running he couldn't stop.

Now that he gave it its full expression, the panic was almost total, yet there were still a few signs of control of which he found time to be proud even as he was charging away. He didn't wet himself and he didn't cry out. A scream had risen up behind his lips, but he kept it there, somehow feeling that this was proof of his continuing sanity.

He ran out of the room, across the picture gallery, and down the stairs, interested that his legs still had the co-ordination to manage them. This was proof of another level, a kind of humanity, which went on no matter how bad things were. A wooden griffon wheeled past, snarling at him. Then he ran across the dining-hall, his footsteps thundering in his ears. Continuing, he got a glimpse of the white alarm with its flashing lights. Suddenly he was out in the moonlight and the freezing air, and the panic stopped.

The calm was abrupt and total. Father Snow stopped running and immediately felt ashamed of himself. His first impulse was to go back inside, to prove to Vincent that he really hadn't been afraid. For a moment he stood there panting, then decided it would be best to collect his thoughts for a few moments, to understand exactly what had happened to him.

Taking deep breaths of freezing air, he walked past the huge antlers, across the courtyard and out through the giant's doors. Then he crossed the newer courtyard and emerged into the luminous expanse of the park. The 2CV was still parked where they had left it, as silly and incongruous as ever. The moon was still in its place, and all the stars.

Father Snow decided to sit and think about things in the car. As soon as he was inside, however, he was distracted. Looking through the windows to his left, he saw a huge stag with majestic antlers cantering up towards the house across the snow, its snout smoking in the moonlight. There was a weightless quality about the way it moved. It floated past the car, so close that he could hear its hooves crunching the snow, and straight into the building. He watched it cross the first courtyard. In the second, it came to an abrupt halt and stood facing the Tudor house with its head slightly on one side, as deer do in the split second after hearing a noise.

After that, Father Snow couldn't take his eyes off it. He also knew somehow that there was now no question of his getting out of the car. All he would be able to do was sit there till Vincent's return. He began to rationalise the fear which had taken hold of him in the house. Perhaps it had been something to do with Vincent, the utter certainty with which he did things, his ability to communicate faith. At the moment when the holy water had been cast, Father Snow had been able to do nothing but believe. From that, his imagination had created the whole thing.

Even as he thought all this, though, there were images going through his head. He saw himself and Susan leaning like children over a book in the British Library. Then he saw the sneering portrait, transparent, overlaid against the intricate darkness he'd imagined behind the wall. Susan walked out of the Happy Eater into the first fall of snow, lifting her head into the flakes: You see? This is a fairy tale, after all. Vincent leaned on his stick and stared up at the lights of Flamstead from the village green. Hands went up in the classroom. A giant with long white hair sadly explained that deer often came into the courtyards, especially in winter. A huge stag stood facing the house, feet astride in the snow, its snout smoking in the moonlight.

At that moment, the animal seemed to wake up and realise where it was. Looking curiously around, it walked slowly back towards Father Snow, crossing the two courtyards, passing in front of the car, then disappearing the way it had come.

About a minute later, Vincent emerged from the building. His little black figure seemed to be thrown forwards by the snow. With the bag in his hand, he looked like an exhausted old doctor returning from a long night at a deathbed. He trudged across the courtyards and out of the building, bent over, barely lifting his feet. Then he suddenly dropped the bag, turned around and vomited into the snow. Father Snow sat and watched.

Vincent came towards the car, wiping his mouth, his face twisted and tired. Father Snow, still staring through the courtyards, heard movement on his left. Then there was an endless silence.

'How do you feel, Julian?'

'I'm fine,' said Father Snow. 'I'm fine. I just —'

'Not many people, even priests, ever have to see what you've seen tonight.'

Father Snow wanted to explain that he hadn't seen anything. Instead he sat there in silence. Vincent sighed.

'I've never had to deal with anything quite like it before. Old Everard was a giant in more ways than one.'

Father Snow sat and stared through the courtyards. Eventually Vincent said:

'Damn. We forgot to turn that blasted alarm back on.' Father Snow didn't speak or even move his head. 'Still, I pity the burglar who tries to steal anything from that place, eh? Good luck to him, that's all I can say!'

Then Father Snow felt movement in his arm.

'That was a joke, Julian. You could at least pretend to be amused.'

At last he turned away from the house, aware that his face was inappropriately blank, but not knowing what to do about it.

'Don't worry,' said Vincent. 'You'll be all right in a couple of hours. But perhaps, for the moment, you'd better let me drive.'

After that, there were images of trees, houses and snow, all in a spreading embrace of light. They passed through his mind without affecting it, yet they must have had some effect, since it knew that they were there. Otherwise, it was blank. Then, at last, an image swung into the light which connected with him on another level, and he soon understood that it was the presbytery. Strangely, it was this homely sight, which should have been a comfort to him, that brought his panic flooding back.

Light died around him, and silence grew. The presbytery disappeared then resolved itself into something pale and gloomy. A moving shape which he identified as Vincent passed in front of him. Then there was cold against his skin.

'Come on, Julian. We've arrived.'

Things began to shift around, and he knew that he was moving, though he didn't understand how this had been achieved. The presbytery door approached.

'Got your keys?'

For some reason, this caused a fresh wave of panic. In the midst of it, his hand reached into his pocket and encountered a cold, hard sensation: keys.

When they were inside, Vincent made Father Snow sit down on the sofa. He went obediently, feeling like a child, but without the comforts of childhood.

'Have you got any alcohol in the house?'

'I don't know. I don't think so.'

'You must have some somewhere. This is a presbytery, after all.'

Then Father Snow was alone with his terror for a certain amount of time. The memory of the ogre filled his mind. Words started to pass through him, though whether he spoke or simply thought them he didn't know. At first he didn't even recognise them as the Our Father, since it had been so completely stripped of its old meaning and associations. Yet, perhaps simply because it filled his head, it brought a slight diminution of his terror.

While all this was going on, images were still being fed to him, of Father Conner's armchair, the fireplace with its brass tools. Then there was the image of Vincent, squatting down in front of him and handing him a tumbler.

'Drink this.'

Father Snow took a sip, shuddered, and lowered the glass.

'All of it. Go on, gulp it down.'

Father Snow obeyed. Warmth coursed through him, bringing a little comfort. As if by magic, Vincent produced a bottle and refilled the glass. Then he went and sat down in the armchair opposite, raising his own glass in congratulation.

'You did well tonight, Julian.'

Father Snow hung his head.

'I ran away.'

'Few could even have managed that. No, for someone with so little experience, you did well. I'm proud of you.'

Father Snow looked up. As soon as he set eyes on Vincent, he remembered what else he'd seen at Flamstead: the tiny, bright light sustaining itself against the darkness. It had been as mysterious as anything else, but somehow not frightening. All he could see now was an old man, small and wizened, smiling from an armchair. If it hadn't been for his oversized clerical clothes, he might have been a tramp or an absent-minded academic.

'Ralph told me some strange stories about you,' Father Snow heard himself say. 'I didn't really believe them at the time.'

'Ah! Ralph loves to talk.' He leaned forwards. 'Listen to me, Julian. I'm going to tell you a little secret: all priests are romantics. They have to be. That's why it's all too easy for them to get carried away with things. That's why this girl of yours is so dangerous to you.'

For a moment, Father Snow couldn't even remember her name. She seemed unreal and irrelevant.

'I'm not a romantic,' he said, finding that these simple things somehow required a lot of thought at the moment. 'If anything, I'm a cynic.'

There was a subtle change in the nature of Vincent's smile.

'Of course you are. The perfect, cold rationalist.'

'What happened tonight?' said Father Snow suddenly.

Vincent leaned back in his chair, his face serious.

'When you go into a church,' he said, 'you immediately feel the goodness of the place. Anyone with any spiritual sense feels the same thing. That's the most obvious example of the connection between the spiritual and the physical worlds, but all places, all of them, have a –' He paused and gently circled his hand as though to indicate that what he wanted to express was too ethereal for words. 'A spiritual tone. It's usually too delicate for most people to notice. But that particular room, like a church, had been deliberately coloured. It had undergone an inverted consecration.'

'How?'

'I don't know,' said Vincent, 'and trying to find out would be dangerous. All I will say is this: you've seen part of the darkness, but it's nothing compared to the light. Some of us, the fortunate few, are allowed to experience goodness with the same direct intensity that you've just experienced evil.'

'Have you ever done so?'

'Only once.'

'And how did it make you feel?'

Now for a moment Vincent lapsed into one of his intense silences, so that Father Snow was afraid to move, hanging on the reply.

'It made me feel that I could never be really unhappy again,' he said at last, then smiled. 'And I never really have.'

When Father Snow had finished his drink, they knelt together and said the Rosary. Then Vincent commanded Father Snow to go to bed, and he obeyed, since Vincent obviously knew what was best for him.

As soon as he was alone, walking up the stairs, Father Snow's panic and disorientation returned, though they were slightly weaker than before. Lying in bed, he stared at the ceiling, trying to think logically about what had happened. It seemed to him that he'd been allowed to climb for a short time to a different level, where things were not rational or irrational, but simply beyond reason. He'd thrust his head above the clouds and seen one of the monsters that lived there.

After a few minutes, the door opened and Vincent came quietly in.

'Still awake?' he said softly.

'Yes.'

'I thought you might be.' He crossed the room and

threw the curtains open, so that moonlight fell at an angle across the desk. 'It's always good to look at the sky when you can't sleep, I find.'

So Father Snow stared out of the window at the few stars whose light managed to battle its way through the wide glow of the moon. Once more, as he had been before they'd entered the house, he felt strangely close to God, yet infinitely distant at the same time, so that the stars filled him with an unaccustomed yearning.

Taking the chair from the desk, Vincent came and sat down at the bedside.

'What are you doing?'

'I'm going to stay here till you're asleep.'

Father Snow didn't protest. When he spoke, it was in an uncertain, almost humble voice, which didn't seem his own.

'What happened?'

'There are mysteries about which it's best not to be too curious,' came the reply. 'Such curiosity was probably instrumental in Everard's damnation. All will be revealed, in time.'

The voice which spoke these words was so steady and sure that Father Snow's eyes closed of their own accord.

'Do you think he made the children dream?'

'That's another mystery, Julian.' Now the voice was soft and musical, a spoken lullaby. 'All will be revealed, in the fullness of time.'

Once or twice while he was going to sleep, Father Snow secretly opened his eyes to check that Vincent was still there. Each time, he was, sitting motionless in the chair, staring down at the floor, or perhaps asleep.

In the middle of the night, Father Snow awoke with a start from some nightmare he couldn't remember. The sheets were clammy with sweat. Instantly, he looked towards the chair at his side, but it was empty. All he could see was the digital clock beyond, showing that it was almost half past three. Then, looking across the room, he saw Vincent, standing by the window and staring up into the sky.

When he awoke the following morning, or rather in the gloom before the winter dawn, Father Snow at once felt ashamed of the way he'd behaved the night before. Downstairs, he found Vincent up and dressed. There was only time for one last, short conversation before Mass.

'I've got to go back today, Julian. I really wish I could stay, but it's simply impossible. I've upset far too many people by being away even this long.'

Although he'd known this, the hearing of it disappointed Father Snow. He realised that he'd secretly been hoping that Vincent would find an excuse to stay.

'Of course,' he said, 'I understand. I've been lucky to have you here at all.'

The words were spoken like an adult, but they still masked some of the pathetic childishness he'd felt the night before. He was being abandoned. With a little of his old discipline, he straightened his back and clenched his jaw. Vincent laughed.

'It's a relief to see that you're still the same old Julian. I was beginning to worry that I shouldn't have let you come last night.'

'Don't worry about me,' said Father Snow, a little coldly. 'I'm fine.'

Vincent nodded.

'On the whole I think this kind of shock is good for a priest like you. If you should have any problems, though, you can always take them to Ralph.'

'Yes.'

'Don't underestimate him, Julian. For all his apparent faults, he's got enormous experience and the resilience of a rock. When I visit again, I expect to find you two the best of friends.'

Remembering how Vincent had lost his temper the night before, Father Snow lowered his chin.

'I'll try.'

'Even more importantly, I want to find that you've sorted everything out with this girl. Though you may not see it at the moment, she's by far the greatest threat you face.' Vincent smiled. 'Anything can happen when a cynic changes his mind, particularly about love.'

Father Snow straightened again.

'I find it hard to imagine myself changing my mind on that particular subject.'

Vincent laughed delightedly.

'Oh, Julian, I've really enjoyed this weekend, in spite of everything. I'm going to miss you.'

This embarrassed Father Snow so much that he couldn't reply. He just gave a little cough and looked uncomfortably away. But when the moment had gone, when it was too late to respond, he was saddened that he hadn't been able to find some formula, some acceptable words to express his friendship and regard.

The feeling stayed with him through Mass. Vincent was leaving. Since it was a Monday morning, the congregation was small. Even so, the little old man was unnoticed at the back. There was nobody here who could begin to take his place. When he was gone, there would be very little real faith remaining in the village. Father Snow would be left again with his tiny daily congregation. Ralph, for all Vincent had said, was no replacement.

Somehow, the most painful moment was Vincent's communion. Father Snow's sadness was mixed with a sense of unworthiness, and he was reminded of Vincent's surprise appearance at Mass in the old parish, in the other life before he'd come to Wodden. Now, as then, the solemnity of the occasion meant that no sign of friendship could be shown. In a few moments, Vincent would be gone for a long time, perhaps for ever. Only now that he was denied the opportunity to express his emotions did Father Snow feel ready to do so. Instead, his face solemn, he simply raised the host and laid it on the trembling tongue.

Vincent, entirely concerned with his communion, didn't even look up at Father Snow. As soon as he'd received, he lowered his head, walked slowly back to his place, and knelt down to pray.

He was still there, hunched over, when Father Snow left the sacristy after Mass. Hearing him, Vincent stood stiffly up.

'I think it's time to go.'

When they emerged from the church, they found that a black car had appeared in the lane. Seeing them, the driver nodded to Vincent, got out, and opened the passenger door. He was a young priest, barely older than Father Snow.

'They've come for me, you see,' said Vincent regretfully. 'I was hoping, though I'm sure I shouldn't have, that they'd be late. That way we could have had breakfast together.'

The sun was up by now. Although it was early in the day, the snow had already begun to melt. They could hear it dripping all around them like the ticking of a thousand clocks. Vincent sighed and looked into the clear sky.

'I have this dream of taking a holiday, a real one, resting my poor old bones on a beach somewhere. Something tells me it will never come true.'

As he lowered his gaze, he seemed already a different man, more serious, concerned with important matters of which Father Snow knew nothing. He was like a father setting off for work, leaving his son alone and not really understanding the anguish that this caused.

'I'm proud of you, Julian,' he said as they shook hands. 'You've lived up to all my expectations this weekend.' Father Snow couldn't speak, and Vincent must have noticed the look on his face, for he said: 'Don't be downcast. All partings are temporary.'

'You're my best friend,' said Father Snow.

Vincent laughed.

'Thank you, Julian! That sends me away with a slightly lighter heart.' As soon as he'd said it, though, his smile

vanished and he looked seriously into Father Snow's eyes.
'Pray for me.'

Then he was gone, walking quickly towards the car and crying in a completely different voice:

'David! Thank you so much for coming all this way. I'm sorry to drag you out so early.'

'That's all right, your grace,' said the driver, holding the door open for him. 'It's always a pleasure to see you.'

Father Snow felt a pang of jealousy at this. It was as though Vincent had forgotten him already. But as he was driven away, his small face, not far above the bottom of the window, stayed fixed on Father Snow. He was still leaning forwards to catch a last glimpse as the car rounded the bend in the lane and disappeared.

As he went back into the presbytery, Father Snow saw in the porch the tall stick Vincent had found when they'd gone for their walk on the first night. He took it through to the study and leaned it in the corner, where he would be able to see it while he was working on his sermons. Then he sat and stared at it for a long time, listening to the steady drip of water from outside.

PART TWO

16

THOUSANDS OF BLUEBELLS were spread out beneath the trees at the top of the hill, a vast crowd all nodding their heads in gentle agreement. The breeze could be seen moving across them as though across water, although water only had that kind of vibrant blue in postcards and children's paintings. The huge maples and copper beeches were like giants who had stopped to cool their feet and been turned into trees, condemned to stand motionless for centuries, bewitched.

Sitting with his back against one of their trunks, Father Snow just looked, the book he'd brought up with him forgotten at his side. On a Sunday the solitude of this spot would be constantly disturbed by groups of mountain-bikers in muddy lycra shorts and hikers with plastic-covered maps around their necks. But today was Monday, Father Snow's day off, and he was entirely alone. When he'd seen the sunshine that morning, he'd been unable to resist disappearing to explore the hills which surrounded Wodden, but he hadn't been expecting to find anything like this.

The air was comfortably warm. The leaves were swaying slices of light. Only a few slim bolts of sunshine found their way through the dense foliage, illuminating insects and the floating dust of pollen where they slanted down. As he watched, the wind picked up. The beams all flickered and changed places as though they'd been shot through the surface of an agitated sea. The bluebells nodded a little more enthusiastically. The trees sighed with pleasure.

All of it filled Father Snow with a yearning which there was no way to satisfy. Some childish part of him wanted to go and roll around in the bluebells, to luxuriate in them. Instead, he prayed, giving thanks until it seemed that God was revealed all around him, immediate yet unobtainable.

In the midst of it, an expression of wonder came over his face. It seemed only yesterday that the whole place had been covered in snow.

He was filled with nostalgia for his first few weeks in the village. He remembered Flora opening the door to the presbytery on his arrival there. She had seemed so strange to him then, with her oddly shaped glasses and permed hair, so normal now. He remembered the British Museum in the rain, his first awkward drink with Ralph, his first lunch at Flamstead, his first visit to the school.

Things had changed since then, but not dramatically. Wodden itself seemed a normal village now. Father Snow was an established part of the community, treated perhaps with less affection than respect. He couldn't walk from the presbytery to the Old Mill without greeting five or six people.

In his personal life, too, things had changed, but not dramatically. He was perhaps slightly more relaxed with Flora and Ralph, but not close to either of them. Visiting Ralph for a drink was still less of a pleasure than a chore. Each Friday, he still met Susan at the Happy Eater as they had agreed, though his feelings for her had cooled. After his experience at Flamstead, he'd had nightmares for a while, but they were behind him now. Yet that night had reordered his understanding of the world. Spiritual things were more immediate and tangible than he'd thought, and more mysterious. The knowledge that some trace of Everard had survived the centuries had made Father Snow feel that his own past was more immediate, too.

The human mind itself is perhaps like a vast honeycombed building whose whole atmosphere can be dictated by the events of its most distant history.

Now, while his mind went on raking over the past, his eyes instinctively looked through the trees towards the hills on the other side of the village. After a few moments, they found Flamstead, high on the far wall of the bowl, a hundred windows shining in the sun. These days he was slightly more willing to admit the possibility of things he would once have dismissed as absurd. There seemed a slim chance that this was the place from which the famous fairy tale had come.

He was still squinting across at the house when his thoughts were interrupted by the sound of somebody approaching. Irritated that another human being had arrived to spoil the perfection of the place, he looked around and saw Susan.

She was walking towards him slowly and thoughtfully, not seeming to notice her surroundings. Father Snow's first impulse was to call out to her. This was immediately followed by the contradictory impulse to get out of sight before she saw him. In the end, he just sat there in silence and watched her approach through the bluebells and the bolts of sunlight. It was the first time he'd seen her outside the Happy Eater since they'd agreed to meet there each week. She was wearing a long, light dress. Her hair had grown since their first meeting and now fell over her shoulders, though it was still as straight and neat as before.

Whatever thoughts filled her head were so engrossing that it seemed she might walk straight past Father Snow without noticing him. At the last moment, though, she looked in his direction. When she saw him, she stopped walking and just stood there in silence. Somehow Father Snow found that he could do nothing but stare back. He felt vulnerable sitting down and wanted to stand, but couldn't do that either. They seemed to look at each other for a long time. The trees sighed and the bluebells in their thousands gently nodded. The beams of light shifted and flickered. Susan's hair stirred on her shoulders.

'Is that really you?'

Father Snow smiled.

'To the best of my knowledge.'

'I can't believe it. I've been thinking about you. I –' She stopped, embarrassed at herself as usual, and made a gesture over her shoulder. 'I've been walking.'

Unable to think of a suitable reply to this, Father Snow just sat and looked at her. The leaves and light flickered dreamy warnings.

'Can I come and sit with you for a minute?' she said. 'Or do you want me to go away?'

Then Father Snow found himself giving the answer that any young man would have given on seeing the girl he loved in a place like this.

'I don't want you to go away.'

When he heard himself say that, Father Snow felt he'd been beguiled. Smiling, she came and sat down in the flowers at his side, curling her legs beneath her. The breeze died down so that the beams of light settled back into focus. In the silence, he heard the distant buzzing of a bluebottle or a bee.

'Why aren't you at work today?' he said.

'I've taken the day off. I've got an interview with a paper up in London this afternoon. That's why I was thinking about you, wondering what will happen if I get the job.' She looked away from him, down at the flowers. 'I don't know if I'd be able to leave.'

Father Snow smiled.

'I think you'd manage.'

'You'd be pleased if I did, anyway,' she muttered, still looking downwards.

'Yes,' said Father Snow, wise enough at least not to fall into this simple trap. 'In a way, I would be pleased.'

262

Yet when she looked up at him, Father Snow suddenly felt he was in peril. The careful routine through which he'd controlled their relationship had been interrupted. Months of seeing her only in the Happy Eater had almost convinced him that the battle was won. Now he felt it beginning again, and knew that he would have to struggle to reassert control.

'It's funny,' she said. 'All my life I've wanted to get away from this place, and now I'm not so sure.'

Father Snow looked around him.

'Who could want to get away from here?'

'Oh, I know it's pretty, but that doesn't seem so important when you've grown up with it. I used to play up here all the time when I was a child. I hardly notice it all now. And I'm so sick of writing about village fêtes and local schoolboys winning swimming prizes. I want to do some real work.'

There was something charmingly childish about her grown-up ambitions. Even the way she was sitting, legs curled and weight on one arm, was somehow immature. It was hard to imagine her holding her own in the big bad world.

'In one way, I'd be sorry to see you go up to London. It would change you.'

From the way she was looking at him, Father Snow saw that she'd taken this as a declaration of affection. He coughed and looked away. Susan sighed.

'Have you seen anything of Gerald Pitman recently?'

'No. He's been to Mass up at Flamstead a couple of times, but that's all. I haven't spoken to him.'

'No gossip then?'

'Well, according to Trevellyan, there's going to be an election. Pitman told him they'd be making the official announcement this week.'

'This would be the ideal time to dig something up on him, then.'

'Why don't you just forget all that? Stay here writing

263

about your village fêtes. It's a pleasant, uncomplicated way of life.'

She shook her head.

'I need to get away. Perhaps I need to get away from you, as well.'

This time, although Father Snow couldn't say anything, he didn't look away.

'I never thought I had it in me to love anyone so much,' she said. 'Perhaps it's just because you're the perfect gentleman I've always dreamed of meeting. You really are gentle, too, though I know you wouldn't like to admit it yourself.'

'You're confusing the priest with the man,' said Father Snow.

'There's no difference. Only a man like you could have become a priest in the first place, and only you could be quite the kind of priest you are. And because you're a priest, we can't do anything about it, which makes it all much worse.'

This was true. Father Snow still believed that, if they'd been able to sleep with each other, all they felt would have evaporated in a matter of weeks, or even days. As it was, the fairy-tale period had been artificially extended and intensified.

'It seems like a long time,' he said, 'but it's only been a few months.'

'And you'll keep your promise to think about it all after a year?'

'Of course, but you'll have got over it by then. You'll meet somebody else. I'm surprised you haven't already.'

Susan shook her head.

'I can't even look at anybody else.'

She was sitting about a yard from him, but it suddenly struck Father Snow as dangerously close. He drew away a little, straightening his back and hardening his face into its old expression.

'We shouldn't be having this conversation.'

'But I need to have it. It's so difficult to talk in that horrible café. I need to tell you what I feel.'

'All right, you've told me, but it doesn't change anything. Nothing's going to change. You should just go and find somebody else, because I can't do anything for you.'

'There is one thing you could do,' she said, looking at him quite seriously. 'Pick me some flowers.'

'Don't be ridiculous.'

'Please.' She sounded almost desperate. 'I mean it. I'd really like you to.'

Father Snow was horrified. It seemed to him that, of all her generation, only Susan could have made such a romantically anachronistic request. Now she was staring at him as though everything hinged on his agreement. If he did it, all her girlish dreams would come true.

'No, I can't. It's silly.'

'Why? It's nothing to be ashamed of, it's certainly not a sin, and it would make me happy. Are you really too proud to do that?'

So Father Snow stood up. As he did so, he became aware of his surroundings again. The beams of light were flickering, the bluebells all bowing repeatedly in the same direction, as though worshipping some being hidden out of sight among the trees. In his old, upright way, he paced a few yards off, wading through the shallow blue. To pick the flowers, however, he had to bend down in an undignified act of homage. As he did so, he saw the windows of Flamstead in the far distance, a flashing beacon. By this time he was accustomed to pushing away the memory of that night, and did it now with an almost instinctive mental shrug. Whatever had happened was over. The village and his own life had returned to normal.

Yet when he returned to the present and found himself picking flowers, he wondered if things were quite so normal, after all. He had never felt so ridiculous in his life. Yet the bluebells seen close to were so alluring that after a few moments he forgot his embarrassment and began to enjoy the process of picking them. When he finally stood up, he had a bunch of about twelve in his hand. Then the breeze picked up again and for a moment he forgot himself entirely. The touch of it against his cheek was so soft that it was almost painful. The beams of light shifted slowly. The trees sighed with pleasure or regret. As he had before Susan's arrival, he wanted suddenly to embrace it all, to hold all that beauty which would not be held. If he'd been alone, he would no doubt have started praying again. As it was, he had to take Susan her little bunch of flowers.

When he turned and saw her, however, he was struck powerfully by the realisation that she was not an intrusion on the place, after all, but a part of it. There was something strangely natural about her sitting there surrounded by the blue flowers, something almost wild. Her hair stirred in time with the leaves and the light in the distance. She was looking up at him and smiling as though she understood what he was thinking.

For some reason, he didn't then return to his place at the foot of the tree. Instead he went and sat down in the bluebells himself, much closer to her. He had never had such a sense of being entirely alone with another human being. A bee meandered lazily past, not noticing them. All the yearning he felt focused itself on her, the part of all this which it was possible for him to embrace, which had been created for that purpose. Looking into her familiar face, he realised that the past was to be captured there, too. She was a part of his early weeks in the village, his visit to the British Museum and his discovery of the fairy tale.

As he handed her the flowers, he had a vague sense of taking part in some ancient ritual which he'd needed to see as ridiculous precisely because he feared its magic. Solemnly, as though she too were playing out a timeless role, Susan smelt the flowers and looked at him in silence over their heads. Then she lowered the bunch to her lap. He didn't know whether it was her face or his that

266

moved closer. There was a faint scent about her which overwhelmed him, a tiny dose of some narcotic that caused the eyes to close. At the same instant, their lips met. His tongue felt her teeth around it like a hard gate on the other side of which it found its twin waiting, soft and barely moving, stirring with the same sweet, unconscious rhythm as the petals and the leaves. Yet the touch of it seemed more than physical. There was a coming together on some higher level, the sort of contact that Father Snow had never really believed possible between two human beings. For the second time he understood that the spiritual world was more immediate and tangible than he'd imagined, and more mysterious. As he had been outside the laboratory with Vincent, he felt shaken and shocked. Susan's tongue pressed against his a little more firmly, suggesting a slight increase in confidence, and he suddenly felt that her entire personality was being revealed to him. That tiny movement communicated more effectively than any words her vulnerability, her shyness and the almost brash need that lay behind it. There was also, besides an overwhelming love for him, a kind of tentative respect that he felt would break his heart. All of it was there. In all those months of blurted words and embarrassed glances she had simply been pleading for the opportunity to express herself in this more direct and devastating way. Yet he knew that this contact, for all its power, was just a shadow of the union available to them. The desire for it glowed in him, gentler than lust. The breeze filled his ears and the light swooned across his eyelids.

When it was over, he barely recognised her face. Everything seemed to have been rearranged into a different kind of beauty, at once grave and surprised. Only when he saw her expression did he realise that his own personality had been communicated as powerfully as hers. He understood then that it is impossible to touch without being touched in turn, and that this is true not only of the body, but also of the soul.

'I love you,' she said.

Father Snow drew away and straightened his back, but he was shaking, full of love.

'I've got to go.'

'No! I mean –'

Then she just looked at him hopelessly. Father Snow saw that she felt hurt and rejected in spite of his fall. Like us all, she needed to believe the fantasy that in the end, when it came to the crunch, she was irresistible.

'I'm sorry.' He stood up. 'I don't know what came over me.'

He went and retrieved his book from the foot of the tree. When he turned around, she was still sitting there, the flowers in her lap, her enchantment broken.

'Can I still see you on Friday as usual?'

'Of course.'

For a moment, he paused, looking down at her with a mixture of admiration for her power and pity for its limits. Pleading with her eyes, she made one last desperate try.

'You can't just leave like this. At least stay for five minutes more.'

Father Snow shook his head.

'No. I'm going back now. Good luck with your interview.'

Ignoring this pleasantry, she stared up at him.

'What are you afraid of?'

'It's nothing to do with fear,' said Father Snow in his old, measured way. 'I'm a priest.'

Susan gave him an ironic look, as though to say that this had simply begged the question. Father Snow turned from her and began to walk giddily away through the flickering beams of sunshine, back down the hill towards the order and safety of the presbytery.

After that, he felt for the first time that his vocation might be under threat. The scene kept returning to his mind during the week, bringing with it an emotional and physical craving that drowned logic. All the old lies filled his head. He and Susan had been made for each other. What he felt for her would never disappear. She offered him a lifetime of happiness. If he could only be with her, even for a few minutes, the world would turn into an earthly paradise.

In his worst moments, it seemed to Father Snow that giving up the priesthood for her was nothing. He would gladly have laid down his life, his immortal soul.

Even now, however, he had moments of lucidity. He continued to fight as best he could. There was still a tiny shred of logic in him which knew that the mirage would disappear as soon as he allowed himself to chase after it. He would be left to years of dissatisfaction and regret. Yet he feared that in kissing her he'd taken some irrevocable step. A process had been set in train which he had no power to halt and which would lead inexorably to his fall. When the fall came, Father Snow knew that it would be total, all or nothing. Having slept with her, he would simply be unable to continue as a priest.

Again and again, he remembered how her face had looked magically changed at the end of their kiss. Each time in his imagination he said the words he'd been too strong or too cowardly to say in reality, the last words of enchantment. They were so sweet that he was often unable to resist mouthing them silently, savouring them. Then, opening his eyes and finding himself alone in the presbytery, he would be frantic at the idea that he couldn't see her now, immediately. At the same time, the remaining core of logic and strength, old Father Snow, would be full of disgust and despair.

All week, he waited for her to phone him. She didn't, and he realised how effective his display of strength had been. It would have to wait until Friday. Everything hinged around that. He felt certain that when he saw her again she would turn back into an ordinary girl, just another part of the humdrum, unenchanting world. Once the old routine had been restored, this brief madness would pass.

Yet Father Snow didn't eat or sleep much that week, nor did he go and talk the problem over with Ralph. Instead he went about his duties feeling like a fraud. When he walked to the altar to say Mass each morning, he was reminded of an adulterer creeping home to bed. In the midst of it all, he continued to fight, spending long hours on his knees before the God he'd almost betrayed.

By the time Friday came, however, he was unable to go on fighting. The knowledge that their meeting was so close left him unable to think, hardly able even to keep still, let alone pray. He was beside himself. The day seemed to pass at an unbearable crawl. When Flora had at last been and made his supper, he decided to set off at once. He would be early, of course. Instead of driving to the Happy Eater, it would be pleasant to walk up through the village, taking his time.

As he always did for these meetings, Father Snow took off his dog-collar and dressed in ordinary clothes. Outside, the air was almost mild. The sky was still clear. The stars were beginning to shine. Lights were on in most of the cottages, but there was hardly anyone around. As it had on Monday, the whole world seemed to be encouraging Father Snow to give in, to fall entirely in love. He walked slowly down the lane and over the bridge by the Old Mill. On his way across the twilit green, he stared up at the cluster of dim lights in the hills. There was an orange smudge above them where the sun had been, the glow of a fire reflected from smoke.

After forty minutes of very slow walking, he arrived at the café. He was still early. There was no sign of Susan. Father Snow chose a table facing the window and ordered coffee. Then he sat and watched the cars speeding down the A25. When he looked at his watch, he found that time, having dragged all week, had miraculously speeded up. Susan was ten minutes late.

He instinctively turned in the direction of the door, but there was no sign of her. It was the first time this had ever happened. If anything, she tended to be early for their meetings. He would arrive and find her there already, staring at one of the tasteless laminated menus. Now it seemed to him that her lateness had something to do with what had happened on Monday. She was doing it deliberately as a punishment for the way he'd left her sitting there with her bunch of flowers.

Turning back towards the road, Father Snow settled down to wait. As he did so, other explanations began passing through his mind. Susan was afraid of him. The strength of her feelings on Monday, combined with his power to walk away, had made her wary. By arriving late, she was proving her own independence. Or perhaps she'd given up on him at last. Perhaps by walking away he'd finally convinced her that the whole thing was hopeless. In that case, she wouldn't just arrive late. She wouldn't arrive at all.

The idea brought an unexpectedly sharp anguish. Aware of the impression he was making on the other customers and the waitresses, Father Snow sneaked a secret look at his watch. Now she was fifteen minutes late. Casually, he looked towards the door, hoping for the relief of seeing her come in, but there was still no sign of her.

After that, the pain grew until he was frantic, in a kind of panic. She'd met somebody else, somebody able and willing to give her what Father Snow could not. Now she was in his arms, all thoughts of Father Snow lost in selfish happiness, while he sat here alone in this unexpected desperation.

Once the suspicion had started, he couldn't drive it away. Time seemed to be measured by his surreptitious glances at the door. Each time, he expected the pain to stop. At each disappointment, fury rose in him, making him vow that he would never forgive her for this. He told himself that if she did arrive he would simply walk out, though he knew that in fact his anger would be far outweighed by happiness and relief. He tried to make himself feel glad

271

that she hadn't arrived. It was what he'd always wanted, after all. The whole thing was over. He could return to his normal life as a priest. The problem was that he no longer felt like a priest as he sat there and watched the traffic, wondering when it would next be safe to glance at the door. He was just a lover who'd been stood up.

In the end, after an eternal half hour, Father Snow gave up. As he got up from the table, he was filled with something which might almost have been called despair. It drained the strength from his limbs, so that he wanted just to sag back down into his seat and abandon the idea of doing anything.

Even as he walked towards the door, he was still hoping she would arrive. Then, on his way back through the village, he really began expecting to see her walk past arm in arm with another man. He peered around him, thinking he might catch them kissing in a gloomy corner. Yet there was no sign of her at all. As soon as he got back to the presbytery, too desperate by now to begin an internal battle on the rights and wrongs of the action, he rang her.

'What happened to you?'

'I had to work late. I –'

'Don't you ever do that to me again.' Father Snow felt his limbs begin to shake. 'Never, ever put me through that again.'

'I'm sorry.' She sounded offended, as though he were the one who should be apologising. 'I tried to ring you but you were out.'

This was plausible enough, since he'd left so early. His anger began to recede, but it only left more room for other, more painful feelings.

'Will you come next week?' he said.

'Of course.'

It wasn't enough. He needed to hear more. For a few moments he was silent, struggling with the last remnants of his pride. In the end, he said:

'Do you still feel the same as you did on Monday?'

Susan didn't answer at once. Father Snow felt himself sliding back into panic and despair. At last, the word came down the wire.

'Yes.'

It was said unwillingly, a grudging admission, but it was enough. The relief left Father Snow gasping. He closed his eyes, beyond embarrassment for once, hating himself.

'Thanks.'

'How have you been, anyway?' said Susan lightly. 'Have you had a good week?'

This was somehow like a mortal insult.

'Not bad,' he said, trying to match her tone. 'What about you? How did your interview go?'

Only now did Susan herself sound really unhappy.

'Don't ask.'

Father Snow's first thought was that, if she hadn't got the job, she wouldn't be leaving Wodden after all. He felt relieved, then dismayed at the extent of his relief.

'Well,' said Susan, 'I suppose I'd better . . .'

Desperately he cast around for a way of prolonging the conversation, of winning more assurances from her. Nothing came to him, so he just stood there in frantic silence.

'Goodbye, then,' said Susan, as though addressing a stupid child, showing by example the way conversations were supposed to be conducted.

'Goodbye.'

As he put the phone down, Father Snow realised that he was exhausted. He sank into the chair behind the desk and swivelled it so that he could look out into the darkness of the garden. For some time he went over what he'd felt that evening, the anguish of waiting and the despair of getting up to leave. In a way, it had been an echo from another night in his distant past, from childhood. Perhaps for a normal man simply being stood up like that wouldn't have been such a traumatic thing. He remembered Susan sitting in the flowers with her legs folded under her, looking up at him and asking what he was afraid of.

With an abrupt movement, Father Snow stood up and began to pace jerkily around the room, as though in a parody of his usual controlled movements. There was a look of horror on his face.

'No, no,' he muttered. 'No, no, no. That's got nothing to do with it. It doesn't work like that.'

He stopped, closed his eyes and took a deep breath, lowering his hands palm-down towards the floor as he did so. It was over. Things had gone too far. He'd been pushed to the edge of some chasm into which he didn't want to stare.

Now it really was over. The following week, he would be the one who didn't turn up. He would punish her for what she'd done to him, for understanding nothing, for being barely more than a child, for having power she had done nothing to deserve, for humiliating someone who was so much more knowledgeable and mature than her, so far above her in every way. No matter how cruel he had to be, he would drive her away from him as he had in the early days. No matter how she implored and beseeched him, no matter how softly she looked into his eyes and stroked his face, he would drive her away, and the more vicious she forced him to be, the more he would enjoy it. That was how he should have dealt with her all along.

When the doorbell rang, Father Snow managed to walk from the study with something like his old calm. But in the corridor he broke into a run, overcome with joy and relief. The danger into which he was careering didn't cross his mind. He had no idea what he would do when he saw her, and didn't care. All he wanted was an end to the anguish of being abandoned.

17

WHEN FATHER SNOW opened the door, he found Melanie Histon waiting there. The disappointment was so sudden and violent that at first he simply didn't believe his eyes. He couldn't take it in.

'Hello, Father,' she said. 'Are you all right?'

Only then did he really remember that he was supposed to be a priest, that certain things were expected of him. He thrust down the awkward lump of his disappointment.

'Of course, Melanie. I'm fine. Come in.'

As she stepped past him, he assumed once more the persona of Father Snow. This was something he now found he was able to do quite consciously and deliberately. He put on the expression, the posture and the calm certainty of voice almost as though they were not his own. It was like climbing into a suit of armour which forced him to move, and even to think, with a certain stiff precision.

The sitting-room was no longer charged with Father Conner's presence as it had once been. The newcomer had by that time made a few acquisitions of his own. The empty rectangle above the fireplace had been filled by a large Victorian print of Regent's Street, which reminded him both of history and of home. In the centre of the room he'd put a new coffee-table. On this was an ashtray for the use of visitors, beside which lay the neatly-folded newspaper he'd been unable to read that morning.

Melanie went and sat on the sofa, placing her bag on the floor at her feet. Father Snow sat in the armchair by the fire which he'd once been unable to use, looking on it as Father Conner's. Now it was his. He rarely thought about the dead priest these days.

'I've come to say goodbye,' said Melanie. 'I'm leaving Wodden tomorrow.'

Father Snow, for all his outward composure, was still numb. It took a moment for her words to sink in. When they did, he had to make an effort to focus his mind on the situation and produce the appropriate response.

'Oh. I'm very sorry to hear that, Melanie.'

She shrugged.

'Yes, it's a pity, but I just can't go on working in a place where I know I'm not appreciated or even wanted. People like me are outcasts wherever we go, I suppose, but it's even worse in a place like this. It's unbearable, in fact.'

This was the first reference to her sexuality she'd ever made outside the confessional. It was excruciatingly embarrassing to Father Snow. He gave a little cough.

'So you're going back to London.'

'Yes. At least there, where there's no community as such, you don't notice it so much. Everyone's an outcast there.'

'Yes,' said Father Snow. 'Perhaps they are.'

'Things haven't been going at all well with Bill, of course. He hasn't actually asked me to leave, but he's done his best to make my life a misery. And I know there's been a lot of gossip about me in the village. It's starting to make me paranoid. I think people are watching me all the time.'

At the mention of paranoia, the shade of Father Conner seemed to return for a moment to the room.

'I'm very sorry that you're leaving,' said Father Snow, 'but I can't help feeling it's for the best. There's no point staying in a place which is affecting you like that. As long as you realise it's the village that's at fault, not you.'

'It's not even so much the village, Father. It's Bill. He's the one who's turned them all against me. You've got

276

no idea how I hate that man. He's so bloody smug and hypocritical, so —'

Suddenly Melanie seemed to realise that these were not appropriate things to say to a priest. She shifted, changing her position on the sofa.

'Anyway, there's something else. This may be paranoia, too, but I've slowly come to believe that there's something unpleasant happening here. I haven't got the expertise to deal with it, certainly not with the amount of support I'm likely to get. Bill's reaction when I told him about it was the reason I finally decided to pack it all in.'

Melanie bent down and opened her bag. As he watched her, Father Snow had to struggle not to start thinking about Susan. He was a priest, a priest. It was his duty to focus on the business in hand, which might be important.

'This is rather unfair on you, Father, but you're the only person I can really trust. So I'm afraid I'm going to just dump the whole thing in your lap, as it were.'

When she straightened from her bag, Melanie was holding a thick sheaf of plain paper.

'What whole thing?'

'Well, let me begin at the beginning and see what you think. You'll probably tell me that I'm wrong, and I certainly hope I am.' She paused and closed her eyes, as though she had a long and complicated story to tell and wanted to collect her thoughts. At last she said: 'Some of the children in my class are still having nightmares about Flamstead House.'

As she spoke, Melanie opened her eyes to gauge his reaction. It seemed to disappoint her slightly that there was none. Father Snow's face remained as impassive as ever. But in his mind's eye, he saw himself running away from the laboratory and charging down the stairs, a scream behind his lips.

'I see,' he said. 'Go on.'

'I got them to do pictures of what they'd dreamed about. These are some of the results.'

With that, she opened the sheaf of papers and began laying them out on the coffee-table. The pictures were done in crayon. Each had the child's name written at the bottom, along with the number of the class. Not all the figures were immediately recognisable as giants. Some of them had the requisite long hair, boots and club. Others, though, might have been no more than children's drawings of grown-ups. In many of them, the children had represented themselves, little stick-figures in triangular skirts running away with their mouths open, waving their spindly arms.

Soon the coffee-table was full, the ashtray and newspaper invisible.

'Does anything strike you about any of these pictures?' asked Melanie when she'd finished laying them out.

Father Snow stared dutifully down at them.

'Not really.'

'All right. The next thing is that four or five of the girls in my class seem strangely anti-social and withdrawn. I noticed it when I first arrived last year, of course, but either it's been getting worse, or I've been getting more alert to it, because now it seems to me that there's something seriously wrong with them.'

'What connection could that have with their nightmares?'

'Wait. Just hear me out and tell me what you think. Last week I found two of these girls doing a striptease for some of the boys behind the bushes in the playground. And when I say a striptease, I don't just mean a quick jerk of the skirt. This was adult stuff, Father. Yet these girls are only eight years old.'

Remembering his own first visit to the school, Father Snow went rigid with embarrassment.

'So what?' he said. 'I still don't see the connection, I'm afraid.'

'Isn't it obvious? These so-called nightmares aren't nightmares at all.'

'What are they, then?'

Melanie leaned towards him with a strange agitation, her eyes shining.

'Memories,' she said.

'Of what?'

Before she could answer, the doorbell rang. Both their heads jerked in the direction of the sound. There was something guilty and conspiratorial about the silence that followed. Hope had quickened Father Snow's heart. This time, it would certainly be her. He'd only been through all those disappointments to make this moment more sweet. Then he remembered his visitor, and realised that he would have to send Susan away.

When he looked back at Melanie, he found she was staring towards the door with a kind of horror.

'Hang on,' he said, getting up. 'I'll just see who that is.'

A moment later he found himself face to face with Bill Saunders.

This time, Father Snow didn't have much time for disappointment. The headmaster, his thick lips smiling and glistening, was his usual over-friendly self.

'Father! Hope you don't mind me barging in on you like this, but I was wondering if I could have a quick word.'

Father Snow wasn't quite sure what he should do. He just stood there, blocking the doorway.

'Of course.'

'Well, do you mind if I come in?'

'It's a bit awkward, actually, Bill. I've got Melanie Histon here.'

The glistening smile lost a little of its warmth.

'So she's here already, is she? I had a funny feeling she might be.'

'Would you rather come back later?'

Saunders retrieved his geniality.

'Of course not, Father! There's nothing awkward about

it at all! Melanie and I are still the best of friends, in spite of our little differences.'

With great reluctance, Father Snow stood aside to let him pass. When they entered the sitting-room, Melanie didn't make a very good job of hiding her shock and dismay. She just stared up at Saunders from the sofa. The brightly-coloured pictures were still spread out before her on the coffee-table.

'Been having a little art class, have we?' said Saunders, as cheerful as ever. Neither of them spoke. 'Well?'

'Melanie's a bit worried, Bill. Some of the children in her class have been having strange nightmares. These are pictures of them.'

'And why should dear Melanie want to show them to you, I wonder?'

Father Snow glanced at her, then back at Saunders.

'She thinks they might not have been nightmares at all, but memories of some kind.'

'Ah yes! Melanie is a firm believer in the theory of repressed memory, which is so popular in the United States.' He turned to Father Snow and lowered his voice, as though the thing should remain confidential between them. 'The idea is, Father, that the brain records every single event of our lives. The records can never be destroyed, but they can be buried or reinterpreted. The incredible thing is that such an innocuous little fallacy should have led to such an enormous amount of suffering.' He turned back to Melanie, raising his voice again and forgetting for a moment to smile. 'Well, Miss Histon, am I right? You believe that a memory can be repressed, or partially buried so that it takes on the appearance of a dream?'

Melanie met his eyes for a moment, then looked away.

'And have you told Father Snow,' Saunders went on, 'just what you think the meaning of these dreams or memories is?'

There was silence. Saunders went on staring down at Melanie. He was smiling again now, but Father Snow saw his thin fingers twitching at his sides. Melanie didn't look at him. In the end, the priest felt he'd better intervene.

'No. She hasn't told me yet.'

'Oh, but she must! Go on, Melanie. Tell Father Snow what you told me last week.' There was silence. 'You had no hesitation then, did you? Oh no! In quite a state about it, you were, if I remember right. So tell us: these dreams are in fact memories of what?'

'Sexual abuse,' said Melanie quietly.

'Well, and aren't they always? Isn't it funny how every time a memory gets repressed it turns out to be one of sexual abuse. Hit a child as hard as you like, and he won't repress the memory. Pour boiling water over him, and he'll remember it for the rest of his life. But if you so much as unzip your trousers, the poor little mite goes into trauma and immediately represses the whole thing.'

There was silence. The headmaster's hands trembled. He was staring down at Melanie, who still refused to look at him.

'Why don't you sit down, Bill?'

'No, thank you, Father. The fact is that I don't feel very relaxed just at the moment. I think it's rather important that we all realise exactly what we're dealing with here. I want us to remember the thousands of families that have been torn apart by these ideas in America, daughters severing all relations with their parents because of these so-called memories of abuse uncovered on the psychoanalyst's couch, these imaginary monsters of the past. I want us to remember the insane allegations of Satanism which have destroyed communities in our own country. It only takes one person like Melanie, with a little too much enthusiasm, or perhaps a little too much ideology, to set that madness off. And once it's started, it can't be stopped. It devours everyone in its path with its baseless allegations. Just one person, that's all it takes. One little feminist down from London with her big ideas.'

Leaping up, Melanie snatched one of the pictures from

281

the coffee-table and brandished it in the headmaster's face so violently that he flinched away.

'What do you think that is?' she screamed, pointing at the picture. 'Go on, you tell me!'

'You know what it is as well as I do.'

She swung round and presented the picture to Father Snow. It was one of those which showed the giant chasing after a little girl. He had a club in his hand, held at waist level, rising up at an angle which made the phallic associations all too obvious.

'What do you think it's supposed to be, Father?'

'It's a giant's club,' said Saunders, 'such as you can see in any book of fairy tales.'

Melanie turned back towards him.

'This is one fairy tale that's just a little bit too convenient, Bill,' she said, spitting his name out as though it was something unpleasant she'd just brought up into her mouth. 'How strange that this place has to have a fairy tale all of its very own. How handy that it should be based around a real house.'

Father Snow coughed.

'Perhaps I should say that I've done a bit of research into this, and I do believe the legend of the Ogre Earl to have been based on a real person.'

Melanie swung back.

'And what did that person do?'

Father Snow avoided looking at either of them.

'He abused and murdered children.'

'There you are!' cried Melanie triumphantly.

'And when did he commit these crimes, Father?'

'In the sixteenth century.'

'Do you see any way in which that could possibly be connected to present-day abuse?'

Father Snow turned and gave Melanie an apologetic look.

'Of course not. What connection could there be?'

'Neither of you understand how child abusers work,'

said Melanie. 'Perhaps neither of you want to. But the fact is that they congregate together so that they can organise and protect each other. The legend itself would be enough to attract them to this village. That monster would be a hero to them. The house itself would be more or less a place of pilgrimage.'

'Don't you think somebody would have noticed?' said Saunders.

'Somebody just has, and look at the response she's got.' She turned back to Father Snow, speaking rapidly. 'These people are a society within society. They have their own information network, their own culture. Believe me, every one of them will have heard of Flamstead House. Now they're cleverly using the monstrosities of their great predecessor to cover up their own. If any of their victims should make an allegation connected with Flamstead, which would inevitably be garbled and unclear, they have only to point at the fairy tale.'

'There's just one flaw in your theory,' said Saunders quietly. 'It all rests on the absurd assumption that memories can be buried or distorted beyond all recognition. If that's true, then Father Snow and I could claim to be victims of abuse just as much as any of the children who drew those pictures. We're all potential victims. That's the real fairy tale.' He spread his hands as though to emphasise how calm and rational he was being. 'It's one of the most dangerous myths of our times.'

'They use drugs, like diazepam,' Melanie went on, addressing Father Snow as though Saunders hadn't spoken. 'If the dose is right, even an adult doesn't remember what happened to them, though they were completely conscious at the time. Imagine yourself as an eight-year-old child, drugged and carried off in the middle of the night to a house of which you were already terrified, where things were done to you that you simply didn't understand. If you did remember any of it the following morning, the only way of explaining it would be as a nightmare.'

She stopped, as though suddenly realising how loud her voice had sounded in the silent room. Turning towards Saunders and seeing his look of scornful disbelief, she sat back down on the sofa, obviously making an effort to appear more reasonable.

'I accept that I may be wrong,' she said, 'and I certainly hope I am. But none of us is in a position to ignore the facts. In my opinion, they merit further investigation.'

'Then I'm afraid to say it's just as well you're leaving us. If you were to stay here, there's no telling what damage you might do.'

Melanie didn't reply. Father Snow felt tired, buffeted into exhaustion by the feelings of the other two.

'Well,' said Saunders at last, 'you've said your piece, Melanie. You've done your worst. Now, if you don't mind, I'd like to have a word alone with Father Snow.'

Melanie hesitated, then looked imploringly towards the priest.

'Perhaps it would be better if you went, Melanie,' he said. 'I'll do my best to sort everything out.'

'All right.'

She bent to start collecting the pictures from the desk.

'Those pictures are school property,' said Saunders. 'I'd appreciate it if you left them here.'

So Melanie just picked up her bag and left. Father Snow went out to see her to the door. When he'd opened it, she stepped outside, then turned around.

'There's systematic child abuse going on in this village, Father. These people organise themselves like cells of terrorists, invisible to the casual eye. The latest evidence also suggests that the tendency to abuse is passed on genetically. That means it's probably endemic in a place like this. There's no telling how many centuries it's been going on, hidden quietly away.'

Seeing that Father Snow's face was still impassive, showing neither belief nor scepticism, she suddenly changed tack.

'I must admit,' she said, glancing towards the door of the sitting-room, 'that Bill's arguments seem very convincing. He's remarkably informed on this particular subject. And it's a strange coincidence, isn't it, that he happened to turn up just as I was going to tell you about it?'

Then she said it with her eyes: he's one of them.

'Goodbye, Melanie,' said Father Snow. 'And good luck.'

'You're the one who needs luck now, Father. I shouldn't really be walking out on it all like this, but, as I say, I wouldn't be able to achieve anything here. And I'm really coming to the conclusion that it might actually be dangerous for me to stay.'

As she walked away, Father Snow couldn't help thinking again about Father Conner, slipping from paranoia to insanity, and at last into despair.

When he went back into the sitting-room, it seemed full, as it had in the old days, of the dead priest's presence. Saunders had collected all the pictures from the coffee-table and was standing with them folded under his arm. His glistening lips were smiling again in their usual way.

'Those feminists!' he said when Father Snow came in. 'They still haven't forgiven us for the witch-hunts!'

He laughed. Father Snow sat down without even smiling.

'Don't tell me you believed any of that paranoid nonsense, Father?'

'Of course not, Bill. It's just rather shocking to see the sort of state people can work themselves up into, that's all. I think it all just came from the fact that Melanie never felt she belonged to the community here.'

'It's partly that,' said Saunders, taking Melanie's place on the sofa. 'Partly the bitterness of a departing employee who made a mess of her job. This is her last shot at us, her last attempt to land us all in it. Partly, too, it really is a witch-hunt. That's the level it's reached in America. The feminists are turning the tables. Some of the so-called victims over there make allegations against entire towns.'

Father Snow shook his head.

'Incredible.'

'In this particular place, of course, we also have to consider the political dimension. Gerald Pitman, a senior minister, is a close friend of Lord Trevellyan's. With the election campaign just starting, you see how potentially explosive the situation might be.'

'Indeed I do.'

'That's why I need to rely on your complete discretion, Father. Even if it were no more than a rumour, all this could be most damaging.'

'Don't worry, Bill. I'll keep it to myself.'

Saunders smiled.

'Good man!' After that, he became thoughtful for a while, a peculiar expression of distaste on his face. 'The unfortunate thing about Lord Trevellyan is that he has certain . . . eccentricities which might make such a preposterous story all the easier to believe. They also, I'm afraid, frighten the little ones. Fortunately, he's rarely seen in public, but I still can't help feeling that he could make more of an effort to at least appear normal. As it is, he actively seems to invite comparison with that ancestor of his.'

As he spoke, Father Snow remembered how Everard's chief delight had been in the terror of children. If Melanie's suspicions were correct, then that would be the explanation for Trevellyan's long hair and fingernails. Once he got his victims, drugged and confused, up into that huge house of which they were already so afraid, he would want to look like a real monster, to terrify them completely. He would set them loose and hunt them down through the acres of empty corridors, lumbering after them with his long white hair flowing behind him and his fingers hooked like claws, bellowing and snarling as he came.

'Well, I can only speak from my own experience,' said

Father Snow reasonably, 'and I've always found him the most charming of men. A good host, and a good Catholic, too, come to that.'

But he was thinking about Melanie's claim that the tendency to abuse was in the genes. He remembered how he'd surprised Trevellyan looking up at the picture of Everard and laughing.

'I'm sorry you've got sucked into all this, Father.' Saunders stood up to leave. 'I'm very glad, though, that you've taken it all so sensibly.'

'Not at all, Bill. If you need my help in any way, don't hesitate to get in touch.'

At the door, Saunders paused and looked around the sitting-room.

'I had a feeling she might come here. She always spoke so highly of you.' He gave a broad smile. 'But then, everybody does.'

As soon as he'd gone, Father Snow went through to the study and rang Susan again. She didn't sound particularly pleased to hear his voice, but his head was now so full of other things that he hardly felt hurt at all. It was as though he'd got over her already.

'There's something I want to ask you,' he said.

'Fire away.'

'Have you ever heard any rumours of child abuse going on in Wodden?'

'Why do you ask?'

'Just tell me. I'll explain next time I see you.'

'I did hear something actually, about a year ago. It was a girl called Jackie who used to be in the year above me at school. I didn't know her personally, but a friend of mine told me about it. I can't really remember the details, but basically she was in therapy because she'd been abused by her father.'

'Is she still in Wodden?'

'No, she's living in London. I seem to remember

that part of her treatment involved not coming back here.'

'Did she always remember the abuse, or did it only come back to her when she went into therapy?'

'How should I know? We only had a quick gossip about it in the pub one evening.'

'So you don't know her father's name?'

'Only his surname, which was Dugdale.'

Father Snow sat down.

'Hello? Are you still there?'

'Yes, I'm here.'

'So what's it all about?'

Amazingly, he felt once more the desire to punish her for what she'd done to him that evening.

'I'll tell you when I see you next week,' he said coldly.

'Can't you tell me now?'

'No.'

When he'd put the phone down, Father Snow returned to his place in the living-room. Flora had never mentioned having a daughter. He would have thought she was the type to go on about her children, to show you photographs of them and tell you what they were doing. Yet perhaps the fact that she hadn't done so was simply due to his own failure to become friends with her. It might be nothing more sinister than that.

The room still seemed charged with energy left by Melanie and Saunders. Closing his eyes, Father Snow prayed for the strength to find out what was happening and deal with it as a good priest should. In the end, he realised that he had to talk it all over with someone who was not directly involved. Since he could only be completely open about such matters with a fellow priest, he decided to go and see Ralph.

All the way there, he turned it over in his mind. At the same time he found himself thinking about Susan and the echoes she had awoken from his childhood. In the end, self-analysis became confused with the problems of the village, nostalgia changing places with history. He saw Everard's crimes as a trauma from the childhood of the place which somehow continued to have an effect now in its adulthood, in the world of computers, cars and televisions.

Ralph seemed pleased to see him. When he opened the door of the presbytery, his red face broke into a smile.

'Julian!'

Although he knew that the pleasure was probably affected, Father Snow was ashamed that he couldn't return it. He couldn't even bring himself to pretend.

'I hope I'm not disturbing you.'

'Don't be a fool. Come in.'

As Father Snow walked past him, Ralph slapped his back. It was what he always did these days. Since Vincent's visit, Father Snow had felt that they were like two feuding children who'd been ordered to make up by their teacher and were now forced to pretend a friendship they didn't really feel.

The large, empty front room was as depressing as ever. Father Snow wondered how Ralph stood it all alone. Then it struck him that visitors to his own presbytery probably had the same feeling when they saw the shabby armchairs, the photocopier in the hall. That was the problem with visiting Ralph. The older priest was a mirror that revealed too much. Perhaps it was partly this that held Father Snow back from liking him.

Following the usual routine, they sat at the table. Ralph produced a glass for Father Snow and began to pour whisky into it.

'Say when.'

'When,' said Father Snow immediately.

Ralph rolled his eyes, but he was smiling.

'Pushing the boat out tonight, I see.' He sat down and took a swig. Father Snow sipped politely. 'So, how are you, you miserable old bugger?'

'Well, I've had rather a disturbing evening, actually,

289

Ralph. I was hoping you might be able to give me some advice.'

'It must be bad, if you've been driven to ask the old soak for help.' He put on a posh voice. 'Tell on, dear boy. Pour out your troubles to old uncle Ralph.'

So Father Snow told him about the visit from Melanie and the intervention of Bill Saunders. As he listened, Ralph began to frown, which made his widow's peak look even lower and more exaggerated than ever. Father Snow noticed that his bulbous nose was full of little black holes, like a red rubber which had been kneaded into a strange shape then repeatedly stabbed with a biro.

'So,' said Father Snow when he'd finished. 'What do you think?'

'Sounds like nonsense to me,' said Ralph, his face still serious. 'Dangerous nonsense, mind, but nonsense nonetheless.'

'What do you think I should do, then?'

'What can you do, when all you've got to go on is a few dreams and some dodgy psychological theory? Just sit tight and see what happens. I certainly wouldn't tell anyone else about it. The chances are that the poor girl's simply nuts.'

Father Snow nodded.

'I think you're probably right.'

With a sigh, Ralph leaned back in his chair.

'It reminds me of the crackpot story poor old Charles came out with just before his death.'

Then Father Snow realised that he was once more playing out a scene from his predecessor's life. Father Conner, too, had come round here and poured out his story to Ralph. He had probably sat at this table with a drink in front of him, just as Father Snow was doing.

'He didn't actually mention child abuse, though?'

'No, I don't think so. But, to be honest with you, he was barely making sense.' Ralph smiled. 'Something tells me you won't be going that way.'

'I sincerely hope not.'

Picking up the bottle from his side, Ralph leaned forwards across the table.

'Top up?'

Without thinking, Father Snow covered his glass.

'No, thank you.'

Ralph sagged back in his chair, looking at him with a strange smile.

'When will you ever unbend?'

'What do you mean?'

'You know perfectly well what I mean. In these past few months I've done everything I could to make you relax, to be friends with you. I'm starting to think that it's hopeless.'

Father Snow's back stiffened and he began to blush. At the same time, he wanted to apologise to Ralph, not for anything in particular, but just for the way he was. Of course, this was impossible. The best he could do was to purse his lips and nod his head regretfully, as though lamenting some minor misfortune over which he'd had no control.

'You're a funny chap, Julian,' said Ralph, watching him. 'The strange thing is that I've grown to like you. Don't ask me why.' There was an unbearable pause. 'You don't believe that, do you?'

By this time, Father Snow's embarrassment had taken him beyond the point where he was able to speak. All he could do in answer was to jerk his shoulders. Ralph laughed.

'Ah, well! I'm sure we will be friends, in the end. I know we will.'

There was another silence. Father Snow was desperate to escape, but didn't see how it was to be done. In the end, he resorted to the rather obvious trick of looking at his watch.

'I think I'd better be off, Ralph.'

Again, Ralph laughed, and this time it did seem almost affectionate.

'All right, Julian! You –' He stopped and shook his head, as though realising it was hopeless. 'Come on, I'll show you out.'

As Father Snow drove away, Ralph stood on the door-step and raised his fist as he had done on the night of their first meeting.

'Fly like the wind!'

To his own surprise, Father Snow wiggled the wheel so that the 2CV rocked from side to side.

That night, he lay awake for a long time, staring up at the sky through the window and wondering. It reminded him of how he'd awoken in the early hours to find Vincent still standing there, gazing upwards. He remembered the hands going up in the classroom. He wondered about Trevellyan and Pitman, about Jack Dugdale hunched in his dressing-gown in front of the TV. Behind it all, so huge that those other figures in his imagination crawled like insects before it, was Everard's sneering face, knowing and sardonic. Again he remembered the terror in which he'd run away, out into the snow.

As he drifted towards sleep, in spite of all that had happened, his thoughts managed to return in their usual way to Susan. He began to develop a complicated fantasy in which she was offered the job in London, but turned it down to stay near him, even though he'd made it clear that he would never leave the priesthood for her. Her love for him was such that she gave up everything just to stay in the village and spend the rest of her life watching him from afar, content with no more than their weekly meetings. She would never abandon him. In the midst of it, though, he remembered how she'd stood him up that night. The despair of it came back, so that it seemed to him that there is only one kind of sorrow, which is the sorrow of separation.

Then his eyes opened of their own accord and fixed themselves on the drawer in the desk which he hadn't opened since his transfer to the village. For a long time he stared at it through the gloom. Some sentimental part of him wanted to open it and look at the photograph inside. He even imagined himself standing the picture up on the desk so that it would be watching over him as he slept.

Assuming the cold expression of Father Snow, he turned towards the wall and closed his eyes. Only when he'd been lying like that for some minutes did he unclench his fists.

18

EVERYTHING BECAME IMMEDIATELY clear to Father Snow when he woke up. Melanie's suspicions were absurd. It was pointless to waste time thinking about them. As for the other events of the previous day, he felt nothing but shame and disgust. He'd allowed Susan to humiliate him. Remembering how he'd leaned across and kissed her among the bluebells and the shafts of sunshine, he was sickened.

That day, he did his best to bring himself back under his old iron discipline. Since it was a Saturday, he had to hear confessions. Then he returned to the presbytery and spent the rest of the morning in spiritual reading and prayer. Yet it wasn't easy. The anguish of the day before slowly grew in him again, the longing to get in touch with her and find out exactly what she felt. The good weather didn't help. The sunshine in the garden was a constant temptation to go outside and just sit there thinking about her.

Father Snow resisted for as long as he could. Then, in the afternoon, when it had simply become impossible to read or pray any longer, he went for a walk through the village. The papers outside the newsagent's were full of the election. Stickers supporting the Conservatives had appeared in the windows of the pretty cottages. Father Snow walked around for an hour, but he didn't see Susan. He was tormented by the idea that she was doing something else, not thinking about him.

Back at the presbytery, he switched on the television

in the hope of distraction and was immediately presented with the sight of Gerald Pitman in an exquisite suit walking down the steps of number ten. A bristling thicket of reporters crowded behind a barrier across the road, shouting and taking photographs. The camera lingered on them as though they were as much a part of the news as the minister himself. After hesitating for a moment Pitman walked smoothly towards them. He did it without smiling, with such condescension that Father Snow was surprised the journalists didn't just pack up their kit and leave.

'Are you worried by the latest polls, Mr Pitman?'

Pitman's face filled the screen. Father Snow was amazed, unable to accept that this was a person he'd actually met. He spoke with complete self-assurance, apparently in no doubt that his words were significant and original. The reporters fell silent as they listened, but their cameras went on clicking, as though this were an involuntary noise that they were unable to suppress.

'I've never set too much store by the polls. There's only one poll that counts, and it's some time away yet. The British people aren't stupid. They realise that Labour in government would be an economic disaster. When the time comes to decide, I have every confidence that they'll make the right choice.'

As soon as he turned around, commotion broke out. The reporters shouted after him with that particular frenzy which only comes over them at election time. Ignoring them completely, Pitman got into the Daimler and swept away.

For the first time since he'd woken up that morning, Father Snow began to wonder about Melanie's accusations.

When Flora came round that evening, he went out into the kitchen to talk to her. She was at the sink, peeling potatoes, and the sight of her working for him like that made him feel guilty.

'How are you today, Flora?'

She glanced over her shoulder at him, perhaps surprised by this uncharacteristic attempt to start a conversation.

'Oh, not too bad, thanks, Father.' She shook the excess water from a potato, expertly cut it in half, and put it in the saucepan on the draining-board. 'A bit tired.'

'And how's Jack been?'

She shook her head, staring down into the sink. Her hands were slightly coarse and reddish, middle-aged hands which had been overworked. It was impossible to say what they, or she herself, might have been like in youth. Looking at her face now, Father Snow didn't have the imagination to strip away the double chin, the looseness and wrinkles, the peculiar glasses.

'Not well,' she said. 'I don't know how long he's got left.'

This called for a moment's sympathetic silence.

'You've never told me what he did before he retired.'

'He was a mechanic when we met. Used to work on the buses over in Dorking. He didn't really enjoy it, though. He was always a bit of a gardener, so in the end he got a job as a groundsman, up at Flamstead House. He carried on with that until it got too much for him.'

Father Snow was silent for a moment, digesting the implications of what she'd said, thinking about Trevellyan, Pitman and the election. He watched Flora carefully as he asked his next question.

'And you never had children?'

She shook, cut and dropped another potato.

'Yes, we had a daughter. She lives up in London now.'

If Father Snow hadn't been looking for it, he would have heard nothing strange in this. As it was, he sensed a certain tension in her voice, though there could have been any number of reasons for that. He hesitated, wanting to ask more, yet reluctant to upset her. In the end, he said:

'I think it's time I had another word with Jack.'

Flora stopped peeling, lowering her hands so that her

shoulders sagged, and turned towards him. There was relief and gratitude on her face.

'Would you, Father Snow? I've been meaning to ask you, but I wasn't sure. I still think you might be able to bring him round.'

'Well, I don't know about that, but I'll have a try.'

'You can come back with me tonight after supper, if you like.'

'If you don't mind, Flora, I'd rather go and see him alone. I think that when you're there, he feels he's got to keep up appearances, as it were. After years of telling you how much he hates religion, it would be difficult for him to suddenly backtrack before your very eyes. You see what I mean?'

Flora nodded.

'You're quite right. When do you want to go?'

'I might as well go now, if that's all right with you.'

In answer, she dried her hands on a teatowel, went to the kitchen table and started rummaging around in her large leather handbag.

'I'd better give you the keys. He has problems getting to the door.'

When he'd taken the keys, Father Snow paused for a moment, looking at her.

'Flora . . . is there anything you feel you should tell me about your husband before I go?'

'No, Father. Why should there be?'

Father Snow shrugged.

'I just don't see why he should have such a violent hatred of the Church.'

With an abrupt movement, Flora turned and went back to the sink. She picked up a potato and begun to peel.

'Oh, people get these ideas, you know.'

It took Father Snow fifteen minutes to walk to the Dugdales' house. Wodden seemed to be making a special effort to appear innocent and picturesque that evening. The sun was just setting as he left. A few pink clouds hovered above the trees on the horizon, above the twinkling lights of Flamstead, as though reluctant to be on their way. Dusk poured through the village below, flooding the gardens and the narrow lanes.

Using the key Flora had given him, Father Snow quietly let himself into the Dugdales' house. As soon as he did so, he heard the sound of the television.

'Mr Dugdale!'

There was no answer; he had it on too loud. Father Snow walked down the corridor and called his name again, knocking this time on the sitting-room door.

'Who is it?'

The priest opened the door and stepped inside.

'Father Snow.'

The first thing to hit him, as before, was the heat of the invalid's room. Although there was no fire in the grate this time, the radiators must still have been on. Dugdale was sitting on the settee, bent over, wearing his dressing-gown and tartan slippers.

'What the bloody hell do you want? Who gave you the right to come barging in here?'

'Could you turn the television off, please?' said Father Snow, raising his voice above a gust of canned laughter.

Pulling a face, Dugdale groped for the remote-control. He didn't turn it off, however. That would have been too much of a concession. All he did was to turn the sound down. The pictures would still be there, something for him to stare at, an escape from the room if he found himself cornered.

'No,' said Father Snow. 'Turn it right off. I won't be here for very long.'

After glaring up at him for a moment, Dugdale complied. Father Snow was slightly heartened. He seemed more reasonable than he had been when they'd last met. Perhaps he'd finally accepted that he was approaching death.

298

'Now, tell me what you're bloody doing here.'

'May I sit down?'

'Can't stop you, can I?' This seemed to open a well of self-pity in him. As Father Snow sat down, he whined: 'How can I stop you, when I don't have me strength any more? It's not right, your coming round here like this and pestering a sick old man.'

'I'm not pestering you. I only want a chat.'

'That's what disgusts me about you people,' spat Dugdale, suddenly converting his self-pity into venom. 'You act all friendly, but all you want is to stuff us up with your religion.'

'What greater act of friendship could there be than that?'

'Listen to you!' He gave a thin but unpleasant laugh. 'Just listen to yourself!'

'I'd like to hear your confession, Mr Dugdale, if you'll let me.'

'Bugger off.'

'This could be your last opportunity. A few minutes, and it would be done. You may be dead next week. You may be dead in an hour.'

'Charming!'

'I haven't come round here to make you feel better by telling you lies. I've come to save your soul.'

Again he laughed, but briefly.

'There's no such thing.'

'There is,' said Father Snow, allowing his face and voice to express uncompromising certainty. 'And you know that there is.'

'Look, we went through all this last time. I told you then that I wasn't interested, and I'm telling you again now. How many times will you have to hear it before you finally leave me in peace?'

'Peace is what I'm offering you.'

Father Snow stared at the wasted man in his dressing-gown, praying for the power to be able to love him.

Everything he saw, from the small eyes to the thickly veined hands, made this more difficult. Eventually, he leaned back in his chair.

'All right, then. Tell me about your daughter.'

Dugdale flared up.

'What bloody right have you got to go poking around in my family? It's none of your business.'

'Do you see her often?'

'Often enough.'

'Do you get on well?'

The old man seemed to dwindle back into the sofa. His voice fell.

'She's barmy. Goes to see some bloody shrink who fills her head with mad ideas.'

Father Snow nodded, watching carefully.

'Yes, I've heard about that. A friend of hers told me everything.'

Dugdale's head jerked round.

'What do you mean?' Father Snow just sat and stared at him in silence. 'It's not true. None of it. I loved that girl more than my own life, and now she goes and stabs me in the back like this.'

'I'm not accusing you.' Father Snow leaned forwards. 'But be certain about one thing: if what I heard was true, then you're going to hell.'

Dugdale was silent, so Father Snow went on, pushing home his advantage.

'I've heard the allegations about you. Nothing you have to confess could be worse than that, so why not just do it? You have to understand that hell is a choice, Mr Dugdale. God doesn't send you there, you send yourself. This is your opportunity to choose.'

For a moment, the old man seemed to waver. His eyes wandered in the direction of the television, but there was no comfort there. Then suddenly his head snapped round. His eyes stared straight into Father Snow's. There was a leer on his face.

'I'd rather go to hell,' he said, 'than get down on my knees to you.'

As he spoke, the barriers came down. The last pretence of civilisation between them was gone. All Father Snow could feel before him was naked hatred and scorn. It reminded him of the moment when he'd turned and fled from the laboratory.

'With those words, you damn yourself forever.'

'Good,' said Dugdale. He laughed. 'Good!'

'If you won't confess to me as a priest, then just tell me man to man. Did you abuse your daughter?'

Something seemed to die in Dugdale. He retreated back into his sofa, just a grumpy invalid again.

'I told you, all that is rubbish. It's rubbish that's been put into her head.'

There was silence. Father Snow looked at the dying man in his misery. Dugdale himself was staring at his knees.

'You want it so much, don't you?' said Father Snow.

'What?'

'Confession.'

Dugdale snorted.

'I don't want it, and I'll tell you why: I know about priests. You're no better than the rest of us. If anything, you're worse. You're the ones who really do abuse children, then cover it up. Aren't you, eh? Aren't you?'

'Nobody is more tempted than a priest.'

This delighted Dugdale. He gave an ecstatic, wheezing laugh, leaning back and slapping his knee.

'That's rich! What an excuse!' Abruptly, he stopped laughing and glowered. 'Bunch of pompous bastards.'

Father Snow stood up.

'You can call me any time,' he said. 'If you ever change your mind, I'll drop everything and come round here.'

In spite of himself, Dugdale was slightly embarrassed by this. He gave a little nod which might have been taken as one of thanks, but remained silent.

'I'll pray for you,' said Father Snow.

'Keep it, mate. I can look after myself. I know about priests.'

'Goodbye, Mr Dugdale.'

Father Snow left the room and walked down the corridor. Closing the front door behind him, he went down the garden path in the mild evening air. Then, when he was opening the gate, he heard, across all that distance, through the curtains and closed windows, a bellow of hatred which couldn't have come from any normal invalid. It was an ogre's roar.

'I know about priests!'

Back at the presbytery, Father Snow found Flora sitting with her elbows on the kitchen table and her head in her hands. As he entered the room, she looked up. She was crying. Her glasses were on the table in front of her. Father Snow had never seen her without them on. It made her face look younger, yet strangely sheepish. Everything else in the room was as he'd left it, the potatoes lying half-peeled in the sink.

'Well?' she said. 'Did he . . . ?'

Standing upright at the door, his mouth set in an uncompromising line, Father Snow shook his head. Flora's face twisted and she hid it once more in her hands. The priest just stood there in silence, watching her sob. Eventually, she spoke in a muffled voice, without lifting her head towards him.

'Will you hear my confession?'

Father Snow took his stole from his pocket, draped it around his neck and sat down at the head of the table. Moving slowly and stiffly, as though she'd just run a marathon, Flora knelt on the tiles and placed her thick red elbows on the table.

'Bless me, Father, for I have sinned. It's been a month since my last confession.'

There was a long silence. Father Snow wasn't looking

at her now. He was staring across the room without seeing anything.

'My husband's a bad man, Father.' He could hear how difficult it was for her to produce the words, as though she were forcing stones up through her gullet. 'I didn't realise how bad until it was too late. Even then, I should have done something.'

'In what way is he bad?'

To his shock, Flora wailed. The noise was so horrible that it sent an involuntary shudder through Father Snow's body. Then Flora was silent, staring blankly down at the table as though the discovery that she was capable of producing such a sound had sent her into shock.

'Well?'

'He did things . . .' she said softly. She swallowed and closed her eyes. 'To our daughter.'

After that, she began to sob heavily, causing the table to tremble beneath her. Father Snow clenched his jaw and stared at the sink.

'And you didn't know about it?'

'I worked as a nurse in those days. It used to happen when I was on night shift. I didn't find out until Jackie had grown up and gone to London. One day she rang me and told me about it all.' Once more, her voice rose to a wail. 'She said I must have known about it, that I must have been involved. She said she never wanted to see me again.'

After that, realising that she was beyond speech, Father Snow let her sob for a few moments. Quite soon, though, his mercy ran out.

'So then you confronted Jack with it?'

Flora brought herself under some kind of control.

'Yes.'

'And what did he say?'

'In the end he admitted it, but he said there was nothing I could do. There was a whole group of them in the village.'

303

'Did he tell you who the other members were?'

'No. But he said that if I tried to expose him, they'd find a way of dealing with me. He said they had very important friends. The one name he did give me was obviously a lie.'

'Who was it?'

Flora shook her head.

'It wasn't true, Father. I know it wasn't true.'

Father Snow decided to let it go. Flora was supposed to be confessing for herself, not anybody else. Now she was staring down at her interlaced fingers, her face covered in tears. His expression only hardened still further. He was full of a remorseless fury.

'You should have taken action.'

'I know, Father, but what could I do? Jack was already old and ill by that time. It seemed pointless to hound him. I thought the best I could do was try and bring him back to the Church.'

Father Snow's mouth twisted with revulsion.

'You were afraid of scandal.'

Flora started to sob more violently than ever.

'I knew I wasn't strong enough, Father. That's why I took this job. I wanted to try and be a good person.'

'Being good isn't just a matter of belief. It requires action. There's no telling how much suffering you've caused by doing nothing.'

Flora gasped as though he'd stabbed her.

'I'm so sorry,' she cried. 'You can't know how sorry I am. This has ruined my life.'

At last Father Snow softened.

'You're not a saint, Flora, but few of us are. You've laboured under this burden for a long time, but in a few moments it's going to be removed. Remember what we say in Mass: only say the word, and I shall be healed. When God has said the word through me, your soul will be healed even of this unbearable wound.'

Flora sobbed so hard that it sounded as if she was trying to be sick.

'Your penance is to make things up with your daughter. Explain everything to her as you have to me.'

She rolled her head like someone trying to awaken from a nightmare.

'She won't even talk to me.'

'Then keep trying. Go to her house and wait there until she agrees to see you. Go to her with humility and she'll eventually come round.'

'I'll try.'

'You're a good woman, Flora, and you've made a good confession. Bow your head now while I give you absolution.'

When it was over, Flora stood up, taking the deep breaths which come after tears. She dried her eyes and put her glasses back on, so that she was suddenly once more the homely middle-aged lady who'd greeted Father Snow on his arrival in the village.

'I haven't made your supper, Father,' she said, looking across at the sink. 'Haven't even finished the spuds.'

'Don't worry about that tonight, Flora,' said Father Snow, meticulously folding his stole and putting it in his pocket. 'You've done more than enough for one night.'

She turned and looked down at him, imploring. Father Snow realised that she was looking at him now no longer as a priest but as a man. The priest had given his forgiveness. Now she needed the man to do the same thing. She needed also the human sympathy and warmth which Father Snow was incapable of giving.

He stiffened under her gaze, not knowing what to do. After a moment, he stood up so that his chair scraped loudly against the tiles. Then, to his own surprise, he found a formula.

'You can cook me an extra big meal tomorrow.'

Flora looked away as though embarrassed.

'Yes, I'll do that.' When she looked back, the tears were

rolling down her cheeks again, and this was something he could only cope with in the context of confession. 'Thank you so much, Father.'

Then she just stood there, wanting some other sign, but Father Snow had reached his limit.

'Go home now,' he said. 'Tell Jack about what's happened. Who knows? It may even be an inspiration to him.'

'All right.'

She picked up her bag. Showing his warmth and forgiveness in the only way he could, Father Snow walked with her to the front door and politely opened it for her.

'Tell Jack that I know what's going on in this village,' he said before she left. 'I knew before tonight. Tell him that from now on none of his important friends are safe.'

The truth was, however, that Father Snow had no idea what he was going to do. There was only one proven case of child abuse in Wodden, and his evidence for that couldn't be repeated. The rest, as Ralph had said, was still just nightmares and a dubious psychological theory. Even now it was possible that the whole thing was simply paranoia. If he acted without proof, the consequences might be disastrous, not only for the families who got sucked into the witch-hunt, but also for himself and the Church.

All evening, he thought about it, praying for guidance. Although he wanted to pace frantically from room to room, he forced himself to be still, to remain in control. Once he went out into the garden and stared up at the lights in the hills, wondering what would happen when he went to say Mass there the following day. He wondered, too, about that one name Jack had given his wife, the allegation she'd been unable to believe.

The result was that he didn't think about Susan all evening. At two in the morning, however, just as he was at last dropping off to sleep, the doorbell rang.

306

Father Snow himself was surprised at the frantic speed with which he leapt out of bed and pulled his trousers on. He saw that the anguish Susan produced in him hadn't gone away. All he'd done was ignore it for a few hours. Now that her own feelings had driven her round here in the middle of the night, he was desperate to get downstairs before she changed her mind. He felt sure he only needed one conversation with her for everything to go back to normal.

Buttoning his shirt as he went, Father Snow ran downstairs. When he opened the door, he found a large man in a black uniform. As he peered through the gloom, his first thought was that it was a policeman come to report some terrible tragedy. Then he saw that the man wasn't a policeman at all, but a chauffeur.

'Sorry to disturb you so late at night, Father,' he said, not sounding in the least bit sorry. 'Gerald Pitman wants to see you.'

Father Snow remained calm.

'What about?'

The chauffeur shrugged his big shoulders and lowered the corners of his mouth regretfully, as though to say that these things weren't for the likes of him or Father Snow to know.

'And what if I don't want to see him?'

This idea seemed to amuse the chauffeur. He raised an eyebrow.

'I think you'd better come, Father.' There was quiet satisfaction in the man's voice, the pleasure of borrowed power. He was obviously in no doubt that being Gerald Pitman's chauffeur put him far above Father Snow in the scheme of things. 'You'd better be quick, as well. We're running to a very tight schedule tonight.'

'Wait there,' said Father Snow, and closed the door in his face.

Deliberately taking his time, he went back upstairs and dressed in his dog-collar, stock and black jacket. Then he went into the bathroom and combed his hair into its usual perfect parting. He still felt strangely calm.

Downstairs, he found the chauffeur pacing agitatedly in front of the presbytery. Hearing Father Snow close the door behind him, he stopped and turned around. Father Snow walked slowly towards him, taking his time. The chauffeur seemed about to tell him to hurry up, but changed his mind when he saw Father Snow's expression. At the priest's pace, they strolled into the lane.

There they found a black Daimler waiting, its engine running. The chauffeur opened the back door for Father Snow. Then, finally able to move at his own speed, he ran round to the front and leapt in. The car sped away so that Father Snow was thrown back in his seat. Trees and houses flashed in the headlights. By the time he'd recovered from the shock of the acceleration, they were already crossing the bridge by the Old Mill.

'Slow down,' he said. 'This is a built-up area. The speed limit is thirty miles an hour.'

The chauffeur laughed.

'Sorry, Father, but as I say we're running rather tight tonight. Mr Pitman changed his schedule at the last minute to come down here.'

'When I lay down my life,' said Father Snow sourly, 'it's going to be for something more meaningful than Mr Pitman's schedule.'

'Don't worry, Father. I know what I'm doing.'

After that, Father Snow fell silent and stared out of the window. There was something unreal about the drive. They seemed to sweep across the deserted green, along the High Street and up onto the A25 in a matter of seconds, as though the point of the whole exercise had been to demonstrate what a small and insignificant place the village really was. Then they screeched through the gates of Flamstead, so that Father Snow was thrown against the door, and began to hurtle uphill through the park. He suddenly felt trapped and powerless, as though he'd been kidnapped.

The car rose and fell with the undulations of the ground, so that Father Snow began to worry he might be sick. In a few moments Flamstead was growing ahead of them, filling the windscreen. Another Daimler and a Range Rover were parked in front of the building. Four tall windows were lit on the first floor, but the rest of the huge house was dark.

Bringing the car to a halt so abrupt that it seemed intentionally rude, the chauffeur leapt out and ran round again to open the door for Father Snow. Then he walked rapidly towards the house. Following more slowly, Father Snow looked up at the four lighted windows, then at the stars. They seemed closer from up here, only just out of reach in the mild air. He remembered standing side by side with Vincent on that night long before, when they'd looked out across the snow and prayed for strength before entering the building. This time, he had to pray alone.

When he lowered his gaze, he saw that the chauffeur had reached the door and was ringing its ordinary little plastic bell. It was opened immediately, as though someone had been waiting for that sole purpose, and the chauffeur began to walk slowly back towards his car. There was an expression of relief on his face; the burden had been passed on. He didn't look at Father Snow.

As he approached the building, Father Snow saw a fox standing in the moonlight of the seventeenth-century courtyard, staring at him. Their eyes met for a moment. Then the fox turned and trotted calmly away through the enormous wooden doors which led to the Tudor part of the house.

Only when he turned to face the door did Father Snow see who had opened it. It was the smart young man who had sat next to Pitman on the day Vincent had lunch at Flamstead. Like the chauffeur, he seemed to have an air of urgency and the complacency of reflected power. Yet he seemed to wear it all with a slightly ironic air, as though keen to show that he was aware of the impression he made.

Father Snow realised that he was an apprentice Pitman, working for the master while he learnt the ropes.

'Sorry to have to drag you out of bed like this, Father.' Closing the door behind Father Snow, he began to lead the way along the corridor. 'It's very good of you to come. Gerald's waiting upstairs.'

As they walked along the red carpet, past the friezes and the antiques, Father Snow remembered his first visit here, when he'd stopped Pitman's son in his pedal car. Looking back, it seemed like an act of incredible foolishness, the foolishness of a newcomer who hadn't really known what he was risking.

At the end of the corridor, the young man turned and led the way up a staircase which Father Snow had seen but never used. This led onto another corridor, slightly lower and less grand than the one downstairs. As they started down it, a door opened up ahead and two men in suits came running towards them.

'It's still on for tomorrow,' said one of them to Father Snow's escort, without slowing his pace.

'Right. I'll be down in a minute.'

They ran past, glancing at Father Snow with a mixture of condescension and curiosity. A moment later, he heard their footsteps going down the stairs. Reaching the door they'd appeared from, the young man opened it and let Father Snow walk in. As soon as he did so, the door closed behind him and the young man was gone, as though Father Snow had been no more than a parcel he'd been ordered to deliver.

The first person he saw, sitting on the window-sill directly opposite the door, was Trevellyan. He was wearing a large, flowing white shirt, open at the neck, which gave him a rather historical air, as though he'd just come away from fighting a duel in the grounds. His heavy face was framed by the two curtains of white curls which fell to his shoulders. Something about him convinced Father Snow that Melanie had been right, and he found himself at once powerfully attracted and repelled. As their eyes met, an inexpressible sadness came over the ogre's face. Then, almost awkwardly, he turned away.

Looking around, Father Snow realised that he was in a library. On his left was a large fireplace with griffons carved into its wood. All the other walls were lined with books from floor to ceiling. There was even a pair of library steps in one corner. In the centre of the room was a huge dark table, on which lay two telephones, a laptop computer and a closed file. Apart from Trevellyan, the only person there was Gerald Pitman.

He was standing in front of the window at the far end of the room, staring out at the distant lights on the horizon, or at his own reflection in the glass. His beautiful suit was without any trace of a rumple or a crease, as though he'd just put it on. He was speaking on a mobile phone, standing elegantly with his hand in his pocket and most of his weight on one leg.

'Just tell him to have it ready first thing tomorrow,' he was saying. 'Yes, I know it's two in the morning, but there's an election on. What the fuck does he expect? He can go to bed when I do, which won't be tonight . . . No, I'm down in the country. Something's come up.'

As he said that, he seemed to remember Father Snow. Turning from the window, he gestured to an armchair which had been positioned in front of the gigantic table. Father Snow went and sat down. The moment he did so he felt dizzy and sick.

'I've just about had enough of this crap. Either he has it ready on time, or I send someone round there to cut his balls off.' Closing the phone and slipping it into his pocket, he smiled at Father Snow. 'Metaphorically, of course.'

As Pitman came across the room, Father Snow straightened his back and clenched his jaw as though preparing to receive a blow. Pitman, though, was all smooth politeness.

'I do apologise for my strong language, Father,' he said,

approaching the table. 'But sometimes one has to be firm to get things done. I'm sure you understand.'

Father Snow stared at him and said nothing. Pitman slid into the chair on the other side of the table and leaned forward to press a button on the laptop. He managed to make the action seem completely insincere, so that Father Snow wondered whether the computer was even switched on. It had been like a newsreader's mime of pressing a button, whose only purpose was to give the impression of control.

'Thank you so much for letting me drag you out of bed like this, Father.'

'It's no more than I'd do if any of my other parishioners called on me.'

Pitman smiled.

'Of course. All of us here have been most impressed by the way you perform your duties. I do assure you, I wouldn't have asked to see you except on a matter of the utmost importance.'

Father Snow didn't make things easier for him by asking what it was. He just sat and waited, meeting Pitman's eye, trying not to be awed.

'There's an election on, Father,' said Pitman conversationally, 'and, as I'm sure you'll appreciate, we politicians tend to get rather jumpy at election time. Now the thing is, I've recently been hearing things about you which have made me, if not jumpy, at least a little concerned.'

'That's strange, Gerald. I have almost no interest in politics.'

Pitman laughed.

'Just like your friend Vincent, eh? Well, that's good, that's good. All the same, I'd just like to set my mind at rest. The first thing I found out about you was that you had a bee in your bonnet about all this Jack and the Beanstalk stuff. Nothing wrong with that, of course. You're interested in history.' He glanced towards Trevellyan, who was still leaning motionless against the window-sill. 'And whatever else this house may have, it has a history.'

There was a silence. Father Snow also looked towards Trevellyan, and found that he had turned to stare out of the window.

'Then I hear,' Pitman went on, 'that you've been having weekly meetings with a local journalist.'

Father Snow's head jerked round.

'How did you find out about that?'

Pitman smiled.

'This is a very small community, Father. In fact, I always like to think of it as a tight-knit community. A man in your position can't conduct a friendship like that without attracting comment.' He stared at Father Snow as though everything were to be read on his face. The priest felt himself begin to blush. 'Of course, I'm sure it is just a friendship. Nobody could doubt your probity. In any case, I'm not concerned with your private life. All I ask is that you don't concern yourself with mine. That's fair enough, isn't it?'

Father Snow said nothing, but went on meeting Pitman's eye.

'Anyway, now we come to the disturbing part. It turns out that there have been certain very unpleasant accusations made here and there, and that you seem to have been at the centre of it all.' Still smiling, Pitman leaned back in his chair. 'When you put all these things together, you can see why I'm uneasy, can't you? That's why I've asked you up here. I'm giving you the opportunity to set my mind at rest.'

'How could I do that?'

'Well, you could start by telling me exactly what these allegations are.'

Father Snow was silent for a moment. He found that his mouth was dry, as though he was about to address a large crowd. It was almost a shock to hear his usual, measured voice come out.

'The allegation is that there is systematic child abuse going on in the village, with this house as its focus.'

'I see,' said Pitman. 'Now just tell me that you know it's all nonsense, and you can go home to bed.'

'I'm afraid I can't do that, Gerald. After tonight, I'm almost inclined to believe it all. Your own actions have hardly been those of an innocent man.'

There was silence. Father Snow realised that he'd stepped over the line and that now there was no going back. When Pitman eventually spoke, it was in a different, more business-like voice.

'All right, Father, let's be realistic about this. You'll never be able to prove your nonsense any more than I can disprove it, so the argument would be pointless. If you won't take my word that it isn't true, nothing I can do will convince you. So it all comes down to this: what do you intend to do?'

'I'll do what's right.'

'And what might that be?'

'I haven't decided yet.'

'But you intend to take action?'

'I'm afraid I may have to.'

Pitman stood up and began to walk round the table.

'That's a real pity,' he said, shaking his head and looking at the floor. 'I must say, I'd never have expected anything like this to happen in my own constituency.'

When he reached the front of the desk, he stopped and turned around. Father Snow could have leaned forward and touched him.

'Don't you fuck around with me, you jumped-up little shit.'

Trevellyan stirred by his window, but Father Snow found himself unable to move. 'As a priest, you have my respect, but as soon as you cross the line into politics the cloth will be no protection, believe me. Smear me and I'll smear you back before you know what's hit you. You'll be disgraced and defrocked, and there'll be a scandal the

like of which even the Catholic Church has never known.
You throw a turd into my garden, mate, and I'll unload a
lorry load of manure on yours.'

'Gerald –'

Pitman swung towards the window.

'Shut up, Nick. Let me deal with this.' When he turned
back to Father Snow, he was smiling. 'You've just climbed
your beanstalk, sonny, and I'm the giant who's going to
grind your bones. If it was your friend Vincent sitting there,
I might have a battle on my hands, but I know you, little
boy. I know you. You're just a midget. You look tough,
but you're brittle. You're going to crack as soon as I put
the pressure on.'

Father Snow couldn't reply. His face was red, as hot as
if he were sitting two feet from a fire.

'Now get out.' Pitman turned and began to walk back
round the table. 'Go home and get praying.'

Father Snow's body obeyed before he had time to think.
He stood up with a jerk and began to walk to the door,
aware only of his need to escape from the hot pressure of
the room. He didn't look round as he left. In the corridor
he began to walk quickly away. He felt numb and confused.
At the same time, he had a sense of himself as completely
worthless, less than human. It was as though he'd just been
beaten up.

Before he reached the end of the corridor, he heard
heavy footsteps behind him.

'Father Snow!'

Almost in terror, he swung round, and saw the extraordinary figure of Trevellyan coming towards him with large
strides. There was something like anguish on his face.

'I'm so sorry about all that, Father. I should never have
allowed such a thing to happen in my house, but, as you've
seen, Gerald can be rather difficult to control. In any case,
let me see you to the door.'

All the fury and revulsion which Father Snow had been
too cowed to feel for Pitman now focused unfairly on

Trevellyan. He was still unable to speak, however, as, humble and gentlemanly, the ogre escorted him along the corridor. In silence, they went down the stairs. As they headed for the front door, Trevellyan said:

'Don't take any of it too seriously, Father.' He was walking with his hands behind his back, staring at the floor. 'Gerald's just a bit worked up at the moment. It'll all blow over, believe me. I'll have a quiet word with him when you've gone.'

This comforted Father Snow, so that he felt an unreasonable gratitude. Nobody as worthless as him deserved such sympathy.

'Would you like a lift home?' said Trevellyan when they reached the door.

'No. I'd rather walk.'

Trevellyan nodded, understanding. Then he gave an encouraging smile.

'We'll talk after Mass tomorrow. Until then, don't worry. You're going to be all right.'

The walk to the presbytery was like a slow descent back down into the normal world. Father Snow went quickly, without looking back. All the way his mind was filled with images from the fairy tale. It hadn't so gripped and fascinated him since those childhood evenings when he'd insisted that his father read it for him again and again. Now he saw it was no coincidence that Gilles and Everard had both been aristocrats. Physical size is not enough to make a real fairy-tale giant. One needs the trappings of power, the clothes, the riches, the enormous castle. Without these, no monstrosity, however gigantic, will ever acquire the power of enchantment.

For a long time after he'd gone back to bed, Father Snow lay awake, thinking about Everard. There was no doubt in his mind now that Melanie had been right. The giant's evil had outlived him in more ways than one. Flamstead was a place of occult pilgrimage, the ogre's Mecca. Pitman, Saunders, Dugdale and probably many more had gathered here, attracted by the legend, to continue their great predecessor's work. At the centre of it all was Trevellyan himself, who carried Everard's blood in his veins and stood guard over his monstrous legacy. Father Snow had appeared the midst of these monsters as the child who'd somehow been chosen to do battle with them all, to break their ancient spell. Remembering how he'd seen Pitman on the television, striding down the steps from number ten, he realised that the enchantment spread far beyond Wodden, that the spell held millions in its grip.

On the edge of sleep, Father Snow wondered if he'd finally followed his predecessor into madness.

19

IN THE MORNING, Father Snow could only see his nocturnal journey to Flamstead as a dream. He had to struggle to convince himself it had all been real, and he realised that his own reaction was an echo of the children's. Melanie had been right. What they described as nightmares had been no more than their interpretation of abductions more confused and horrific than his own. He'd uncovered a nest of ogres.

He had to go back up to Flamstead that morning to say Mass. When he drove through the gates, he found the whole park full of movement. It almost felt like summer now. A warm wind harried flocks of little clouds across the sky. The huge faces of the trees turned pale beneath it. Birds were constantly flying from one to the other, while the deer roamed calmly underneath, slower than the clouds. All that movement only served to highlight the stone stillness of the house, giving it the air of something that had passed beyond age.

During Mass, Father Snow watched Trevellyan singing the Latin Creed. He did it with his head lifted upwards towards the sunny window behind the altar, not needing to look down at the missal gripped in his long-nailed hands. Mournful yearning twisted his face, raising his eyebrows in the middle, so that it seemed he was on the edge of tears.

When Mass was finished, Father Snow went and had lunch with the Trevellyans and the usual collection of local worthies. He looked at them suspiciously today, wondering how many of them were involved. Most of the conversation concerned the election, which they all hoped the Conservatives would win. Trevellyan himself remained silent through it all, though there was nothing unusual about this. Today he was wearing a pale summer suit and a cream cravat which emphasised the whiteness of his skin. For all his silence, his presence seemed to fill the room, huge and moody, yet somehow gentle.

After lunch, Trevellyan spoke for the first time.

'I'm going out for a walk in the grounds. Won't you come with me, Father?'

Father Snow gave a small, unsmiling nod.

Everything seemed to have quietened down when they got outside. The wind had died, giving up on the little groups of clouds and leaving them to laze above the house. The trees were still, their leaves lolling like idiots. Even the birds had settled down to rest and sing. It was as though, after centuries of trying, the building had at last imposed its stillness on the surrounding countryside. The deer were reclining in the shade of the trees, so that they reminded Father Snow of unicorns in a medieval painting.

They went a long way down the hill in silence. Trevellyan walked with large, slow steps, his hands behind his back, his white hair rising and falling around his face.

Eventually they stopped beneath a tree and both turned back to look at the house. Trevellyan sighed, as though about to perform an unpleasant duty.

'I'd like to apologise again for what happened last night.' Father Snow was silent, so he went on. 'Gerald senses that he can't really control you, and I think that makes him uneasy. And he's absolutely terrified of bad publicity, particularly at the moment.'

'So what do you think he'll do?'

Trevellyan turned away from the building to look at Father Snow.

'Nothing. I had a word with him after you'd gone and

managed to convince him that he'd over-reacted. As long as you don't do anything foolish yourself, he'll leave you alone. That would be the course I'd advise you to take.'

Father Snow said nothing.

'None of it's true, you know. It's sheer madness.' Trevellyan shrugged. 'My family has been subjected to this kind of nonsense a number of times over the years. That's one of the reasons I'm usually so reluctant to talk about Everard. Some people will always be ready to believe that I've inherited his tendencies, even across all those centuries. But I haven't. It really is sheer madness.'

Turning towards Father Snow, Trevellyan lifted a white, clawed hand and placed it on his shoulder. 'I could never hurt a child.'

His voice had been perfectly gentle, more mournful than ever, but Father Snow shuddered at his touch.

After that, Father Snow felt powerless, both as a citizen and as a priest. He had no evidence. If he tried to explain his suspicions to anyone in authority, they would simply think him insane. He had entered a fairy tale which no one else would understand.

When he returned to the presbytery after saying Mass the following morning, he found a white envelope on the doormat. It had been delivered by hand. His name was typed on the front, not followed by an address. He took it through to the study and opened it at his desk.

There was a photograph inside. A split second after he'd seen it, Father Snow jerked it away from him so that it skated across the desk and landed on the carpet. He'd acted with the instant disgust of a man spitting a maggot from his mouth, yet it was still too late. The image had entered his mind. It showed a girl of about eight with a man in late middle-age. Both of them were naked. The girl was sitting on a sofa, facing the camera with her legs apart. Her head was turned towards the man who stood next to her, so that her face was hidden by her hair. She had lifted one hand to hold his penis.

Father Snow stood up, taking deep breaths. Then, feeling that there wasn't enough air in the room, he went and walked around the garden. His first thought was that now he had a piece of concrete evidence, though he wasn't sure how it could be used. Nor could he understand why it had been put in his hands.

After a while of pacing around the garden, Father Snow realised that he was beginning to lose control. Then he forced himself to stand perfectly still and upright, eyes closed and face calm. As soon as he did so, the sickening image leapt back into his mind. It seemed to him now that there had been something familiar about the man standing by the sofa.

Father Snow went back inside. He forced himself to move calmly, yet he felt a strange excitement as he picked up the photo from the floor. The man had grey hair. His head was lifted, his eyes squeezed shut. Under other circumstances it would have been taken as an expression of extreme pain or grief. Though Father Snow had never met him, there was definitely something familiar about the face, so that he felt sure it was one he'd seen in the village from time to time.

In the end, he put the photo back on the desk and examined the envelope in which it had arrived. There was nothing to be seen on the outside except his own name. When he looked inside, however, he found a small strip of paper. On this a message had been typed in block capitals: THE FIRST OF MANY

In horror, Father Snow understood why the photograph had been sent. They were trying to corrupt him. Now that he'd found out about them, they would have to make him one of themselves. They would bombard him with temptations until he broke. At the same moment he realised that, in some awful, smothered way, the photograph had excited him. After years of solitude and celibacy, he'd suddenly been subjected to a powerful sexual stimulus, and his body had responded.

Shaking and panting, Father Snow replaced the photo in the envelope and slammed it away in the drawer of the desk. Then, almost in a panic, he fled from the presbytery. He wasn't sure why he did this, unless it was that the solitude of the place had become unbearable. Without any clear intention, he got the car out of the garage and drove round to the Dugdales' house in a kind of fury.

There was no answer when he rang the bell, so he shouted and hammered on the door. Eventually, one of the neighbours came out and informed him that an ambulance had arrived shortly before. Dugdale had been carried out on a stretcher. Flora had gone with him.

As soon as he got back to the presbytery, Father Snow called Ralph. Although he allowed the phone to ring for ages, there was no answer. So Father Snow went into the church and knelt there, praying for peace, but the image of the child's body kept hanging itself on the air in front of him, obscuring even God.

In the end, in desperation, Father Snow did what he had done on the previous Monday, exactly a week before. He escaped up into the hills which surrounded Wodden.

The walk itself did something to calm him. It was a hot day and the hill was steep. The ferns on either side of the path reached his shoulders. Birds and insects were the only signs of life. As he climbed, Father Snow found himself looking around for Susan, and realised that he'd come in the hope of recreating their last meeting. He wanted to escape back into that perfect world where to kiss a girl among the bluebells had seemed the most awful crime of which he was capable.

When he reached the top of the hill, he found that the bluebells had died in their thousands, as though they'd been subjected to some kind of chemical attack. All that remained was a crowd of drooping stalks. The petals lay on the ground, their colour faded. He hadn't realised they lived for such a short time. Everything else, though, was as it had been that day. The beams of light still slanted down, shifting when the breeze picked up as though they'd been projected through waves. Looking at the thousands of headless stalks, he wondered what Susan had done with the bunch he'd picked for her, whether they'd somehow survived the holocaust.

Father Snow went and sat down under the same tree. As he did so, it all came back to him. He remembered exactly how she'd walked towards him, the exact spot where she'd sat down. Then he saw himself picking the flowers and sitting down beside her. Remembering their kiss, he closed his eyes as he had done that day. This time, though, he didn't force himself to get up and walk away.

When he at last opened his eyes, he could hardly believe she wasn't there. The longing to see her overcame him, and he didn't fight it, pleased now that she should have that power. Everything else was driven from his mind. All he wanted was to see her, and the need was so great that his imagination tried to meet it, so that she was almost there, coming towards him through the trees.

He would have given anything to go back, to get away. Now he felt that he'd done the wrong thing that day. Life had offered him one of its few perfect moments, and he'd turned it down. Even a priest is still a man, and perhaps everybody has a duty to live. Those rare moments must just be taken as they come.

Much later, as he was getting up to leave, Father Snow saw a bunch of headless stalks on the ground near the tree.

Everything down in the presbytery was as he'd left it. The appalling photo was still hidden away in the study. The same claustrophobic solitude filled the building. As soon as he got in, Father Snow dialled Ralph's number, but there was still no reply.

Twenty minutes later, the phone rang. It was Flora Dugdale, calling from the hospital to tell him in a tearful voice that she wouldn't be round to make supper that night as her husband had just died.

In the early evening, Father Snow finally got through to Ralph, who agreed to see him. Taking the envelope from the drawer in the study, he left immediately. For once he drove fast, with the window down, as though the breeze against his face would cleanse him. The A25, with its steep hills and sharp corners, was dangerous at that speed. At one point Father Snow, unable to keep his mind entirely on the road, almost turned the little car over.

Ralph greeted him with his usual expansive bonhomie. He was already drunk. Only when they were inside, sitting at the table in the large living-room, did he seem to notice anything strange. Father Snow's carefully combed hair had been disordered by the wind in the car. His movements were jerky, his expression distracted, his composure gone.

'What's the matter, Julian?' said Ralph, becoming suddenly serious. 'You seem in a bit of a state.'

Father Snow would have liked to explain, but found the thing too terrible for words. All he could do was produce the envelope and push it across the table.

'This arrived today.'

Giving him a curious look, Ralph picked up the envelope and opened it. When he saw the photograph, his red face twisted into an expression which seemed to convey grief as much as disgust. After looking at the picture for a moment, he put it gently on the table. Father Snow glanced down at it. Now that someone else had seen it, the horror of the thing was slightly lessened.

When he looked back, Ralph had hidden his head in his hands.

'Oh my God. This is awful.'

'I know. There's no doubt in my mind that it came from Pitman. He called me up to see him late on Saturday night.' Father Snow shifted in his chair. 'It's all true, Ralph. There really is a group of them here. What can we do?'

But Ralph was still hiding his face.

'It's awful.'

'Do you recognise the man?'

Ralph lifted his head. He looked at once haggard, horrified and surprised.

'You mean you don't know?'

'Know what?'

'It's Charles.'

Father Snow still didn't understand.

'Charles who?'

'Charles Conner.' As though to check, he turned his twisted face back down towards the picture. 'That's Father Conner.'

'No!'

Father Snow snatched the picture up and examined it. Now he saw why he'd vaguely recognised the face. He'd seen it in another photo, in Eileen Dodson's house. It was the same face that smiled shyly down from her mantelpiece. Now he knew the one name Jack Dugdale had told his wife, and knew too why she hadn't believed him. Even now, with the evidence in front of him, he could hardly accept it himself.

'Oh my God,' said Ralph again. As though not fully aware of what he was doing, he got up to fetch a bottle and two glasses. For once there was no protest from Father Snow as he poured them large measures, sloshing whisky over the table. 'I can't believe it.'

'Everyone says he was such a good man,' said Father Snow, as though that would prove it all untrue. 'Everyone agrees.'

Ralph took a deep swig of whisky. Then he put the photo back in the envelope, holding it by the corner as though it might infect him. When it was hidden, a presence seemed to have vanished from the room.

'He was a good man,' said Ralph quietly. 'Some of these people become priests precisely because they are good men, but saddled with an evil tendency. They see the disciplines of the priesthood as a way of controlling themselves.'

'Perhaps he wasn't one of them before he came here, though. Perhaps finding out what he did about the place awoke it in him. Or perhaps they deliberately corrupted him when they realised he was onto them.'

Ralph nodded.

'Priests are particularly open to that kind of pressure.' He spread his hands, indicating the huge, empty presbytery. 'Look at the lives we lead. We have to live constantly under the strain of loneliness and celibacy. Perhaps you'd have to be a bit of a weird bugger in the first place to even contemplate such a life.'

As he spoke, Father Snow became quite still, watching him with fresh horror. His head span.

'There was a message with the photograph,' he said.

'What did it say?'

'"The first of many."'

Lifting his head, Ralph saw the look Father Snow was giving him and understood.

'Julian!' His shock seemed genuine enough, but Father Snow just sat there, staring at him. 'If you think that I'm involved, then you really are getting paranoid!'

'I sincerely hope so.'

The heavy face in front of him looked hurt, the little eyes twinkling as though with drunken tears.

'Think what you're saying, man!' Ralph leaned forwards and slapped him on the shoulder. 'This is your old friend Ralph you're talking about!'

Then he stayed there like that, leaning across the table to grip Father Snow's shoulder and stare into his eyes. Father Snow felt all his old calm and coldness coming back. He was repulsed by Ralph's boozy warmth.

'I'm afraid,' he said quietly, 'that you and I have never really managed to become friends.'

The hand fell from his shoulder and, in the same movement, clasped Ralph's glass of whisky with equal force.

'Not from want of trying on my part.' He drained the glass and slammed it down on the table. 'Believe what the hell you like about me,' he said, starting to get angry. 'I never thought I'd live to see the day when I had to endure such suspicions from a fellow priest.'

Then, as he leaned forwards to pour himself a refill, his anger gave way to depression. A morose, drunken expression came over his face.

'Perhaps you're right to suspect me though. I mean, if a man like Charles can do it, anybody can.'

Father Snow shook his head and stirred as though waking up.

'I'm sorry, Ralph. Of course I don't suspect you. I don't know what came over me.'

Ralph looked over the top of his glass.

'Do you mean that?'

'Yes. I'm really sorry.'

'Thanks, Julian.' Now it really did seem that Ralph was on the point of tears. 'You don't know what that means to me.'

Father Snow shifted uncomfortably.

'And I didn't mean what I said about us not being friends.'

Ralph smiled, but his tears were still dangerously close. Father Snow sat there stiffly, full of dread that Ralph might now get up to try and hug him or make some other awful display of emotion.

'We are friends, aren't we?' said Ralph, and he had never seemed so pathetic to Father Snow. 'We have to be. When things like this happen, we priests have got to stick together.'

'Yes.'

Then Ralph was silent for a while, staring blearily across the room.

'It makes you wonder what the point of it all is.' He turned back to Father Snow. 'Do you ever think about leaving? Leaving the priesthood, I mean?'

This was somehow the most shocking thing that had happened all evening.

'Not seriously.'

Ralph was looking at him with exaggerated steadiness.

'Perhaps you really are the perfect priest that you appear. How do you do it? Is it just that you don't need the things the rest of us need?'

Father Snow shrugged and coughed.

'I don't know.' He remembered himself climbing the hill that morning. 'Perhaps I just know those things wouldn't bring me any lasting happiness.'

'It's not to do with happiness,' said Ralph. 'It's to do with human warmth. I think that even poor old Charles was looking for that, in the only way he could.' He raised his glass. 'I find my consolation here. Where do you find yours?'

'Only in my faith,' said Father Snow.

'Perhaps you really are one of the rare ones like Vincent, then. But there's a difference between you.' He leaned forwards with drunken wisdom. 'Vincent has transcended the human level. You have simply kept away from it. Am I right? Is that the secret of your strength?'

'Perhaps.'

'There's a key to every priest, you see. I've known enough of them, and there's always a key. Some of them are genuinely holy men. Many are just unable to find their happiness in the normal world. They can't form ordinary relationships. After what I've seen tonight, I think Charles fell into that group. He probably had some deep-rooted fear of women. Others have suffered some great calamity and decided to retreat from the world. In a way, I suppose you could say that the priesthood itself was a sign of perversion.'

Father Snow was silent, staring at the envelope on the table and remembering his own arousal on first opening it, horrified.

'I often think of leaving, anyway,' said Ralph. 'But what

kind of life would there be for me outside at my age? It's too late to start again.'

He was looking intently across the table, and Father Snow realised that he was hoping for help or advice. If it had been one of his parishioners, or if Ralph had been younger, there would have been no problem. As it was, Father Snow felt unable to start a lecture about the power of the sacraments or the refuge of prayer.

'When something like this happens,' Ralph went on, 'I feel like giving up hope.'

There was nothing Father Snow could say. He left a short time later. Ralph saw him to the door, slapping him on the back as usual, but Father Snow had never known him so subdued. The shock would be even worse for him, since Father Conner had been his friend. As they walked towards the door, he realised how much Ralph needed him, so he forced himself to say:

'It was nice to see you, Ralph, in spite of everything. It's always nice to see you.'

Whether Ralph believed this or not, he smiled.

'Thanks. Come again soon.'

They had paused in the hallway. Father Snow felt crushed by the huge, hopeless atmosphere of the presbytery.

'Yes, I will. You must come over to me one day, too.'

Where he would once have laughed uproariously, Ralph gave a small smile.

'I thought you'd never ask.'

Then the worst happened: Ralph stepped forwards and hugged him. Father Snow stood there and endured it, patting him on the back as though he were some great diseased dog.

'I'm sorry things never worked out between us, Julian.'

When Ralph stepped away, there was no doubt that he was crying. Father Snow had never seen a man of that age in tears. He pretended not to notice, but was unable to speak.

'I know it must be hard for you to respect a man like me,' said Ralph. 'I know what a mess I am. You deserved somebody better here to help you.'

'Don't say that, Ralph.' The stocky man just stood there shaking his head as though some spring inside him had broken. Father Snow felt that the battle which had started with their first argument was finally over, and that he had won. 'Don't say that. You don't know how much I do like and respect you.'

Even to his own ears, it wasn't very convincing. Unable to bear it any longer, he turned and walked away. It wasn't really dark outside. The sun was only just setting. As Father Snow drove away, there was more than enough light to see Ralph, standing at the door as always to see him off. He didn't raise his fist in farewell, or even wave.

When he got back to the presbytery, Father Snow went through to the living-room and burnt the photograph in the grate. Father Conner twisted and buckled. Then his grimacing face erupted as the chemicals began to boil. The girl went with him, and Father Snow watched intently, as though this would enable the image to be burnt also from his mind.

Afterwards, all that remained was a few black curls of ash which couldn't be burnt. Crouching there at the fireplace, Father Snow remembered his arrival in the presbytery. He had found black traces identical to these among the white ashes of Father Conner's last fire. Perhaps the dead priest had destroyed a similar photograph before he'd gone out to the garage.

20

AFTER HE'D BURNT the photograph, Father Snow just sat on the sofa and did nothing. He hadn't said his Office for the day, but now there seemed no point. It was the first time since his ordination that he'd failed in this duty. The whole business of being a priest seemed polluted to him now. His whole way of living, his very existence, had lost its meaning. In some vague way he realised that he'd fallen into the sin of despair. Yet he saw, too, that the nature of despair is that there can be no resisting it.

Everything in the room, as it had on the night of his arrival, seemed connected to Father Conner. He imagined that weakest of men, corrupted and probably blackmailed, crouching down to burn a photograph of himself in the grate. Then, almost as a vision, he saw him leave the room and walk out to the garage. Remembering the excitement which had stirred in him as he looked at the photograph that morning, Father Snow felt his despair deepen. There was a desperation about it now. He felt the ogre in himself had been awakened.

Now it seemed that there was only one hope left. He went through to the study and phoned Vincent's residence in London. He was unsure of what he would say, but knew that, if he could just hear Vincent's voice, a little courage would return. However, the voice that eventually answered was not Vincent's. It informed him that the archbishop was out of the country and wouldn't return for a fortnight.

His despair deeper than before, Father Snow went out into the garden. Things were little better outside. Night had fallen completely by now. Only a few bluish clouds on the horizon gave any hint of which way the daylight had gone. The lights of Flamstead were glimmering between the trees. Father Snow didn't look at them. He knew that it was hopeless to think that anything could be changed.

Suddenly he was filled with an urge to leave, to get in his car and drive away from Wodden without a word to anyone, to leave his responsibilities behind and play truant for the rest of his life, to disappear. Perhaps he would have done it if he'd been able to think of anywhere to go. But all he could think of was the way Ralph had looked, drunk and hopeless at the door of his presbytery. Then it seemed to him that not only he and Ralph, but everyone, everyone alive, has to find some way of dealing with what Father Conner felt as he walked to the garage. That was why Ralph drank and he himself so longed to get away. All of us have to find a home for that despair.

Feeling worse, even worse than before, Father Snow went back inside. In the study he lingered, unable to face returning to the living-room with its brass tools and silent armchair. But then he realised that the whole presbytery was corrupted. There was no escape. All of it was somehow part of Father Conner and shared in his crimes, in his search for human warmth.

As he was standing there, plummeting into the pit, the doorbell rang. The sound seemed to come from a long way away. A tiny, forgotten hope leapt up in him before he'd even realised what it was he hoped for. He had to think before he saw that he was hoping it would be Susan. By this time, though, he knew how cruel a hope it was. Instead of her, he'd find someone else waiting there, come to burden him with some fresh horror.

Father Snow stood for a few moments in the study, not wanting to answer. He knew by now the anguish which followed when the hope of seeing her was dashed, the despair he felt when she didn't appear. It seemed to him now that he no longer had the strength to bear that disappointment.

The degree of courage required to go and answer the door surprised him. Once he would have scoffed at the very idea. Now he was so weak that he had to concentrate on the simple process of walking. As the door approached, it seemed to offer the promise of escape. Though he knew that this was illusory, he was filled once more with the desire to run away and leave it all behind – Father Conner's desire.

When he opened the door, he found that it was her. In that first instant, he felt that the sheer shock of it was worse than any disappointment. He just stood there, unable to take it in. She was standing at the bottom of the steps, looking up at him without smiling. She was wearing a sober blue suit, perhaps the same one she'd worn for their first meeting.

'Don't be angry.'

Father Snow found that he couldn't speak. Looking down, he saw her sensible, middle-aged shoes and was filled with love. His arms and legs went weak, trembling so that he doubted his ability to go on standing there. He managed to shake his head.

'I just want to talk to you for a few minutes. I won't be long.'

Silently, he stood aside to let her in. Then he closed the door and followed her through to the living-room. Susan sat on the sofa as she always had, her knees together and her hands folded neatly in her lap. Instead of taking his usual place in the armchair by the fire, Father Snow went and sat down beside her. An image of trees and bluebells flashed for a moment through his mind. Then he found he had put his arms around her. His whole body began to shake violently. He couldn't breathe. Screwing his eyes shut, he pressed his face against her shoulder. He heard her voice, soft and surprised.

'What's happened to you?'

Father Snow just shook his head. Then the trembling of his body increased so that it seemed he was having a fit. There was nothing he could do to control it. Even he was surprised. But Susan just put her arms around him and began to stroke the back of his head. She did it kindly and calmly, as if she understood everything, though he didn't really understand himself.

All the same, he wanted to understand and to explain. At first he thought he should tell her about Father Conner, but he found he didn't want to pollute her with all that. In any case, he somehow realised now that everything that had happened since his arrival in the village had been only a tiny part of it. The grief was endless. There was no way to explain. Eventually, when his body had calmed under her touch, he drew back so that he could see her and said what would once have been impossible:

'I need you.'

There seemed strangely little shame in it now, and Father Snow vaguely realised that he'd been broken at last. He'd lost his pride. Without saying anything, Susan drew his face towards her own. Again he had a brief image of the bluebells and the trees, the beams of sunshine. After all the anguish she'd made him feel, there was nothing now but relief that she was there, that, in the end, she hadn't let him down. The feeling so overwhelmed him that for a time he was hardly aware that he was kissing her. When he did become aware of it, he felt he would never be able to get enough of her coolness, her taste and her smell. There was stirring and growth in his body, and this produced no guilt in him, but only gratitude.

Eventually, after a period that defied the normal measurement of time, Susan drew away from him. Then, lying back on the couch and looking solemnly up into his eyes, she raised her hands to her neck and undid the first button of her modest white blouse.

*   *   *

For a long time after it was over, Julian remained unaware of his surroundings. He was somewhere far away, high up, descending very slowly through warm clouds. Then suddenly he found himself lying on the floor by the cold fireplace, facing the window. The curtains had been drawn and the lights turned off, though he couldn't at first remember doing these things. Gentle light filtered into the room from the hall, through the half-open door. The coffee-table was on his right. Susan lay on the left between him and the fireplace, her head on his shoulder, one leg lifted over his body, so that he felt enfolded in her warmth. Their clothes were strewn over the sofa. He could see his white dog-collar shining through the gloom, the black priest's jacket and trousers lying like a cast-off skin. Susan's dull outfit and sensible shoes lay nearby, and when he saw them he was filled with renewed love, because he realised that he and Susan were both anachronisms, in a way. A girl like her, making no display of herself but just waiting quietly to be swept off her feet by some fairy-tale gentleman, had as little place in the modern world as priests themselves.

For a long time he just lay and looked around him, full of a strange, child-like wonder. The coffee-table seemed to tower over him, huge and unfamiliar when seen from down here. There was a chink in the curtains through which he could see a slither of blue night sky. Then he looked down at Susan's body, taking in the curve of her hip and the line of her leg which rose across his stomach. He'd never allowed himself to imagine her naked. Even if he had, he would never quite have been able to picture this. The soft shapes were unlike any other object in the room, as though the gloomy light itself had coalesced at his side. When he thought of how much trouble she had taken to disguise this beauty from the world, he knew that the desire he felt for her would never be put out. It was insatiable. Looking across her body at Father Conner's brass tools in the fireplace, he found that they had lost their magical power to disturb him. He could think of the awful photograph now without fear. Julian was perfectly normal, not an ogre after all.

Remembering the despair he'd felt before her arrival and comparing it with this happiness and peace, he was amazed. It was a miracle. Gratitude overwhelmed him, yet it was nothing compared to what she had given, to her great generosity. He felt that, unless he gave it some expression, his heart would break.

'I love you.'

Susan stirred against him, as though disturbed in sleep. Now that he'd said it at last, the magic phrase, which had once been so repugnant, seemed indescribably sweet, so that he felt he could repeat it forever.

'I love you,' he said again, propping himself up on his elbow to look down into her face and stroke her hair. They were the last words of enchantment. 'I love you.'

Susan turned to lie on her back and looked up at him seriously. Julian's hand moved, attracted by the shiver of her breasts, and held one of them gently.

'I can't believe it,' she said. 'You seemed so strong when we met. I thought you were impregnable. I could never have believed that anything would break you.'

Then some buried grief rushed up through Julian, forcing him to close his eyes and speak without thinking.

'I was broken all along.'

'What do you mean?'

Without opening his eyes, Julian shook his head. He didn't know what he meant himself. All he knew was that it was true.

'It's easy to appear strong when you keep yourself apart from people.' He couldn't stop shaking his head. 'Nobody can break what's already broken, and I was broken all along.'

He lay back down and stared up at the ceiling, unable to understand his own grief. After a moment, Susan's face

336

appeared above him, her hair hanging down, as straight and neat as ever.

'What happened to you?'

Julian started shaking his head again, rolling it on the carpet.

'I don't know, I don't know.'

This wasn't true. He did know, but he didn't want to face it, least of all in front of her. It would involve a nakedness far beyond the removal of clothes, a vulnerability much worse than any declaration of love.

'Why did you become a priest?'

'I don't know,' said Julian again, but she just looked down at him, waiting. Then something about the expression on her face and the warmth of her body made him feel entirely safe, so that he looked away from her and said: 'My father died when I was six.'

When he looked back, he found Susan nodding her head above him as though this were only to be expected. Then, perhaps sensing that it would make things easier for him, she lay back down by his side, her head on his shoulder.

'How did he die?'

'He had a heart-attack. He was much older than my mother. I was always afraid that one day he'd just go away and never reappear. Perhaps all children feel the same way about their parents, I don't know. One night there was this commotion in the house. I can't remember it very well. I got out of bed and found Mum getting ready to leave in a panic. She told me to wait in my room, because my auntie was coming round to look after me. So I waited. I was terrified that all my fears were coming true, and that time they really did. He never came back. I never saw him again.'

It was the first time Julian had told the story to anyone. He felt pity not for himself, but for the poor child waiting in the house. It seemed too terrible to be true, so terrible that it couldn't be a part of his own past. If he'd been alone, he would have wept, but only for the child.

'Do you remember him well?'

'No,' said Julian, and this one word somehow seemed the most terrible thing of all. 'Not very well. My clearest memory is that before I went to sleep each night he used to come and tell me a story. It was usually a fairy tale.'

Then his stomach contracted and he realised that he had begun to cry, after all. Freezing lines ran straight down the side of his face towards the carpet. His throat tightened painfully. As this happened, he saw himself as a boy, lying in bed with his father sitting at his side. He remembered the little lamp which had sat on the bedside table and the gentle light it had given. His father had always used to tell the stories without a book, as though he was making it up as he went along. At the end of each story, Julian had always asked the same question: Is it true? And his father had always given the same reply: Of course it is, son. Every word of it is true. After he'd died, Julian had refused to listen to any such stories again. He felt he'd been betrayed through them. Somehow he knew that they hadn't been true, after all.

While these things were passing through his mind, his body went on weeping. Susan moved closer and put her arms around him, accepting it with such kindness and understanding that Julian didn't feel any shame.

'He was so gentle,' he said, speaking as his body would allow. 'He was a lovely man.'

As he spoke, he realised that he'd waited all his life to say those words to somebody, and the grief was too much. He rolled away from her, curling up into a naked ball on the carpet, and for some time was aware of nothing.

Eventually, it passed, but Julian knew that he would never be the same again. Some kind of exorcism had been achieved. The monsters of the past had lost a little of their power.

When he was quite calm, Julian turned to find Susan lying naked by the fire.

'I'm sorry,' he said. 'I've got no right to burden you with this.'

She shook her head.

'Don't be silly. As long as you don't feel guilty about tonight.'

'No, I don't feel guilty.' This was true, and it suddenly struck Julian as very strange. He thought about it for a while. 'Perhaps the priesthood was just something I had to go through. I didn't want to put my trust in anything which would let me down again, so I had to devote my life to the eternal. I had to undergo a period of being Father Snow.'

'And now?'

With a sudden, harrowing doubt, Julian looked at her.

'You remember our agreement? All or nothing.'

Susan nodded.

'Yes, I remember.'

When she took him in her arms, Julian felt his anguish disappear and knew that it was for the last time in his life. As he held her, he had once more a vision of the trees and bluebells, but this time it was his father sitting there among the flowers where Susan had been. He was telling a story to the child who sat with his back against the tree. Now at last Julian believed that every word of it, from once upon a time to happily ever after, was true.

Later, not wanting to put his black suit back on, Julian went upstairs and dressed in ordinary clothes. When he came back down, he found that Susan had moved two chairs out into the garden and was sitting there, staring up at the hills that surrounded the village, a wave of ink that threw the complicated tendrils of trees into the sky.

Julian took his place next to her. Neither of them spoke. The stars were out as though in welcome or in benediction, and he stared up at them for a while. He knew that there would be lots of evenings like this, spent side by side in silence, enjoying solitude but not alone.

After a while, his eyes were drawn, as they always were, to the lights of Flamstead in the hills. He remembered their visit to the British Museum. It had been a fairy tale that had brought them together, in a way. All of it had turned out to be true. The discovery of that fairy tale had led him on to this one. Even now, it was still going on around them all the time. The ogres congregated up there in their castle to perform their hideous deeds. The ancient monster still held Wodden in his spell, as no doubt he always would. The time had come to get away.

Even so, he couldn't remove his eyes from the lights. As he stared up there, a breeze wandered through the dark garden, fingering the leaves like a browsing shopper. It stroked Julian's face and moved on as though he wasn't what it was looking for. The warmth of it surprised him, and he thought again of Father Snow. One of his characteristics had been to channel nostalgia into history, to repress his own past just as he'd repressed all human warmth. Now, with the onset of summer, he'd melted away. The magic kiss had done its work.

'If I had a son,' said Julian at last, 'and I wanted to explain things to him, but was afraid that I might die before he was old enough to understand, then I would tell him fairy tales.'

Susan said nothing but, stirring in her chair, she reached out and took his hand.

'There's so much truth in them.' For a moment, he was tempted to explain to her all he had discovered, to recount the experience of being summoned to see Pitman in the middle of the night, but he somehow knew that it would spoil the perfection of everything. In the end, he just said: 'There really are giants in the world, beside whom the rest of us are children.'

Susan laughed.

'I used to think that you were one of them.'

'Oh no,' said Julian. 'In fact, I think that I'm more of a child than the rest.' He turned towards her, suddenly struck by something. 'Why did you come round here tonight, in any case?'

'It doesn't matter,' she said, giving him a smile that was full of warmth. He realised that she, too, didn't want anything external to intrude between them, and this made him even happier than before. 'I'll tell you next time I see you.'

'And will that be soon?'

'Yes. Very soon.'

Shortly afterwards, she left. They stopped for a long kiss in the hall. When it was over, she looked up at him with the same yearning he'd seen on her face in the old days, when she'd known she couldn't have him.

'I love you,' she said.

Then, having completed his happiness, she left without another word. He went back outside to enjoy the mildness of the garden for a while. Although he was tired, it seemed a shame to waste the opportunity. After all, there are not many such nights in an English summer. So he sat there, staring up at the sky and the hills around the village, turning away occasionally to look at her empty chair.

Before he went to bed that night, Julian opened the desk-drawer in the bedroom and took out the photograph. He hadn't looked at it for years. The first thing to strike him about the face was its similarity to his own. The dark hair was the same as his, if slightly thinner. There were the same lean lines, which would have been hard and uncompromising if they hadn't been warmed by the beginnings of a smile. The eyes which stared into his own were at once strong and kind. Julian realised that this was how he'd always pictured the eyes of Christ when, as Father Snow, he'd knelt for long hours at prayer. Yet there was something knowing about them, too, so that he felt his father had somehow predicted this exact moment and been thinking about it when the picture was taken.

Julian put the photo gently down on the desk, so that it was facing in the direction of his pillow, and went to bed.

21

THE CHURCH WAS a leaky old hulk that let in sunshine. It spread as a glowing puddle beneath the doors. It pawed against the stained-glass windows as though making a dreamy effort to attract somebody's attention and be let in. The handful of people scattered around the pews didn't notice. They were kneeling with their heads bent and their faces covered, so that they had all the outward devotion of saints.

At the altar, a young man in vestments was bowed towards the circle of bread in his hands. As far as anyone could tell, he was identical to Father Snow, who had said Mass here the previous day. He spoke the words as Father Snow would have done, giving each its solemn weight, though there was perhaps an unaccustomed degree of emotion in his voice.

'This . . . is . . . my body . . . which will . . . be given up . . . for you.'

Then he elevated the host in his unworthy hands. He held it there for slightly longer than usual, staring up at it.

My Lord and my God.

A short time later, as he went down to distribute communion, Julian glanced around the church. He almost expected to see Vincent, magically returned to England at the moment of crisis to make him stay in the priesthood. The congregation formed a short line before the altar. As he raised the host for each of them, Julian looked into their faces, trying to apologise. He knew that he would soon be letting everybody down. Yet there was nobody there with the power to save him. As far as he could tell, there were no saints waiting in the line.

Back at the presbytery, Julian had his usual solitary breakfast. Strangely, he still felt no guilt. Perhaps this was because he had no choice in the matter. He had to be with Susan. Without her, he was incomplete. Sitting alone at the table, he realised that he'd only been half a person all along. All his life, the priesthood included, had been no more than a prelude to their meeting.

It was impossible to feel guilty about the inevitable, but he did feel a kind of regret. That morning he was full of nostalgia for his life as a priest, particularly in Wodden. Soon he found himself pitying poor, crippled Father Snow in the same remote way that he pitied his childhood self.

When he'd finished breakfast, he went out into the garden. There he found the two chairs they'd used the night before, close together, facing outwards in the same direction. He decided to leave them there as symbols of his new life.

The sun was stronger now outside. Everything seemed more intense to Julian that morning, perhaps because he was in love. He was vividly aware of the perfume in the garden, the sound of insects, the colour of the sky. Everything was magnified. He saw a bluebottle settle on a swaying leaf and crouch there with exaggerated stillness, like a child playing a game, watching for some imaginary foe. Green waves melted across it, as though it was charged with some molten electricity. Suddenly it disappeared. When Julian looked up, he found that the breeze had carried into the garden large clumps of dandelion seeds, which floated in the summer sunshine like a parody of snow.

Julian said a short prayer for forgiveness as he walked across the lawn. He still believed. For the rest of his life, he would always be a Catholic, but just an ordinary one.

At the bottom of the lawn, he paused and looked upwards. The trees on the horizon lifted their heavy arms and went pale, as though drawing away from him in feigned horror.

'I did my best,' said Julian. 'But perhaps you just asked too much.'

The sound of his voice seemed to emphasise the silence of God which lay behind the buzzing of the insects and the breaking waves of wind in the leaves. He saw that God was a spurned lover, accepting his rejection with a quiet nobility no human lover ever shows. Then for a moment his love of God seemed even more powerful than his love for Susan, so that he was almost tempted to change his mind.

Turning his head, he saw the windows of Flamstead glittering like water through the leaves. He realised that Pitman had been right: Father Snow had melted away at the first sign of pressure. One photograph was all it had taken.

Ten minutes later, he was still standing there, but all of it had been forgotten. He was thinking only of Susan. When the telephone rang, his first inclination was to pretend he hadn't heard it. He felt instinctively that it wouldn't be her, but a call connected with some parish business requiring him to act out the role of Father Snow.

The sound from the study came and went with the vagaries of the breeze, as small and distant as the voice of conscience. Eventually, Julian walked slowly in to answer.

It was the hospital, ringing to explain the manner in which Ralph, too, had tried to make his escape.

The drive to the hospital was by now so familiar to Julian that he did it without noticing. None of it seemed real on such a perfect day. He drove slowly across the bridge, past the village green, along the High Street and up onto the

A25. As he went, he tried to make himself feel shock and grief, but he couldn't pretend an affection for Ralph he'd never really felt.

Even when he'd actually arrived in the hospital, none of it seemed real. Julian, knowing his way around, went through to the small intensive-care ward. Before going in, he had a quick word with the sister on duty. She explained that Ralph had driven into a tree at high speed. He hadn't been wearing his seat-belt and had gone through the windscreen.

'He's in a bad way, Father. Multiple fractures and severe brain-damage. We've done a scan, and it doesn't look too good, I'm afraid.'

'What do you think his chances are?'

'Very slim. We'll give it another couple of days. He may stay as he is, or there may be further brain-swelling, or he may develop a clot. If there's no improvement, we'll have to switch the respirator off.'

Julian nodded and went into the ward. There were only six beds. All the patients were on respirators. The hiss and suck of the machines was clearly audible, suggesting a sleep that was far deeper than normal. The noises of the world outside sounded distant against the silence of the room. Apart from the steady action of the respirators, there was absolutely no movement or sound. The sunshine at the window made it seem unnatural, as though there was a spell on the place, the patients all locked in an enchanted sleep.

Ralph was lying flat on his back. There was a corrugated plastic tube going into his mouth, linked to the hissing and sucking machine. Six tubes entered his neck. Others emerged from under the sheets, feeding things in and taking things out, so that his body was festooned like some macabre fallen maypole. There was a large bandage on his head, which seemed faintly absurd, a bandage from a school-play or a cartoon. His eyes were taped closed under pads of cotton-wool.

Father Snow had been prepared for all this. He'd seen enough people in intensive care. Yet none of them had been people he'd known, and what he wasn't prepared for was how much of Ralph had survived the transformation. It was still obviously Ralph lying there. It looked as though he was subjecting himself to some drastic hangover cure. Julian expected that at any moment he would stir, remove the pads, and get up, rejuvenated and refreshed.

But, while Julian administered the last rites, Ralph just lay there, outstretched and motionless, an eyeless effigy. The ceremony reminded Julian of the naming of a ship. When it was done, he knelt down by the bed to pray. All of this was somehow his fault. Nobody drives their car into a tree if they have a real friend. His first prayer was for his own forgiveness. Then he prayed for Ralph's recovery or, failing that, the salvation of his soul.

Eventually, he opened his eyes and looked around the ward. The others all lay in a similar condition to Ralph, moored by tubes between this world and the next, ships waiting for the tide. Above each bed was a television screen with silent green lines, making a public display of what their bodies were up to. The sound of respirators filled his ears, waves at the shore. Again, he felt that the sunshine made it all unreal. He couldn't believe that Ralph or any of them was really dying. All he had to do was stand up and call to them in a loud voice, telling them that it was daytime, that the sun was shining, that it was time to get up. Surely one loud noise would break the spell. They would stir slowly, remove the tubes from their mouths, and sit up in bed, rubbing their eyes.

Julian looked at Ralph's face. It was as red as ever. The black pockmarks in his nose were still there, having survived the wreck of more important things. Suddenly he wondered whether, somewhere deep in that catatonic frame, there was still some kind of consciousness. He leaned closer.

'I'm sorry, Ralph.'

346

He would have liked to say more, to make the unambiguous declaration of friendship and respect which Ralph had always needed. What held him back was not so much the idea that Ralph couldn't hear as the knowledge that it wouldn't have been true. He forced himself to kneel there in silence for some time longer, but it was as it had always been with Ralph: he wanted to get away. In the end, he stood up. For a moment he stared down at the huge, barrel-chested figure on the bed, amazed that it could have remained so entirely unchanged since his arrival.

'I'm sorry,' he said again.

The sound of his voice, though it had been barely more than a murmur, emphasised Ralph's complete stillness and silence. At that moment, all Julian's suspicions returned. Ralph's stillness grew in intensity until it reached a pitch at which, almost as though Ralph had silently communicated with him, the suspicion turned into certainty. He knew not only that this had been no accident, but also that loneliness and depression alone had not been enough to cause it. Remembering the expression on Ralph's face when he'd seen the photograph of Father Conner, he felt entirely certain. Ralph had been one of them.

When he realised that, Julian's guilt disappeared. He saw now that he'd been right in instinctively disliking Ralph from the start. The tubes and bandages were suddenly like proofs, symbols of his monstrosity. For a moment more, Julian stared down, no longer trying to deny what he'd always felt for the decaying old drunk, which was disgust. Then he turned and left the ward.

For the rest of the day, Julian couldn't escape the image of Ralph lying there with his eyes covered and his lips puckered around the tube. The shock of it all had been greater than he'd realised at first. It soured his happiness. He hated Ralph now not only for whatever crimes he might have committed, but also for having got himself into that condition, for having turned himself into a horror that made a mockery of mortal love.

At the same time, it increased Julian's desire to make his own escape out into the ordinary world. The priesthood seemed more impossible and unnatural than ever. If it hadn't been for Susan, the sight of Ralph in the hospital would have thrown him into despair. As it was, he simply felt an urgent need to see her. When he did, all his happiness would return. She would hold him as she had the previous night, but it would be better this time, even better than before.

By the time he rang her that evening, he was desperate. She didn't answer immediately, and a little of his old anguish returned. It was still light in the garden and through the french windows he could see the two empty chairs which stood there side by side, facing the hills. When she at last answered, he was staring at them as though for reassurance.

Julian didn't waste any time being embarrassed or dignified.

'Can I see you?'

'It's a bit difficult tonight. I'm meeting some old friends for a drink over in Dorking. Tomorrow would be better.'

He was crushed.

'Just five minutes.' There was a silence. Julian was confused, simply unable to understand what was happening. He began to feel frantic. 'Please. Something terrible has happened.'

'All right, then. I'll come round.'

While he was waiting for her, Julian paced around the presbytery, unable to keep still. All the discipline he'd had as Father Snow was gone, and he knew that this was the result of trusting another person at last, of putting his happiness entirely in someone else's hands. There was no longer any possibility of self-control, since so much of himself had been given away.

When the doorbell rang, he hurried to answer. The first

thing he noticed was that she'd driven round. There was an old Mini parked in front of the presbytery. Susan herself was dressed as he had never seen her. As it had been for their visit to the British Museum, her hair was swept up and away from her face, making her seem at once more childish and more sophisticated. This evening, though, she was wearing make-up that was almost heavy. In place of the usual prim clothes she'd put on a close-fitting black dress that was daringly short by her standards. The sensible shoes had given way to heels. She had a little handbag over one shoulder.

Julian's first impulse was to ask what had happened to her, yet the transformation itself left him incapable of speech. He just stood and stared. The clothes and make-up seemed to create an invisible barrier around her. He could never have any contact with such a woman. It was incredible to him that he'd made love to her the night before. The tight dress and high heels even made her move in a different way. As she swayed past him, he smelt perfume.

She went into the living-room, but didn't sit down. Julian followed. Seeing her inside, he realised that her appearance had done what it was supposed to do. Besides making her unobtainable, it had made him desire her more than ever. The presbytery had never looked so shabby and sad.

Standing in front of the sofa where the old version of herself had undressed the night before, Susan turned to face him. When she spoke, he could tell from her voice that she was in a hurry.

'So, what's happened?'

As he told her about Ralph's accident, her expression softened slightly, filling him with hope.

'You poor thing,' she said when he'd finished. 'You've really been having a rough time of it, haven't you?'

'We weren't very close,' said Julian, wanting to tell the truth. 'Still, it's shaken me up all the same.'

Then he couldn't bear it any longer. In desperation, he walked towards her, opening his arms. Yet when he tried to kiss her, she turned her head as though to protect her lipstick. Julian ended up clumsily kissing her jaw. She gave a little laugh, so that it became impossible for him to hold her with the intensity he would have liked. She put her arms loosely around him and they stood there for a while. Julian didn't know what to do.

Eventually, Susan stepped away. When he saw her face, as perfect as before, he knew that the invisible barrier would never be broken. No matter what he did, she would somehow elude him. He had the sensation of flailing, scrabbling for a hold at the top of a cliff, about to fall.

'You look lovely.'

She turned away when he said that, staring down at the carpet with a trace of her old embarrassment. It was as though the Susan he loved was in there somewhere, struggling to express herself. Julian forgot everything then in the sadness of seeing her so transformed.

'What's happened to you?'

She looked up at him with a strange defiance, as though determined to play out the role she had set herself.

'Sorry, but can we go out? This place depresses me.'

The insult to the presbytery was somehow unbearable to Julian. For a moment he said nothing, hoping by his silence to communicate all the pain she was making him feel. He didn't see how else it was to be expressed, since it was obviously impossible to talk to this creature about his feelings.

'All right, then,' he said. 'Where do you want to go?'

'I don't know. Let's just get out.'

Evening was falling as they left the presbytery, though there was still some light in the sky. They got into the Mini and Susan sat there for a moment, staring over the steering-wheel, thinking. At last she said:

'I know where we can go.'

She started the engine and they drove away, all the way through the village and up onto the A25. Both of them were silent. Being driven by her was strange. The car itself was a kind of revelation about her. There was a packet of boiled sweets in front of Julian, a map by his side, a sticker he couldn't read on the rear window. All these things shared in Susan's transformation, so that they seemed to mock and look down on him. There was a howl in his mind. All the same, he continued to hope. It was absurd to worry like this just because she'd dressed up to meet her friends. That he took it as a sign of anything deeper was just a result of his old, morbid fears.

After a while, they turned into a lane that was unfamiliar to him. The sky was hidden by trees which met overhead. Susan put the headlights on, illuminating the trees, which seemed startled by the light, as though they'd spent centuries in darkness. The car was like a submarine crawling along the bed of a dark sea, light pushed in front of it, black water closing in behind.

They stopped in a car-park that was no more than a clearing in the trees. There was only one other car there. Julian wondered whether it contained a pair of lovers, then had the crazy hope that she had brought him there so that they could be somewhere isolated and romantic together. Susan drove to the far side of the car-park and stopped. There was a steep hill in front of them.

'I've always wanted to bring you here.'

She reached across into the back of the car. After a few moments, she turned round, and through the gloom he saw that she was holding a pair of her old, flat shoes. She leaned forwards so that her face was close to the steering-wheel. There were small noises. Julian, who had slept with her the night before, now felt privileged to be there while she exposed her feet.

'Come on,' she said when she'd finished. 'I'm going to show you something wonderful.'

They got out of the car and began to walk up the hill. There was barely enough light to see where they were going. After a long, silent climb, they emerged onto a flat clearing. Out of the trees, there was a little more light.

'Look,' said Susan. 'This is the highest point in Surrey.'

The world was spread out at their feet, a pale area as huge as the sky. He could see the lights of cars moving slowly along the roads far below.

'That's the airport.'

Susan was pointing at a cluster of fierce, livid lights on the horizon. Julian looked dutifully. He felt she'd brought him up here in the absurd belief that it would cheer him up. After a few moments, she led the way to a bench which had been put there so that people could enjoy the view. Before sitting down on it in her smart dress, she brushed at the wood. Julian sat down close to her, and she didn't move away.

'I love this place,' she said. 'I always come here when things are getting on top of me.'

Perhaps because of all the space around them, her voice sounded softer than it had done in the presbytery. Encouraged, Julian looked at her. She was staring out at the wide expanse of land beneath them. After a moment, though, she turned towards him. As he had the night before, Julian broke and put his arms around her. For the second time, she avoided his lips, and he knew that it was hopeless. Releasing her, he said:

'What's the matter?'

Susan sighed and shifted as though preparing herself for some long-awaited ordeal.

'I don't think it's going to work.'

A dead weight dropped inside Julian as though a trapdoor had been opened. He saw the lights below him and the pale sky in the distance. It made him feel giddy. His mind flailed as he fell, still scrabbling for something to hold onto, although he knew that there was nothing. The drop was bottomless.

'Why?'

'I don't know. Perhaps you just need too much.' She was silent for a moment. 'There's some kind of absolute need in you. God might be able to satisfy it, but I don't think I can. Not now, at least.'

'You didn't feel like that yesterday.'

'How could I have said no to you then? You were in such a terrible state.' She looked towards him. 'That was why I came round last night, to tell you. I can hardly bring myself to say it now. I'm so sorry.'

'I don't understand. What about all those months you came after me?'

She gave a little smile, which might have been one of embarrassment.

'Perhaps I just didn't know what I really wanted. After my fiancé left me, I thought I never wanted to be with a man again. I just couldn't believe that anyone would ever really love me. Then, when I met you, I just kind of clung onto you. You seemed so different from other men, so distant and strong. Perhaps I just felt safe in the knowledge that nothing serious could ever come of it. I never thought that I might hurt you.'

'Nor did I,' said Julian, looking away from her. 'But you have.'

'I'm sorry. It was the last thing I wanted to do.'

They fell silent. Julian worried that she might get up and leave. He wanted to look at her again, but felt it would be too painful. Images passed through his mind. He saw Ralph lying among his tubes. Then he saw the photograph of his father, smiling. In the end, he decided that he had to look at her, no matter how painful it was. Soon she would be gone.

When he turned, he found that she'd been watching him all along, smiling with a sad sympathy which filled him with self-pity and love.

'I love you.'

The words reminded him of the night before, when they

had seemed so full of happiness and truth. Susan went on smiling at him.

'I do love you too, in a way. I think that, underneath it all, you're the most gentle, caring man I've ever met. Our time together has been like the courtship I always dreamed of. Perhaps the problem is that I feel you're just too good for me.'

Hope leapt in Julian. It seemed to him that, given time, things might be all right, after all.

'Can we still see each other?'

Susan pursed her lips regretfully and looked away.

'You remember that, when I met you up in the woods, I was going for an interview? Well, I got the job. I'm moving to London next week.'

'I see.'

It was the end. This really was the end, after all. This was what he'd been afraid of all his life. He was reliving that night when his mother had ordered him back to his room and he'd waited there alone, knowing that all his fears were coming true. It had been the same room where his father had used to sit and tell him stories, leaving him to sleep each night with a happily ever after in his mind and the assurance that it was true, that every word of it was true.

Julian thought frantically. It seemed to him that, if he could only say the right things and behave in the right way, he could still win her round. She would turn back into herself, into that modest girl who had so respected and loved him. It was impossible that she, who the night before had lavished happiness and pleasure on him with apparently endless generosity, should suddenly now subject him to this final and irrevocable pain. It was simply impossible.

'Who are you meeting tonight, then?'

Susan shook her head.

'Nobody important.'

Something about her tone produced a new kind of

anguish in him. He was struck again by the way she was dressed, and it filled him with fury.

'Just tell me.'

'All right, then,' she said, sounding irritated. 'I'm going to see a man I met when I went up for my interview. You had your chance that day, remember, and you decided not to take it.'

Julian was too stunned to speak. The sheer pain of it might have killed his anger if Susan at that moment hadn't peered through the darkness at her watch.

'Leave, then,' he said. 'Go away.'

As though realising what she'd done, she leaned back heavily on the bench.

'I'm really sorry.'

'Just leave.'

'Don't you want me to give you a lift back? It'll take you ages to walk from here.'

'I don't care,' he said thickly. 'Just as long as I never see you again.'

'Julian —'

It was the first time she'd ever used his name, and her voice was full of pity. There was surprise, too, as though she'd never expected to see him reduced to this. He leaned forwards and hid his face in his hands. A moment later, he felt her stroking his head, and knew that she was only doing it to make herself feel better. She wanted him to feign acceptance so that she could go on to her new man without the burden of guilt.

For all that, it was impossible to resist the touch of her hand, which seemed so understanding and kind. Julian's eyes screwed up and he concentrated just on that touch. Out of it he produced a desperate fantasy that nothing had happened, after all, that she still loved him. It only lasted a few seconds. Then she destroyed it all by speaking.

'Please don't be like this.'

With a sudden, violent movement, he shook her off.

'Go away!'

'I can't,' she said. 'I don't care if I'm late.'

'Thanks a lot.'

'I'm not leaving you like this.'

Julian lifted his head and shouted at her.

'Can't you understand? You've used me, you've led me along for months, and now you've ruined everything for me. I can't stand the sight of you. Just go away.' She didn't move. 'Fuck off!'

With a jolt, she stood up. Julian turned away. He couldn't bear to see her leave. She didn't say goodbye. All he heard was the sound of her walking back the way they had come. Now that it was done, he couldn't believe that it was happening. He couldn't believe that he'd sent her away for ever. Even though it was hopeless, he should have tried to make her stay. Even those last few moments with her would have been better than this.

Darkness was falling. The stars were coming out. The last pallor of the land was gone, so that it was now just a dark expanse which stretched to the horizon. The lights of the houses were like those of boats that had dropped anchor for the night. Looking down at them, he slowly realised that her last memory of him, of Father Snow, would be an unworthy one.

Suddenly he got up and ran after her. It turned out that she hadn't gone far. Near the edge of the clearing, where the descent began, she stopped and turned towards him. Julian slowed his pace and walked towards her with a strange, sudden calm. She waited in silence. When he arrived, she said:

'What do you want?'

There was still anger in her voice, but Julian maintained his composure. As he stood there, stiff and upright, with his hands by his side and his mouth compressed into a line, he realised that he'd adopted the old posture of Father Snow.

'I'm sorry I shouted at you,' he said. 'I'm sorry I used bad language.'

To his surprise, Susan ran up and threw her arms around him when he said that, pressing her head against his shoulder. Julian suffered it as Father Snow would have done. He stood like a pillar.

'I do love you,' she said, and he heard that she was crying. 'I could never love anyone as much as I love you. But if I tried to have you, you wouldn't be yourself any more, and I couldn't stand that.'

As she said it, Father Snow saw that she was right, and understood everything. Then for some reason he remembered the photograph of his father which was still standing on the desk in his bedroom.

'You've done a lot for me, Susan. You've made me happy.'

Crying harder, she shook her head against his shoulder.

'No, you're the one who's made me happy. You've restored my self-respect, my faith in people. I can't bear to think that we won't see each other any more, but we can't. We just can't. Tell me you understand.'

'Of course I do,' said Father Snow, giving her an awkward pat on the back. 'There's no need for you to be upset, you know. I'll be all right.'

Then it seemed to him that his father had been right, after all. Every word of it was true. In this life, happily ever after can only mean a finite time, and one finite time is much the same as another. These last few moments in themselves would be enough to prove that it was true.

'There's only one thing I'd like you to do for me.'

Susan removed her head from his shoulder and stared up at him. He was struck, as he had been on first seeing her, by the strong line of her jaw.

'What?'

'Don't go round dressed like that. It doesn't suit you.' She suddenly lowered her face, ashamed. 'I don't mean that unkindly. I just mean that I prefer the way you usually dress. When I first met you, you were so —'

Father Snow found that he was unable to go on.

357

'You're right,' said Susan quietly. 'I've never really felt comfortable done up like this, in any case. It isn't really me.'

Then she lifted her head, put her hand behind his neck, and kissed him. Father Snow unbent a little, lowering his head. He was reminded of their first kiss, which had seemed at the time to him almost a communion of souls. There was something of that spiritual dimension now, though it was not a union he felt this time, but a sundering.

When it was over, he saw the pale shape of her face in the darkness, and understood how much of himself had been invested in her. Their moments of nakedness and trust, no matter how brief they had been, had indeed been for ever and could never be undone. When he said it now, he knew it was for the last time in his life.

'I love you.'

Susan stared up at him.

'I know I'm doing the wrong thing,' she said. 'I know I'll never meet another man like you. Perhaps the problem is that I'm just afraid. Do you understand that?'

Father Snow smiled.

'I, of all people, understand.'

'So you won't be angry with me?'

He shook his head.

'Never.'

At last she turned and began to make her way between the trees, still crying. It took Father Snow a while to accept that his moments of human happiness were gone. He walked back up to the bench at the top of the hill. It was the emptiest place he'd ever known.

He sat there for a long time, watching the lights of the planes. They descended slowly, so that it seemed they were hanging on the air, until they were eventually swallowed by the larger light of the airport on the horizon. In the end, he turned and looked at the place next to him on the bench. It was impossible to believe that she'd ever been there. At the same time, it was impossible to believe that she was gone.

Beside the grief of losing her, Father Snow still felt his old despair. He thought of the life which was waiting for him, and knew that there would be no escaping from it now. Then he thought of Ralph lying in the hospital, suspended between life and death. Lifting his head, he saw a plane hanging above the airport. He wondered where it had been.

When the plane had landed, Father Snow stood stiffly up and began the walk back to the presbytery.

Susan had been right: it took him ages to get back. Walking took his mind off things a little, so that he felt that perhaps the pain wasn't so bad, after all. He would recover quickly and go back to the old life, the old satisfactions. From time to time, though, he couldn't help thinking of her, having a drink with her new boyfriend while Father Snow walked back to his empty house. There was no jealousy or anger now, but only grief. He told himself that she would never forget him, and knew it wasn't really true. Her brain would remember, but her emotions would soon move on and forget. Perhaps they had already done so. But his own feelings for her, as he returned to the suspended world of celibacy, would never be replaced. For his own part, he would never forget.

It was past midnight by the time he got back to the presbytery. As soon as he stepped through the door, the intense loneliness of the place settled on him. All the old problems came with it. He remembered the suicide, the photograph of Father Conner, the monstrous evil that existed in the village. It only made him long to see her even more, to share the problem with her.

Without thinking, he walked into the living-room. It was a mistake. He immediately pictured her standing there in her make-up and black dress. Then he saw himself, desperate, crossing the room to try and kiss her. Worst of all was the carpet in front of the fireplace where they had lain together. She had been present in that place more intensely than anywhere else. Now her absence focused itself there, an absolute lack.

Looking at the place, he wondered if perhaps some tiny trace of her, a scent or a strand of hair, had remained there to comfort him. He almost went and lay down there as he had the night before, staring up at the coffee-table and the curtains. Instead, forcing himself to behave as Father Snow, he straightened and walked into the study. There, in the light which fell from the french windows, he saw the two chairs standing side by side in the garden.

Then Father Snow knew that he had to get out of the presbytery. He also needed to see somebody. Even a drink with Ralph would do. He was on his way to the phone before he remembered that Ralph wasn't at home, but lying in a hospital bed, his heart and lungs kept going by machines. Only now did he really begin to see the horror of it. Whatever sins Ralph might have committed, he had surely received ample punishment.

Catatonic or not, Ralph was all that Father Snow had left. Before self-pity could get the better of him, he straightened his back and went upstairs. There he changed into his black suit and dog-collar. A few moments later he was driving to the hospital, back to the post he should never have deserted, at the deathbed of his fellow priest.

22

THE INTENSIVE-CARE WARD was a very different place by night. There was muted illumination inside, as though dying were something best accomplished in a discreet twilight. Total darkness waited at the windows. The hiss and suck of the respirators was louder now, sustaining the silence of the six unconscious figures.

Calm and upright, Father Snow paced between the beds. Perhaps because of his own loss, he no longer had the feeling that the patients were simply sleeping, waiting to be woken up. The unreality he'd felt about it all that afternoon was gone. They were really dying, after all. Their souls hung above the beds like six loosely-tethered balloons, tugging gently, waiting to float away.

The shocking thing about Ralph now was the fact that he hadn't moved an inch. He was lying exactly as Father Snow had left him all that time before, flat on his back with his arms at his sides, his barrel-chest rising under the sheets, an effigy of Ralph. The bandage was still wrapped around his head, the pads of cotton-wool still covered his eyes. The numerous tubes still hung in exactly the same position. To Father Snow, after all he'd been through, it seemed incredible. The world had changed, but Ralph had just lain there motionless, sleeping through it all. It was as though he'd already entered eternity.

When Father Snow sat down in the chair by the bed, he began remembering his time with Susan. Yet all the while he was looking at Ralph's face, staring fiercely, as though he wanted to explain how it had all happened. He thought of her standing outside the presbytery in her demure clothes, then sitting inside with her knees together, as though he were the one who might make advances. By the dual carriageway, as he leaned down towards the car, she said she was falling in love with him. The rain soaked through his jacket. In the Happy Eater she explained about her fiancé, screwing up a little packet of sugar and grinding it into the ashtray. She stepped out into the snow, telling him it was a fairy tale. Somehow she'd made him believe it all.

Still staring at the macabre figure on the bed, he found that his thoughts had taken on a kind of frantic intensity. He realised that he was still trying to explain. Now that it was too late, he wanted to open his heart to Ralph. In this perfect loneliness, he would have given anything to see him as he had done in the old days, slapping him on the back and filling his glass with drink in that large, empty living-room. It seemed to him now that, if he'd been allowed to go back, he'd have been able to find a way of liking Ralph, after all. Yet he knew that such things are easy and convenient to believe when there's no risk that they'll come true.

Father Snow sat quite still, as though the perfect stillness next to him on the bed was infectious. If anything, the suspicions of the afternoon were stronger than before. He felt certain that Ralph and Father Conner had been in it together. When he'd seen the photograph, Ralph had feared impending discovery and humiliation. He'd known Father Snow to be implacable. His tears on the doorstep at their last meeting had been tears not only of despair, but also of repentance.

None of this seemed to change Father Snow's desire to see him again. He leaned forwards, close enough to see the pock-marks in Ralph's nose, as though the answer to some mystery was there to be read on his catatonic face. As he did so, he understood that his dislike for Ralph had never been the result of a difference in spiritual development or of Ralph's drinking. It had all been more simple and fundamental than that, a question of loneliness and need. Ralph had simply been the lonelier of the two. Father Snow had still been young and sexually attractive. He'd still had options open to him, and the presence of Susan in the background had been a constant proof of this. Ralph's need had been repulsive, as the need of the lonelier always is.

Now that Susan was gone, they were equals at last.

'I'm sorry, Ralph,' murmured Father Snow. 'All of this has been my fault, in a way.'

Ralph lay flat among his tubes, so motionless that it seemed he was deliberately ignoring Father Snow, playing some childish game. Again, his suspicions returned, and again they seemed unimportant. Remembering how he'd been preparing to leave the priesthood for Susan, Father Snow shook his head.

'What would Vincent say about all this, eh? We've made a proper mess of things.'

Then he was silent for a while, thinking about the night when Vincent had arrived at Ralph's presbytery. Ralph had been boisterous and amusing that night, telling endless stories. Father Snow, consumed by petty jealousy for Ralph's relationship with Vincent, hadn't understood. Through it all, Ralph had been trying to show the kind of friend he might have been.

Suddenly feeling it was too painful to go on looking at Ralph's silent face, Father Snow turned away. He found himself staring at the big red hand lying on top of the sheet. Somehow that hand seemed to reveal Ralph's personality better than anything else. All of it was there: his morose moods, his insecurity, his crude bonhomie. Yet perhaps it was also a hand that had committed the most awful of sins, the ruin of innocent lives.

'I don't care what you've done,' whispered Father Snow.

Without thinking, he reached down and took the hand in his own. It was surprisingly, almost shockingly warm, but it was completely limp. He remembered how firm its grip had been, how Ralph used to raise it in a fist as he said goodbye from his presbytery door.

Then Father Snow found that he had raised the hand to his face. This surprised him, so that he wasn't sure if he really was Father Snow any more, or simply Julian again, the man who had fallen in love. He kissed the hand and pressed it against his cheek. There was a strange, sweet smell from Ralph's skin that was not entirely unpleasant.

'Come back,' said Father Snow, then smiled. 'Come back, you old soak. All is forgiven. I'll do everything I can to protect you.'

There was no movement in the fallen frame. Father Snow replaced the hand on the bed, but found he didn't want to leave. For the first time since they'd met, he didn't want to get away from Ralph. Perhaps Julian's feelings for Susan were still spilling out of him, or perhaps it was Father Snow's nature to feel friendship only at a safe distance. The catatonic are undemanding and can never make you ill at ease. It was almost pleasurable for Father Snow to sit there. Ralph was like a sympathetic and respectful audience, listening in on his thoughts. Though he didn't speak, Father Snow felt he was revealing things to Ralph that he would never have revealed in life. Without shame, he showed himself bending down to pick bluebells for Susan. Then they were sitting side by side in the garden, and Father Snow made no secret of the enormous happiness he'd felt. Nor did he attempt to hide the grief of that evening, when she'd eluded him at last. It felt to him now like the end of the world. At the centre of it all was the image of her face, grave and changed after their first kiss.

Returning his attention to the bed, Father Snow wondered if it was wrong for him to sit there thinking about Susan when Ralph lay on the edge of death. Surely any grief he felt should have been reserved for this greater tragedy. Yet he felt then that death is not a tragedy, after all. Death is simply the end of tragedy, the absence of it. All the tragedies take place in life, and they are all to do with separation, with saying goodbye.

After that, Father Snow sat and stared at Ralph for a long time, wondering what his life, or at least his existence on this earth, had amounted to. As he did so, he realised his almost complete ignorance of Ralph. He knew nothing about his background, his childhood, his family, the place where he'd grown up, because he'd never thought to ask. Now that it was too late, Ralph seemed the most fascinating of people, a mystery he would have given anything to unfold. All he could do was imagine. Ralph would have played conkers and had fights in the playground. No doubt he had also fallen in love and undergone, like Father Snow, like everyone, the anguish of being abandoned. At some point, he would have turned to God. Perhaps he had been fiery as a young man, perhaps morose. Corruption and despair might have started in middle age, or they might have been there since the beginning.

In the end, all Father Snow could understand of Ralph's life was its enormous size. There had been a vast number of experiences and emotions. Father Snow saw them passing in front of Ralph like a long carnival procession, a line of fabulous floats, the beautiful and the grotesque. All of it ended here, in this particular hospital bed among these particular machines and tubes, with Father Snow, this particular, peculiar man as the only witness.

When he realised this, Father Snow was awed by the sheer solemnity of what was happening. Ralph lay silent, playing out his part, holding in his catatonia the whole secret and mystery of a human life, the dream of a deep sleeper. Looking at him, Father Snow realised that everything between them had changed. Although Ralph might not have known it, some communication and union had taken place. In some strange way, Father Snow had revealed his innermost self, and felt that Ralph had done the same. If Ralph ever did recover, Father Snow would treat him in a very different way. Tonight had been the beginning of their friendship.

Father Snow stayed there for a long time. In the end, he reached out and squeezed Ralph's hand.

'Goodbye.'

The word stuck in his throat, because he saw that this particular scene was not Ralph's tragedy, after all, but his own.

The grief was worse next day. As soon as Father Snow woke up, it all came back to him. He remembered Susan in her black dress and Ralph lying among his tubes. In Ralph's case, at least, there was still a little hope. Father Snow decided to go back and see him again immediately after morning Mass. In a strange way, he found himself looking forward to it.

Before he set off, Father Snow tried to eat breakfast, but he could only force down a few mouthfuls. Then he sat there and wondered when he'd last had a proper meal. He couldn't remember. For all that, he didn't feel dizzy or ill. Yet there was a light, hallucinatory clarity about everything, as there had been the day before when he'd walked through the garden, in love. Perhaps it was a version of what the ancient saints had felt after their days of fasting.

The telephone rang. It was the hospital, calling to tell him that Ralph was dead. As he was listening, Father Snow looked out through the french windows and saw the two chairs which were still standing side by side in the garden. He had reached the end.

When he put the phone down, he went outside, folded up the chairs and put them away. Somehow he had lost himself. He was neither Father Snow nor Julian any more. He had reached the end. Even grief seemed to have deserted him. He felt light and empty. In a dream, he went round to the church and knelt down for what might have been a very long time. Eventually, he began to see as he had done outside the laboratory with Vincent, not knowing whether his eyes were open or closed. He saw his father by his bedside, Ralph laughing, Susan floating towards him over clouds of bluebells. He saw a tiny figure curled on the carpet in the living-room, weeping, and realised it was himself. Then everything dissolved into pure light, which was like starlight, but immense. The weeping, foetal figure was a speck in the midst of it, but not invisible, curled in the aisle of the church. Father Snow understood then his own importance. He had an overwhelming sense of himself as a creature, entirely dependent and infinitely weak. At the same time, he looked into the light and knew he would never really be unhappy again.

For some days after that, he brooded, leaving the presbytery only when absolutely necessary. He still ate little. For hours on end he would sit motionless, losing track of time, meditating on the way his vocation had been finally secured. It seemed to him that God had sent Susan as proof that, even with the best of women, Father Snow would never find happiness. With her departure, any last hopes of an ordinary life had been removed. Ralph's death had tied the final knot. All he could do in his allotted time was try to make amends.

At the same time, Father Snow brooded also on the situation in the village. There would be no running away from it now. A strength had appeared in him that was far greater than his old rigidity, and he knew that it had been given for a purpose. He was the one who, after all those centuries, would finally break the ogre's spell.

Some days after Ralph's death, Father Snow rang Flamstead House and asked Trevellyan if he could come up to see him. Though it was the first time he'd made such a request, Trevellyan agreed with a kind of mournful resignation, as if he'd been expecting or dreading such a visit.

Father Snow set off in the early evening. Before he left, he saw the stick Vincent had used on their walks, still leaning where he had left it in the corner of the study, and decided to take it with him. Outside it was windy, but mild. There was that perfume in the gardens and the lanes which he was coming to associate with Wodden in late spring. Swinging his stick, Father Snow strolled down the hill and across the bridge by the Old Mill. For some reason, there were more people than usual walking up and down the lane. Everything seemed full of a strange anticipation. On the village green, he saw a sign pointing in the direction of the school: POLLING STATION.

Father Snow had entirely forgotten about the election. He paused on the green and watched for a few moments, leaning on his stick. The whole thing now seemed perfectly meaningless to him. He supposed the Conservatives would win as usual. Old England always does win, in the end. In worldly terms, it would be a disaster. Spiritually, he wasn't so sure.

As he watched, he was suddenly struck by the quintessential Englishness of the scene. Singly or in twos, the voters made their way across the twilit green. The war memorial seemed to watch them come and go with silent approval. Two of them deviated on their way back, attracted by the muted lights of the pub. There was no sound of merriment or revelry from within. High above the village, Flamstead House was still visible, throwing out the peculiarly English spell which kept it all in place, the enchantment of the centuries.

After a while, Father Snow moved on. He walked along the High Street and up onto the A25. A part of him still hoped to see Susan on the way, but he was almost relieved when it didn't happen. Even if they did bump into each other, there was nothing to be done. The following week, she would be gone. Even so, he paused on the A25 to look down at the gaudy lights of the Happy Eater, remembering his happiness. He knew that he could never really have loved Ralph, or even God, if he hadn't first loved her. There had been a purpose to it all.

At last Father Snow dragged himself away. A short while later, he had reached the snarling griffons. Here, too, he paused to look up, remembering. He wasn't sure whether the carvings were so impressive in spite of their age or because of it. It was amazing to think of the centuries they had stood there, posturing at the road. Almost as amazing was the time that had elapsed since he'd first seen them himself, the changes that he'd undergone. Leaning back to look up at them, he found his sense of history got joined with his own nostalgia. From now on, now that Susan and Ralph were gone, this was the feeling which would dominate his life. There was no way it could be controlled. The best of life is always in the past.

The park was at its best in twilight. The deer, gliding silently between the trees, seemed barely physical, mere spirits or illusions. The grass was pale, losing its colour as the sun went down, but still managing to capture and project the last of the light. The huge trees themselves, though, had fallen into perfect darkness, swaying and sighing in their sleep. There were only a few lights on in the great house at the top of the hill.

Father Snow walked slowly, savouring it all. When he at last arrived, Trevellyan himself answered the door. As he had been on their last meeting, he was dressed in a flowing white shirt which gave him a faintly historical air. This evening, though, he was wearing black jodhpurs and knee-high riding boots.

'Good evening, Father. Do come in.' Leaning his stick against the wall, Father Snow stepped into the house. 'I thought I might go out for a ride later,' Trevellyan went on, as though apologising for his appearance. 'Do you ride?'

'No.' They were walking down the long corridor where he'd first met Gerald Pitman. 'I don't know one end of a horse from the other, I'm afraid.'

'You should learn,' said Trevellyan sadly. 'It's the most wonderful thing, especially at night.'

With that, he folded his hands behind his back and stared down at the red carpet as though embarrassed. They paced on in silence. Eventually Trevellyan led the way into the living-room where they'd gone with Vincent long before. Here they sat down facing each other.

'So, Father,' said Trevellyan quietly. 'What can I do for you?'

Only now did it strike Father Snow that he hadn't planned this conversation at all. In the old days, he would have constantly rehearsed it in his head before coming. This evening, though, he'd just turned up, trusting that he would be guided to do the right thing when the time came. Now the right thing seemed just to sit and look at Trevellyan quietly. This evidently made Trevellyan uncomfortable. After a few long moments, he stirred, refusing to meet Father Snow's eye.

'Well?' There was an unfamiliar edge to his voice. 'What do you want?'

'Somebody recently sent me a photograph,' said Father Snow. 'It showed my predecessor abusing a child. A young girl.'

'What's that got to do with me?'

Father Snow shook his head, almost disappointed at the clumsiness of this answer. The long silence that had preceded the conversation had obviously left Trevellyan too rattled even to erect the most rudimentary defences.

'You're not shocked? Most people would be outraged to find out that the man who'd been their parish priest for ten years had been doing such things.'

Trevellyan scowled down at his long fingernails.

'There have been other such cases . . .'

'No matter how many there had been, a Catholic would always find it shocking. Unless, that is, he had some prior knowledge.'

Trevellyan looked up.

'What are you trying to say?'

'That you're somehow involved,' said Father Snow

gently. 'I've come here so that you can tell me the exact nature and extent of your involvement.'

'You're wrong. You've got caught up in some crazy paranoia.'

Father Snow smiled and shook his head.

'You won't put me off so easily, I'm afraid. I'm going to hound you until I've got what I want.' The priest himself was surprised at the implacable calm of his voice. Trevellyan's huge frame seemed to sink back into his seat as though he really were being hounded. 'Let me assure you, though, that I seek a solution to these things purely on the spiritual plane. I have no desire to inflict public humiliation on you. I have no interest in seeing justice done as the world perceives it.' He smiled. 'And still less in shaking governments.'

Trevellyan was silent.

'Best to do it now,' said Father Snow. 'You'll feel better once you've got it over and done with. That's why I'm here.' He leaned forward and spoke quietly. 'Put the burden onto me.'

After that, they both sat motionless, Father Snow still leaning forward, Trevellyan staring at the floor. When Trevellyan eventually tried to speak, all that emerged was a croak, as though he hadn't used his voice for years. He coughed and tried again.

'Jack Dugdale took the photograph.' Father Snow sat perfectly still, suddenly horrified, as though he'd never really believed that any of it was true. 'The girl with Father Conner is Dugdale's daughter.'

'And did Dugdale send it to me?'

'No. I did that.'

'Why?'

'Because I thought you'd want to avoid bringing scandal on the Church. I thought it would keep you quiet.'

He paused. Father Snow waited patiently, taking in the long white hair and fingernails as though seeing them for the first time. It struck him that he'd climbed the

371

beanstalk at last. He was in the presence of a living ogre.

'I've always been obsessed by Everard,' said Trevellyan eventually. 'Even in my childhood, I knew a version of his story, although it was one from which the sexual aspects had been expunged. Then, at the age when most boys are reading girlie magazines, I found and read Everard's own account of his crimes.' He looked up. 'It changed me forever. What had started as fascination with a fairy tale turned into a more sinister obsession. I became prey to another kind of fantasy. I began to see myself as a freak, the victim of some genetic evil. In my worst moments, I even believed myself a reincarnation. Even now, I can't quite shake off that belief.'

'No matter what you've done,' said Father Snow, 'I can't believe you come anywhere close to him.'

'No, I don't. My monstrosities are . . . pathetic compared to his. Perhaps I'd almost feel less ashamed of them if they were greater. For a long time, you see, I led an outwardly normal life. I got married and made love to my wife in the ordinary way, though I had the most extraordinary fantasies while I was doing so. I thought I'd go on like that forever, being a monster only in my mind. Then I met Jack Dugdale.'

'When he came to work here as a groundsman?'

Trevellyan nodded.

'He, too, knew the story of Everard and was fascinated by it. Whenever we met, he'd bring the subject up. He dropped careful hints that his sexual interests might lie in the same direction as Everard's. Eventually I found myself dropping similar hints. Then one day a letter arrived containing a photograph far worse than the one I sent you of Father Conner. After all those years of just imagining, it was the most arousing thing I'd ever seen.'

Trevellyan stopped and swallowed. Father Snow was silent, choked with pity and disgust.

'When I next saw him, Dugdale asked me if I'd liked

the photograph. That was how it started. After that, he sent me huge numbers of them.'

'Where did he get them from?'

'I don't know exactly. Somewhere up in London. He said they were very expensive, and I ended up paying more and more money for them. Of course, it horrified me to think that they were photographs of real abuse, and to imagine the effect it had had on the victims, but. I just couldn't help myself. I couldn't say no. Then one day Dugdale asked me if I'd be interested in having a real child, one who had already been broken in, as he put it, and would do whatever I wanted. He assured me that there was no risk. As long as I was prepared to pay him, I could have what I'd always dreamed of.'

After that, Father Snow tried to stop himself from listening. He was afraid that Trevellyan would at any moment break down. Staring out of the windows at the twilit park, he heard Trevellyan explain how Dugdale had brought his daughter to work with him one day during the Easter holidays. He'd disappeared into the grounds, leaving Trevellyan alone with the child, assuring him again that he could do what he wanted, that she was used to it.

'But instead of that, I found myself having a conversation with her. More than anything else, I felt embarrassed. I asked her about her school work, her friends, her favourite television programmes. She was so sweet.' Trevellyan's voice broke. Yet when Father Snow turned from the window, he saw no tears trickling down the ogre's face. 'I knew that I didn't have it in me to harm her.' He shook his head. 'That poor child.'

'So you just let her go?'

'Yes. And after that, I was sickened by the whole thing. It was as though I woke up. I sacked Dugdale and told him never to send me any more pictures. I wanted to go to the police, but I couldn't have exposed him without exposing myself, and that's the one thing I couldn't have stood. I've always been terrified of that.'

'But you kept the pictures he'd already sent you?'

'Only one or two of them. I thought it best to have something there in case . . . the pressure ever built up.'

For a moment Father Snow was simply too disgusted to speak. All Everard's monstrosities were somehow better than this.

'And the picture of Father Conner was one of the ones you kept?'

Trevellyan nodded.

'I don't know how Dugdale got to him. Probably as he did with me, first with hints, then with photographs, and finally with the offer of his daughter. The only difference was that Father Conner took the offer up. It astonishes me, even now. He seemed such a kindly man. But then I suppose none of us can know what sort of pressures he was under. When I heard he'd killed himself, I was simply horrified.'

'You don't know what finally drove him to it?'

'No. But my guess would be that he believed, as you do, that he'd uncovered some vast conspiracy. He would have felt himself surrounded by evil but unable to act without exposing himself. It probably drove him mad.'

'And is there a conspiracy?'

'Not as far as I know.'

'But Dugdale apparently claimed to be part of a wider ring.'

'Knowing Dugdale, it was probably all talk. That, and a way of protecting himself.'

Father Snow was astonished.

'So Pitman was never involved?'

For the first time, Trevellyan smiled.

'Oh, no. Gerald is purely interested in other kinds of power. So much so that I think it's made him almost asexual.'

'And Saunders?'

Trevellyan shook his head.

'Innocent, to the best of my knowledge. There's no

monstrous network here, Father. It all went no further than Dugdale, Father Conner and myself. The only victim was that one poor girl.'

Father Snow was quiet for a few moments, taking this in. None of it had really been true. The children's nightmares about this house were really just nightmares, after all, the product of a fairy tale. The modern version of the story was a dirty, squalid thing, because the real giants are always in the past.

'Yet the message you sent me with the photograph suggested that there were others.'

'Only to frighten you. I wanted you to think that other priests might be involved, you see, though none of them ever were.'

So Ralph had been innocent, too. Simple loneliness, depression and despair over Father Conner, the despair of a good priest for one of the bad, had driven him to end his life. Father Snow thought the guilt of it would cripple him. Perhaps he'd been so willing to believe Ralph a monster precisely to avoid this guilt, to shift the burden away from his own inhumanity.

Father Snow found himself shaking his head.

'How could I ever have believed all that?'

'It's simple.' Trevellyan spread his long nailed hands. 'Everyone needs a fairy tale.'

As soon as he heard that, the thought of Susan leapt into Father Snow's head.

'There is a kind of truth in them,' he said. 'I know there is.' Trevellyan smiled.

'You must think me a very poor successor to Everard.' He stopped smiling and stared straight at Father Snow. 'How you must despise me.'

'No, I don't despise you.' The thought of Ralph once more crossed his mind, and he smiled warmly at Trevellyan. 'Judge not, lest ye be judged. Even a priest can forget that simple rule.'

His tone and expression seemed to amaze Trevellyan.

'You don't find me disgusting?'

'No. Everyone has to struggle with their own weaknesses. Who's to say that, in God's eyes, you haven't struggled harder and better than me?'

Trevellyan's big face screwed up at this, and he looked away.

'What do you want me to do now, then, Father?'

'You've confessed to me as a man,' said Father Snow, 'and I admire you for it.' He removed his stole from his pocket and draped it around his neck. 'Now I think it's time you made your peace with God.'

With a single nod, the huge man got up, lowered himself to his knees, and began to weep.

Afterwards, it seemed that Trevellyan was unable to look at Father Snow. He stood up, went to one of the windows and stared out into the darkness of his ancestral grounds. Father Snow watched and waited quietly, not feeling awkward. Trevellyan was standing with his feet apart and his hands behind his back, his face hidden by two wings of white hair. In spite of everything, although his sins had been the tawdriest that Father Snow had ever heard, Trevellyan managed to retain a kind of fairy-tale charm. Perhaps the aristocracy will always have that, no matter how low they sink, since they are a kind of living history. Only priests have quite the same air of anachronism.

'When did you last visit Everard's room?' said Father Snow.

'Oh . . . more than twenty years ago.' Trevellyan was still staring outside. 'The very idea of it terrifies me.'

'Then I think perhaps we should go up there now.'

Trevellyan turned from the window.

'Is that really necessary, Father?'

'I think so,' said Father Snow calmly. 'I think it's important that you go there with me and see that it really is no more than an old room.'

'Father,' said Trevellyan suddenly, 'I've never asked you —'

'Asked me what?'

'What happened when you went there with Vincent.'

Father Snow was silent for a moment, trying to find the best words to explain.

'We did away with a piece of the past,' he said, then smiled. 'Or rather, Vincent did away with it. I was afraid, so I ran away and waited in the car.'

Trevellyan turned back towards the window.

'It's very strange . . .'

'See it as a sign. All of us are to some extent the prisoners of history. Perhaps it's a peculiarly English thing. But it doesn't have to be like that.' He paused, looking at Trevellyan's back and wondering if he'd understood. 'You have to live with the past, but there's no need to live under it. Each morning, we have the power to recreate the world anew.'

'I hope you're right,' said Trevellyan quietly.

Satisfied with the tone of his voice, Father Snow stood up.

'Come on,' he said. 'Let's get it over with.'

So they left the room and walked silently down the corridor. Outside, Trevellyan went into the little National Trust booth. A moment later he emerged holding a bunch of keys and a rubber torch, and they walked side by side towards the old part of the building. Dusk was falling. The huge antlers on the wall still looked impressive, if rather theatrical today.

When Trevellyan opened the door, the alarm on the wall began to beep. He stepped forwards and keyed in the code. All of it reminded Father Snow of the night he'd visited the house with Vincent. He hadn't been back to this part of the building since. Watching the giant with his mane of white hair, he began to feel a little of that fear.

Trevellyan turned on the lights and strode quickly across the main hall. Then he led the way upstairs into the long gallery of portraits. Both of them glanced up at Everard's sneering face as they passed, but neither of them stopped. At the end of the gallery, Trevellyan unlocked and opened a window.

'This isn't as difficult as it looks, Father.'

Sitting on the window-sill, he swung his legs outside. Then, holding onto the frame, he stood up so that he was facing Father Snow with the drop to the courtyard behind him. He shuffled to the end of the ledge, leaned his arm across to hold something out of sight, and disappeared.

Father Snow went and clambered up onto the window-sill. When he swung his legs out, he found the drop far greater than he had imagined. Above him, he could hear Trevellyan grunting and scrambling. Feeling giddy, he clung onto the window-frame and stood himself up. When he'd done so, he lifted his head and saw that there was a ledge above the window on which Trevellyan was now standing.

'It's easy from here, Father. You just have to climb the ivy then step across. After that, it's simple to get onto the roof.'

Having shuffled to the edge, Father Snow reached across to get a handhold. Then there was an unpleasant moment while his legs were scrabbling in the air. After that, though, it was plain sailing. Father Snow had never climbed ivy in his life before, or even believed that such a thing was really possible. As he stepped onto the ledge above the window, he felt an unexpected elation.

Trevellyan by that time had climbed up onto the roof. As he'd promised, this part was easy. A moment later, they were standing side by side, looking at the vast net-work of roofs and courtyards spread out beneath them. The moon was up. Away in the distance, hidden from public view behind the house, Father Snow could see a swimming-pool.

When they'd looked for a moment, both of them turned round. They were standing on a huge, flat roof surrounded by a low parapet. In the centre of it, Father Snow could just make out the trap-door. Trevellyan led the way. The door was protected by an ancient, rusty padlock, which he bent down to open. After fiddling for a moment, he lifted the door and laid it down flat on the roof. A square of perfect blackness had opened at their feet. Trevellyan produced the torch from his pocket and shone it down into the square, illuminating the first few rungs of an old iron ladder which disappeared into the darkness.

'The ogre's laboratory.'

After that, they both just stood there and stared downwards. Cold, musty air seemed to rise up across their faces. Father Snow felt his courage begin to fail. Darting's account of the horrors he'd seen down there passed through his mind. He remembered also the horror he'd experienced himself, and began to fear that Vincent might not have succeeded that night, after all, that Everard had somehow survived.

When they'd been staring at the entrance for a few moments, Trevellyan handed him the torch.

'I'll go first.'

So Father Snow shone a soft, egg-shaped light into the dark while Trevellyan began to climb down the ladder. It was far longer than he'd expected. The sound of Trevellyan's feet on the iron was soon inaudible. The egg of light got slowly larger and weaker as he descended, trembling against the wall. While he was watching, Father Snow realised that the wind had picked up. He could hear it roaring softly through the distant trees. His black jacket flapped around his hips and he felt for a moment that he was standing on some enormous ship, staring down into the hold.

When he at last reached the bottom, Trevellyan lifted his head and shouted up for Father Snow to drop him the torch. A moment later, the light was wheeling and spinning through blackness. Then Trevellyan shone it up onto the ladder and Father Snow climbed down.

When he'd reached the bottom, Trevellyan gave him the torch back so he could have a look around. Father Snow swept the light across the walls. The laboratory was far smaller than he'd imagined. After the long climb down, it was more like examining the bottom of a lift-shaft than a room. The walls were flaking. As he moved the torch around, expecting some nightmarish vision to appear at any moment, Father Snow began to lose his bearings. It seemed to him that the light stood still while the room revolved around it and objects moved themselves into its illumination. A wooden workbench slid into the motionless circle of light, kept sliding, then vanished. There was nothing on its surface. Old tea-chests jumped upwards. They were full of peculiar glass jars, many of them broken. A fantastic pile of metal struts suddenly appeared and stood still in the light while Father Snow wondered if it might once have served some occult or scientific use.

After a while, Father Snow began to feel calmer. It was just a lumber room, full of old junk. He was almost disappointed. But at that moment, as though acting of its own accord, the torch swung round towards the corner of the room beyond which Vincent had stood with his black bag. When it reached the place, the light seemed to dim. It took Father Snow a moment to realise that the light was in fact as strong as ever, but the wall itself was darker, as though it had been burnt.

While Father Snow was standing there, staring at the scorch-mark, which was like the negative image of a gigantic candle, he heard a bellow from behind him.

'Fe, fi, fo, fum!'

The room swung madly round, making Father Snow feel giddy. When it all jerked to a halt, an enormous man had appeared in the light. He was wearing high black boots and a white shirt. White hair fell around his shoulders and in his long-nailed hands he was holding a gigantic wooden club. Seeing the astonishment on Father Snow's face, he smiled.

'Only joking.'

'Let me see it,' said Father Snow, stepping forwards.

When Trevellyan handed him the club, his arm dropped with the weight of it. Letting it fall to the floor, he shone the torch across its varnished wood, an expression of wonder on his face.

'Is it real?'

'I doubt it,' said Trevellyan. 'It probably dates from the eighteenth century. My family used to bring their friends up here in those days. This place was a kind of aristocratic tourist attraction. They filled it up with all sorts of marvels.' Both of them were silent for a moment, staring down at the tapered hunk of wood. 'Still, you never know.'

Father Snow said nothing.

When they had climbed up onto the roof and put the padlock back on the trapdoor, Trevellyan walked away towards the front of the building. Father Snow followed. At the parapet, they both stopped. Below them were the two courtyards. Beyond that, the park fell away down towards the A25. From up here, they could just make out the lights of the cars passing the wall. The wind was still rampaging through the trees. Looking upwards, Father Snow saw that the stars were out. There were a few wispy white clouds riding the wind, reclining ghosts on the black air. When he saw them, all his grief returned, and he realised that the fairy tale was over at last. He was returning to the ordinary world.

'Father —'

There was a strange expression on Trevellyan's face as he stared out across his beautiful park. The wind sent his white hair fluttering behind him. At that moment, he seemed suddenly like no more than a sad old pervert, affected and rather absurd.

'Yes?'

'You were right.' Trevellyan lowered his head, apparently embarrassed. 'It's just an ordinary room. Perhaps

I've allowed myself to believe a number of preposterous things.'

'You're not alone in that.'

A few minutes later, they climbed back down into the house, went downstairs, and walked across the two courtyards. At the front door, Trevellyan said goodbye hurriedly and disappeared inside. Father Snow picked up his stick from where he'd left it and began to walk home across the park.

It was the ordinary world. When he thought of the emptiness which awaited him at the presbytery, Father Snow didn't see how he was to go on. Ralph and Susan were gone. The only thing he'd salvaged from it all was a photograph of his father. Yet for all his grief, Father Snow still wasn't really depressed or unhappy. He was just sad, which is a very different thing. God was with him, and he knew that God would be enough, even in the ordinary world.

As he walked, Father Snow had the strange feeling that he was leaving Flamstead for the last time. In a sense, this was true. He would never see it in the same way again. The place had lost its enchantment. He remembered his first visit to the house. It had fired his imagination that day, filling his head with all sorts of vague ideas for historical projects. They would never be written now. Somehow or other, he'd lost his old interest in history. At the same time, Father Snow knew that Everard's magic, when subjected to the rigours of historical analysis, would simply disappear. Any serious investigation would prove that, whatever anyone might like to think, he had no connection with the famous fairy tale. Its true origins long pre-dated him, and they were not real or historical at all, but purely a thing of the imagination. The only truth of the story was psychological, but it was a truth so deep that it had been formulated long before Everard, beyond the reach of any written history, far away in the dark childhood of the race.

As he was nearing the gates, Father Snow seemed to hear beneath the raging of the wind another sound, at once more distant and more powerful. He turned around. On a huge white stallion, Trevellyan was galloping across the moonlit grass, away from the house, about to disappear among the distant trees. The deer were cantering away from him. He was leaning forwards towards the horse's neck, his white hair and shirt fluttering in the wind. Though he was so far away, Father Snow felt he was able to make out a wild expression on his face, his mouth open and roaring in a giant's voice. Then the illusion passed and he could hear nothing but the bellow of wind in the trees.

23

'THIS WEEKEND,' SAID Vincent, 'we must indulge ourselves.'

They were the first words he'd spoken for some time.
On the way from the bed and breakfast, Father Snow
had been explaining about Father Conner. Vincent had
listened to it all in silence. Now, as he leant on the blue
railings and surveyed the beach, he began to smile. His
expression seemed to say that, having finally managed to
come on holiday, he was determined that nothing would
spoil his enjoyment.

The pier was on their right. Below them, a huge crowd
of people was spread out across the beach. The children
were playing games or splashing about in the water. Some
of the adults were playing with them. Most, though, had
made themselves as comfortable as possible on the pebbles
and were smoking, talking, shielding their eyes to read the
newspaper, or simply snoozing. On the horizon was a boat
from a primary-school picture, with two triangular white
sails. The sea itself was calm. Its slow movement, huge and
effortless, lent an unreal quality to the human activity at its
edge, as though it were some vast sleeping mind which had
dreamt these peculiar little creatures. If it ever awoke, all
of them would disappear.

As they walked down onto the beach, Father Snow was
aware of what a strange couple they must look. Everyone
else seemed to be part of a family. The only other men of
Vincent's age were there with their grandchildren. Father

Snow's generation had come with their children and wives. All the same, no one seemed to pay them any attention as they spread out their towels. The person nearest to them was a fat woman, sitting under a sunshade and rubbing cream into her legs, glancing up from time to time to check on her children.

'Poor old Charles,' said Vincent, lying back and closing his eyes.

'I wonder what drove him to it.'

'A psychiatrist would probably say that he was unable to form normal relationships with adults. That would explain both his vocation and his attraction to children.'

'And what do you say?'

'That he was a good man, far better than most in that he tried to devote his life to God. It's upon such people that the devil mounts his fiercest attacks. You have to expect some of them to fall.' Without opening his eyes, Vincent waved his arm to indicate the beach. 'Why should the devil bother with the vast majority of people? The most charitable way of describing them would be as spiritually neutral beings. They're not part of the war. People like Charles, who stick their heads above the parapet, are the ones who get shot down.'

Then, as though to prove this to himself, he lifted his head and looked for a few moments around the beach. To Father Snow, perhaps because of the bright sunshine, he was suddenly more old and frail than ever. His hair was so white that it almost hurt to look at.

After a few moments, he lay back down.

'But it's Ralph I'm going to miss.'

'Me too,' said Father Snow, and it was true. 'It's not the same in Wodden without him there.'

Vincent had come down for the funeral a few weeks before, but he'd had to leave almost immediately, and they hadn't really had a chance to talk. Until now Father Snow hadn't been sure whether he would explain the exact circumstances of Ralph's accident to Vincent: that he'd been depressed about Father Conner and the priesthood generally, that he hadn't been wearing a seat-belt, that he'd driven into a tree on a straight part of the road. Now, though, as he looked at Vincent lying there in the sun, Father Snow decided not to explain. Ralph was gone and nothing else really mattered.

The new priest over in Dorking was a much younger man. For some reason, he had conceived a respect for Father Snow which was far more embarrassing than Ralph's overt friendliness. He deferred to Father Snow in everything, asked his advice on every point. Perhaps he was the sort of priest Father Snow would have been happy to find when he'd first arrived in the village. Now that it was too late, of course, he would have liked to have Ralph back. He felt sure that if he'd handled things better, if he'd only been more human, Ralph would never have died.

Father Snow had already been over this a hundred times, but being with Vincent somehow made it worse. Now he felt he wanted to explain, after all, to tell Vincent everything. Perhaps what held him back as much as his own shame was the idea that he'd somehow have been betraying Ralph, exposing his final weakness to the man he'd so idolised in life. Perhaps, too, he was silenced by Vincent's age and vulnerability. He couldn't bear the idea of Vincent knowing that another priest and friend had been driven to despair. In the old days he would have told him without hesitation, would have gone to him with any problem. Yet Vincent seemed smaller and weaker now, a little old man whom Father Snow didn't want to lean on, but to protect. Either he'd shrunk, or Father Snow himself had grown. In any case, it seemed that, somewhere along the line, even Vincent had lost a little of his magic.

So in the end, Father Snow just said again:

'It's really not the same without him there.' Vincent lay in silence, so he went on. 'He was a great guy. I thought when I first met him that he was a bad priest, but that wasn't true. It was just that all his weaknesses were on display, while mine were more complicated and hidden. I only wish I'd got to know him better.'

Vincent turned his head to look up at Father Snow with that direct softness of which only he was capable.

'You mustn't blame yourself, Julian.'

Father Snow looked away. Vincent, being Vincent, had understood the whole thing. Perhaps he hadn't quite lost his magic, after all.

'How can I not blame myself? If I'd just spent more time with him, if I'd been a better friend . . .'

'It's not your fault. You were very inexperienced. I think Ralph was going through the kind of crisis a man of your age, no matter how perceptive and sensitive, can only dimly imagine.'

Father Snow shook his head.

'I'll never forgive myself.'

He turned back to find Vincent lying with his eyes closed.

'Well, perhaps that's for the best.'

For a while after that Father Snow looked across the beach, watching the children play and thinking about Ralph. There was no one but himself to blame. He remembered the time he'd spent sitting by Ralph's bedside, and found it peculiarly moving. Then he realised that, of course, it had been an echo of those other moments from his distant past, when his father had come into his bedroom to tell him fairy tales. It was strange to think of the earliest memories of life being recreated at its end, with a similar intimacy and warmth.

On the sea there seemed to be one flash of sunshine which teleported from place to place, playing games with the eye.

'Anyway,' said Vincent, 'this is supposed to be a holiday. We have a duty to forget our problems and enjoy ourselves. Let's go for a swim.'

Father Snow was reluctant, but Vincent persuaded him in the end. When they'd changed into their costumes,

Father Snow saw that there were burn-marks on Vincent's back, as though the flesh had melted. Apart from that, it was just the body of a small old man, thin but loose-skinned. He looked unbearably vulnerable as he led the way down to the sea, hobbling over the pebbles. Father Snow noticed people glancing at his melted back, and wished there was some way to tell them who he was.

It turned out that Vincent's idea of swimming was to lie staring into the sky and wave his arms limply in the manner of a jellyfish. Father Snow soon got bored with it and went back up onto the beach, where he sat and shivered in his towel. In the end, a delicious warmth came over his body. The movement of the sea seemed to relax his mind, and he found himself thinking about Susan. Although Ralph now seemed by far the greater loss, he still missed her, if less than before. Like all feelings, it came in the form of waves, in peaks and troughs, so that some days were worse than others, but they were smaller waves now. Even grief, which is for some people the most powerful of the emotions, slowly disappears. Perhaps he only missed her at all now because she was associated with his own past, with those strange months after his arrival in Wodden, when it seemed his life had become a fairy tale. Yet that couldn't be the whole explanation, because he still wondered where she was and what she was doing now, at this precise moment. All he knew for certain was that she wouldn't be thinking about him.

After a while, he found himself just sitting there and watching the repeated movement of the waves. It was as though the sea were trying to explain something, putting on a demonstration for the benefit of the people on the beach. A wave approached, rolled effortlessly over, and threw itself flat on the pebbles. Realising that nobody had understood, the sea patiently produced another one. Father Snow felt that he could almost hear it trying to explain: It's so simple. You do it like this. The wave rose up, glittering, and collapsed. Like this.

Sometimes the sea, like any frustrated teacher, would lose its patience and fly into a rage, producing enormous waves which crashed right over the front. At other times, it would give up, and hardly bothering at all. Today, though, it just went on, patiently explaining again and again: Like this. Then it sighed and tried again. Most of the people on the beach paid no attention, but one or two, like Father Snow, sat there and stared as though desperately trying to understand.

When Vincent had finished swimming, he wanted to go on the pier. Once there, he insisted on sampling every entertainment on offer. It was all terribly embarrassing for Father Snow. The old man ate ice-creams, won a cuddly toy on the shooting range, played video-games in the arcade. For the most part, despite Vincent constantly encouraging him to have a go, Father Snow just stood to one side, rigid with embarrassment and praying for the whole thing to end.

It was the dodgems that Vincent enjoyed the most. Father Snow, watching from the sidelines, felt like a father watching his son. It seemed to him that perhaps there is a part of a celibate man that never really grows up. Vincent went round and round, studiously avoiding collisions, yet laughing delightedly whenever anyone bumped into him. He seemed blissfully unaware that people were staring. Each time the cars came to a stop, he turned to Father Snow and called out:

'Just one more go!'

In the end, it dawned on Father Snow that this was Vincent's last holiday. When he eventually walked away from the dodgems, it would be for the last time in his life. The long procession was coming to its end for him, the carnival floats were moving on. He had to enjoy them while he could. Perhaps when one got to that age and looked back, the whole thing would seem a fairy tale, a parade of fabulous illusions.

After that, still standing in his usual calm way and with

his usual grim expression, Father Snow watched without embarrassment.

At last Vincent had had enough. He approached with a broad smile on his face, which Father Snow did his best to return. It was difficult, because he felt at that moment that grief is cumulative. The waves may seem to get smaller, but the tide is always coming in. After a certain point, all of us are overcome.

Seeing the expression on his face, Vincent laughed.

'Look at you, you old wet blanket! Even on holiday, you're the same old Father Snow. Won't you ever change?'

'No,' said Father Snow. 'I don't suppose I will.'

'Good,' said Vincent, apparently without irony. 'Come on. Now you can watch me go on the ghost train.'

That evening, after supper, they went back to the beach. It was almost deserted. The sea, dark now, still moved calmly, in the same effortless and patient way. Father Snow and Vincent walked slowly along the promenade. Vincent was serious again, almost solemn, a dignified old man.

When they'd walked for a while in silence, they stopped and leaned on the railing, side by side. The tide had come in and covered most of the beach. The sea stretched almost to their feet, a dreaming darkness. There were a few lights out in the distance.

'Things have gone badly on my watch, Julian.'

'How do you mean?'

'The Church is in retreat. Vocations are down to a trickle. Society is almost entirely secular. People satisfy their need for belief with any number of empty superstitions. When I think of poor Ralph and Charles, I could almost despair.'

Father Snow couldn't answer. He'd never have imagined Vincent was capable of even saying the awful word.

'I still believe that you're the man to put it all right,'

Vincent went on. 'You have it in you to revitalise the Church.'

Father Snow shook his head.

'Why have you always thought so highly of me?'

'Because it's true.'

'No, it isn't.' Father Snow turned to look at him. 'There's more to it than that.'

Vincent, still staring at the sea, gave a little shrug, as though annoyed by Father Snow's persistence.

'I can't go on much longer,' he said. 'Perhaps I just need to feel that the torch will be passed on. I need to hope that someone will make a better job of things than I have.'

They were silent for a while, listening to the sound of the waves. When Vincent next spoke, it was in a quieter voice.

'When you're young, it seems that sex is the greatest sacrifice demanded by the priesthood. As you get older, though, all that gets less and less important. It's having children that you start to miss.' He turned and smiled at Father Snow. 'Perhaps I just like to see you as the son I never had.'

As he said that, Father Snow remembered the moment when he'd first seen Vincent. The old man had been walking down the aisle of the cathedral, pacing at the back of a long procession in all his fabulous pomp. His eyes had gone straight to Julian's, as though picking him out of all the congregation. The look had seemed to tell, with complete conviction, the one fairy tale that all of us would like to believe.

'How old are you, Vincent?'

'Old enough.' Vincent smiled. 'Old enough to be your father, anyway.'

When Father Snow looked back out at the sea, the darkness shocked him. The day had passed so quickly. It seemed only a few moments ago that they had been lying in the sunshine. Once more he saw how grief is cumulative. The losses pile up. We must somehow find the courage to say what has to be said while we still have time.

'Don't worry, Julian,' said Vincent cheerfully. 'I've got years left in me yet. You wait and see.'

But something in his tone seemed to prove that he knew it wasn't true. They wouldn't be together very long.

'You're my best friend,' said Father Snow. 'My only real friend, now that Ralph has gone.'

When he looked back out across the sea, Father Snow found himself having a kind of vision. In it he saw all of them pass by as participants in a carnival parade. Ralph was a sad dancing bear with bells around his neck, Susan a beautiful princess riding a gorgeous float, Trevellyan a shaggy monster, half giant and half beast, tamed and paraded in a cage for the pitying revulsion of the crowd. Father Snow himself was a kind of ice man with a frozen heart who could only melt around the eyes, walking jerkily along and leaving pools of water in his wake. Vincent, of course, was the little magician, wizened and wise. He paced quietly at the back, hunched over and leaning on a staff, his long, royal blue robe sprinkled with silver stars. Nobody really noticed him, but it was his enchantment that leant a wonder to it all. In fact, he was what Father Snow's own father had always been, the man who made people believe in dreams, the teller of fabulous tales.

The vision passed, melting away as such carnivals do. When he looked at Vincent, he saw nothing but a little old man, leaning on a railing and staring out to sea. Yet it seemed to Father Snow that, if you once can believe in life as a fairy tale, even for the shortest time, things are never the same again. He saw that this was really what he'd been trying to do all along. From the moment when he'd first set eyes on Vincent, he'd seen the old man as a substitute for his father, somebody who would make him believe the most unlikely and marvellous of things.

Vincent turned towards him, his face serious. He seemed to glimmer in the dark, a dissolving vision, about to fade away. In years to come, Father Snow would look back and wonder whether such a creature could ever really have existed any more than a griffon or a unicorn.

'Don't be downcast,' said Vincent, having used his mysterious powers to look into Father Snow's morbid, sorrowful mind. 'All partings are temporary.'

But they were silent for a long time after that, both staring blankly out at the sea, watching the movement of the waves like a pair of backward children struggling to understand a simple lesson.